I0778392

Praise for *Dandelion Wine*

"In his masterful debut novel, Jon writes a coming-of-age story with a twist that will have you aching to turn the page."

– Elizabeth Davis

"I really enjoyed this book. A wonderfully creative adaptation of a true story with the debut author honoring his mother's fifty-year secret: a southern coming-of-age story set in the 1940s with a gothic underbelly. I was rooting for Shirley from the first page to the end. The prose was densely beautiful, and the plot carefully executed to bring about an ending that is both surprising and delightfully ornery. I stayed up all night to finish it. I still cannot get the characters out of my head."

– Margaret J. Baker

J.C. White is an American suburban planner, technical writer, and fiction novelist. He's a lifelong lover of words and worlds, traveling the world with his loving wife, Emily, and coming home to write about it. His career spans the shadowy worlds of undercover drug and violent crimes enforcement; private investigator at home and abroad; a defense contractor; real estate developer; a technical writer in various briefing books and comprehensive plans; lobbyist/advocate for public safety; and the most dangerous world of all, suburban public planning. Through it all, words were the one honest thing—sharp when they needed to be, gentle when they could afford it.

A national award-winning planner and debut novelist at sixty-one, Chris is not starting a writing career. He's finally clearing the table for it. His style has been characterized as: *"Prose that thinks in memory and speaks in confession."* But according to Chris, "It's just writing that's been fully lived-in."

Chris writes Southern fiction—Southern Gothics and historically, regionally bent threads. What binds it all together is that none of it is pretend. Chris writes Gothic tropes that are awkwardly true but told with blurred faces and alias names. His stories, like the man, are Southern to the bone. Walking the line between grit, grace, and humor. He writes like a man who knows what time costs. Who's seen enough of the world to have been forged anew but misses the Chris he left behind. He understands that fiction—real fiction—is just truth with its mask off.

DANDELION WINE

J.C. WHITE

Published by
Southern Narratives
117 Public Square South
Shelbyville, TN 37160
southern-narratives.com
chris.white@southern-narratives.com

Hardback ISBN 979-8-9990281-0-5
Paperback ISBN 979-8-9990281-2-9
eBook ISBN 979-8-9990281-1-2

Cover design by Navigation Advertising, LLC

First Edition

AUTHOR'S NOTE

While Springfield is the county seat of Robertson County, Tennessee, a real place, and while the Raglands were a real family living on Willow Street in Springfield, in 1942, and, while Shirley was my real mother—Ora and Jim, my grandparents—and while this story is loosely based on true events that were shared directly with me from my mother's memory, I have taken great liberties in the writing of this novel.

Each character, including my mother's character, is fully a creation of my imagination and in no way represents any person, living or dead. Every word, every sentence, and every plot twist in this story is the result of my mother's memory and countless hours of human thought, effort, and passion. Other than real places, events, and names, this story was crafted solely by me, with no assistance from artificial intelligence or language models.

This book and its enhanced story are entirely a work of fiction, although it is loosely based on a secret my mother kept from us, her family, for fifty years.

Other names, characters, places, and incidents are either the product of my imagination or used fictitiously.

Any resemblance to actual events or persons, living or dead, is purely coincidental.

*"The woods are full of regional writers,
and it is the great horror of every serious
Southern writer that he will become one of them."*

—Flannery O'Connor

To Josh Carney,
the friend whose kindly voice
inspired my timid pen with hope.

And

To my wife Emily,
my companion in calm or chaos,
brave enough to be true,
true enough to be singular,
one who says what she thinks
and very often thinks what she says.

IN DEDICATION TO MY MOTHER

To some, she was Shirley Lucille Ragland. To others, Shirley White. For a short season, Shirley Shannon. To me, she was just Mom.

She was a great many things to surprisingly few people. A woman both remote and magnetic. She could be warm when she chose, like a fire that crackled just long enough to thaw your hands, and in an instant, vanish into smoke. To some, she was cold. To others, divine. She was a constellation of contradictions—aloof yet all-seeing, tender only in passing, brilliant in ways that made people uneasy. She read between lines you didn't know were written and pointed out truths you didn't know you'd told.

Tennessee Williams, our fellow Southerner and lifelong student of the wounded heart, once wrote, *"When so many are lonely as seem to be lonely, it would be inexcusably selfish to be lonely alone."* My mother understood that line better than most. She wore her solitude like armor, her distance mistaken for disdain. But inside, she was a storm of thought and ache and private dreams she nurtured in silence.

She kept her circle tight and her affections tighter. She didn't need friends the way most people do, and she sure as hell didn't need applause. Her world was internal, and she ruled it without council. She liked her coffee strong, her convictions stronger. And when it came to mothering, she did not swaddle or soothe. She did not coddle. She demanded. She trained. She made warriors out of worriers and thinkers out of feelers. And if you came crying, she'd wait patiently for the moment you pulled yourself together. Then she'd ask what you'd learned.

She nurtured ambition, not affection. And yet, buried beneath the sharp edges and cool assessments, was a woman who dreamed in secret. Who wanted to be wild. A provocateur who loved to be dangerous. And in those rare moments—when who she was collided with who she wished she could've been—she became something unforgettable.

She dreamed for us, too. For her children. She saw talent before it knew its name, and she watered it—expecting, knowing—that it would one day bloom. When she saw me, the caboose in a long line of siblings, treading water, she didn't reach out. She just told me to swim harder.

She believed I could write fiction. She told me, every time she gazed above glasses and closed a favorite James Patterson novel. "You could do that," she'd say. "Better, if you had the guts."

I'd laugh. "James Patterson's a machine, Mama," I'd tell her. "That's a big pair of boots to fill." She didn't flinch. Her kind of confidence could blister paint.

Well, Mama, here it is. I hope it doesn't disappoint.

And James Patterson?

Relax. You're safe.

And with my deepest respects—go to hell.

CONTENTS

ONE

ECHOES OF UNHEARD APPLAUSE

Saturday, Second Week in May 1942

THE FORMAL LIVING room was embalmed in a velvet stillness, sunlight pooling across the hardwood like spilled gold, as young Shirley Ragland sat before the polished, battle-weary baby grand, her small hands trembling above the stained ivory like a beekeeper on the edge of madness—braced to command a choir of weaponized fleas. The air, thick with the scent of furniture polish and aged wallpaper, wrapped around her as she began to play *Gaspard de la Nuit*, an intricate tapestry of sound that spun from her nimble fingers. Shirley's teacher, Ms. Thatcher, an unvarnished woman fashioned from a distillate of music and self-discipline, observed Shirley's playing with a practiced eye, her presence a blend of patience and opulent expectation.

With each sonorous note, Shirley's right hand leapt across the keys in daring arcs, bridging chasms of silence with the fluent certainty of someone who had long ago surrendered herself to the mathematics of music. Ravel's chaos unfolded beneath her fingertips like a battlefield map drawn in candlelight, and still she moved through it, flawless, instinctive, her mind so quick it might've rewritten the laws of motion without breaking rhythm. And beneath the elegance, beneath the grace and control, something wordless surged through her, some deep, raw ache to be seen, to be named, to be enough. Burning steady and small in her chest like the flickering bulb above, trembling with the effort not to burn out, as if straining to shine a little brighter just for her sake.

As she approached the climactic section of Scarbo, the piano seemed to vibrate beneath her fingertips, a creature alive with the pent-up energy of its creator's heart. The notes cascaded, rapid and repeated, requiring a dexterity she feared would elude her; yet, still she pressed on, intently aware of a figure lingering at the threshold, casting a silhouette of telltale curls against the dimming light of the wall. Ora stood in the archway like a woman waiting for a verdict, her arms folded in the quiet armor of disapproval, eyes fixed not on Shirley's hands, but just above them, watching without seeing. The girl felt it like static in her lungs, that fragile space between triumph and collapse, her fingers suddenly too aware of their own daring. She did not need her mother to speak; the silence bore teeth.

The piece came to its breathless conclusion, the final notes floating through the room like wisps of smoke trying desperately to find an escape. Shirley released the last chord, feeling a swell of triumph as she turned to catch Ms. Thatcher's astonished expression, the music still reverberating within her. But the joy that ignited within her heart flickered, threatened by the chill of Ora's pickled voice.

"Too soft at the end, Shirley," her mother said, a matter-of-fact draping of words that landed heavily in the room, snuffing out the fragile light of triumph Shirley had held. Ora stood there, unyielding and oblivious to the brilliance that had blossomed between the notes. No hint of praise for the Herculean climb Shirley had just traversed—only an expected bite of critique, sharp and unrelenting.

Ms. Thatcher's generously freckled brow furrowed in disbelief, her voice rising in defense. "But it was precisely how we practiced it, Ora. The delicacy at the end is not merely an option; it is integral to the piece," she said, her tone tinged with a protective fervor.

Yet, Shirley watched as her mother, indifferent as air, dismissed it all with a distracted wave, the hem of her apron brushing against her as she turned to leave. "You'll do better next time," she muttered, already drifting away, oblivious to the torrent swirling inside her daughter.

In the vacuum left by her mother's retreat, Shirley sat frozen; a web of turmoil tightened around her heart. She tried to reclaim the joy that had at once surged then dissipated like the last breath of the afternoon sunlight. Instead, a silence gathered; a raw, resounding silence that rang louder than applause. The piano, still trembling from her touch, its keys faintly humming with memory, bore witness to the depths of Shirley's disillusionment. Her fingers, once aflame with intention, now lay folded in surrender, resting like fallen petals across the ivory keys, not from exhaustion but from something heavier, something tender and terrible lodged beneath the skin, the way a child might bury a love note they were too ashamed to send.

SISTER AGATHA

Monday, Second Week of May 1942

I WAS BORN WHEN my parents had already lived too much and not enough. My three brothers, big and loud and feral as men are, were all grown, married, and settled before I even knew the world. They'd carried away with them my parents' purpose, their connection, their reasons to stay under the same roof; maybe even their hope of starting again separately. And then there was me, my late arrival a cruel trick played by time. What folks 'round here call a mistake, what Mother calls "an unexpected blessing," though she can't quite meet my eyes when she says it out loud.

I wonder what I am to her. A child born too late, too redundant, uninvited, but still planted smack in the middle of Mother's endless ambitions. She parades me around town like a prize pumpkin. My face in the *Springfield Herald* so often, folks don't even bother to read the captions anymore: piano recitals, summer Latin camp at Sewanee, Sunday school ribbons, a beret or dubious fascinator hat perched on my head just so. I often feel like the preface of a time-worn book, pushed out front, the only pages no one cares to read.

Every photograph in our house bore her signature, each frame arranged like a scene in a play she cast me in, all smiles measured, every moment lit just so, as if perfection might heal something we never spoke of. But I was never her star. I was a stand-in for some unnamed dream she couldn't quite bring to life, playing a part in a language that I never learned, mouthing lines that never felt like mine. And still, she pressed on, relentless in her direction, handing me the weight of her unfulfilled years like an armload of books in a language I couldn't read, expecting me to carry them into a future she no longer believed in.

Sometimes I wonder if she sees me at all, or just the blueprint she's drawn in her head: the girl with perfect manners, perfect posture, and immaculate thank-you notes. The kind of daughter who never asks to be known. She says she's proud, but I don't think she knows I love the piano more than I love anything, or that my dance teacher makes me want to cry in the bathroom stall. She doesn't see the way the spelling bees twist knots in my belly, or how sometimes, in the stillness of church, I wonder if even God has forgotten I'm here. The weight of being her hope feels like one of those old hymnals Father Schadenfreude makes us hold high during Lent, arms burning, legs locked, no end in sight. And though I haven't dropped it yet, I've started thinking how easy it might be to let it fall.

Even Ms. Thatcher, my piano teacher, sees it. She would never say it out loud, but her writhing body language screams to me. I'll admit it is sometimes difficult to hear her thoughts over the shrill of her appearance. Ms. Thatcher is unfortunate to suffer from a skin condition that leaves her with a ruddy complexion, something that has eluded her pursuits for marriage no doubt. And she has freckles laying atop scars.

Not freckles, not the innocent copper scatter you'd expect on a child's cheeks. No, these looked like the afterthoughts of a painter's brush, careless and divine; golden flecks spattered across her face as if God had once tried to make her laugh and forgot to clean up after Himself. They ran like constellations, familiar and wild, the kind you couldn't chart but somehow knew by heart. And though her face fought itself in stillness, her expressions landing somewhere between stern and startled, there was a symmetry to the rest of her that felt carved, composed, like something built to outlast its first impression. I have to believe that will be enough. That some good-hearted man will one day see past the hesitation and find what the rest of us already know: she is capable of pulling miracles from the deep.

Although I wouldn't wish to share the same problems Ms. Thatcher suffers, I do find her admirably knowable. I'm almost sixteen, and for all my ostensible accolades, I remain a mystery to myself. Who is this girl so polished and praised, the darling of Robertson County? And who is this woman who curates her so carefully? I can describe her titles, her manner, the shape of her smile, the arc of her posture, but none of these tell me who she really is. Will I ever know, really know?

This is the essence of being a daughter to a mother so dispassionate and glacial, living in a world where everyone knows me while I'm left a stranger unto myself. Where I can recount the details of every neighbor's life, yet remain utterly bewildered by my own mother's distance. It's a perplexing truth, a puzzle that seems forever undone; with pieces scattered in the corners of both my heart and this trifling, yet torrid town.

Someday, I hope to bloom into whatever shape she's imagined for me; some truer version of myself she swears she can see, hidden behind the hard lines I wear like armor. But today I drift through hours like a girl misplaced in someone else's fairytale, unsure if I'm the one building the castle or just sweeping its floors. There's a pressure in my chest I can't explain, like the ache of holding back a name no one's ever called me, and I wonder if the truth, whatever it is, will still know how to stand when it finally steps into the light.

I have taken piano lessons since I was six years old. Most folks would say I possess a natural talent; a gift. In Mother's eyes, nothing is ever enough. Lately, she's been harping on me to take up the pipe organ at our parish, her lofty vision of me someday wrangling that grand, wheezing, dreadnought during Sunday Mass burning brighter than ever. Clearly, this is a dream for her, not me, but I've always been game for trying new things, things that let me poke and prod and find out how they work on my own terms. But that colossal pipe organ with its iron-maiden liturgical music feels like a heavy, gilded door slamming shut on whatever creativity I might one day conjure up.

The piano, now that's a different creature. It breathes when I do, lets me talk to it and have it answer back in ways that surprise us both. But that otherworldly church organ? It seems like all law and no grace, like being handed a stone tablet carved with Thou Shalts and Thou Shalt Nots, without so much as a sliver of wiggle room for doubt or imagination.

Still, when Mother pushed me out of the comfort of my nest, dropping straight down to Tom Walker, our new Yankee organist, I gave in. I figured one close-up look at the thing might confirm my suspicion that it and I were never meant to be friends. Let it groan and moan for someone else, I thought. Besides, there's a certain thrill in proving the suspicions of your distaste by staring a hideous thing dead in the face.

You could tell right off that Tom didn't belong, not by the way he dressed, but by the sound of him. His voice had the sharp, nasal edge of city winters and polished concrete, like someone who'd never once pulled honeysuckle off the vine or been whipped for sass in Sunday clothes. Father Schadenfreude brought him down from Philadelphia after old Mr. Gaines keeled over cold at the foot of the altar, hands still inked from the morning's music. No one much asked where Tom came from or how the priest found him, just that he showed up with a suitcase and a way with Bach. Folks forget how rare a pipe organist is, especially one who can breathe life into that old beast like it's more idea than instrument. Rarer than hen's teeth, I suppose.

Our congregation had a way of meddling too hard in things that didn't rightly concern them, or things that did, but maybe just a little too much. Strangely though, no one meddled with Tom Walker. He was single, never married, and handsome in that tightly wound, over-scouted and overweighted kind of way, if you liked men who looked like they ironed their socks. But he played the pipe organ like a river beneath winter ice; slow and certain, like it remembered something the rest of us had forgotten. And when the congregation spoke of him, it was always in tones hushed and half-hearted, as if their admiration lived in the music alone, not the man; each note lifting, drifting, then falling quiet, like a blessing whispered by someone who never quite believed in it.

I'd seen Tom many times, sitting upright on his stool, always looking like he was waiting for a cue, like the Mass was just a rehearsal and he was already thinking of the next show. He was an awkward fixture at church socials, polite but distant unless you talked to him; then he'd never stop talking. While his music filled the vaulted ceilings with something close to holy, he and I didn't know each other, nor did I have a reason to speak to him aside from our mutual interest in the piano. 'Least, not until today.

The church seemed empty when I arrived early for my first lesson, its silence stretching wide and deep, clinging to me like the incense still hanging in the air from yesterday's service, thick with layered odors of beeswax and the dark scent of old decomposing oak; producing a rich, almost cloying scent of vanilla and equally imposing. That's when I saw Bo Harris. He stood in a corner with Father Schadenfreude, their heads bent together in the kind of conversation that needed distance from curious ears like mine. Bo's posture flickered between defiance and unease, his hand animated; slicing the air as though his words demanded punctuation. Bo wasn't intimidated by the Father; steady as a psalm held too long in the throat before it dares to break free.

I froze where I was, one hand gripping the brass floor lamp beside me, cold as a church rail in January, steadier than I was. I couldn't tell if stepping closer would make things worse, or if standing still had already done the damage. The air between them crackled, the way a room holds its breath when something sacred is about to shatter.

Father Schadenfreude saw me first. His face tightened, folded in on itself like parchment too often creased; irritation tempered by something that looked a lot like defeat. He muttered a benediction meant for no one and brushed past me without pause, like I was an open window he'd forgotten to shut.

Bo didn't follow right away. He lingered a second too long, the silence around him loud enough to drown me. Then he moved—slow, precise, like a man walking a tightrope no one else could see. He passed so close his cologne cut the air between us—sharp, clean, and too grown for the boy I used to think I understood. He didn't look at me, didn't need to. That scent said enough: whatever thread there'd been between us, someone had cut it.

I stood there, adrift in the rousing scent and the moment. He hadn't said a word, but his presence hung dense, like an apparition. Did he still—like me? Did he even see me? Bo is impossible to read. Sometimes, he looks at me like I am the only thing worth noticing, and other times, I may as well be one of those creaky wooden chairs stacked behind me. I wanted to follow him, to impose something close to an answer, but the weight of the Father's earlier glance kept my feet nailed stiff to the floor.

Tom Walker greeted me in the dim light of the storeroom, his sickly-sweet grin an unexpected relief from the lingering silence left by the Father and Bo. "Ah, there you are. Ready t-t-to meet Sister Agatha?" he said, his voice like the crack of a match, but with an obvious stammer. His speech impediment, like a sore thumb, caught me off-guard and impolite.

I blinked at him, still caught between the beats of what I'd overheard and the weight of Bo's cologne still permeating the air. "S-i-s-t-e-r Agatha?" I asked, my words slower than I intended.

Tom chuckled, a sound that danced between patience and pity. "The organ, Shirley. That's h-her name, m-m-m-my little joke."

I followed him through a narrow side door I'd never noticed before, tucked beside the grand double doors leading from the narthex, trying my best to ignore his stammer. The staircase spiraled upward, tight and breathless, until it spilled us into a hidden loft. The air there was different, old and heavy, as though unable to exhale, sitting too long without anyone to disturb it.

Sister Agatha stood waiting, looming in the chancel like some monstrous, wheezing contraption of divine engineering, its controls a labyrinth of knobs, pedals, and keys that might have easily been plucked from the fevered dreams of a lunatic clockmaker. She looked like something alive, her dubious controls labeled in a language that might as well have been ancient scripture.

Tom spoke about the "manuals" and "stops" as though he were describing a puzzle box only he could solve. His voice filled the space, but I was somewhere else, imagining how the venerable walls of the organ loft must shudder when she roared to life.

Now, sitting next to Tom, I noticed the way his hands moved over the stops with an ease that made the instrument seem like it was part of him. It wasn't just skill, it was a kind of authority. He didn't say much at first, just showed me how to place my hands, how to listen for the notes to settle, like dust after a storm.

I respected him for that. For the way he let the music do the talking, for the way he didn't treat me like a child even when my playing faltered. There was something in his manner—calm, assured—that made me want to learn from him, even as I wondered what had brought him here, to this little town and this little church. I didn't ask. It felt like the kind of question that hung in the air, unspoken, not meant to be understood, like so many things in this place.

"P-play something else, s-s-something you'd play at home," he encouraged, and before I could think of an excuse, I played the *Tennessee Waltz*! The sound didn't pour out of the pipes; it leapt. The notes felt too big for my hands, too much for my chest; and yet, they came. Tom watched me with something like approval, though I caught him adjusting the stops now and then, a silent nudge in the direction he thought best.

By the time I left my first lesson, my head was swimming with new sounds and questions. I told myself I'd come back, if only to learn more about how Sister Agatha worked, how she could be both mine and not mine at all.

Downstairs, Bo waited like a shadow against the light of the narthex. I nodded at him, polite but distant, and kept walking. He'd upset me, made me feel small. Invisible, like I feel at home. It wasn't until I was nearly out the door that I heard him.

"Hey," he said, soft and detached, but still enough to pull me back.

I turned, not quite looking at him, crossing my arms. His hands shoved deep in his pockets, hair a mess—and his face carried the kind of trouble that sticks to people like him. The silence between us stretched, thick and taut, until he broke it.

"You was good, up there," he said, his voice rough but sincere, his command of the English language expected, but not as polished as I would prefer in a potential suitor. "I heard you."

"Thanks," I said, my own voice thinner than I meant it to be.

"You ever been all the way up in that belfry?" he asked, his words casual, but his eyes too sharp to match.

"No," I said, taking a step back without realizing it. "Maybe next time, if I'm worthy of your time."

"Sorry… I was just mad, you know, earlier. I'd like to show you… the belfry," he offered, his hand brushing his neck as though to shrug off the weight of the moment.

"Maybe," I said again, not wanting to promise more than I could handle, "tomorrow, after my lesson."

Before I changed my mind, I decided to turn and leave. When I left, the door behind me stayed open longer than it should have. He watched, his presence pressing against my back like a second shadow.

WHERE SECRETS WAIT

I WALKED STRAIGHT HOME from church. Earline was waiting, her voice lilting, soft and steady like a song, the kind that could soothe a restless heart without it ever asking; the way it always did when she spoke my name. The smell of hot butter and caramelized sugar trailed her from the kitchen, warm and thick in the air.

"Miss Shirley, is you hungry? Lord, I made your favorite, butter pecan bread puddin'."

Earline's fingers found the little gilded cross at her throat, thumb and forefinger turning it slow, careful, the way she always did when she spoke, like it might whisper something if she held it just right. I'd watched her do it for years, that quiet habit of hers, and wondered what lived in the space between her touch and the cross. Maybe it was faith? Maybe it was habit? Or maybe it was just something to keep her hands from feeling empty when she wasn't working?

Earline's love had been there longer than my memory, wrapped around me like a second skin. She'd held me when I was fresh to this world, and somehow, she still held me now, though I wasn't so easy to carry anymore. Her care was so steady, so unshaken, that I didn't think much on it; like the ground under my feet, I assumed it would always hold.

"And your poor mother," she said, shaking her head like she had a secret she couldn't share. "Lord, she sure has been wondering 'bout your organ lesson. I swear, if your mama'd let me up in that place, Miss Shirley, y'all know I'd be proud to hear my baby girl play that fancy organ."

Her excited words settled in my chest, warm but also heavy, though I didn't know quite why. I just nodded and smiled, letting her love wash over me. I had to let myself believe that the simple weight of it might be enough to hold me steady, even as the rest of the world started to tilt. I quietly enjoyed a small portion of bread pudding before finding a quiet place and a book to process my day.

I shut my bedroom door and leaned against it, the muffled sound of the organ still thrumming through the floorboards, humming faintly in my fingers like a song I hadn't learned the words to. Bo's voice lingered too; quiet, low, close enough to make the hairs on my wrist stand up like they were listening. I could still smell him, like soap and cedar and something I couldn't name, and when I breathed in, it settled somewhere deep in my chest, like a kind of drunkenness, where the edges of my heart felt strange and warm, like something had just begun but didn't know what to call itself yet.

Until now, the church felt like a place to hide. But there was a kind of holy ache blooming inside me, and it wasn't just Bo Harris, though his name was the only one I could say out loud without the room shifting.

What really stirred in my chest carried the scent of something much older, something buried, something I wasn't allowed to speak of anymore, 'least not since that summer when discovery meant ruin, and Earline's hands, trembling not from anger but from some horrible unspoken fear, pulled Benji away from me like he was a match I'd struck too close to the curtains.

He'd looked back once, just once, his face a knot of questions I wasn't old enough to answer, and I learned then that silence could be an inheritance too. I hadn't said his name, not in a long time.

Wouldn't now.

It hurts too much.

Instead, I let the weight of Bo's smooth voice settle over me like a quilt in August, too warm, too much, and I folded myself down to the floor, dress crumpling beneath me like an unopened love letter, still half-written, still afraid of what the ending might be.

What sort of precarious dance was unfolding between Bo and the Father? Their private quarrel felt steeped in something personal and emotional, the tension so thick it hung in the air like summer humidity.

It was not anger alone, nor was it duty. It ran deeper. It was enough to keep Bo mute as a stone, personal in a way that made me feel like an intruder. This was our church, not a public meeting hall. Bo had turned from me, silent, his shoulders set in a way that told me not to ask.

I didn't cry. Not because I wasn't close to it, but because something colder moved in first, a kind of stillness I didn't have a name for yet. I stood, brushed the wrinkles from my skirt like I was smoothing over something more fragile, and reached for a *Reader's Digest* off the shelf. I didn't want truth or beauty or meaning. I wanted distraction, just enough story to keep my mind from circling the edges of what I'd seen, and what I wasn't ready to understand.

*

THE NEXT DAY, I RETURNED for another lesson with Tom, or so I told myself. The truth trailed behind me with a weighty pull. It wasn't Sister Agatha or her mighty pipes that had me touching up my lipstick and smoothing my hair and dress before entering the church, nor was it Tom's meticulous corrections that had me quickening my steps up those dreaded spiral stairs.

The staircase twisted upward in a tight coil, each step worn smooth by years of passage. The wooden treads and risers, darkened with age, creaked like an old ship adrift in slow waters, the boards bending and settling with each ascending step, murmuring their quiet protest beneath even the lightest touch; their edges rounded from countless feet pressing forward, climbing higher, turning ever inward. The sounds rose and fell; a weary complaint echoing through the narrow shaft, as if the wood itself remembered every foot that had ever pressed upon it. The railing, polished from touch, curved along the spiral like a serpent's spine, its balusters spaced close, their carved forms catching thin slivers of light that slipped through the narrow gaps between steps.

The walls pressed close, thick with old plaster, cool beneath the fingertips, the scent of aged wood and dust lingering in the narrow air. The ceiling above shrank as the spiral tightened, pulling inward, folding upon itself until the last steps seemed to disappear into the dimness beyond reach. The climb felt endless, each turn pulling the body forward, demanding trust in what lay unseen above. It was a passage built not for haste but for patience, where each step marked another turn away from what lay below and toward the unknown above.

Bo's troubled voice lingered in my mind like the echo of a song half-heard. He was older, sharper at the edges, with a way of leaning into words that made them seem important and unnecessary at the same time. I imagined the girls he probably spent time with, girls who didn't blush when he touched their shoulders or look away when his eyes held theirs too long. Girls who didn't have mothers that prayed out loud at the dinner table or older brothers with fists that knew their way around a fight.

What would he even want with a girl two years younger? And if he did want me, what kind of wanting would it be? The question clung to me, heavy and damp, tangled up with the image of Father Schadenfreude's solemn but suspiciously jealous face. A triangle came to mind, uneven, Gothic and grotesque, its angles and spires sharp enough to cut and gore.

I shook the thought loose, ridiculous and unwelcome, and climbed the last step to the organ loft. Tom would be waiting. But when I stepped into the loft, the air felt wrong, heavy in a way it hadn't before. Tom was hunched over an unfolded letter, penned with sharp, angular and weighty handwriting, as well as a book, a diary. He was scribbling furiously, the movement of his pen so fierce I could almost hear it lacerating the paper.

It wasn't sheet music—not the kind you'd play, anyway. I'd seen that book before; brown leather binding with a small gold monogram, sitting neat on the stand. Never thought once to ask what it held.

And then I saw his face. Cheeks wet. His shoulders shook, just a little, but enough for me to know I wasn't imagining it. Tom was crying. My breath held tight, and before I could step back unseen, he slammed the book shut like a mink trap, the letter inside it. The sound rang out sharp against the quiet, and the wooden bench creaked under the immense weight of his hulking frame. He looked up, his face blank and pale, save for the pink that edged his bloated eyes.

"Tom? Are you... are you alright?" The words felt small as I said them, like they didn't fit the room.

He straightened too quick, brushing past the question like it wasn't there. "S-s-stops and m-m-manuals today," he said. His troubled voice came in fits and starts, halting before they could take full shape, as if caught on the jagged edges of his own hesitation, already turning to the organ. His hands darted across the keys, showing me something I couldn't see through the fog of what I'd just witnessed.

I followed his instruction, stiff and fumbling, and when I made mistakes, his corrections came sharp; not cruel, but not kind either. The warmth he'd shown before had dried up, leaving only efficiency in its place. I tried to focus, tried to let the music pull me back into something steady, but my eyes kept wandering to the door at the far end of the room. It sat deep in the shadows, as if daring me to wonder where it led.

The door to the belfry.

Tom grabbed his diary while lecturing me about my technique, his consonants doubling back on themselves, stumbling out of his mouth like loose stones kicked down a hill, uneven and uncertain. The pauses between syllables stretched way too long, straining the air with an unspoken battle between his mind and his tongue. His breath hitched before each attempt, a sharp intake as if gathering courage, only for the word to break apart in his throat, splitting into fragments before he could force it forward.

When he finally spoke, his voice wavered, heavy with effort, each sound pushed past an invisible weight, a tremor of frustration and something like melancholy lingering in the silence that followed. Though his anger was directed at me, I knew there were other stressors afoot that had nothing to do with the organ or me, and for that, I took the stuttered lashing straight-faced and with a sense of sorrow for him. In haste, he abandoned me with an urgent determination, leaving me to contemplate both the lesson and his emotional state, his weighty footsteps fading down those arrogant stairs. I stayed behind.

My heart pummeled my chest unevenly as I stared at the door that led to the belfry, its brassy handle worn smooth from hands long gone. Bo had mentioned he went there to think; he'd invited me to join him, and I wondered what kind of thoughts filled that space. Did they match the ones circling in my head now, or were his darker, more dangerous?

WHAT THE RAIN TRIED TO WASH AWAY

I STEPPED CLOSER TO the door, hand hovering over the latch. My breaths catching, domed my upper chest with a persistence of a false rumor, as I imagined him waiting there, leaning against the stained glass, his eyes lit with something implied. The thought warmed me, but it also prickled at the back of my neck.

I opened the door; its worn, boisterous hinges hadn't felt the solace of oil since Sherman set the South afire. The stairs were steep and uneven, the kind that made you question each step; I hesitated, glancing back at Sister Agatha. The organ loomed behind me, silent but alive, its pipes a witness to my delicious irrationality. I climbed higher.

The railing, smooth and worn, felt warmer beneath the fingers, slick with the sweat of effort. Each turn looked the same as the last, an endless spiral pulling the body higher, the destination unseen but near, or so it seemed, though the steps never quite surrendered their end, until they did.

Through the wooden slats of the bell tower, sunlight fractured into thin lines that danced on the worn floorboards, tracing the uneasy rhythm of my breath. I saw him before he saw me, standing there; leaning with studied indifference, one hand gripping the other arm like he was keeping himself from reaching out.

Bo. What a strong name. The sound of it breaking free of my lips alone seemed to carve heart shapes into the air. And I, who had been told a hundred times that purity was armor and temptation the sword, felt explicitly, worthlessly naked—as though the opaque material of my dress had somehow dissolved in the warm, honeyed light of the sullen chamber, leaving me more exposed than I'd ever known.

I hesitated. It would have been better to turn and leave; to let this gloriously misguided moment pass unspoken, like so many confessions unuttered in the silence of pews. But something in his posture, in the way his head tilted ever so slightly, as if listening for something just beyond my grasp, drew me forward. My sandals made no sound on the uneven wood, yet he turned, his eyes catching mine with a brightness that seemed to disarm the very air between us.

"You came," he said, softly, as though he'd been rehearsing the words but hadn't meant to say them out loud.

I wanted to laugh, or scoff, or do something that would keep me from stepping closer, but my feet betrayed me. His smile flickered, not bold, but curious, like a boy daring the edge of a frozen pond. And then his hand lifted, not quickly, not carelessly, but with the deliberation of someone tracing the outline of a thought they refused to make whole. The back of his fingers brushed my cheek, and I felt the pulse of my heartbeat leap to the electrified surface of my skin.

I should have turned. I should have spoken some word of scripture, something firm and final, but instead, my voice faltered, whispering only, "We shouldn't..." The words hung there, incomplete, as though even they had lost their resolve in the stillness of that place.

He stepped closer, the rough wool of his shirt brushing against the thin edge of my sleeve. His hand, warm and certain now, lingered on my face. I felt the faint scrape of his calluses, the remnants of work or play, or whatever it was boys did when they weren't here, unraveling girls like me. My knees trembled, not from fear, not entirely, and I realized I was holding my breath, waiting for something; something magnificent.

"You're beautiful," he said, as if the words had slipped out before he could stop them. It wasn't the kind of beauty I'd heard preached against in church, the vain kind that fades and damns. No, his voice made it sound like a discovery, like he'd found something buried and couldn't believe his luck. And for a moment, I wanted to believe him. I wanted to take his words and wear them like the pearl necklace my grandmother left me, the one I never dared to touch but always kept close.

He bent his head, his lips so near my temple that his breath stirred the fine hair that lived there. I thought of the sermons, of Mother's warnings, of the words that should have come to me then, sharp, clear, unyielding. Instead, I stood there, caught in the peculiar gravity of him, the way his presence seemed to fold the room inward, pulling me to a center I couldn't see but felt with every inch of my skin.

And then, his lips brushed mine, so lightly that I wondered if I had imagined it. The contact was fleeting, hesitant, as if he, too, was unsure of the boundary he might have crossed. But it was enough to set something loose inside me, something I had been told to bind and bury and never say out loud. Just like I had to do with Benji. But Benji's gone.

Now, there's only Bo.

My hands, of their own accord, rested against his chest, feeling the warmth of him, the steady rhythm beneath the coarse fabric.

There, in that stolen moment, I forgot myself. I forgot the church around us, the light slanting through the beams, the warnings of my mother, the lessons of Sunday school. All I knew was the weight of his hand at the small of my back, the way his thumb moved in slow, unconscious circles, as though trying to memorize the curve of me.

And then, just as quickly as it began, it ended. He pulled back, his face like a forgery of Rodin's *The Thinker*, a study of conflict, part wonder, part regret. His hand lingered on my arm, his fingers brushing the edge of my sleeve as though reluctant to let go. "I'm sorry," he whispered, but it sounded like he was speaking to himself.

I didn't know what to say. I stood there, trembling and speechless; the warmth of him fading too quickly in the coolness of the imposing tower. I opened my mouth, but no words came. Only silence stretched between us, thick and heavy and alive with all the things he, we hadn't said.

And then he turned, his footsteps echoing as he descended the stairs, leaving me alone in the quiet aftermath of what we had done—or almost done. I touched my lips, still warm, still tingling, and wondered what it meant to feel so alive and so lost all at once.

I was still tingling from the ghost of his kiss, fixated on the tiny dust motes hanging like stars in a galaxy only I could see, each one catching the golden slant of sunlight pouring through the window, spinning slowly, like time had lost its footing. The beams didn't frame the belfry like the bars of a cage; not anymore. They felt like the strings of a harp, stretched tight and humming with a music I couldn't hear but somehow understood. I pressed my fingers to my mouth again, not to erase the feeling, but to memorize it, like I could hold the moment in place, so long as I didn't breathe too hard.

The silence settled heavy, the kind that demands you pay attention to what's just happened. My cheeks burned, though I wasn't sure if it was shame or exhilaration, or both tangled up in some dense and unyielding knot I couldn't begin to unravel. I wanted to run after him, to demand he explain why he left, why he stepped back from something we'd both leaned into. But my legs wouldn't move.

I felt caught between two worlds: the one I'd been raised in and the one I was only just beginning to glimpse. It wasn't so much about Bo, though his shadow lingered in every corner of my mind. It was about the space he'd opened, the seeds planted and reawakened; the questions he'd allowed to slip through the cracks.

The sunlight had shifted, casting longer shadows now. I adjusted my clothes, smoothing the fabric of my dress with trembling hands, still tingling in excitement with the memory of his. My pulse was unsteady, a drumbeat or two louder than the church bells that had yet to ring. I stayed in the belfry, unable to follow him, unable to go back down the way I came. The moment felt as fragile and brittle as old paper, as though moving too quickly, any sudden motion might crease it, tear it, leave it illegible in ways that could never be mended.

I leaned against the rough wood of the tower's upright beam, staring out through the slats at the small town spread below me. I've never seen the town from such an elevation, never in such a splendid light.

Everything looked the same as it always had, yet different; better. Neat rows of houses—the collective assortments of porch columns: Doric, Ionic, Craftsman— standing like steadfast sentinels guarding Willow Street, with the distant tannery's faint spiral of chimney smoke braided into the lead-gray clouds; the clock tower of the courthouse ticking on like it always would, only sweeter. It all seemed different. Or maybe, somehow, I was.

I thought about Bo's expression as he left, the way his mouth had softened into something like appreciation, maybe recognition. I didn't fully understand what had passed between us, whether it was something real or just something he was curious about, a selfish game boys play when they realize the power they hold over girls like me, burning with a disobedient curiosity. But in those moments, I choked out all traces of negativity and doubt, and tried my best to focus on the way my stomach bubbled up to the point of burping, but instead, butterflies flew 'round popping the bubbles to save me the embarrassment.

It had sure left its mark, faint but there, like the pressure of his fingers on my arm. It made me wonder if I'd been fooling myself all along, thinking I couldn't stand apart from the Jennifers and Trixies and Barbaras of the world, at risk in the safe judgments and observations that kept me hiding from boys in my books and in my bedroom. Maybe I wasn't so clever or steady as I had persuaded myself.

The summer sun finally warmed the air around me even as I felt a chill settle deeper inside. I knew I couldn't stay much longer. If Mother found out I'd been in the belfry, if she even suspected I'd been near Bo, the consequences would be worse than any sermon Father Schadenfreude could conjure. I wasn't sure I could face her sharp eyes, her disappointment, certainly wrapped in scripture—and delivered with the precision of a prison guard.

I descended the stairs slowly, each step feeling heavier than the last. When I reached the bottom, the organ loft was empty, silent as though it had never held a single sound.

Sister Agatha loomed there, her pipes dull in the fading light, her keys untouched. I felt a strange pang looking at her, as if she, too, knew something had changed with me, but wouldn't say a word. Shrugging off the weight of a possibility that Bo might have been waiting in the organ loft, I descended the second set of stairs with neglectful steps.

When I stepped outside, the air was heavy with moisture, wrapping around my skin like damp wool. A storm was brewing in the distance. Sweat rose before movement, beading at my temples, tracing slow paths down my face.

The sky had quickly turned a tumbling dull gray, the kind that always made me feel like the earth was holding its breath. I glanced down the road, half-hoping to see Bo leaning against the churchyard fence, waiting for me, his expression perhaps unreadable but undeniably his. Of course, he wasn't there. The only thing waiting for me was the too-short walk home and whatever questions Mother would hurl my way when I arrived.

The house was quiet when I opened the door, the kind of quiet that feels intentional. Earline was in the kitchen, humming softly to herself as she stirred something on the stove. She glanced up when she saw me, her eyes narrowing just enough to let me know she'd noticed the flush in my cheeks and the slight tremor in my hands. But she didn't say anything, at least, not yet.

I collapsed into the kitchen chair, scooting up to the table.

"Miss Shirley," she said, drawing out my name like a slow melody, "y'all been out longer than usual. That organ sure be keepin' you busy."

I nodded, trying to force a smile, but it felt brittle on my lips. "Tom had a lot to show me today. He's fat and he stutters, Earline. It takes a while," I said, my voice too quick, not too eager to explain.

Earline's gaze lingered a moment longer before she turned back to her pot. "Well, good," her tone light but knowing. "Long as y'ain't lettin' nobody distract you from what matters. Ain't nothin' good comes from wanderin' eyes, you hear me, child?"

I nodded again, swallowing the lump in my throat. I didn't trust myself to say anything more. Earline fixed me a saucer plate with three perfectly arranged peanut butter'd crackers, and poured me an ice-cold glass of milk.

Later, when I was alone in my room, I lay on my bed staring at the ceiling. The weight of the day pressed against me, heavy and unrelenting. I replayed the moment in the belfry over and over, dissecting every glance, every word, every touch. Part of me wanted to believe it meant something big; that Bo had seen something in me worth wanting. But another part, the part Earline's voice had shaped and sharpened, told me to be careful. Boys like Bo didn't give without taking, and whatever they took, they rarely gave back; I was more than excited to find out.

The storm broke later that night, rain hammering against the windowpanes, thunder rolling low and steady like the organ's deepest pipes. I lay awake, listening, wondering if Bo was lying awake too, if he was thinking about me or if I was already forgotten, just another young girl caught in his orbit for a moment.

I didn't have answers, not for that, not for anything. All I had was the exquisite memory of his touch, the questions it had stirred, and the uneasy feeling that whatever came next would demand something from me I wasn't sure I was ready to give.

TWO

EMPTY WORDS

Wednesday, Third Week of May 1942

IT'S A STRANGE kind of loneliness—not knowing who you are, not really, not down in the marrow. Stranger still is living among people who claim to know you better than you've ever dared to know yourself. In town, they'd tip their hats with practiced grace, their smiles folded neat as Sunday napkins, and offer up praise sweet enough to rot your teeth. "Pretty thing," they'd say, nodding toward the ribbons in my hair, the way I held my shoulders like I knew I mattered. But their words floated too easily, too polished to belong to me. They settled around me like dust on glass—proof of a reflection I'd learned to keep spotless, even if I never believed it was mine.

I used to imagine love was something so natural it didn't call for proving, like the way your lungs just keep breathing whether you ask them to or not. Natural in the way something can just exist in the quiet balance of things untouched, where wind moves through tall grass without resistance and rivers carve their paths without instruction; like the scent of earth after rain, rich and unforced, or the taste of fruit ripened under the sun, unaltered by hands that would want to make it sweeter.

But with Mother, it's different. Her love, if it's there at all, feels more like an obligation, stretched tight over us like the Sunday tablecloth, meant to make the jagged edges of life appear smooth and just as thin.

I squander most days walking around with a hollowness that feels almost physical—hollow and veritably oblique, hollow like the remnants of a burned-out tree—as though loneliness were a place inside me, carved out, echoing, and waiting to be filled by someone. But there's no one to fill it. Not really. Not aside from Earline and Daddy, my dog Cousin Ralph, and a few girlfriends—Phylis and Bridgette. Two loathsome names Mother can't hear without making a face, disapproving of the very air I share with them.

It's a type of surreptitious loneliness. A diluted woe from missing out on so many things that I never possessed, or knew I needed; not until now, and I can't see myself ever taking grasp. A torment that comes from almost being an adult and not knowing who it is I will marry, what will become of me, and the absence of a mother's nurture, of supportive companionship. My girlfriends seem to have this with their mothers, each with boyfriends they intend to marry after or before graduation. Perhaps this is why Mother doesn't like my friends. Or perhaps it is Bridgette's smutty mouth and Phylis' hilariously raucous snoring.

Not only is Bo treading the floorboards, he doesn't know what he wants. Mother despises him anyway. But Bo—Lord, Bo—sometimes he'll look at me with a softness so fierce it stops the air in my lungs. And just when I start to believe he sees me, really sees me, he pulls back into himself, quiet as fog peeling off a river, like loving anything too much might burn a hole clean through him.

Sometimes he'll say something sweet, like how the sun catches bits of auburn in my sable hair or how the sound of my voice reminds him of wind chimes. Other times he'll act like I'm just another girl at the end of the dirt road, someone to pass the time with until something better comes along. It makes me feel like I'm always standing on the edge of something, never sure if I'll fall or be pulled back to safety. I wish he'd never kissed me, 'least not in the way he did; the way Clark Gable kissed Vivien Leigh, for God's sake.

One minute I'm skimming through catalogs looking for wedding dresses and the next I'm crying, face down on my grandmother's quilt.

Mother says I'm too young to know anything about boys or love, but what she doesn't understand is that I know more than I'd like to. I know how Bo smells like summer, like hay and dirt and the faintest hint of something sharp, like dark chocolate drenched in a bath of ginger. I know how he gets thunderously quiet when he's thinking, his lips pressed together like he's holding back words he's too proud or too scared to say. And I know how my heart twists like a carnival pretzel every time I see him walking away, leaving me to wonder if he imagines me as his one-day bride, or if he'll ever come back at all.

But it's not just Bo. It's this town, this house, this suffocating life of a well-dressed cadaver I'm living that cages me in, feels too small for me. Sometimes I think about running away, just walking until my legs give out and I find a place where nobody knows my name. But then I remember Mother and her tired eyes, the way she wipes her hands on her apron and looks out the kitchen window like she's waiting for something that'll never come. I wonder if she ever thought about leaving, too, before she had me. Maybe I'm the reason she stayed. Maybe I'm the reason she's so tired.

I laughed at myself this morning, thinking how funny it is that a person can be so lonely they start talking to themselves just to fill the quiet. I told that old pier mirror in my room, "Well, Shirley, looks like it's just us," and for a moment, I thought it might talk back. It didn't, of course, but wouldn't that be something? To have someone, even your own reflection, tell you who you are—who you're supposed to be, when you don't have the faintest idea.

Until that happens, I reckon I'll keep my head up and drift through the places where he might be, half-hoping to see Bo in a crowd, half-dreading what I'd do if I did. That's the trouble with being fifteen and unsure of your own shape in the world. It's standing barefoot on the threshold of a hundred different wide-open doorways, wind pulling at your clothes, and wondering if you're meant to walk through any of them or find your way to the middle of just one.

I desperately needed to get out of my room this morning, to do something, to get out of this house and away from my books and thoughts.

In the living room, Mother sat in her corner chair, sewing with such precision it seemed her needle moved to a metronome I couldn't hear. I leaned against the doorframe, watching her hands work the thread through cloth like she was stitching her past back together with a different trim. I wanted to say something, anything—but words with her always seemed to get caught in my throat, tangled like burrs. Finally, I spoke.

"Mother, do you think people ever wonder if they're... enough?"

Her needle paused mid-air, her sharp eyes lifting to meet mine. "Enough for what, child?" Mother has a cool and airy voice, meted out with a misplaced fervor, the tone of a lady well beyond her station, yet hopelessly trapped in the one she'd ended up.

"For anything," I mumbled, shifting my weight, "for love, for success, whatever?"

Mother resumed sewing, her voice even. "People waste too much time on questions that have no answers, Shirley. You'd do better to keep your mind on what you can control."

It wasn't the answer I wanted, but it was the answer I expected. That was the peculiar essence of Mother: her words flowed from her lips as if chiseled in granite, her movements imbued with a certainty that felt both preordained and unshakable, like the church hymns she sang every Sunday without glancing at the pages. I ached for her to utter something along the lines of, "Why, of course, sweetheart, we all ponder such things, but fret not, for everyone loves you, especially me!" Alas, she remained trapped within her own fortress of reticent strength, seemingly loath to bestow upon me even a solitary crumb of assurance, leaving me to grapple with the jagged edges of my own vulnerability in silence.

"Do you ever feel like… maybe there's more?" I ventured, knowing I was pressing my luck.

Her lips tightened. "More of what?"

"I don't know. Just… more than this."

Mother set her sewing down and fixed me with that look, the one that could silence a room. "This is what there is, Shirley. Wishing for more is a fool's errand. And I didn't raise you to be no fool. You're the top of your class; you're fishing for something, it's both obvious and annoying. Just say what you're thinking, child."

I heard her, but I plucked a word that struck me odd. She hadn't really raised me at all, had she? Not in the way other mothers did. She'd orchestrated my life, yes, like a conductor leading a symphony where every note was hers to dictate. But I wasn't sure if it was love or duty—or maybe the two had become so intertwined in her that even she couldn't tell the difference. My dog, Cousin Ralph, trotted up behind me, nuzzling his way between my legs and sitting there, as if waiting for a treat. In that tense moment, Ralph's presence provided a sense of comfort, an unconditional support system that shows up with slobber and butt-wagging just when I need it most.

"Do you ever wish grandmother were still here?" I asked softly, almost afraid of the answer.

Her face didn't change, but something flickered in her eyes, gone so quickly I might've imagined it. "Wishing doesn't bring people back. We have what we're given, and we make do."

I nodded, though her words felt hollow, like an echo in an empty room. Mother might've believed them, but

I wasn't sure I did. What I was sure of was that Mother was never going to voluntarily say what I most needed her to say to me.

She picked up her sewing again, signaling the conversation was over. "Run into town and make yourself useful. And don't dawdle, Shirley. Here's my list. You've got better things to do than stand around questioning things you can't change."

I bit back a retort, swallowing the bitterness that rose in my throat. She didn't see it, the weight of her expectations, the way they pressed down on me like the heavy hymnals at church. She didn't see me, not really.

As I leave the house with Mother's list—navy blue thread, ochre thread, and four packs of needles—I feel the weight of it all pressing on me like this oppressive summer heat. It's not that I mind running errands. It's just that I sometimes wonder if she even notices I'm growing up, almost an adult. Or if she's more interested in the spools of thread than in me.

Most mornings, I'd cut through the square, past the white clapboard Baptist church with its peeling steeple, my shoes scuffing out a rhythm on the uneven road, counting the steps to the stop sign, like I'd not done the same thing a hundred times, wondering if the number would change. The errands were never much: flour for biscuits, a tin of lard, a fresh loaf of bread, whatever Mother needed.

The town square sits at the heart of Springfield like a clockface, orderly and unchanging, four blocks from our house. At its center is the courthouse, a proud and stony thing with tall columns that seem to look down on the rest of us. Around it, the shops form a tidy, orderly circle. The CeeBee Store, Finch's Pharmacy, and The Lady Bug—a seamstress shop—my first stop today, to name a few.

On the edges of town, the hills roll on forever, green and dappled with the light of the afternoon sun. They seem to hold the town in their arms, even as they turn their backs to it. Walking through the square, I can smell the mingling of fried chicken, car exhaust, and the occasional sweetness of magnolia blossoms. A stroll through Springfield can be as exciting as it is mundane; one never knows what peculiar scents await.

People move through their daily routines with a rhythm as predictable as the tolling of the church bells. The Baptist church, whitewashed and sagging at the corners, looms over one side of the square, its steeple casting a long shadow. Father Schadenfreude's parish, St. Cecilia, smaller but statelier, sits two blocks away, its stained glass catching the sun like jewels.

The movie theater marquee catches my eye as I pass. *Casablanca* is playing. I don't have the money to see it, but I can imagine what it's like—Humphrey Bogart's gravelly voice, the swirling cigarette smoke, the kind of romance that exists only in dreams. A thought enters my mind the perhaps Bo might ask me on a date to the movie—a fine thought but unrealistic, considering Mother doesn't approve of him. Just as I think about walking on, I reach into my purse and feel for whatever it is that's been crinkling. Fifteen cents. Daddy must've slipped it in. For once in a long while, I smile. I'll get a Coca-Cola on my way home.

It's funny how a town so small can feel so big when you're walking alone. Each building, each person, seems part of some unspoken story, one I'll never quite be able to read. But today, my story leads me to The Lady Bug, where Ms. Trixie Simpson waits, ready with her sharp eyes and even sharper tongue.

Ms. Trixie, Patricia Simpson, runs The Lady Bug like a queen ruling over a realm of silks, satins, and threads. Her shop is tucked between The CeeBee Store and a florist, its window filled with mannequins dressed in her latest creations. The bell above the door tinkles as I step inside, and the scent of fabric, clean and comforting, wraps around me like my daddy's hug. My love of fabric must have been inherited.

Ms. Trixie herself stands behind the counter, a vision of confidence and beauty in a dress she surely made herself, the cut sharp enough to slice through the gossip that follows her like a shadow. Her bright silk scarf, today a bold crimson, flutters as she turns, her smile half amusement and half something else I can't quite place. She always seems to know something you don't, as if she's holding the last piece of a puzzle you didn't even know you were working on.

"Why, it's Shirley Ragland," she says, drawing my name out like three wraps of yarn. "What brings you here today?"

I hand her Mother's list and watch as she moves with the kind of grace that makes you forget she's human. Her fingers, with perfectly manicured nails, are quick and precise, the seams of her stockings in perfect vertical lines, pulling spools of thread from shelves with exactness, her bewildering eyes darting between the colors like she's weighing their secrets. "Navy blue and ochre," she murmurs. "Your motha' has impeccable taste, I do wonda' what it is that woman's making?"

Ms. Trixie isn't like anyone else in this town. She's a creature of such elegance and refinement that it feels almost indecent to look directly at her, like staring into the sun. She's the kind of woman who could turn a trip to the grocery store into a parade, her heels clicking like a metronome that sets the pace for everyone around her. Her hair is always perfect, a glossy brunette wave that defies the humidity we all wrestle with. Her lipstick is a shade of red that would look garish on anyone else but on her. It's commanding—a flag planted on a battlefield, daring anyone to challenge her.

The grown-ups talk about Ms. Trixie in hushed tones, their words dripping with judgment and curiosity. They say she doesn't go to church regularly, and when she does, she sits in the back, her head held higher than it should. They whisper about the expensive dresses she wears and the gentlemen callers who come and go like fireflies on a summer night. Mama calls her "shameless" but always says it with a pinch of envy, like she's wondering what it might be like to be shameless, just for a minute.

And it's not just Mama. The other women in town—Mrs. Hargrove with her starched collars and Mrs. Ellis, who's forever clutching her pearls—they can't stop talking about her either. "A widow shouldn't carry herself like that," Mrs. Hargrove said once, her voice tight as her bun. "She's practically asking for trouble." But I think what they mean is that they're scared. Scared their husbands might look at Ms. Trixie and see all the things they've forgotten to want.

To me, she's something else entirely. She's everything I want to be. Confident. Graceful. Unafraid. I wonder what it'd be like to have even a fraction of that confidence.

She doesn't hide behind the opinions of others like the women here do, folding themselves into neat little boxes marked "decent" and "proper." Ms. Trixie lives like she doesn't know what the box is, or if she does, she's already turned it into kindling.

She is Mother's cousin too, though I can't see them having much in common besides a bloodline and a tendency to sigh when the subject of men arises. I've always wondered what she sees when she looks at people. Her eyes linger too long sometimes, as though she's stitching together a story from their inseams and hems. Does she see me the way I see her—strong, untamed, and unwilling to fit into the neat little boxes the town has built for us? Or does she see something else, something I'm too scared to confront?

I'm not sure what's more intoxicating: the way she carries herself or the way she's entirely unbothered by the consequences. It's not that she's reckless; it's that she's free. Even now, as she glances over her shoulder, her eyes narrowing in thought, there's a quiet assurance about her. She knows exactly who she is and doesn't seem to care if anyone else likes it.

She hands me the thread, her fingers brushing mine for just a second, and I feel a rush of something I can't quite name. "Tell my cousin Ora I said hello," drawing out the words, her lips curving into a smile that feels like a secret. I nod, clutching the thread like it's a treasure, and turn to leave, but not before stealing one last glance at her.

Ms. Trixie Simpson, unshakable and unapologetic, standing there like a queen in exile, daring the world to doubt her. Oh—would I love to have a glamorous name like that.

As I leave the shop with Mother's thread and needles tucked safely into my purse, I glance back and see her through the window, bent over her sewing machine, her hands moving with the precision of an artist, wondering if there's something in the way she moves, the way she lives, that I might learn to borrow for myself. I wonder if she's happy, or if she's simply learned to live with the restlessness that comes from being too much for a town like Springfield. Whatever the answer, I admire her. And in a small, secret way, I hope someday I'll be as brave and bold as Ms. Trixie.

Thread in hand, I move down 7th Street. The sound of my footsteps echo against the brick walls of the alley. The air thickens as I near the door to Sadie Cooper's salon, freighted with lilac water and the acrid sting of something chemical—hair tonic or bleach or whatever it is that eats the shine out of things.

"Shirley Ragland!" Sadie sings my name in a cadence of a primitive meter, voice high and hollow. She stands by the chair like a monument raised by habit—apron streaked with pomade; hands planted on her hips like they're keeping the building upright. "What brings you in, darlin'?"

"I need an appointment, Miss Sadie," I tell her, not quite meeting her eyes. "Tuesday morning. Next week. Nine, if you've got it."

She tips her head, smile crawling slow across her face. "Piana' recital, huh? I heard 'bout that. Your mama's been ringin' it through to town like a church bell."

I nodded, and already I'm wishing I'd stayed home, let my hair go flat and limp and unnoticed.

"Well," she says, thumbing her appointment book with nails that look dipped in something dark, "I reckon I can squeeze you in. But only 'cause I want to see you shine, honey. You're the pride of this place, you know that?"

I don't feel like the pride of anything. Not town, not family, not even my own reflection. But I give her a smile. Polite. Hollow. The right thing to do. "Thanks, Miss Sadie."

I turn toward the door, but there he is—Mr. Cooper, framed in the threshold like he's been standing there a while, listening. His grin is too wide. "Now, Shirley," he says with a grin, slow and smooth, "you tell your daddy I said he owes me a game of checkers. Been too long since he's had his tail whooped fair and square."

"I'll let him know," I say, my voice sounding light. I even laugh a little. But something cold moves up my spine, and I don't look back when I step out. Not once. Not even when the door clicks shut behind me.

On the way home, I stop by The CeeBee Store. The worn-out wooden screen door jerks from my hand and slams against the frame with a hollow clap that rattles the pane. Inside, the air clutches at my lungs—sawdust and bleach and the raw, sweet tang of cured meat, all mingling into something that feels more alive than inert, like it's been waiting for me.

"Shirley!" Cousin C.B. calls from behind the counter, wiping his hands on a rag that's already dirty. "Well, don't you look like the spitting image of your mama today. How's Jim?"

"He's fine," I say, fishing a nickel from the small zip pouch in my purse I keep just for errands like this, thanks to my good daddy's generosity. "Just here for a Coke."

C.B. strolls over to the bright red Coca-Cola chest and brings me back an ice-cold bottle. He flips the cap off and slides the bottle toward me, flicking the cap across the room to a large waste bin. "Tell him I said hi, and don't let him forget about Sunday dinner. Your mama'll have my hide if he does."

"I'll remind him." The glass sweats against my palm, damp and slick, as if the bottle wants to escape my grip.

I walk home sipping the Coke, the fizz sharp against the back of my throat. Around me, the street feels too quiet, like the world's taken a breath and held it. I think about the day—the drag of Mother's hopes pulling tight across my shoulders—and the other thing too: the glittering, gummy strangeness of Trixie Simpson. A world that smells like lipstick and cigarette smoke and trouble. A world that grins when you look away.

A PERFORMANCE OF PIETY

Sunday, Fourth Week of May 1942

SUNDAYS, AS MOTHER always reminded us, were the Lord's day. Though to me, they felt more like her day, a grand performance in which Mother played the starring role. The St. Cecilia parish itself stood there like a weary sentry, its paint peeling, the smell of mildew mingling with the perfume of overdressed ladies and the faint tang of varnish rising from the pews. Those pews—sticky and shining, as though they'd been dipped in molasses—creaked under the weight of peckish, pious bodies shifting, moaning, sighing and "Oh Lording" through Father Schadenfreude's absurd sermons.

The Father, with his Polish accent and his dramatic gesticulations, never failed once to choose the most peculiar passages from scripture. It was as though he'd spent the week spelunking through the Bible's darkest caves, emerging with treasures meant to warn us against everything from greed to an improperly buttoned blouse. These sermons were not so much lessons as they were a tightrope walk—balancing just enough fire and brimstone to keep us upright but never so much as to send anyone fleeing in fear. Mother, naturally, found in them endless inspiration.

Each obscure biblical reference seemed to light up her face with revelation, her eyes narrowing in that certain way that made me brace myself. By lunchtime, whatever the Father had said would be recast as her personal wisdom, wielded like the sword of a Teutonic knight, against me or anyone else who dared deviate from her script for moral living.

Poor Daddy, never in attendance—born into, I hate to say it, the Baptist cult—knew to run for cover or the old outhouse when he saw Mother and I walking home from one of Father Schadenfreude's ridiculous sermons. But it wasn't just her preaching that wore me down; it was her obsessive need to embody the very spirit of the sermon in public.

"Look at me, everyone! Aren't I just the picture of piety?"

I could practically pluck those words from her thoughts, as she nodded enthusiastically during the service in a manner that bordered on the comical. Her hymnal was pitched one note too bright, her "Amens" punctuating the air like a conductor's baton, precise and demanding, yet dripping with an insistent sweetness that grated on my nerves like an uninvited itch in an inappropriate place to scratch.

When Father Schadenfreude spoke of humility, she ached to embody it, sitting tall and poised with a regal air. I could see it so clearly: her eyes cast downward like a queen bestowing charity upon her loyal subjects. "Oh, Father, your words are pure nectar for the soul!" she might have declared with all the earnestness of a kitchen prayer meeting, saccharine enough to invite the skeptical to lean in and catch a whiff of her insincerity.

It bordered on parody, really—each gesture an exaggerated stroke of virtue, a fine painting crafted with too much paint and too little primer. Yet to the congregation, brave souls clinging to beliefs more fragile than blown glass, she was the saint—their saint. "She is simply filled with the Holy Spirit!" they'd coo among themselves, eyes gleaming as if they'd lost the ability to see properly outside the brilliance of Mother's blinding stage light.

Perhaps it was humor that kept me afloat in the swirling tide of resentment and affection, sarcasm serving as a life ring tossed my way in turbulent times. I could not escape the irony—the view of my mother being a shining beacon of piety while I remained a flickering candle, desperate for just a whisper of light from the holy woman herself.

But as her amen crescendo echoed through the sanctuary, I held fast to my secret hope: that one day I might emerge from those shadows unafraid and perhaps, just perhaps, make my voice rise above the racket to whisper a truth that could shatter the gilded glass of pretension that cloaked our lives. What a spectacle that might be!

To me, however, she was insufferable, a living testament to piety worn like a costume rather than a heartfelt adornment. Her faith shimmered with an artificial sheen, heavy lace draped over a too-tight corset that constricted her true self, stifling any hint of authenticity lurking beneath. It felt less like a guiding light and more like an intricate trap, turning faith into a mere performance rather than genuine conviction—a well-rehearsed act that danced dangerously close to hypocrisy.

"Did you see how she practically radiated holiness today?" I could hear the whispers of adoring parishioners nearby, eyes gleaming as they idolized the spectacle she made of herself. Their admiration twisted like vines around my neck, suffocating and leaving no room for the more honest shadows of holiness.

Each time she raised her hands in testimony or gazed heavenward with a look of rapturous bliss, I wondered if she truly believed the script she played or if she too felt the suffocating weight of expectations pressing in—all those watchful eyes yearning for her to validate their own insecurities. A part of me held deep resentment for her ability to command such adoration while I wrestled with a burgeoning spirit dimmed by her brilliance.

As Father Schadenfreude wrapped up his weekly warning—a convoluted metaphor involving sheep, gold coins, and an inexplicably lost candlestick—I found myself lost in thought. It wasn't about salvation or the wages of sin, but rather the enigma standing before us. His face bore the weight of untold stories, each wrinkle a testament to burdens swallowed in silence, hinting at tragedies far removed from Springfield's narrow confines. With every fervent word that spilled from his lips, flames of urgency swirled around him, but it felt more personal than spiritual; it was as though he preached not to save our souls but to rescue his own from the cavernous depths of whatever despair that loomed just outside the shining façade he maintained.

I watched, caught in a tension I couldn't quite pinpoint, as he leaned into his sermon, his eyes shimmering faintly with conviction. A prickle of unease skittered down my spine, the warmth of his faith obscuring motives that felt murky and less than pure. I caught the way his gaze sifted over the congregation, darting from face to face, assessing us like an amateur gambler weighing his odds at a crooked table. The room felt thick with the weight of understated power, and my gut twisted into an anxious knot that mirrored the tension in his stance. But it was the way he gazed at Bo, caught somewhere between the fervent flames of passion and the shadowy depths of perdition, that stirred the deepest unease within me.

Could it be that beneath those finely woven robes, rich with the shimmering threads of piety, lay tangled truths—a desperate man grasping at the last vestiges of authority as the world around him felt hell-bent on unraveling? His voice, commanded with charisma, painted grand realities in vivid strokes; still, I couldn't shake the sensation that with each deliberate pause, he was weaving an intricate web that bound us tighter to the very church we should be seeking escape from. The rhythm of his speech, confident and commanding, masked a restlessness that left an echo of mistrust dancing in the air and settling into my bones like a menacing wintry chill.

In these flickering moments that should have bristled with grace, I began to recognize the double-edged sword of his craft. It was not mere scripture he wielded; it was power—the power to control thoughts, the power to invoke fear, the power to define worthiness.

His lessons dripped with a bittersweet poison, laced with a need to dominate rather than uplift. I felt it settle deep in my stomach, a foreboding unease that whispered of Bo—trapped like a canary in a cage with an indifferent lion, the taste of ash lingering in my mouth. There was a hint of something unholy nestling itself among the shadows of holiness, taunting me with the notion that perhaps even those who purported to guide us had murky intentions cloaked in the guise of benevolence.

With every whispered prayer and fervent "Amen" that echoed off the heavy church walls, I questioned where the true intentions of Father Schadenfreude lay. Did he truly seek to shepherd us into a better life, or were we but pawns in a game rigged with deception? I envisioned Bo's hopeful, earnest eyes, and the way his laughter would shimmer like sunlight on water. I feared for him, trapped as he was in the Father's line of sight—a target for every arrow marked with judgment wrapped in satin piety.

As Father Schadenfreude concluded his bombastic warnings, his voice melted into the air heavy with artificial tension. On cue, Mother leaned slightly forward, her hands clasped tightly in her lap and her girdle stretched tight across the burgeoning swell of her middle. With a smile that shimmered with feigned warmth, she turned toward me, her voice ringing with the glassy timber of someone convinced of their own righteousness.

"Ah, my dear, our dear Father reminds us," she declared, her tone dripping with sanctimonious glee, "that the good book teaches us that even the lost sheep must learn to find their way, lest they fall amongst the gold coins and candlesticks of life's distractions. We must stay ever so vigilant, for piety is the only true coin worth collecting!"

With that, she settled back into her pew—the flicker of her smile a mere mask, betraying a spirit thrumming nervously beneath layers of devotion and barely concealed something akin to scrutiny.

Then, as the Father closed his bible, the parish congregation lapped it up like hungry hens. When he'd finished, they'd clamor to shake his hand, their mouths dripping with compliments that sounded more like confessions. And there was Mother, front and center, bestowing upon him her most radiant smile— the one she saved for anyone she deemed worthy of her approval, or her influence. My name was conspicuously not included.

SEEKING WHOLENESS IN SHADOWS

LATER, THE STILLNESS of my room presses close like a too-warm blanket, heavy but familiar, a kind of refuge from the rawness Mass leaves behind. The air hangs flat, unmoving; dust motes drifting like thoughts too small to have anyway. Here, among my books and the vague comfort of Cousin Ralph—a wiggly brindle boxer with the unfortunate face of a blood relative we no longer talk about—I try to gather what's left of my strength. What light remains in me clings to the edges like a fog to glass.

But peace doesn't last. Not really. Not here. The silence breeds new unrest, a slow infestation of doubt and dread. I lie still beneath the scratchy afghan, Ralph's head, warm and too heavy, parked on my chest like he's trying to crush the unease out of me. He smells like sleep and dried slobber and the faint, unshakable scent of Earline's bacon. I don't mind. He's ridiculous and loyal and utterly useless against the thing swelling in my chest: Mother's contempt for Earline.

It festers there. A storm that hasn't broken yet.

The air thickens, charged like just before lightning. I hear Mother's voice from the hallway—sharp, clipped, just loud enough. Complaining to Daddy about how Earline didn't oil the dining room table yesterday. Her words aren't just criticism; they're calculated. Cruel. She peels at Earline's dignity like old flaky paint. But Earline moves like someone who knows no other way—always in motion, always tending, always putting me before herself. A ghost with a dishcloth.

How does Mother not see that?

Does she truly not see her—the devotion cinched beneath her ribs, the kind that breathes in cautious silence, held tight by the invisible corset of her station? Does she not sense the strength veiled in her stillness, the kind of faithfulness that doesn't call attention to itself but seeps, steady and unshakable, into every motion she makes? There's a power there, quiet and dignified, stitched into the way she pours a glass, folds a cloth, bows her head—not the kind that roars, but the kind that lasts.

Or maybe she sees it too well, and it stings her. Maybe it reminds her of everything she once had—ambition, brilliance, a mind too big for linens and casserole dishes—and how it all calcifies inside a box being built by men, bound by marriage and expectation. Mother seems a woman too burdened by her own disappointments; disappointments in herself, in her life, in the metastasizing misogyny of this horribly unfair world, strapped in so tightly she can barely breathe?

Maybe that's what makes her so cruel. She looks at Earline and sees a kind of freedom dressed in servitude. Something she gave up long ago. Something that still breathes in her.

I don't know. I don't want to know. All I know is this: Earline gave me herself. Freely. Without condition. And in doing so, she shaped me in ways Mother never will.

Cousin Ralph, with his insistent need for attention and his ridiculously cute, but intolerably heavy head resting upon my chest, provides an uncomfortable but welcome distraction from the tempest of thoughts swirling within me. This faithful pet had an uncanny knack for bestowing affection that is as palpable as Earline's hot buttered pancakes. His floppy ears, soft as a lamb, a warm furry balm against the chill of my worries.

Yet, despite his noble efforts to soothe my restless spirit, his steadfast loyalty did little to quiet the clamor of my busy mind, which buzzed incessantly like a hive of honeybees, flitting from one anxious thought to the next as if in a whimsical dance, a dance that Cousin Ralph—dear stinky soul that he is—could only observe with a bemused tilt of his head, as though pondering the folly of it all.

If I strip away the polish Mother insists that I wear—her lessons in posture and silence, in polite deception—what's left of me feels like a hollow frame. A lamp flickering behind boarded-up windows. Something unfinished. Something watched but not seen.

It wasn't something I could explain, not to her, not to the priest, not to anyone who seemed to think the shape of a girl could be drawn out by rules, ribbons, and a decent Sunday dress. And so, I played the part, the dutiful daughter, all shining shoes and straightened spines, while inside, the shadows of my self-restraint stretched long, growing restless with every passing day.

Mother says it's selfish to want to be seen. "God sees you," she's quick to remind me, her voice thick with that churchy certainty that always seems more for her own benefit than mine. But God feels too far away to notice, and what good is being seen by someone who won't speak back?

I want something different, something closer, warmer, messier. I want someone to look past the curated hair and books, past the practiced posture, and find the girl who doesn't have all the answers. The one who isn't even sure she wants them at all.

Something like Bo Harris.

With his slouched shoulders and careless hair and that grin that acts like it owns the hour. Bo, who slides into pews like they belong to him, who doesn't care about sermons or science or the slow rot of expectations. He's the only breeze in a room that never opens its windows.

I know what I am supposed to know about Bo. And I know what I actually feel.

He touches my shoulder to grab a hymnal, and it sparks something behind my ribs. A slow burn. He catches my gaze across the chapel and holds it just a beat too long, and it's like a dare I can't walk away from. But then he's gone again, watching Father Schadenfreude with that strange intensity, as if Bo knows something I don't.

He's a contradiction wrapped in Sunday clothes. I keep trying to quit him, and I keep failing. I build my walls just high enough to feel safe, and he topples them with a single smile, a brush of fingers, the way he leans too close when no one's watching.

And maybe I hate that. Or maybe I don't.

Maybe that's where Bo fits in—near sin, up in the belfry. In all this, I'm just a girl trying to figure out who she is, and whether she's allowed to be more than what the world's already decided for her. A search for something real, in a place that feels like it's built entirely on maxims and façades. Maybe it's selfish, or maybe it's brave, but all I know is this: I don't want to keep living my life as a hollow frame. I want to fill it with something wild, something burning, something unmistakably mine.

In all honesty, the only reason I can bear to step foot in that suffocating church is Bo Harris. Bo is dangerous in the way that beautiful things often are. He makes me see parts of myself I'd rather keep locked away. The hunger, the doubt, the part of me that's always asking: *What if?*

I know I shouldn't think about him the way I do, shouldn't feel the way my chest tightens when he glances my way, but I can't help it. Bo makes it all bearable, even when everything else feels like it's unraveling.

I can't pin him down, and maybe that's why I keep circling back, how he hypnotizes me—that stupid belfry. At once, he's all warmth, his hand brushing the loose strands of hair from my face as if he had some claim to it. Those moments catching me off-guard, leaving me blinking in their wake, sure something bigger is just around the corner. But then, just as the heat begins to simmer, he'll freeze me out again, his words short, his gaze skipping over me like I'm no more than an empty beer can.

I tell myself I don't care. For days, weeks sometimes, I'll build my resolve, harden it like the bread crusts Mama saves for the birds. I'll steel myself against his half-smiles and fleeting touches. But then comes the moments, the ones that tear through me like a crack in stained glass, letting the light flood back in. A brush of his hand, the faintest curve of a grin, and all that resolve crumbles, brittle and useless.

I hate the game, but I hate the silence more. Each time he draws close, only to retreat again, I feel myself pulling taut, a string snapping. It ain't just Bo, it's what he makes me see in myself. How easily I bend toward his flickering flame, only to be fumbling in the dark when he turns away. How much I despise that about myself, and how powerless I feel to change it.

Bo is just old enough to be dangerous, the sort of boy who walks through a room and leaves it tilting slightly off-balance. Soon to be a senior when school kicks back off in August, an athlete, tall and lean, already confident in his movements like he has the world all figured out. The kind of boy who makes ninth-grade girls like me sit up straighter and whisper into cupped hands.

He probably isn't for me; I endure that much, but the idea of him is something else entirely. He stirs a rebellion in me that I don't yet have the courage to voice, though I carry it around like a stone in my pocket—heavy, hidden.

He looks at me sometimes, a certain way—not often, but just enough to plant a thought I can't quite shake. That maybe, despite the gaps I feel, my age, my shape, the immature angles of me that are yet to soften into what his crowd of girls already have; there is something about me that catches his eye. Not enough to keep it perhaps, but enough to brush against it like a moth testing a flame.

Despite his distance, we sometimes meet down at the creek or at the courthouse steps to talk and get away from our parents. He flirts, and I let him, happy to have his teetotal attention even if just for an hour. At the creek yesterday, he asks if I ever think of disappearing. Like a joke. But words like that lodge themselves curiously deep.

"Shirley," his voice low, the sunlight filtering through the leaves above us like whispers of fate, "you ever wonder what it'd be like to just... disappear for a while? You know, like those dandelion seeds blowing in the wind?"

The way that single glance stays with me feels absurd, and yet there it is, humming under my skin.

"I'd probably land right in a field full of wildflowers," replying nonchalantly, though my pulse rises to my temples, racing like a trapped bird at the thought of being wherever he might wish me to wander. "And what about you, Bo? Do you dream of floating away with the clouds?"

Laughing, Bo injects a teasing lilt to his voice. "Nah, I might get tangled up in a damned old tree and end up stuck there for good. Not exactly adventurous, not the kind I'd like to be known for."

"Maybe you'll just become the brave tree climber," countering and being cute, then lifting an eyebrow. "Someone has to be there to save the lost souls from then on, right?"

"That's the plan," Bo says, leaning a little closer, the unsteady air between us thrumming with something electric. "But if you're one of those lost souls, I might have to take a different route." The weight of his words settles like a shiver across my shoulders, and I catch myself smiling, even as I ponder over the promises hiding behind his jest.

At home, I wear my good-girl mask like it is stitched to my skin. I say "Yes, ma'am," and "No, sir," with a polish that makes Mother beam in front of the neighbors. My hands stay folded like I'm carved out of porcelain, skirts pressed sharp enough to cut. If obedience has a face, it's mine. But inside? Inside, I am a riot waiting to happen.

My thoughts don't march in straight lines. They bite, they bloom, and they wander into places no good girl is supposed to know about. And in those places I meet myself—not the Shirley Mother wants, not the Shirley the priest preaches to, but the real me, wild and sharp-edged, flickering in the dark. Sometimes my thoughts are playful, sometimes they're the kind filled with perversity and contrariness that make my heart race just imagining it.

And in that dark, I think always of Ms. Trixie Simpson.

She's what freedom looks like if it wears lipstick and heels. She moves like music, unapologetic, a symphony of don't-give-a-damn. Even the way she crosses her legs in church feels like defiance. Every man looks. Every woman pretends not to.

Bo looks, too. I see it. I feel it. A cold thing blooms inside me every time his eyes follow her instead of me. I don't hate her. I can't. Not when she moves with the kind of power I crave to drink like fine Kentucky whiskey. Not when she walks into a room and makes everyone else a supporting character.

One day, I'll take pieces of her and build something of my own. Not a replica, but a reckoning. A woman who doesn't beg to be seen.

Until then, I carry that image like a secret—close to my chest. A pulse beneath the fabric of my life. A promise I make to myself, again and again:

I won't be a hollow frame on the wall.

I'll be something wild. Something that burns hot. Something *mine*.

57

THREE

IN THE MARGIN'S QUIET

Wednesday, Fourth Week of May 1942

THE BREAD DOUGH in the Ragland kitchen swelled under Earline Johnson's gaze, rising slow as the sun through the trees at dawn. Her hands, roughened by years of service, smoothed a light coat of flour over its surface, her fingers moving with the same unthinking rhythm she'd used when patting Elijah's back as a baby. Outside, the oaks swayed with a lazy indifference, the kind that made Earline feel smaller than usual. She caught sight of her own reflection in the glass, faint and wavering, as though the woman staring back were someone she barely knew.

Ora Ragland's voice floated in from the parlor, light as chiffon but with the weight of command beneath. "Earline, don't forget the silverware before you leave today. It's tarnishing something awful."

"Yes, ma'am," Earline replied, her words a practiced melody. She reached for the rag and polish she'd left on the counter, the smell of ammonia rising sharp in her nose. Polishing the silver wasn't hard work, but today it felt heavy, like the air before a storm. The Ragland house buzzed with its usual tension: Jim's distant footsteps, Ora's sharp commands. But beneath it all lay the unspoken grief of two sons drafted and gone to war. She could feel it in the way Ora's hands lingered on the piano keys too long after finishing a hymn.

"Miss Ora, you got yo'self a house full o' boys going off to save the world," Earline had said a week ago, half to break the silence, half to see if Ora would bite.

"Well, Earline, I guess it's the price we pay for freedom," Ora had answered, but her smile had faltered, and her eyes had drifted to the photograph of her oldest, Thomas, in his uniform on the mantle. "I just pray they all come back. Your boys too, Earline."

Earline nodded, not trusting herself to speak. Prayer was the only weapon left for mothers these days, and even that feels a bit blunt sometimes. Earline couldn't help but think of her own boys, Aaron and Isaiah, their names fresh on the draft board's list. The delivery of the letters came weeks ago; the thin dog-eared papers trembling in Mun's hands like dry leaves in a breeze. The sound of distant thunder rolling low across the horizon as if the earth itself mourned what might come.

The storm threatened, but Earline's thoughts carried their own weather, a swirling mix of hope and fear. She turned her attention back to Ora's silver, the soft rag gliding over the tarnished surface. "Ain't no piece of silver this house owns that could shine bright enough to ward off what's coming," she muttered under her breath, half to herself, half to the storm outside. But she polished anyway, the rhythmic motion grounding her as much as it cleared the tarnish. She imagined a home of her own, small but sturdy, with silver she could call hers. The thought was fleeting, almost foolish, but it lingered just long enough to warm her hands as they worked.

"Miss Ora," she called out, raising her voice over the sound of the wind rattling the windows, "I'm done with the silver. Anything else before I head out?"

"No, Earline, you go on home," Ora replied, her voice carrying the faintest tremor, as if she, too, felt the storm's approach.

Earline nodded, wiping her hands on her apron and folding it neatly on the counter. The rain had started, a light patter against the roof that promised more to come. She grabbed her coat and stepped into the soft drizzle, the damp air wrapping around her like a second skin.

The walk home was familiar, each step marking the divide between servant and self. Her mind drifted to her sons Benjamin and Elijah—they ought to be home by now; school let out nearly an hour ago. The two attended The Tate School for Coloreds, named after her own cousin—Dr. Jessie B. Tate, bishop in the African Methodist Episcopal Church and a man who'd carved out space where there had been none. The schoolhouse was only four blocks from their cottage, but she hoped the boys had managed to dodge the rain on their way home.

Elijah has stayed up late working on the composition for Turner Normal School in Memphis, scribbling by lamplight with this tongue tucked tight in the corner of his mouth. Earline said nothing at the time, only placed a fresh piece of cornbread beside him and kissed his head before bed, but she'd been praying all day he remembered to turn it in.

A scholarship could change everything. Maybe not all at once, but enough. Enough to believe the ground would hold. The walk, the worry, none of it could shield her mind from her older sons Aaron and Isaiah, both drafted and off in Europe somewhere, the weight of their absence pressing tight, the pressure in her chest almost too much to bear.

*

BY THE TIME SHE reaches her door, the rain has turned to deluge, its rhythm a steady drumbeat against the tin roof. Earline steps over the threshold and inhales the familiar mingling of scents; Mun's pipe tobacco, the cornbread she'd left cooling on the counter that morning, and just a hint of silver polish from the Ragland house clinging to her skin. She doesn't sit or settle but rambles her way straight to the kitchen, where a cast-iron skillet waits for its service, its well-seasoned iron contributing its own secret ingredient from years of faithful service.

Mun is preoccupied, busy showing young Benjamin how to clean the damper and flue stack on the potbelly stove, as Earline enters. His jaw tightens as he works, his brow furrowed, hands steady despite the strain.

Without thinking, his tongue slips forward, just past his lips, caught between his teeth as if it anchored his focus. It stays there, motionless at first, then shifts slightly as he adjusts his grip on the tool, his breath pushing out slow through his nose. A bead of sweat traces down his temple, but he doesn't notice, too absorbed in the task, too locked into the precision of his movements.

His tongue presses firmer when the effort peaks, the muscles in his forearm tensing, his fingers working with measured control. And then, as the last turn, the last pull, the last push, settles into place, he exhales and lets it retreat, disappearing as if it had never been there at all. "See that, Benji, that bead on the pipe joint, how tight it is? That's how a man do things. Tight is right."

"Benjamin, fetch me that fatback from the smokehouse," Earline calls, rolling up her sleeves and tying on a clean apron, this one frayed at the hem but all the dearer for it. Her youngest scrambles to comply, returning with the slab of salt-cured pork wrapped in a dish towel. She slices it with a sure hand, the knife thunking against the cutting board. The skillet hisses as the pork fat flits about the hot skillet, a savory promise rising with the steam.

The storm rumbles louder outside, the rain now a steady cascade. Earline glances out the window, her eyes lingering on the darkened sky. "Lord," she whispers, her voice low but steady, "keep my boys safe. Keep all these Johnson boys safe." And with that, she turns back toward the stove, the hiss of the skillet and the warmth of the kitchen her only solace against the gathering storm.

On another burner, a pot of greens simmers, the collards swimming with bits of onion and a ham hock salvaged from a week of meals. Earline stirs the ancient pot with a rhythm all her own, the steam curling around her face like a reluctant veil. "Greens 'bout ready," she mutters, more to herself than anyone else, before turning to pat out the cornbread batter in her palms and dropping it into a separate pan of hot lard. The golden patties sizzle and pop, crisping at the edges as they fry.

Benjamin leans against the doorframe, his lanky frame almost too tall for the narrow kitchen. He watches his mother work with a mix of curiosity and hunger, his fingers fiddling with the loose thread on his shirt. "You gon' make that peach cobbler too?" he asks, hopeful.

"Boy, you think I got cobbler money?" Earline shoots back, though her tone has a touch of playfulness. "Be thankful you gettin' this. Ain't nobody got peaches for free."

Benjamin's grin, sheepish. "Yes, ma'am," he replies with confidence, but he stays moored to the doorway, his eyes lingering on the skillet like it might produce dessert by osmosis or spontaneous combustion or sheer willpower. "Mama, can Daddy show me how to cut the ham next time? I ain't too good at it, and I wanna' learn it right."

Earline glances at him, a flicker of approval crossing her face. "Ask your daddy then. Maybe he'll take the time to teach you, so you don't waste half the meat like last time."

"Mun, this boy wanna' learn from you," she calls to her husband over her shoulder. "You gon' teach him or let him hack up another ham bone?"

Mun's deep chuckle rumbles from the next room. "I reckon I'll teach him," he says as he steps into the kitchen. "Come on, boy. Can't have you makin' no mess and callin' it learnin'."

"Mun, don't you leave that sooty tool laying in my kitchen, come put this thing where it belongs."

Benjamin's grin widens as he picks up the dusty tool and puts it in his pocket. He washes his hands then follows his father to the counter, the two of them leaning over the cutting board while Mun's hands guides his son through the motions, firm but patient. Earline watches the two for a moment before turning back to her greens, her lips curving into a small, knowing smile.

When the meal is ready, she calls out, "Y'all come eat before it gets cold!" Plates clatter as Elijah comes in, joining Benji. The boys and Mun crowd around the small table. The space tight, but comfortable, the air warm with the smells of dinner and family. Earline takes her seat last, wiping her hands on her apron and surveying the table with a quiet satisfaction.

It's not much, as Earline often says, but it is theirs. The chipped plates, the mismatched silverware, the way the light bulb above them flickers just enough to remind them of its fragility; it all speaks of a life stitched together not with money, but with care and resilience.

Earline bows her head, extends her arms, and reaches for the hands of her two children on either side. Her leathered hands, still for just a moment, clutching tightly with those of her two boys, as her calloused elbows come to rest on the edge of the table. "Mun, say a prayer for us. For the boys. For all of 'em."

Mun bows his head, and the room falls silent except for the distant rumble of thunder rolling sporadically across the evening sky.

"Lord," he begins, his voice low and steady, "Lord, we come to you tonight with heavy hearts and hope still burnin'. We ask you to watch over Aaron and Isaiah as they head into a world that don't see 'em for what they are: good boys—strong boys. Keep 'em safe, Lord, even when some folks, bad folks, be tryin' to hurt 'em, Lord. We ask you to watch over Benjamin and Elijah too. Keep 'em healthy, make 'em smart, and send good folks their way, folks who'll see what they can be and give 'em a chance to grow into it. And Lord, we ask you to bless this family, Lord, and bless them Raglands too. Keep Mrs. Ora strong, give Mr. Jim a long life, and watch over them Ragland boys fightin' for the same freedom we all pray comes true someday, the same one, Lord, that Aaron and Isaiah be fightin' for. And Dear Lord, bless little Shirley. Lord, give her dreams bigger than this town, and the strength to chase 'em. Bless this food, bless the righteous hands that made it, and bless this roof that keeps us dry tonight. Thank you for your abundance, even when it's small in the world's eyes but big in ours. Amen."

"Amen," the family echoes their agreement in unison, their voices quiet but full. The storm outside deepens, the rain pattering heavy against the roof, but inside, the warmth of the meal and the prayer wraps comfortably around them like a shield. Earline picks up her fork and looks around the table, her gaze lingering on each of her boys.

For a moment, the world outside doesn't matter. What matters most to her is right here, at this table, under this roof, with the storm waiting patiently at the edges of their light. With the Johnson men sated and rising up from the table, Earline stays behind cleaning up the kitchen, then joins her family sitting around the hearth.

"Miss Ora sho' be worrying 'bout them boys, Mun."

Mun grunts, his eyes narrowing. "She got the right to worry. Ain't nobody safe now."

"No, they ain't," Earline murmurs, her hands busy with a basket of mending. Her thoughts drift to Aaron and Isaiah, the way their laughter once would fill the cramped house until it felt almost spacious. Now, their absence echoes louder than their voices ever could. She glances at Benjamin, who lays sprawling on the floor, a comic book splayed open in his hands. His bare feet kicking idly against the floorboards, a boy on the cusp of manhood but not yet far enough to see the dangers waiting for him.

"Benji, you writin' Miss Shirley again?" she asks, her voice casual but her eyes sharp.

Benjamin's head snaps up, his cheeks flushed a deep crimson brown. The comic book suddenly wobbles in his hands, like he'd been caught stealing. "No, ma'am," he says too quickly, his voice cracking on the last syllable.

Earline's lips curve into a knowing smile. "Boy, don't lie to me. I seen you sneak that envelope into the post this mornin'. What you think she gonn' do with it? Frame it?"

Benjamin's eyes dart back to his comic book, but he doesn't dare look her in the eyes. "Mama, she writes me back. We still be friends," he mutters, his voice now something between whisper and whine, as he holds up a handful of Shirley's letters.

"Mm-hmm," Earline says, leaning forward with her elbows on her knees, the fabric of her worn skirt pooling loosely around her legs. "Is that so? But Miss

Shirley, she don't knows you be sweet on her, Benji. She just thinks y'all two friends. She gotta good heart, but she a white girl. She got rules—same as you. And she got her eyes on a boy at church anyhow. When she do write back, what you gonn' say then? Miss Shirley ain't the type to settle for no starry-eyed colored boy with dreams bigger than his pocketbook. Even if he cute as you is, Benji."

Benjamin's chin juts out, a flicker of defiance lighting his eyes. "I'll figure it out," he says, his voice firmer now. "You always say we gotta dream of things, Mama."

Earline's hands lay still on the fabric she is mending. Her face softens, but her tone remains rock steady. "I do," she says slowly. "But I also say you gotta keep your feet on the ground while your head be up in them clouds. Don't be foolish, now. I can't lose my job over you bein' sweet on no white girl. They some lil' black girls at church, pretty as peaches, Benji, them gals be a big deal too. Dreamy if you ask me, Benji. What that one cute lil' gal's name, Mun—Scherrye? She sho enough is a big dream, Benji—sho' e-nuff!"

Mun's laugh rolls out low and steady from his chair by the window, where he sits quietly whittling a piece of wood into something unrecognizable but entirely his own. "Let the boy dream, Earline. Ain't no harm in dreamin'."

Earline casts her husband a sharp look, her eyes narrowing. "Dreamin's fine," she shoots back, "so long as it don't make a fool outta' him. You knows how it is, Mun. Them sweet lil' white kids grow up and turn on ya'. I think it be bred into 'em sometimes. I wanna' believe it ain't so bout Miss Shirley, but—"

Mun shrugs his shoulders, his knife scraping against the grain of the wood. "Ya' think Jim Ragland ever turn his back on me? Naw, Earline, not all white folks the same. Benji got sense. He'll figure his way. And that Shirley, she's her Daddy made over. She might not ever be our daughter, but she a loyal sorta' gall."

Benjamin, growing more embolden by his father's defense, sits up straighter, taller. "Miss Shirley ain't like that," he says. "She would never turn on me. She's still Shirley."

Earline's face softened for a fleeting moment as she looked at her boy, his lanky frame lolled across the worn floorboards, the comic book lying forgotten beside him like a relic of simpler times. The light from the single overhead bulb casted shadows across his face, flickering playfully with each subtle shift of the evening air.

Memories rose unbidden, like the scent of honeysuckle on a damp summer night, Shirley and Benjamin as young children, their laughter tumbling through the yard, weaving itself into the hum of cicadas. They were inseparable then, two halves of some innocent whole, unbothered by the divisions that shaped the adults around them.

But beneath that memory, another surfaced, darker and heavier, like storm clouds pressing down on a brittle roof. She saw them again as they were that day, too young to know the weight of the world but old enough to make her heart seize with a fear she hadn't known she could carry. She'd found them in the bathroom, their small, curious bodies tangled in a moment of discovery that was neither malicious nor calculated, just innocent in the way she knew those two children were. Yet the sight of it had struck her like a stone to the chest, the innocence eclipsed by the knowledge of what could come after.

That bone-deep dread rooted itself in her, spreading like kudzu, choking out all reason. Ora's face flashed in her mind, sharp and unyielding. If she had found them, there would've been no room for explanations, no space for understanding. And what if the children had taken it further, crossed some line they didn't even know existed? The thought gnawed at her, a whisper of catastrophe that kept her awake long after Mun had started snoring beside her.

That was the day everything changed. She stopped bringing Benjamin to work with her, pulling him from Shirley's orbit with a swiftness that confused him but spared him explanations he couldn't yet grasp.

The yard grew quieter after that, its echoes of laughter fading like the evening light. Earline bore the silence like a penance, every step away from that memory a measured act of protection, even if it meant breaking their bond. She told herself it was for the best, though the doubt never fully left her, lingering at the edges of her mind like a shadow that stretched too far.

"Boy, you don't understand," she says finally, her voice low but firm. "The world ain't gonna' see you the way you see her. And if y'all two was together, they sho ain't gonna' see her the way you do, not the same way people does now. You keep writin' if you got'ta, but you best be careful. Words on paper can't protect you when white folks get ugly."

Benjamin's jaw tightens; he nods to his mother, the defiance in his eyes fading to something quieter, something more uncertain. Earline watches him for a moment longer, then turns her attention back to her mending, her hands moving with the steady rhythm of someone who'd spent a lifetime stitching things back together.

Mun's chuckle breaks the silence again. "Don't you worry none, Earline. Benji got more sense than you think. He'll find his way, just like Aaron and Isaiah did. Ain't that right, son?"

Benjamin strategically delays his answer, his eyes drifting to the window where the last rays of sunlight fade through broken gray clouds and into the horizon. "I guess so, Daddy," he says finally, his voice soft but steady. But as he looks back down at his comic book, Earline can see the seeds of doubt and hope, both mingling in his eyes, a boy caught square between dreams and the world waiting to crush them.

The room falls quiet then, save for the faint creak of the floorboards as Elijah paces the small space between the kitchen and the front door. He's been restless since the draft letters came, his movements erratic, his temper quick to flare. Tonight is no different.

"What you wearin' that floor out for?" Mun asks without looking up.

"Just thinkin'," Elijah speaks up, his hands gripping something unseen deep in his pockets.

"You thinkin' too loud," Earline says, her voice edged with humor but underpinned by concern. "Sit down 'fore you dig a hole straight through to the dirt."

Elijah pauses, his shoulders slumping as he drops recklessly into a chair. "I'm just wonderin' what it's gonn' be like," he reluctantly admits, his voice quieter now. "For Aaron and Isaiah, I mean."

Mun's face darkens, the lines around his mouth deepening. "Ain't no use wonderin'," he barks, his tone firm. "They gonn' do what they gotta' do, same as every other man."

"But what if—" Elijah begins, his words faltering under the weight of his own thoughts.

"Ain't no 'what if,'" Earline interjects, her voice cutting through the room like a bowie knife. "We pray, we hope, and we keep movin'. That's all they is."

The silence that follows is heavy, but not without comfort. The kind of silence that holds space for unspoken fears, the kind that wraps itself around a family like a threadbare quilt, warm despite its wear. As the night deepens, the Johnsons settle into their routines, each of them carrying their own piece of the weight that binds them together.

In the corner, Benjamin returns to his dog-eared comic book, his mind wandering far from their small cottage to a world of heroes and villains, where battles are fought and won with a certainty life rarely offers. Earline watches him, her heart swelling with a mix of pride and trepidation. He is her youngest, her last to hold close before a cruel world comes to claim him too.

"Benji," she says softly, her voice almost a whisper. Benji looks up, his eyes wide and questioning. "Don't you ever stop dreamin', you hear me, boy? But don't you forget where you come from, neither."

Benjamin nods, his face solemn. "I won't, Mama. I promise."

Earline reaches out, ruffling his hair with a tenderness that belies the calluses on her hands. She glances at

Mun, who meets her gaze with a small, steady smile. Together, they carry the weight of their family, their dreams, and their fears, brick by brick, day by day. And in the quiet of their small home, they dare to hope that one day, the weight might lift, even if just a little, and they have a home all their own, with kids in college and a yard full of grandbabies.

DESIRE IN A TUCKED-AWAY TOWN

Wednesday, First Day of April 1942

IN THE SLOW and deliberate unfolding of spring 1942, in Springfield, Tennessee, life moved at a languid, syrupy pace, as if it had been held in the gentle embrace of a world untouched by the clamor of war. The town buzzed with murmurs of sons shipped off to far-away lands, of ration stamps, and the righteous echoes of Sunday sermons. Yet it remained snuggled up like an unbroken egg, as though the Almighty Himself had drawn a curtain 'round its fertile tobacco fields and dust-coated streets.

The dogwood is first to awaken, their white and pink blossoms unfurling like quiet benedictions against the deep green of pine and oak. The wisteria is next, draping itself over fences and forgotten porches, and a cascade of lavender blooms spill down like a memory too sweet to let go. Here, spring is not a season but a return, of color, of warmth, of barefoot steps through dewy grass and the sound of children laughing as they chase fireflies through the twilight. It is, above all, a reminder that the world, despite its bruises and burdens, will always bloom again.

And on the spirited fringes of this durable cocoon sat Ms. Trixie Simpson, a widow at forty, her life measured by the rhythmic click of her sewing machine and the soft cadences of the women who drifted into her modest shop, sharing news both mundane and profound. Each conversation was clad in a fragile veneer, the laughter too often strained, as the dread of sons at war loomed ever more pronounced, intruding on their sunny, quilted lives.

Trixie Simpson was a handsome woman, a deep raven brunette whose looks had not yet slipped into the kind of withered elegance middle-aged women feared. She carried herself like a figure carved into a ship's bow—upright, aloof, her eyes sharp as needles. Her widow's attire was, by design, immodest for her age and status. She turned lots of heads, more than she'd openly admit, in a conservative town where the men cast their gazes upon her like mosquitos to an arm drenched in sweat.

Yet she heard the whispers too, the ones that followed her when men stood too long at her counter, or neighbors cast glances at the home she kept alone; her suitors more plentiful than respectable. A beautiful widow with a sizable estate could never rest fully at ease, not in a place like Springfield.

Her troubles began, as these things often do, with something small. Trixie had been in the back room mending a hem when she overheard the voices of the Logan sisters, two giggling girls, barely out of pigtails.

"Bo Harris," one whispered, the name a little breathless, like a secret between friends. "You ever seen him? Good Lord, like Clark Gable, and he's got that smile, too. Makes a girl… well, you know."

The words hung in the air like perfume, tempting a breath. Trixie had paused, hands still on the fabric, her heart giving a strange flutter, like the flame on the tip of a candle. She did not know Bo Harris, though she knew of the Harrises.

Their boy, seventeen and broad-shouldered, had built a quiet reputation as the golden one—dashing, good with his hands, a pitcher for the high school baseball team, and a tight end for its football program. Girls talked about him in a way they did not talk about other boys. He had a way of standing in doorways that drew all eyes to him. Trixie brushed the thought aside, but the whispers lingered in her mind; enfeebled, encircled, entertained by delectable thoughts.

Trixie overheard the Logan sisters speaking of a Shirley, and how she and Bo had been seen talking to each other at church. "Oh, that Shirley," one swooned, her voice dripping with derision. "She's almost as flat-chested as a board. What does he see in her? Surely it's just a fantasy, one that'll never come to pass."

Her sister nodded vigorously, her eyes glinting with the thrill of shared malice. "I heard Jenny Carpenter, that blonde bombshell who practically glows in the dark, has her eyes set on Bo. She's got curves for days. Why would he waste his time with such a—plain girl?"

Trixie took pause for a minute, wondering if the "Shirley" they were speaking of might be her young cousin, daughter to her first cousin Ora, then, in a moment of clarity told herself it was ridiculous, shameful even, to think of such a young boy, especially one that her little cousin might be sweet on. Yet over the next week, her thoughts drifted toward Bo with unsettling frequency.

She pictured him in that clumsy uniform boys wore on Sundays, hat tipped down, a strand of sun-bleached hair at his brow. Her vanity crept up to meet these thoughts—was she still pretty enough? Did she still hold the power to make a young man stumble over his words, the way men used to when her husband Jake was still alive?

The next time Bo Harris came into the store, Trixie saw him differently than she had before. She noticed things. He was no longer the boy who came in with his mother's sewing. A senior in high school, he presented the duality of adolescence and growing manhood, a sliver of testosterone wrapped in the uncertainty of youth. The cowbell above the door clattered, and there he stood, framed by the bright light of day. Bo had that rugged Jack Young, Clark Gable 'look' the girls had giggled about—his jaw firm, his straw-colored hair curling boyishly at the collar, and something easy and careless in the way he held himself.

"Afternoon, ma'am... uh, Mrs. Simpson," Bo said, setting a small basket of mending on the counter, holding an unremarkable bundle of fabric wrapped in brown paper. "Mama says these things need tending to."

"Trixie, please. Mrs. Simpson makes me sound like someone's grandmother." Her voice rolled like smooth honey off her tongue. "Plus, I'm widowed now, everybody knows that; you can drop the Mrs."

Trixie smiled at Bo faintly, her fingers brushing a spool of thread on the counter. She noticed how his eyes dipped to her hands, how her small gesture made him pause. Trixie's gaze narrowed slightly as she dropped her sewing aside, eliciting an almost imperceptible gasp from Bo, who was struggling to maintain his composure—both punctured by her sudden switch from seamstress to the town's seductress.

"Sorry… Trixie. Mama said you'd know exactly what to do with 'em."

"Your mama knows how to flatter," Trixie replied. "Any instructions? What's the trouble, what happened to them?"

Bo had always been aware of Trixie, though he treated her with a practiced distance, one fostered by respect and a faint flicker of fear, fear of crossing unwritten boundaries. Yet there was something about the way she regarded him. He caught glimpses of her curves, the delicate lines hinting at degrees of femininity that left him both mesmerized and dizzy. Trixie's dress clung tightly to her waist, and when she bent slightly to inspect the package in his hands, a slit along the hem of her immodest dress subtly revealed the shape of her thighs and the glimmer of her stockings.

Bo shifted on his feet, his thumbs hooking into his pockets. "She says my sister's Sunday dress tore when she climbed the oak tree. The rest's just patchwork—on Mama's trousers, but Mama says it needs a good hand and you'd done the same repairs for her before."

"Your mother's calling card, Bo," she said, voicing her joviality yet giving it an intentional lilt, every word layered like the fabric she stitched. "She seems to have a knack for tearing clothes right where I wouldn't expect it."

He muttered an embarrassed chuckle, oblivious to his own blushing. "Yeah, she… she does that."

Trixie looked at the boy's face, his handsome awkwardness, the way he couldn't quite meet her eyes without shifting. There was something delicious in it, like seeing a stag pause in the clearing, unsure whether to flee. She leaned forward slightly, just enough to make the space between them shrink.

In that exchange, Trixie made her first move. "You know, I could use an extra pair of hands around here. What if you came by to help out after school?" She kept her eyes locked on his, searching for a flicker of eagerness.

Bo hesitated, bewildered, uncertain of how to read her invitation. "Sure, I guess I could do that," he stumbled, his voice breaking slightly.

"Your mama raised a polite young man, Bo Harris. Tell her I'll have these back by Saturday."

Bo flushed at the mention of his name, and Trixie took quiet pleasure in how his composure faltered. As he left, Trixie's smile lingered, fluttering like a moth's wings in a warm spring breeze, determined to keep him coming back.

In the days and weeks that followed, Bo found reasons to visit Trixie's shop again and again. Each time, the tension thickened. Trixie, skilled in the delicate art of flirtation, unearthed more ways to engage his curiosity.

"Bo, do you think this color would suit a certain type of woman?" she'd ask, draping fabric over herself as a model, encouraging him to step closer without realizing that he was encroaching on dangerous grounds.

The young man's heart raced with each encounter as Trixie revealed various pieces of her charm, inhaling his youth and innocence like rare perfume. He could not help but feel changed every time he left the shop, his mind drifting to fantasies filled with her laughter and warmth, caught in a web of desire he had not known existed until he met her.

One afternoon, Trixie had decided that it was time for an intentional accident. She wore a dress that left her braless, a deliberate choice, one she had planned since the last time Bo left, raptured in her presence. As he entered, the sunlight streamed through the window, enhancing the outlines of her figure. The subtle nudity in her demeanor seemed amplified when she turned to him, a shadowed silhouette glistening in the soft light.

"Bo," she called innocently, "I need your opinion about something. Come here."

His heart thundered as he stepped into an atmosphere thick with unspoken tension. Trixie stood with her back turned, the fabric of her dress barely grazing the edge of her spine, the outline of her soft curves enticingly highlighted. "What do you think of this pattern?" she asked, over her shoulder, her voice a sultry whisper.

He stepped closer, their proximity throbbing with possibilities. The air was electric, charged with the unsaid yearning that lay woven between them, an intimacy that drew taut without touching. As she turned, there was a brief moment where their eyes met, one of innocent recognition and the thrill of something deliciously forbidden. Bo, entranced by her vulnerability, found himself lost.

Sometimes she would bend over at just the right angle, allowing him a fleeting glimpse of the taut garter straps pressing ever so daringly into her willowy legs, as she reached for a bolt of fabric. Or her skirt would catch on a chair, revealing a tantalizing flash of her thigh, just a hint before she adjusted her clothing with practiced nonchalance.

Bo came back, assisting her as needed, then sometimes again in the afternoon under the pretense of running errands for his mother, then without excuse at all. Once he asked for thread, a spool that cost no more than a nickel, fumbling for change in his pocket like a boy caught unprepared.

"You must be starting your own sewing business," Trixie said dryly, watching him with amusement.

"I guess I just like coming by," Bo said, the words rolling out like marbles he never intended to drop. "You're so nice, and real pretty too." Bo replied, his voice was uncertain but direct. He glanced at her then, really looked, and Trixie felt her heart hitch in her chest.

"Yeah?" Trixie responded flirtatiously, "What's so pretty about me, Bo Harris?" Trixie wanted to put Bo on the spot, to make his squirm, make his heart race a little.

Bo was cautious to respond, then—"It's everything, Ms. Trixie. I'm keen on your face, but it's more than that. Your neck is—it's perfect. Your clothes fit tight, so, ugh, your body is so, ugh, curved and—I don't know." Bo's nervousness was obvious, and Trixie lapped it up.

Trixie did not need a mirror to know when a man, or boy, admired her. She'd already seen it in Bo's lingering glances, in the way his hands seemed too big and clumsy for him when he was near her. He had taken the hook, though Trixie told herself she did not want it. At night, lying alone on the big empty bed, she wondered how far she might let things go, and how far Bo would chase what she could never offer him.

It happened on an afternoon thick with heat. Bo stood at the counter, his knuckles grazing the edge as he searched for something to say. Trixie, standing opposite him, smoothed the expensive fabric of her skirt as though brushing off dust. The silence between them seemed to swell, thick as molasses.

"You're too quiet today," Trixie said softly, her voice teasing. "I might start thinking you don't like me anymore."

Bo swallowed. "No, ma'am, I do. I mean… I'd never think that."

"Never?" Trixie murmured, tilting her head. The look she gave him was brief but searing, a flicker of something deeper, hungrier, that passed as quickly as it appeared. It was enough. Bo, entranced by her vulnerability, found himself lost. He leaned forward then, unthinking, and kissed her, softly, tentatively, the way a boy kisses for the first time; a surfacing of the passions held dormant through their playful encounters. Trixie did not pull away. Her heart raced under her rib cage as she felt the tremor of his lips on hers. The intensity of the moment mirrored the fever of their secret, intoxicating them both. And before he could retreat into denial, Trixie pulled him deeper, pushing her desires to a fever pitch that demanded more.

In the stillness that followed, Trixie's voice broke the silence. "Oh, no, Bo Harris!" she said quietly, almost to herself.

What followed seemed inevitable. Trixie locked the door, turned the sign to CLOSED, and took Bo's hand, leading him to the back room where a small bed waited. She told herself she could stop, that they could stop, but the lie unraveled the moment his lips met hers again. Trixie's demeanor danced on the edges of seduction, slow, deliberate, teasing.

"Show me how much you've learned," she whispered, her voice rich with invitation, her fingers trailing along the edges of her dress as it slid away, revealing seductive deep black lingerie trimmed in a lace the color of slaughterhouse red, as if she were a magician unearthing a spell before the audience.

As the seconds stretched into minutes, the spark ignited. Their hearts palpitated, each beat resonating with the thrill of the forbidden. Trixie's slow reveal served a greater purpose than mere physicality; it was a beckoning, a call of womanhood long buried beneath the layers of societal expectation. In Bo's eyes, she saw the reflections of the life she yearned for and the tastes of freedom she had forsaken.

The room was stifling, a tangle of breathless words and hurried movements, framed by the faint musky scent of dreams feeding the atmosphere with unadulterated potential. And when it was over, Trixie sat on the edge of the bed, staring at the closed door as though someone might burst through it.

"Are you all right?" Bo asked, his voice quiet.

Trixie looked at him then, at his flushed face and wide eyes. She reached over and smoothed his hair, her fingers lingering just a moment too long.

"Go on, Bo," she said. "It's getting late."

Their affair continued for weeks, with clandestine meetings growing in heat and fervor, Bo coming by when he could, Trixie allowing herself to slip further into what felt like a dream, a wicked, thrilling dream that might at any moment vanish. Yet dreams, Trixie knew, never lasted.

FOUR

THE SPACE BETWEEN NOTES

Tuesday, Second Week of June 1942

TUESDAYS BELONGED TO the unspoken, to the hollow hours between obligation and expectation, to the things done and left undone. They belonged to the space where guilt was still forming and pleasure had yet to dissolve into regret.

Mother was gone by eight, folded into Aunt Lois's glossy black Studebaker, the two of them crisp and composed, like a pair of hatched eggs, setting off for their rounds, the cemetery first to pay their respects to the dead, then to Aunt Mary Lou's house, where they'd drink Coca-Cola and chew over the sins of the living. These meetings were ritual, immutable, their conversations layered in decades of shared grievances, held together by the adhesive of sisterhood.

Which meant by nine, I was free.

Bo would be waiting, if he came at all. He'd walk the same path he always did, cutting through the square, stopping first at Ms. Trixie's shop, exchanging a parcel of sewing, nodding politely. That was his first obligation of the morning, but not his real one. His real obligation was to himself, to whatever mood had gripped him, to whatever implicit burden he had decided he could bear alone.

I saw him before he saw me, his left hand buried in his pocket, his right clutching something, a dull yellow fruit, the bruised skin of it soft and yielding. His steps were slow, his posture coiled tight.

"Well, there you are," I called, lifting a hand. "You look like you been carrying somethin' heavy."

He looked up, his face momentarily stripped of its personality. "Ain't nothin'," he said, though the lie was thin, transparent as a worn cotton sheet. He lifted the fruit. "You like pawpaw?"

I wrinkled my nose. "Not raw, don't like the texture of it. I like it in pudding. Earline makes it for me sometimes, but not this summer; not yet anyway."

Bo smirked, turning the fruit in his palm. "Yeah, eatin' pawpaws is kinda' like kissin' a mule," he said. "Better the second time around."

I laughed, more at the way his voice softened than at the joke itself, resuming my silliness. "C'mon, let me ride you piggyback to the creek," I said, shifting closer, pressing my hands to his shoulders. "I gotta' see if you'd make a decent horse in case I ever decide to get one."

Bo hesitated, but only for a moment. His mouth twitched, something flickering in his expression, and then I was on his back, my arms looped around his neck, my legs gripping his sides. "Giddy up, Bo!" I hollered. He moved slow at first, testing the weight of me, then broke into a clumsy gallop, his boots kicking up dirt, prancing around like a show pony, the creek rushing close.

"Don't you drop me," I warned, breathless, laughing. "You put me in that creek and I won't let you kiss me later." I giggled, half praying he'd do exactly that.

That stopped him.

The playfulness drained from his posture, the sharp line of his jaw going tight. He set me down carefully, almost reverently, and we sat by the bank, the water churning slow beneath a sky too blue to be trusted.

Bo was brave with his hands, but careful. My mother would not approve. Oh, but I did.

I had a noon lesson with Tom. By the time I left Bo, his shoulders had loosened, the weight of whatever had been gnawing at him shifting to some other place. I took one last look before heading up the trail to town, his figure relaxed, his fingers idly skimming the creek's surface.

St. Cecilia's organ loft sweltered, the July heat pressing into the wooden pews, suffocating the air with something damp and weary. Tom was already there, fiddling with the stops, his movements loose, almost anxious. The fugue we practiced was Bach, precise and unyielding, a tangle of stern, interlocking melodies that demanded perfection with a preacher's conviction, threatening to collapse if you misstepped.

I let my fingers skim the keys, too fast, too careless. Tom flinched beside me.

"L-l-let's t-t-take it from the t-t-top again, Shirley," he said, his voice sticky with the weight of concentration.

He leaned too close, his breath warm against my arm. The sweat pooled at his temples, his collar crooked. I watched the way he worried the hem of his sleeve, as if smoothing a wrinkle in the fabric might erase some deeper fault in himself.

"You make this sound easy," I said, flexing my fingers, "but I'm about to melt trying to get it right."

Tom exhaled, slow and deliberate. "S-sometimes," he murmured, "you g-gotta' let the m-music breathe. It d-don't like to be s-smothered."

His voice wavered, though I couldn't tell if it was the stammer or something deeper, something quieter.

Halfway through the lesson, Father Schadenfreude called him downstairs. Tom hesitated, his hand lingering too long on the organ's edge.

"Don't touch anything," he warned, and I nodded, though my mind had already wandered elsewhere.

The diary was tucked under a stack of sheet music, the leather soft from years of handling. I knew it was Tom's before I touched it, but I opened it anyway, my fingers trembling over the pages, skimming the ink. There were letters, some scrawled, some with beautiful calligraphy, the edges crisp, untouched by dust.

The name William Crayton appeared on one, postmarked from Philadelphia.

A familiar script signed the bottom of another, Father Schadenfreude's hand, sharp, angular, heavy, yet precise.

I had just begun to decipher the words when I heard the creak of the stairs. I quickly stuffed the diary back under the sheet music. Tom stood in the doorway, his eyes unreadable.

"Where w-w-were we?" he asked, his voice stretched thin.

I played dumb, sat straight, pressed my fingers to the keys. "Right where you left me."

We finished the lesson in silence, though the air between us had thickened, brimming with something unsaid. When the lesson was over, I gathered my things, but Tom lingered, his fingers twitching against the side of the bench.

"C-can I a-ask you s-something, Shirley?"

I turned, half-smiling. "Sure, Tom."

"What do you th-th-think about B-bo working with Father Schadenfreude?"

The question sent a flicker of something cold down my spine.

I forced a shrug. "I think it's none of my business."

Tom's face twitched, as if he had expected a different answer. "B-but he is y-y-your boyfriend, isn't he?"

I smiled again, slower this time. "I wish. We're not that serious."

Tom's expression darkened, something unreadable behind his gaze.

"D-do you think Bo l-l-loves the F-Father?"

The words sent a jolt through my bones, something sharp, unexpected. "Love is a strong word," I said carefully. "Why do you ask?"

Tom hesitated. "I j-j-just w-worry about r-r-reputations."

"Whose reputation?" I asked, tilting my head.

He didn't answer right away, just shifted his weight, looked down at the floor. "I th-th-think Bo might have... impure th-thoughts about the F-Father."

My stomach turned. The accusation, so casual, so rehearsed, felt wrong in his mouth.

"That's ridiculous," I snapped. "Bo's not like that."

Tom's mouth twitched. "Y-you don't know that for s-sure."

I leaned in close, my voice low. "And you don't either."

Silence stretched between us, taut as a violin string.

Tom broke it first, his voice strained. "C-can we just... agree to disagree?"

I studied him, his hands tight at his sides, his jaw rigid. His face betrayed nothing but conviction, but there was something else there, something beneath the surface, writhing.

Something that wasn't about Bo at all.

I nodded once, slow and deliberate. "Fine."

But I didn't believe him.

And I didn't trust him.

Not anymore.

That night, I wrote everything in my diary. The name William Crayton. The way Tom looked at me when he thought I wasn't watching. The accusation that didn't feel like concern but something else entirely.

Outside my window, the cicadas droned on, their song slow and unrelenting.

Springfield felt smaller than ever.

And I knew, deep in my bones, that nothing would ever be the same again.

*

TOM WALKED FAST, THEN faster, his breath hitching as if he were fleeing something with teeth. He wasn't, of course. Nothing chased him but his own thoughts, relentlessly as a hungry wolf. His shoes struck the pavement in a sharp, metered rhythm, his whole body tight, like a wound clock nearing the final turn of the key.

The confrontation with Shirley had rattled him, but not in the way he might have expected. It wasn't her words that needled at him. It was her eyes, too knowing, too fixed, as if she'd caught a glimpse of something inside him, something he worked hard to keep buried. She wasn't supposed to question him. She wasn't supposed to make him feel like he was the one being examined.

And then there was Bo.

Tom had seen it. The way Bo looked at Father Schadenfreude. How his eyes lingered too long, his posture hesitant, deferential, the way a moth flutters too close to a lantern. It wasn't right. It wasn't natural. And it had wormed into Tom's brain, into deep places where unease slithered and curled.

Jealousy burned low in his gut, smoldering like an ember in dry leaves. He told himself it wasn't jealousy at all. It was concern. It was duty. Someone had to look out for the Father's reputation, for the church's reputation. If Bo was harboring some—unnatural affections—it was Tom's obligation to snuff it out before it festered, before it tainted everything it touched.

But the thought coiled in on itself, shifting, twisting.

In his weaker moments, the ones he did not acknowledge even in the privacy of his own mind, he imagined confronting Bo. He pictured the other boy laughing at him, those sharp, bright eyes dancing with mockery, stripping him bare without ever laying a hand on him. The thought made his fingers curl into fists. He imagined the moment turning, imagined his own hands moving forward, shoving Bo hard. Hard enough to send him stumbling. Hard enough to erase that smirk, to see his body hit the ground. To watch Bo look up at him, not with amusement, not with defiance, but with something smaller.

The idea horrified him. And it thrilled him.

Tom clenched his jaw, shook his head violently as if he could rattle the thought loose, fling it from his skull like a dog shaking off rain.

By the time he reached his small apartment above the rectory, the stars were hanging sharp and still, scattered across the sky like broken glass. The air was thick, unmoving, pressing against him as he climbed the narrow stairs.

Inside, the room was suffocating. He paced the floor, every pass of his feet against the worn rug carving deeper grooves into his thoughts. He could feel it now, the thing inside him, stretching its limbs, unfurling like something long caged, testing the space it was allowed to fill.

He sat at his desk, pulled a sheet of paper before him, but his hand trembled when he reached for the pen. He would write it down. Yes, that would make it real. That would make it concrete, something outside of himself.

But the words wouldn't come.

The blank page glared at him, white and unyielding. It saw him. Knew him.

His breath quickened.

With a sudden, sharp motion, he crumpled the paper in his fist, shoved it into the waste bin, and pressed the heel of his palm against his forehead.

It was nothing.

Bo was nothing.

This was nothing.

But still, he couldn't shake the feeling that something had shifted. That somewhere, in the heat of his own mind, a line had been crossed.

FIRE BENEATH THE ASH

Wednesday, Fourth Week of June 1942

BO HARRIS HAD been in love before, or at least he thought he had, but love had never felt quite like this. This was something raw and electric, a wildfire burning beneath his ribs, eating through his thoughts, leaving him breathless in its wake. And it was her, always her. Trixie, with the smirk that curled at the corner like a secret she'd never tell, with the way she moved through the world like it was made for her amusement, that undeniable alchemy that turned the mundane into the magnificent.

She had a way of making him feel like he belonged to something greater, something grand. When she pulled him close, whispered his name, he wasn't just Bo Harris, a boy from nowhere special. He was necessary. She made him necessary.

And so, he gave himself to her, the way a man throws himself into a storm, unthinking, limbs loose with abandon, praying only to be carried somewhere worth remembering. With each delicate caress, they entwined together in a dizzying dance of youth and yearning, Trixie, expertly pulling his strings, wrapping Bo snugly around her pinky like a beloved ring, a melody that rang sweet in her ears.

It began in stolen moments, in the hush of afternoons spent pressed against the back wall of her shop, the air thick with the scent of fabric and the heat of her perfume. It was teasing at first, a slow pull, a deliberate unknotting of his restraint. He was seventeen and foolish, but not so foolish that he didn't know he was being played. And yet, he had no power to stop it. He didn't want to stop it.

At first, she let him dictate the terms of their meetings, let him fold up neat little notes and slip them beneath the counter where she'd find them, let him pick the times, the places. Then, when he'd grown comfortable, when his love-drunk certainty began to show in the way he looked at her, she took that power away.

It was always when she wanted now. When she called, he came.

Shirley noticed. Of course, she did.

Bo told himself it didn't matter, that Shirley was sweet and warm and kind, but she was not Trixie. She did not set his nerves alight with just a glance, did not leave him aching with a hunger that had nothing to do with food. So, when the choice came, when Trixie's lips curved, when she tilted her head just so, Bo walked away from Shirley without a second thought. Left her waiting, unanswered. Left her standing in the wake of a promise he never meant to keep.

He told himself it was worth it. That the price of Trixie was one he would pay in full.

But then, something changed.

The weight of her touch pressed deeper, felt heavier. The thrill had begun to carry something else with it, something harder to give a name to. What began as playful encounters a couple of times a week gradually evolved into unrelenting, daily unions that left him breathless and a little bewildered.

He was falling.

He didn't mean to. He hadn't planned for it. But the way she smiled at him after, the way she would sometimes let her fingers linger at the base of his throat, as if measuring the beat of his pulse, had done something to him. The way she sighed when he traced patterns along her bare skin made him believe she needed him. That he mattered.

As the weeks unfurled like the petals of some exotic flower, Trixie escalated her seduction, intoxicated not just by Bo's presence but by her own brazen sense of power. She raided her closet for daring lingerie that leapt well beyond the pages of the Sears catalog, enticing him with a wardrobe that whispered secrets and promises too hot to handle. Not only did her advances become more alluring, but they also transformed into the wellspring of the young man's most salacious dreams.

And so, one afternoon, as they lay tangled together in the quiet hum of the late summer heat, he almost told her.

But he didn't. Not yet.

Instead, he came back the next day, flowers in hand, hope blooming in his chest like something unstoppable.

Sunday afternoon, he found himself outside her shop. The morning sermon still clung to his skin, its words now weightless and irrelevant.

The door was locked.

He knocked once, and she was there. She met him with a look he'd grown so accustomed to, something like lust, like want, something that made his chest tighten in ways that grew into cravings.

"Let me show you something I bought just for you, Bo," she murmured, pulling him inside, locking the door behind them.

He let her take his hand, let her lead him to the back room where the light slanted in through lace curtains, where the scent of lavender and dust curled around them. The bed was waiting. A place he knew well.

She turned away from him, reaching up to pull the pins from her hair, letting the curls tumble down her back like ink spilling onto parchment. The blouse slid from her shoulders, pooling at her feet in a whisper of silk.

Then the skirt.

Then the slip.

She stood before him now, draped in something red and barely there, the lace teasing at transparency, at things he had seen before but never like this.

"Still thinking about that young girl now?" Her voice was velvet and iron, her lips curved, her body an offering.

He swallowed hard.

"I have something important to tell you."

A confession.

The words burned at the back of his throat, waiting to be freed. He had planned to say it differently, softer, but now it surged forward with all the weight of his own reckless heart.

"I love you, Trixie."

The moment cracked.

She stilled, the heat in her eyes flickering, something else slipping in its place.

Bo saw it. Felt it before she even spoke.

She stepped back, folding her arms across her bare stomach as if warding off a chill.

"Bo..."

His name on her lips was a warning now, not an invitation.

"I think we should stop this."

The world tilted.

Bo's breath came too sharp, his heart hammering against his ribs as if trying to escape the cage of his chest.

"But I do understand," he pressed. "I love you, Trixie."

She exhaled, slow and deliberate, then looked at him the way one looks at a dog that's wandered too close to the dinner table.

"You don't," she said, voice clipped, sharp. "And if you did, you'd know how foolish this is, how shameful. You need to forget about me. Do you hear me? Forget about me, Bo Harris."

The words struck like a blow, clean and cruel.

His hands curled into fists at his sides, not in anger, but in something worse.

Loss.

Trixie held his gaze, waiting.

Daring him to fight her on this.

He didn't.

Because for all his certainty, for all the ways he had convinced himself that she needed him as much as he needed her, he saw it now.

The truth.

She had never belonged to him.

And he had never belonged to her.

He was a pastime, a fleeting indulgence, a flame burned too hot, too fast.

And now, she was snuffing it out.

Bo nodded once, sharp, then turned on his heel and left without another word.

Trixie let out a breath when the door shut behind him, pressing her back against the cool wall, her pulse still quick with something she couldn't name.

She had won. She had pulled the strings, played the game, led him exactly where she had wanted.

So why, then, did she feel like she had lost?

*

BO WALKED THROUGH THE streets in silence, the world moving around him, indifferent to his ruin.

The night had never felt so cold.

The church bells rang out across the square—for the town, a simple reminder of time—a tolling steady and distant. But to Bo, a rhythm too slow for his pulse, too measured for the way his chest burned, his breath thin and unsatisfied. The streets and town were uncomfortably familiar for someone wanting nothing more than to be hidden. He stayed away from home too long, the lamplight flickering against the shop fronts, casting long stretches of gold over the brick and cobblestone. Yet nothing looked the same.

His feet carried him forward, not because he had a place to go but because stopping would mean sinking, and he could not afford to sink. He walked past the stores, past the druggist's window where glass jars of peppermint sticks and horehound lozenges stood in neat rows, past the tailor's shop where stiff white collars sat in a basket by the door, waiting to be pressed. The town was closing in on itself, shutters drawn, curtains pulled tight, the late hours claiming it inch by inch.

Bo turned down the alley that led to the creek, the place where he had kissed Shirley time and time again, his hands gentle on her wrists, the taste of salt and honey lingering between them. He had told himself then that he could wait, that he could bide his time and let love build itself slow and steady, like the thick roots of the cypress that lined the water. But then Trixie had called him, and he had run to her, thinking himself a man, thinking desire meant destiny.

Now, he crouched by the water, letting the cool air off the creek move over him, breathing deep, trying to settle the riot in his chest. He dipped his fingers into the current, feeling the pull, the certainty of it, the way it moved forward without hesitation, without regret.

It was a lie, the thing he had built with Trixie. A dream dressed up in silk and lace and whispers, in stolen hours and the rush of her hands slipping beneath his shirt. He saw it now. She had let him believe in something that was never real, had given him just enough to make him chase her, but never enough to catch her.

He laughed, low and bitter, shaking his head.

The truth was, he had been afraid of Shirley.

Not of her softness, not of the way she looked at him like he was something whole and worth holding, but of what she required. She wanted something real, something solid. A love that stayed, that weathered storms. And Bo, he had been too reckless, too caught up in the heat of things, in the thrill of something dangerous, in the way Trixie had known exactly how to pull him apart.

A rustling behind him.

Bo turned.

Shirley stood at the edge of the clearing, arms wrapped around herself, eyes dark in the fading light. She did not speak.

And for the first time, Bo felt it, the weight of what he had done.

He wanted to call out to her, wanted to tell her that he had been wrong, but what would be the point? The words would come too late, their meaning soured by the weeks that had stretched between them.

Instead, he stood slowly, brushing the dirt from his hands, nodding once.

A silent apology.

Shirley did not nod back. She did not move.

And so, Bo turned, walking away from the creek, away from the past, away from the place where he had first begun to mistake longing for love.

The night swallowed him whole.

THE WEIGHT OF CONFESSION

Wednesday, First Week of July 1942

SHE HAD NEARLY talked herself into confession by the time the church bells tolled their slow, deliberate call to evening Mass. Not out of piety. Not for the sake of cleansing her own transgressions, which sat on her shoulders as lightly as a wool shawl in springtime felt, but not unbearable. No, this was for Bo. For the burden he carried. For the way he had turned quiet, his words shrinking into him like a retreating tide, leaving only a vast and empty shore where there had once been easy laughter, teasing remarks, the heat of his hand at the small of her back, absentminded and familiar.

A festering wound between them now. And no bandage in sight.

She felt it most in the spaces where their conversations used to be. The absence, the erosion of something once effortless. On Monday, he had been Bo, the real Bo, the boy she'd known for years, who carried his emotions as loosely as the shirt on his back, buttoned carelessly, always one or two undone at the top. By Tuesday, he had become a stranger in his own body, and now, by Wednesday, she wasn't sure he would ever return to her fully.

She traced the idea of confession, the way a fingertip runs the edge of a well-worn Bible, uncertain if she truly wanted to open it, to lay herself bare in the dark wooden box, waiting for absolution in Father Schadenfreude's gravel-thick voice.

And what would she say? That she had kissed a boy by the creek and let him kiss her back, a whisper too long, a hesitation too soft? That she had climbed the belfry one July night, laughing, slipping on the slick stone, Bo's hands catching her at the waist, steadying her just as she had thought she might fall? That there had been a moment, just a moment, where she might have let herself go entirely, let something forbidden happen, had Bo only asked a second time?

But that wasn't why she needed to speak. It wasn't about her.

Bo Harris was drowning in something thick and heavy, a guilt she couldn't put a name to, a silence more suffocating than any sin she could confess. And if giving her own secrets to the dark might shake loose the ones buried inside him, then perhaps she would do it. Perhaps she would offer up every stolen kiss, every too-tight embrace, every wicked thought in the hope that Bo might be freed from whatever held him.

But what if it backfired?

What if she laid it all at the feet of a priest and Bo never forgave her for the betrayal? What if she pulled at the wrong thread and the whole thing unraveled, both of them laid bare? Not in the safe hush of a confessional but in the ruinous light of public consequence.

She turned it over in her mind, each scenario blooming and wilting as quickly as it came, until the weight of her indecision pressed into her chest, dull and leaden.

And then, as if struck by divine intervention, another thought took hold.

William Crayton.

She had nearly forgotten the name, tucked away in the folds of her memory, the letters she had glimpsed in Tom's hands, the way Tom had paled as he read them, as if the ink itself held a poison he could not stomach.

If anyone knew what gnawed at Tom Walker, it was Crayton.

She would write to him.

Not just about Tom, but about Father Schadenfreude. About the man's peculiar presence in Springfield, his iron-firm grip on the wayward boys of the parish, his sermons edged with something that left her skin cold, even when the summer heat pressed heavy against the stained-glass windows. She would write, and she would ask about the letters, about what had made Tom look stricken, about what past tied the three men together, stretching across states and years like some secret cord wound too tight.

And if Crayton answered, then maybe she wouldn't need confession at all. Maybe the truth would come not in whispered sins but in ink and paper, in words too carefully chosen to be dismissed.

The bells rang again, closer now, signaling Mass was about to begin.

She stood at the church door, hand hovering near the latch, torn between stepping inside and stepping away, between faith and doubt, between silence and revelation.

Tomorrow, she would walk with her father through town, arm tucked through his, his voice warm and steady beside her, and maybe she would find in him the courage she needed.

But tonight, tonight, she would write.

And in the morning, she would send her letter off to Philadelphia, straight into the hands of the man who held the missing piece of a puzzle she could not yet see.

The bells had long since fallen silent by the time she made up her mind.

She would not kneel in the confessional tonight, whispering her misdeeds through the grate, waiting for a mercy she wasn't sure she wanted. No, she would write instead.

The church doors loomed before her, the heavy wood dark with the oil of decades of faithful hands, worn smooth where palms had pressed, where sinners had hesitated before stepping inside. For a moment, she imagined pushing them open, imagined slipping inside to find Bo already there, kneeling next to his mother Blanche, his head bent in prayer, hands folded, lips moving in that soft, urgent way he had when he thought no one was looking.

But Bo wasn't in that church. She knew it with a certainty as strong as the July heat still rising from the stones beneath her feet. Wherever he was, it wasn't here.

She turned, letting the night take her instead.

The street was quiet, Springfield's lamplights flickering in their sconces, casting gold pools onto the brick, the dust, the uneven wooden porches of shops now locked tight against the evening. A dog barked somewhere down by the mill, the sound carrying through the thick summer air, and from the distance, the low murmur of men's voices, laughter tumbling low and familiar from behind the shuttered windows of the tavern.

She walked without hurry, letting the night fold around her, letting the weight in her chest settle.

At home, she climbed the steps to the front porch and made her way inside. Striking a match, she lit the candle on her writing desk. The soft glow stretched her own shadow long across the floorboards, flickering with each small movement as she found a sheet of paper, smoothing it flat with both hands before dipping her pen into the inkwell.

Dear Mr. Crayton,

She hesitated, watching the ink bead at the tip of her pen before it soaked into the paper, a slow bloom spreading beneath her careful script.

How did one begin a letter like this?

She couldn't simply ask, "What do you know of Bo Harris? What do you know of Father Schadenfreude? What did you write to Tom Walker that left him looking as though he had read his own fate scrawled in those pages?"

She chewed her lip, then set the pen back to paper.

I hope this letter finds you well. My name is Shirley Ragland, and I'm writing to you in the hope that you might shed light on a matter that has recently come to trouble me.

She paused, listening to the steady scratch of the crickets outside her window, the slow, rhythmic sound of their nighttime chorus.

I am acquainted with Tom Walker, and in a roundabout way, I came to be aware of a set of letters you had sent him. I do not mean to pry, but I cannot shake the feeling that those letters contained something of great importance. Something I suspect he has been reluctant to share.

She leaned back, pressing her fingers to her temple, trying to quell the slow, insistent pounding there.

How much should she reveal? How much could she afford to?

Bo's name hovered just at the edge of her pen, waiting.

She exhaled, then bent again over the page.

There is someone I care for deeply who seems burdened by something he refuses to speak of. I know I may be overstepping, but I feel that whatever is weighing on him is somehow connected to all this.

Still too vague.

She bit her lip, then continued.

If there is anything you can tell me, about Tom, about your letters, about Father Schadenfreude, I would be most grateful.

She hesitated once more, then finished it with a quick, clean,

Sincerely,

Shirley Ragland

She read the letter twice over before sealing it, pressing the envelope closed with the flat of her palm.

And then she sat there, staring at it, at her own name scrawled in the corner, at the weight of what she had just done.

Would he answer?

Would he ignore her?

Would she receive something far worse, a reply that told her things she wasn't ready to know?

The candle flickered in its dish, the wax pooling warm and liquid at its base, and a breeze from the open window stirred the lace curtains just slightly.

She glanced outside, to the street below.

And froze.

There, standing half in the glow of the streetlamp, half swallowed by the night, was Tom Walker.

His posture was strange; too still.

His hands were shoved into the pockets of his trousers, his shoulders hunched, his head tilted slightly as if listening to something no one else could hear.

She felt a shiver roll through her body, slow and unwelcome.

Tom had no business being outside her house at this hour.

Did he know about her plans? Was he here to warn her about something? Shirley pondered the thought of going outside to greet him, to hear what he might have to offer? Clearly Tom was troubled about something. She rationalized that he couldn't know her plans; no one knew. Shirley speculated that he must have news about Father Schadenfreude. What else could it be?

She edged closer to the window, peering down, her breath caught in her throat.

Tom's eyes lifted.

And for the first time in all the months she had known him, Shirley Ragland felt something she had never once associated with Tom Walker.

Shame.

Not for the man he was.

But for the man he would never be.

FIVE

LETTERS OF VEILED DREAD

Friday, Fourth Week of July 1942

THE LETTER CAME with the morning post, the paper still damp with the breath of dawn, the ink smudged where a hand had pressed it too long, fretted over it, worn it at the edges like a worry stone passed between fingers. Mother did not touch it at first. A mother knows.

The air in the room stiffened around it, the weight of a thing not yet spoken but already shaped. She set it on the lazy Susan, slid the salt cellar over it, let it rest beneath the quiet machinery of the house, the creak of floorboards under the slow movement of morning, the soft rattle of the icebox settling in its frame, the dry clicking of the clock above the stove.

At supper, she unfolded it with the careful precision of a woman peeling back a bandage, smoothing the creases flat against the oilcloth table, hands trembling just enough to make the paper quiver like the thin wings of a trapped wasp.

Dear Mother and Father,

I reckon I'm writing to you with a heart burdened and my spirit no less so. After much soul-searching and spinning in circles, I have reached a decision that I know will change everything. I have enlisted. I will join my brothers in their service of our country.

I know this news will strike you hard, and I beg you to listen. I have found it near impossible to sit idle while my brothers Raymond and Thomas, and the rest of our countrymen fight for the freedom we hold so dear. I would not be able to look at myself in the mirror if I stayed safe at home while they are out there, risking all.

Leaving Sally and Suzanne is no small thing. It is like tearing out a piece of myself. But Sally's folks in Shelbyville will watch over them, and I hope you will visit them while I am gone. Tell my little sister I love her and not to worry.

I ship out next week to Fort Benning. After training, they will send me where I am needed, likely Europe. My boss at Levi's has promised to hold my position until I return. I promise to be careful.

I will try to come home whole. I know the risk, and it weighs on me, but I must go. This is the right thing, and I hope you will find pride in my choice. When we win, and we will, I will come home to you.

With love, your son,

James Winfred Ragland.

My brother's name sat at the bottom like a heavy stone.

Mother folded the letter again, set it on the table, and pressed her hand on top as if to still something alive beneath her palm. Her face did not move. Daddy did not speak. He leaned back in his chair, jaw working, eyes fixed on some distant point beyond the stove, a man who had swallowed something bitter.

I stared at the letter, then at my plate, then at the tight curve of Mother's fingers pressing into the paper. She would not cry. Not yet. Later, maybe, in the hush of the house when no one could hear.

It should have been expected. The world was burning, and men his age threw themselves into the fire like kindling. First Thomas, then Raymond, now James. They fell in sequence, dominoes tipping one after the next.

I could see James in uniform, the khaki stiff at the seams, a sunburn blooming across the bridge of his nose. That same cocked grin, the one he wore when he wrangled a catfish from the river or talked his way out of trouble with Mr. Jeffers at the feed store. He had always carried that wildness in him, a restless thing that made him run headlong at whatever lay in his path, a fire under his skin, something darker beneath it.

The radio crackled, its voice thin and frayed. Reports from the front, names of cities I had never seen but now felt the weight of. A list of the dead. Mother stood, gathered the dishes. Daddy walked to the porch, pipe in hand, though he did not light it. The door hung open behind him, a thing half finished.

I sat at the table, hands curled in my lap, and thought about war.

It had always been elsewhere. In newspapers, in black-and-white newsreels, in places with names that did not belong to us. It did not smell like home, like dust and honeysuckle and fresh-baked bread. But it was here now, in the quiet spaces between us, in the way Mother's sighs stretched longer, in the way Daddy's hands trembled when he reached for his pipe, in the way the house had become a place of listening.

The next morning, I walked to the post office, half hoping, half dreading. No letter yet, not from where I needed it to come. The word *yet* settled in my chest, a fragile hope curled in the shadows of my ribs.

I turned from the post office and let my feet carry me elsewhere, toward St. Cecilia's, where I knew Tom Walker would be, and where I suspected Father Schadenfreude kept his counsel in dark corners.

I did not take the front door. I went round the back, past the crates stacked with hymnals and the storeroom where the air held the weight of old incense and forgotten things. The door gave under my hand, hinges whispering instead of groaning. I slipped inside, moving past the tarnished candleholders and chalices dim with dust.

Kneeling in the quiet, I pulled the small leather book from beneath my blouse. I pressed it against my knee, the spine firm beneath my fingers. I wrote. I listened. And in the dim hush of that storeroom, beneath the heavy air of relics and silence, I waited for something to be revealed.

*

TOM WALKER IS DRINKING alcohol? I should have known. The way his hands shook last week, the way he flinched at loud noises like a man expecting a blow. And the priest knows it, and what's worse, he's using it against him.

I've been crouching in this same patch of shadow for days now, watching and listening to Father Schadenfreude with the quiet obsession of someone who's already made peace with the sin of it, because something in my bones won't let me look away—not until I understand what thread binds him to Tom, and what strange epistle he's preaching to Bo behind closed doors, where the light doesn't reach and the air smells of immorality; I feel the fear of it growing, curling like smoke around the thought that Bo's been drawn into something he doesn't see coming, something that might unmake him before he ever knows what he's worth.

I don't know what Tom did in Philadelphia, but whatever it was, Father Schadenfreude is keeping him here under his thumb, pressing his guilt like a branding iron against his skin, threatening to send him back if he doesn't behave. The priest said as much just now.

Said if Tom couldn't put the bottle down, he'd be on the next train north, straight to his accuser. Accuser? That word makes my skin crawl. What's Tom done that needs an accuser? And why is a priest, the very man who's supposed to stand on the side of right, willing to conceal it?

*

MY HEART POUNDED AS I listened, breath catching in my throat as Tom mumbled something too soft to make out. Then the priest's voice, stern, clipped. "You think you can hide from God behind the bottle, Thomas? That's what the drunkard tells himself—if his mind is too clouded with whiskey, then the Lord won't see the filth in his heart. But I see it. And I can send you back to those who see it too."

My pen hovered over the page. My mind spun in circles, grasping at threads too tangled to make sense of. What filth? What sins? Tom wasn't good, but he wasn't wicked either, not in the way that word meant. And Father Schadenfreude spoke with a certainty that sent a chill through my bones, like he wasn't just aware of Tom's sins, but a participant in their concealment.

I bit my lower lip, forcing myself to stay still as the voices shifted in tone. Tom, pleading now. The strength in his voice, what little he had left, was fading like a tide pulling away from shore. "Please, Father… please. I—I swear I'll stop. Just… don't send me back."

The priest let the silence stretch. "See that you do," he said at last. "Or I won't be able to protect you."

My stomach turned, fingers tightening around my diary. *Protect you.* Not *forgive you.* Not *help you find redemption.* Just *protect.* The weight of his words was incomprehensible. Those weren't the words of a priest. Those were the words of a man with something to lose.

A board creaked, closer than before.

I froze, body tensing like a rabbit caught in low grass. The voices were moving now, footsteps pacing, and I cursed myself for not watching the time. The priest was coming nearer, nearer, his shoes clicking against the stone floor, measured, deliberate.

I shut the diary and pressed myself into the narrow gap between the shelves, breath shallow in my chest. I willed it that I would not be found. I could not be found.

Another step.

The scent of the priest's cologne drifted toward me, sharp, herbal, laced with something metallic, something unpleasant.

Another step.

I squeezed my eyes shut, willing myself into the wood, into the dust, into nothing at all.

A long pause.

Then, the soft intake of breath, an awareness, a hesitation. As if he had sensed something just beyond his reach. His voice, lower now, murmuring almost to himself.

"… Is someone there?"

My heart slammed against my ribs.

The next step would tell everything.

THE BATTLEGROUNDS OF LEARNING AND LEASH

Monday, First Week of August 1942

THE END OF summer drifted in like a slow exhale, soft and inevitable, and with it came a change. Not one I could put a finger on—only feel. Bo had grown strange with me, not cold exactly, but quieter, his eyes elsewhere even when they were looking right at me. We still met sometimes—in the woods, by the creek, behind town where no one much cared—but our time together had thinned, like a sheet worn soft from too many washings. His touches lingered longer now, though he said less. I mistook it for tenderness. Maybe it was.

I never asked where his mind wandered when he went silent. I told myself it was the season, or the way August always made things feel both endless and already gone.

With school coming—Bo back to the public school, me in my stiff gray jumper at Our Lady of Gomer—the hours we had would shrink. No more lazy mornings or slow-moving afternoons. No more ducking behind the sanctuary to talk about nothing that felt like everything. That truth sat in my gut like a handful of river stones. And yet, tangled up in the grief of it, something else stirred—a strange thrill, a pulse of hope I couldn't explain. Maybe because change always comes dressed in both ruin and promise.

And there was that familiar thrill of being around other kids my age, of shaking off the days of loneliness, even if just for a little while. Our first day back! It was a seven-minute walk—seven hundred and forty-three steps—from my front porch that felt like the longest journey I ever made, growing heavier with every step as I slipped back into a routine I craved and dreaded in equal measure.

Before me, the schoolhouse of Our Lady of Gomer slowly arose like some ancient fortress, its weathered stone walls standing resolute and unyielding, much like our headmaster, Father Craig Lynch, whose countless rules hung over us like storm clouds threatening rain.

The schoolhouse had none of the pretense of the church, none of its hollow grandeur or whispering shadows. It sat plain and square at the edge of town, as if to announce its purpose without embellishment, a stern old stubborn teacher in its own right, reflecting that stubbornness like an old mirror, scratched, warped, yet somehow still functional.

Its stone steps, worn smooth in places by a million footsteps, loomed large in my mind. Not as a refuge, not as a place where answers waited, but as a trial to be endured, a summit to be climbed. There was an air about it, unyielding and certain, as though the very walls knew their purpose: to hammer out the crooked edges of the young and cast them into something sharper, harder, though not necessarily better, and certainly not kinder.

The teachers inside were much the same: Sister Bertha Pruitt and Sister Eloise Lytle. They carried themselves with the unshakable authority of roosters in a yard full of chicks—so dominant in their superiority it seemed almost laughable, yet undeniably real. To them, we were soft and pliable, our minds unshaped, mere lumps of clay awaiting their hands, clucking nervously under their all-seeing gazes.

They perched like feral cats on their thrones of books, their voices pruned and measured, their chalkboards full of rules that always seemed to bear down heavier than the heat of summer. They were beings of the impalpable and imperishable sort, soaring far above the muddied mess of our innocence. The ignorance of their own limits was perhaps their truest gift. It made them impervious to doubt, to self-reflection. They knew what they knew, and they would make sure we knew it too, whether it mattered or not.

Father Lynch was the grand custodian of this dogged determination, a figure so rigidly composed that even his shadow seemed straight-backed. He had a peculiar affinity for order, authority, and large German Shepherds, each named after Wagner operas: Siegfried, Brünnhilde, and Parsifal. They were enormous beasts, often seen patrolling the school grounds like loyal sentries, their presence as unnerving as the man who owned them.

He was a man of contrasts: his aftershave carried the cloying sweetness of something store-bought and over-applied, yet it couldn't quite mask the undertone of the whiskey that clung to his words, especially after lunch. He wielded a cane like a king's sceptre, a multipurpose tool for pointing, prodding, and, when the occasion called for it, delivering swift justice to unruly students. It wasn't unusual to see the cane tap against a desk, once, twice—before its final, ominous descent. He didn't need to raise his voice; the snap of that cane spoke louder than any shouted command.

Under Father Lynch's reign, school was a factory, not a sanctuary. It throbbed with the machinery of conformity: rows of desks like assembly lines, faces bent over books, each one learning the art of mediocrity. Curiosity wasn't encouraged; it was a nuisance to be tamed, boxed, and labeled for later use, though what use, I couldn't fathom. Rules weren't just rules; they were gospel, engraved into the very walls of the place.

And yet, for all its grayness, the school pulsed with a peculiar energy, a tautness in the air that made you itch to push against it. It wasn't just the slap of shoes on polished wood floors or the muffled hum of lessons bleeding through the walls. It was the way the building seemed to hold its breath, as if daring you to test its resolve, to toe the line or step boldly over it. The air felt charged, not with excitement, but with the promise of consequences. Whispers flitted like nervous birds in the corners while shuffling feet whispered secrets to the floorboards. It buzzed with the mingled scents of chalk dust, moldy books, and the tangy aroma of boy sweat, a pungent reminder of the years I've spent confined within these hallowed walls.

Father Lynch was the architect of this atmosphere. He was a tall, angular man whose sharp edges seemed carved from the very rules he enforced. His hair, slicked back with precision, caught the light like an oil slick, and his thin lips curved into a permanent half-smirk, as though he were constantly amused by how predictable we all were. His voice, sheared smooth of high notes, walloped with a weight that bruised, leaving no room for argument.

Unflinching and imposing, his cane propped against the desk as if it were an extension of his formidable self, Father Lynch was ready to enforce his dominion at the slightest provocation. His presence loomed large, and I couldn't help but feel as though we were all minor characters in a narrative he alone authored, each word of his countless edicts etched into our minds like the very stones surrounding us.

"Good morning, scholars," he began, his voice smooth but edged with authority. "Or should I say soldiers, for that's what you are, soldiers in the battle against ignorance. And let me remind you, this is a battle we must win, for the good of Springfield, the good of Tennessee, and the good of this great nation."

He paused, surveying the room as if daring anyone to contradict him. No one did.

"Now, who among you can tell me the difference between discipline and punishment?" he asked, his cane tapping the floor rhythmically.

Tommy Brewer raised his hand. "Discipline's when you learn something, and punishment's when you get whupped for not learning it."

The class stifled giggles, but Father Lynch didn't flinch. Instead, he raised an eyebrow. "An... earthy explanation, Mr. Brewer, but not incorrect. Discipline, children, is the foundation upon which success is built. Punishment is merely the hammer we use to remind you of that foundation when you forget." A few heads nodded, though most of us just stared, waiting for the bell to end his sermon.

"Discipline," he added, "is not an action but an atmosphere, one that must be cultivated, cherished, and maintained." To Father Lynch, the world was made of tidy compartments, each locked tight with its own key. There were no shades of gray, only the blinding clarity of black and white.

"And let me remind you," he continued, his voice dropping to a conspiratorial tone, "life is full of hammers. Best learn to avoid them while you're young." The room fell silent, save for the faint scratching of pencils and the occasional bark of one of the dogs outside. Siegfried, probably. He was the loudest.

And yet, even in Father Lynch's fortress of absolutes, cracks formed in the mortar. They were subtle, almost imperceptible, but they were there, waiting for someone with sharp enough eyes to notice. He would let slip a hint of tenderness when he spoke of his dogs, his voice softening just enough to betray him.

Or there was the way he lingered near the grand piano in the assembly hall, his long fingers, like the claws of a bird, reaching out with an almost skeletal grace, brushing its keys as though testing its warmth. Sometimes, his eyes would cloud for a fraction of a second before snapping back into their familiar coldness. Those moments made you wonder what kind of man he had been before he became a tyrant of children. What had bent him so sharply into the shape he was now?

As I sat at my desk, staring vacantly out the window at the world beyond the schoolyard, I couldn't help but wonder if Father Lynch noticed the cracks. Did he feel the weight of them pressing against his rules? Did he fear what might come spilling out? The thought both frightened and thrilled me. Perhaps the real lessons here weren't in the books and desks and endless rules but in the cracks, the unspoken spaces where the light slipped through.

My thoughts wandered, though not far from the topic that had consumed me all summer. Bo Harris. Even in the dull, measured routine of the school day, the thought of him sent ripples through my chest. I imagined what the other girls would say when they found out. When they saw Bo, the golden boy, waiting for me outside the classroom or walking me home after school. I could already feel their jealous stares, sharp as needles, but I welcomed them. It wasn't just about Bo; it was about being seen. Being known. Being worthy.

For years, I'd felt like a ghost among my peers, floating on the edges of their chatter, my voice too quiet to leave a mark. But Bo changed all that. When his attention landed on me, it was like stepping into a spotlight I hadn't realized I'd craved. And if the other girls hated me for it, so much the better. Their scorn would only prove what I already suspected: that I was something more than they thought. That I was someone worth envying.

The bell chimed, yanking me from my reveries, and suddenly Father Lynch's voice reverberated down the corridor, curt and commanding, as if he were trying to orchestrate a symphony of students still dragging their feet in reluctant unison. I lumbered into Sister Lytle's Latin class with all the enthusiasm of a turtle caught in a slow-motion race, one that would likely conclude only when both contestants were declared ancient history. Now, don't get me wrong—I had a fondness for the beauty of the Latin language, but that was before I had to endure Sister Lytle's hubris, which was as thick as molasses and twice as hard to digest.

Being the first day back, Sister Lytle launched into her grand exposition on the syllabus for the year, her expectations, and, of course, her meticulously crafted rules, the kind that felt more like a prison sentence than a lesson plan. As she droned on, I couldn't help but notice that my own private studies in Latin had propelled me light-years ahead of her ambitious outline. I sank deeper into my seat, distracted and detached, praying earnestly for the final bell to ring, as if it were my only salvation from this liturgical obsession masquerading as an educational experience. Oh, the bell—*Tempus ad liberandum!*

I stood, smoothing the front of my skirt, and walked toward the door, my head held high. The cracks in the school walls might never widen, and Father Lynch might never change. But I had Bo Harris, and for now, that was enough to make me feel untouchable. In fact, he was there, waiting on the steps for me as I left the building.

Bo was irreverently leaning against the front steps of the schoolhouse, his arms folded, and his head tilted just enough to let the afternoon sun catch in his straw-colored hair. He looked as easy as a cat in a sunny spot, but his eyes, sharp and steady, found me the moment I stepped outside. My breath caught in my throat. He wasn't just waiting for me; he was waiting for me in front of my peers.

"Well, hey there, Shirley," he drawled, his voice smooth as molasses. He wasn't smart; no, he was built strictly to look at. And that's exactly what I did. "Thought I'd walk you home, if you don't mind." I nodded, unable to summon anything clever to say, my fingers tightening around the strap of my schoolbag. He fell into step beside me, his long stride matched to my shorter, more hesitant one. The gravel crunched beneath our feet, filling the quiet spaces where words ought to go. My heart pounded so loud I was sure he could hear it.

We veered off the main road, surrendering ourselves to the dusty embrace of a narrow path that wound its way toward the creek, each step stirring whispers from the dry leaves carpeting the ground. Here, the trees swelled like guardians of some hinted mystery, their branches arched overhead as if conspiring to keep secrets from curious eyes.

Bo, ever the boy with a wild heart, reached for a low-hanging vine, swinging through the air with a reckless abandon that would have made Tarzan blush with envy. For a brief moment, he was a creature of the wild, before he landed with an exaggerated grace, dusting himself off with the nonchalance only youth and natural athleticism could muster, resuming his idle gait along the path, leaving behind echoes of laughter mingling with the rustle of leaves, as if nature itself chuckled at his audacity.

"So, Shirley," he said, his tone casual but his eyes glinting with something less so, "you ever think about us? I mean, not just sittin' in church or passin' notes. Like—really think about us?"

I stumbled slightly, my shoe catching on a rogue root. "I… I guess I've thought about it," I said, my voice barely louder than a whisper. "Why?"

He stopped, turning to face me. The sun filtered through the leaves, casting his face in soft light that made him look almost too handsome to be real.

"'Cause I been thinkin' 'bout you," he said. "More than I probably ought to. You're somethin' else, Shirley. Prettier than any damn girl I've ever seen. And not just pretty; you've got somethin' in you, a smartness I ain't ever seen. A spark too. Makes a man wanna' get close, figure you out."

My cheeks burned and I looked down at the dirt, unable to meet his gaze. "I don't know if I'm all that," I said, fumbling with the strap of my bag.

He stepped closer, so close I could smell the faint tang of sweat and the sweet scent of his intoxicating cologne. "You're more than that," he said, his voice low and warm. "And I aim to find out just how much."

I wasn't entirely certain what that meant; my cheeks ignited with the kind of heat that would have made a ripe tomato proud—a mix of embarrassment and a peculiar appreciation for the moment. To be truly seen, to feel those eyes probing the depths of my existence, was a rarity in my household; it was akin to finding a three-legged dog at a fancy dinner party—utterly unexpected and yet somehow refreshingly delightful.

We arrived at the creek, where the clear water gurgled softly over smooth stones, its gentle song a balm to the ear. The reflections of reds, greens, and browns waltzed elegantly across the rippling surface, as if the season, fall itself, were tiptoeing through an enchanted ballet, celebrating its fleeting reign before slipping away into the arms of winter.

Bo dropped his book bag by the bank and turned to me, his eyes scanning my face like he was trying to memorize every detail. Then, without another word, he leaned in and kissed me. It was slow at first, his lips brushing mine like they had all the time in the world, coaxing rather than taking. It reminded me of our first kiss in the belfry—untainted, like fresh dewdrops, that sweet, clumsy exploration of something new and exhilarating.

But this time wasn't clumsy; it was deliberate, and the warmth of his mouth against mine sent a shiver down my spine that made my toes curl upward in my shoes. His hands slid to my waist, his fingers firm yet gentle, pulling me closer like he was afraid to let go. My heart thundered in my chest, a wild, untamed thing, and I let myself sink into the kiss, his tongue teasing against mine. The world faded, leaving only the murmur of the creek and the press of his body, solid and certain, against mine, wrapped in all the conservativeness of a school uniform.

His hand moved then, grazing the edge of my blouse, and I felt a spark of something between fear and longing shoot through me. My breath caught, and though a part of me wanted to pull back, a bigger hunk urged me to stay. His hand drifted lower, grazing the curve of my waist and trailing down to my thigh, each touch light but insistent, like he was mapping out something sacred.

My pulse raced faster, my body caught in that strange, electric mix of wanting and not knowing. His fingers lingered, testing the hem of my skirt, searching for a way past it, and my stomach flipped, a mix of excitement and panic swelling all at once.

"Bo," I whispered, my voice trembling, but he didn't stop. Instead, his lips moved to my neck, pressing kisses that sent heat spiraling through me.

"Shirley," he murmured against my skin, his voice low and rough, "you're so damn pretty. I've never wanted anything the way I want you right now."

His words made my knees weak, and I clung to him, torn between the pull of his touch and the quiet voice in the back of my mind telling me to wait. His hand slipped under the hem of my skirt, his fingers slipping just beyond, and I froze.

"Bo, wait," I said, my voice shaky but firm, breaking the spell. I pushed back slightly, enough to put space between us, though my heart screamed at me for it. "I… we can't. Not now. Mama's waitin' for me to go clothes shopping." It was a flimsy excuse, and I knew it, but it was all I could manage.

He blinked, his dark eyes searching mine, and for a moment, I thought he might argue. Instead, he let out a sigh—one part disappointment, one part understanding. His hand slid upward, trailing across my body with a deliberate slowness that made my breath hitch.

Bo's fingers brushed my blouse, grazed the side of my breast, then found their way to my cheek, where he cupped my face and pulled me into another kiss. This one was softer, lingering, as though he wanted to savor it before letting me go. When he broke away, his lips still hovering near mine, fevered sinful breaths filling my nostrils with a type of sorcery I yearned to learn. He smirked, his voice warm and teasing.

"Alright," he said, stepping back and running a hand through his tousled hair. "I'll wait. But while you're out shoppin', pick somethin' pretty, just for me, okay?"

I nodded, trying to smile and unable to trust my voice, not knowing exactly what that would be, but my mind was already spinning. His easy confidence made my knees weak all over again. As we walked back toward the main road, my thoughts churned, torn between the thrill of his touch and the shame of my own fear. I wanted to be the girl he thought I was: bold, fearless, ready. But I wasn't. Not yet.

My chest ached with the tension of wanting and not wanting, of saying no when every part of me screamed yes. As I turned back toward the path home, I bit my lip, my thoughts swirling like the creek behind me. Next time, I told myself. Could it happen twice? I asked myself, afraid to know the answer.

Later that night, lying in bed, I replayed it all in my mind: every word, every glance, every touch. I hated myself for saying no, for letting fear win. I'm stronger than that, I told myself. This fever of a first love is a pounding and unrelenting infection, for it's both a fever and a burden, whatever Emily Dickinson might say.

I made a promise to myself then and there: if Bo Harris ever gave me another chance, I wouldn't flinch. I'd meet him halfway and then some, no matter who was watching. Next time, I told myself, I'd prove I was the kind of girl he couldn't forget. The kind of girl who wears bright red lipstick to the Piggly Wiggly just to stir up trouble. Next time, I'd do just what Trixie Simpson would've done back in her prime—chin up, hips forward, and not a trace of shame in sight. I wouldn't say no.

SIX

THE FRAGILITY OF KINDNESS

Tuesday, First Week of August 1942

EARLINE, WITH HER threadbare frocks and skin the color of polished coal, is the closest thing I have to an obligatory mother. But something about her nurturing ways sets my incredulous mind spinning, as if I am peering through a foggy window, unsure of what lay beyond. To say I have trust issues would be an understatement.

In my quiet observations of the world, I often marvel at the easy, nurturing relationships other girls seem to share with their mothers, a kind of warmth blossoming effortlessly in their homes, like sunflowers turning toward the light, a warmth that never graces my own abode.

I notice it in the way my classmates' mothers smooth their hair or straighten their collars with absent-minded affection, as if love flows from their hands without a second thought. It is evident in their shared looks of conspiratorial amusement or whispered secrets that dance through the air—matters too delicate for young ears, they say.

And yet, those few precious moments of tenderness come not from my own mother, who has long since buried any semblance of warmth, but from Earline, our colored domestic. She moves through the rooms of our house like a wraith born of kindness, her grace and patience, an almost holy contradiction to the weight of indignities she must have borne, yet still I can't help but wonder about her wherefores. What does she see in me, a girl clad in uncertainty and riddled with questions?

It is a strange thing, how her compassion feels almost too effortless, too perfect, as though she's bestowing upon me the kind of love that is passed down through the generations, yet somehow still wrapped in the guise of servitude. Does she love me truly, or am I merely reflecting the kindness she has been taught to give, an obligation dressed up as nurturance? In that strange mix of gratitude and doubt, I feel her comforting presence like a fragile thread from a spider's web, binding us together, even as I grapple with the mist of self-doubt, forever loitering at the brittle edges of my heart.

Earline's husband, Mun, schlepps about with a quiet steadiness, the kind that feels as solid as the earth itself. He's worked alongside Daddy for as long as I can remember, the two of them moving in step like the moldboard of a mule-drawn plow. Their friendship is deep, woven tight like the seams on one of Mother's handsewn quilts, and it doesn't take much for folks around here to start tugging at loose threads with their tongues.

"Mun's been under y'all's roof a long time, ain't he?" Mrs. Lowery had said one Sunday after church, her voice dripping with the kind of sweetness that curdles quick, like lemons in fresh milk. "Looks like he's more family than friend, the way he's always 'round."

Mother hated such unsolicited appraisals, she'd turn three shades of red, a sign to Mrs. Lowry that she'd accomplished what she wanted. Mother would be mad as a wet hen for two days afterward.

Daddy brushed it off with his usual calm, tipping his hat and saying, "Some folks just know where they belong. Some folks don't." Daddy had a way of insulting folks without them knowing. But I'd seen how the words settled on him, heavy as a feed sack.

People around here don't like what they can't understand, and the bond between Daddy and Mun was one of those things. It wasn't just that they work together; it's the way they lean on each other, like two beams holding up the same roof. Mun don't say much, but when he does, it's always straight and true, and Daddy listens like the words mean something.

"Daddy," I asked one evening, as Mun's shadow stretched long across the barn wall, "how come you and Mun are so close? Folks say all kinds of things."

Daddy looked at me, his face calm but his eyes sharp, like he was weighing how much I needed to know. "Shirley," he said, tipping his hat just enough to shield his eyes from the sun, "a man ain't measured by the color of his skin no more than a plow's judged by the color of its handle. What matters is if it cuts the earth true. Mun's been cuttin' true by me since we was boys, and that's all there is to it. Sometimes the best thing a man can do is stand beside another, no questions asked. Let them sons-a-bitches talk; when the wind's change, it'll be them that gets talked about. It don't change a damn thing."

I nodded, allowing Daddy's words to drift into the recesses of my mind, honest as ink blots. Daddy and Mun shared a bond that required no elaborate explanations. It was woven into the fabric of our family, recognizable only to those who truly mattered. In this town, where words flitted about like sparrows in a restless sky, I reasoned that sometimes, silence bore the weight of the strongest loyalty, a steadfast allegiance that spoke volumes without ever needing to utter a sound.

A perfect pair, if ever there was one, were Earline and Mun, creating the semblance of stability in a home that too often felt as delicate as spun glass, ready to shatter with the slightest touch. Mun, ever the silent sentinel standing firmly behind Daddy, worked diligently in the shadows, while Earline burst forth like a blazing sun, a vibrant force of nature, constant and unapologetically present in my life, fiercely illuminating the corners of our fragile existence.

Mun's homemade dandelion wine was the sort of thing Daddy appreciated more than he'd ever admit, though Mother didn't need him to. The smell alone was enough to set her off, a cloying sweetness that carried too many arguments in its wake. To her, the wine wasn't just a drink, it was a breach, a steady drip of sin staining her carefully ordered house.

She blamed Mun for Daddy's weakness; his frequent drunkenness, of course, her dislike for him coiled tight and ready to strike at the first mention of his name. "That colored man's a bad influence," she'd hiss, arms crossed, jaw set hard.

Mother never said it outright, but I knew she thought Daddy didn't need any help finding trouble. She wasn't wrong. Mun's wine was just one more road Daddy could wander down, and even if Mun hadn't laid the path, Daddy would've carved out his own.

The wine itself was a small thing, a few mason jars tucked in the Frigidaire, amber-colored and innocent-looking, like it hadn't upended a hundred conversations. But it was never just the wine. Daddy didn't need Mun or his dandelions to find a drink, and Mother knew that. Knew it and hated it, though I think what she hated more was how it sat between them, something sour and rotting, and neither of them willing to clear it away.

I found myself consumed with a burning desperation to indulge in it myself, a longing that danced at the edges of my propriety. Mother would never stand for such indulgence; that much I knew, while Daddy, ever the keeper of precious things, deemed it far too valuable to share. Yet, each time I opened the Frigidaire door, I was met with that amber-hued sin nestled within its glass confines, a jar of temptation that seemed to whisper sweetly to me, seducing me again and again with the allure of a forbidden fruit, its promise glimmering like a siren's call in the dim light of our kitchen.

"*Sed nocens est, et in tenebris latet,*" I thought, practicing my Latin. "But it is harmful, and lurks in the shadows."

I stand there, tempted by sin, same as every character in the Bible, torn between desire and the stern weight of consequence. Believing that all things cannot be defined in the endless wilderness of faith.

Mother is a figure cloaked in unapproachable aloofness, a presence that fills the room yet remains firmly distant, like a distant apparition lingering just beyond reach. She seldom speaks of her childhood, but when she does, her words emerge with the heaviness of a plow dragging stubbornly through rocky soil, each syllable a testament to burdens rarely lifted. Her father, my granddaddy, was a drinker of legendary proportions, the sort whose thirst seemed insatiable, as if he had tapped a well that ran infinitely deep.

A Lieutenant in the Union Army of Kentucky during the War of Northern Aggression, he carried the scars of violence etched into his very being—not merely those inflicted upon him, but the darker shadows of misdeeds committed in the wake of that tumultuous era. His reputation loomed large over our family, a ghost that whispered of the bad things he had done, casting a pall over the lineage from which I sprang, as if the past were a stubborn weed unwilling to be uprooted.

When Mother was just thirteen, the law finally caught up to him for some hare-brained scheme he'd cooked up with another fellow. They'd been selling shares in a stock that didn't exist, preying on good folks who trusted their slick talk. Granddaddy ended up behind bars for three years, and Mother, being the oldest of six, had to step into his shoes whether she wanted to or not.

She dropped out of school without so much as a second thought, swapping textbooks for dishwater and dances for dirty diapers. It wasn't fair, everybody knew it, but Mother didn't have the luxury of fairness. She took to raising her brothers and sisters like a soldier called to the front line, her days filled with sewing hems and scrubbing floors while her friends went to socials and chased after boys in starched collars.

What cut the deepest, though, wasn't the work or the whispers in town; it was the shame. Mother had been Granddaddy's favorite, the apple of his eye, and she loved him in spite of his flaws, maybe even because of them. His incarceration left her raw and exposed, like a wound that wouldn't heal. Folks talked, Lord, did they talk, and Mother hated the pity in their eyes almost as much as the judgment.

"We couldn't even keep our church," she once told me, her voice low and clipped like she was still trying to wrestle the memory into submission. "Mother said we had to leave the Methodists after Daddy's foolishness. Too many eyes watching us. That's when we switched to the Catholics. Less gossip, more forgiveness."

I tried to imagine Mother as an adolescent girl, her hands busy tying ribbons in her sisters' hair instead of holding a boy's hand under the school bleachers. It didn't seem right, but it made sense, in a hard, Southern way. Life down here has a way of turning girls into women before they've had a chance to dream. Mother was proof of that, and while she might've traded one cross for another, she never let it break her.

THREADS OF TRUST

Wednesday, First Week of August 1942

MOTHER TRUSTED EARLINE enough to place me in her arms but not enough to leave a dollar uncounted.

Trusted her to rock me to sleep but not with the silverware drawer left unlocked. It was a strange thing to see trust and suspicion wrapped so tightly together, one hand offering while the other pulled back. Mother never forgot the time before I was born when she caught a colored housekeeper slipping a jar of preserves into her apron pocket, a pair of gloves folded neat inside. She carried the memory like a coin rubbed smooth, a talisman against generosity.

And yet, she needed Earline.

I was a weak thing when I came, spindly-limbed and wailing, and Mother, too old, too weary, could not bring herself to nurse me. Cow's milk sloshed into glass bottles, forced down my gullet, and came back up curdled. My cries sharpened into something thin and needling, my ribs a basket of kindling waiting to snap.

Earline saw. Earline had milk. She had a baby at home, a boy with a strong grip and a belly full of what should have been his alone. But she took me to her chest, soft and dark, a curve against my paleness, and she fed me. Held me when Mother would not. Let my tiny hand clutch at her, desperate, knowing before I did where life came from.

She never spoke of it. Wiped her breast dry, fastened her blouse, left no trace of what she had given. But Mother walked in once, unannounced, and there I was, my mouth full of what was not mine to take.

She snatched me away so fast I almost forgot to breathe. Stood rigid with fury, scandal slicing through her voice. What would people say?

And yet.

My cheeks had filled, my cries softened. I no longer trembled in my sleep.

Mother looked at me, at Earline, at the space between us. "You can finish what you started", her voice cold as a snapped bone, "but only until she's strong enough."

Earline did not thank her. She did not need to. She only gathered me back in her arms with the kind of finality that made it clear she would have done it anyway, permission be damned.

She rose in the dark to tend a house that was not hers, a child that was not hers, and a life that never would be. Set bread to bake in an oven whose warmth did not belong to her, stirred grits in a pot while her own babies licked sugar from their fingers, waiting for her return.

I used to think her tireless. Now I know better. It was exhaustion she wore, steady as a yoke, shoulders squared against a weight she had no choice but to bear.

Did she think of them, the children she left behind each morning? Hear their voices in the quiet between chores, in the shuffle of laundry, in the hush of sheets smoothed beneath her hands?

She never let it show. If there was sorrow, she hid it well. Her hands moved with the precision of someone who had long learned the art of quiet sacrifice, a seam stitched tight enough to hold against the pull of grief.

I wondered, in the silence of my own restless nights, if she ever resented me. If I was just another mouth to feed, another small voice drowning out the ones that mattered most. Did she tuck me in at night while thinking of the ones she could not? Did she hold me with hands that ached for another?

She never said.

What she gave me was not softness. Not a mother's doting affection, but something stronger, stripped of sentiment, carved from the hard stone of necessity. A love that did not need words, only the rhythm of work, the certainty of care. A love that stayed.

She taught me more than Mother ever did.

Mother gave me manners, posture, the right way to hold a fork. Earline gave me sense.

"Nobody care how good you look, Miss Shirley, if your manners be ugly."

She never raised her voice, never had to. Her lessons landed like coins tossed into a jar, weighty and certain, collecting interest over time.

"Good manners," she told me once, smoothing wrinkles from a freshly laundered sheet, "is how you treat folks who ain't got any."

And wasn't that the truth.

Mother taught me to keep my hem from dragging in the dirt, but Earline taught me not to step on people while I walked.

One morning, I found her in the kitchen, folding linens with a kind of reverence, each crease precise, as though respect could be stitched into fabric. She was not young anymore. The years had curved her back, lined her hands, but she stood steady, unmoved by time's bite.

She was not beautiful by the standards the women in town whispered about—the pale softness, the delicate hands—but there was something about her, some quiet force, some immovable dignity, that demanded attention and made her more beautiful to me than Vivien Leigh. Her skin, deep and rich, caught the morning light like polished mahogany, her hair coiled neat beneath a headwrap, silver threading through the black.

She looked up, not startled, never startled.

"Good mornin', Miss Shirley."

I had always said it back without thinking, but that day, something in me hesitated. The words I wanted to say caught in my throat, thick with something I had no name for.

I swallowed.

"Good morning, Earline."

She went back to her work, fingers pressing fabric into crisp lines, as if she had not noticed the weight in my voice.

But she had. I saw it in the way her lips curved, the barest hint of a smile.

She did not need thanks. She did not ask for gratitude. She did what needed doing, set it right, and carried on.

And yet.

As I stood there, watching her, I felt it settle over me, a warmth unexpected.

What she had given me was not something I could repay. It was something deeper. Something that did not need words.

And so, I did the only thing I knew to do.

I stayed a moment longer.

And then, quietly, I walked away.

CONTRADICTIONS, SCARS, AND SHADOWS

Thursday, First Week of August 1942

THE TOWN WORE its history like a skin, sun-cracked and worn, every inch of it marked by something old that refused to be buried. The great war between the states lived here still, coiled in the loamy breaths of its fields, in the slatted bones of porches sagging under the weight of stories too heavy to be told. The past did not sleep in these streets; it sat wide-eyed and waiting, watching from the magnolia shade with a patience honed by a hundred years of knowing better.

Daddy never spoke of it in any way that mattered, only in ways that let him sidestep the truths nobody wanted to admit, not out loud. The war had come and gone and left behind ghosts that refused to be laid to rest. He called it the War of Northern Aggression when he was being stubborn, the Civil War when he was being polite. But to the bank that had swallowed his family's land whole during Reconstruction, it was nothing but a footnote in a ledger, another broken promise folded into the soil. They had lost everything; not all at once, but in pieces, in crops that never yielded, in debts that thickened like kudzu, in the slow and certain erosion of dignity.

His people, they had owned slaves once, not in Daddy's time, but before. Daddy spoke of them not with shame or pride but with a strange sort of distance, as though they were a thing that had happened to someone else. He never saw himself above a soul on this earth, never dolled up his voice in fancy words or put on airs. When he spoke the names of colored folks, those he loved—those who'd wronged him—they all came out plain and human, like all names should, with no bitterness on his tongue and no holiness either, just respect and memory, with a knowing that the world had its rules and they weren't the ones who had written them.

Mother was different. Her people had fought for the Union, though not for righteousness or the liberation of the enslaved. It had been a matter of principle, she said, "…for the defense of the Republic", she'd say, as though the distinction meant something. Her grandfather had carried a Union sabre, but the blade had never been drawn for justice, only for duty. And if Mother carried any of that fire inside her, it had twisted into something mean and sharp, something that made her purse her lips when the colored folk passed too close, made her grip her pocketbook tight when Earline stood too near. It was not hate, not in the way that boiled over into violence, but something colder, something that had settled into her bones like an affliction passed through bloodlines.

She dressed it in propriety, in rigid posture and clipped words, in the high-necked blouses that left no room for warmth. She kept the house like a temple, every curtain stiff with starch, every floor polished to a blinding sheen. "Elegance," she called it. But it was a brittle thing, that elegance, a structure held together with silence and resignation. There was no breathing room in that house, no place to stretch without knocking something askew.

It wasn't that her immediate family had ever possessed the means or the high status to claim the title of slave owners; no, they floundered around in their own mediocrity, their aspirations suffocated by circumstance. Yet, for reasons long buried with her parents, she harbored a simmering disdain that seemed to challenge the very air around her, driving away anyone, especially coloreds, who dared to occupy space in her world. Even if they were there at her beck and call, working for her, she barely tolerated their presence, muttering discontent under her breath as if their very existence tainted her carefully curated surroundings.

It was a crooked sentiment that bubbled just beneath the surface, a remnant of a bygone era that had ensnared her in its coils, forcing her to wrestle with the dingy silhouettes of her own lineage, and she carried it like an unsightly scar, a betrayal to her family history, yet one she could not shake.

"Don't you go asking questions that can't be answered, Shirley," Daddy would say, his voice light, his eyes heavy. "Ain't polite to stir the pot when it ain't boiling."

But the pot was always boiling in our house, always on the edge of spilling over, steam rising in slow curls from the things nobody would say out loud. The past lay in wait beneath our feet, in the red clay that stained our shoes, in the way people moved through town careful of where they stepped, of who they looked at too long. The fences were not always made of wood and wire. Some were built of glances and quiet warnings, of doors that did not open when certain hands knocked.

At night, the fences blurred in the dim light of the kerosene lamps, the sharp lines of day softening into something less defined. I would stand at the window and look past the edge of our yard to where the town sprawled beyond the reach of Mother's carefully drawn borders. I would think of Earline, her hands smoothing linens, her laughter quiet but whole. She carried herself with a dignity that did not waver, even under the weight of a world that pressed her down at every turn. And I envied her, not for her life, but for the way she lived it, steady and sure, never shrinking even when the walls closed in.

Mother could not understand that kind of strength. Her strength was made of iron and glass, something brittle, something that cut when it cracked. She spoke of colored folk with a tightness in her jaw, a tension that had nothing to do with them and everything to do with what she saw when she looked in the mirror. She resented their presence not because of what they were but because of what they reminded her she was not. Her life had been a series of concessions, of things she had settled for, of doors that had never opened no matter how hard she knocked. And so, she shut them on others first, lest they remind her of what it meant to be left standing on the threshold.

It was a cruel thing, the way the world made people small, how it pressed them into shapes they did not choose. But I would not let it shape me.

In those rare moments, it felt as though I had sprung from one of her meticulous plans, a seed she had sown with care, but I had grown wild, unpredictable, disappointing. Her expectations hung heavy in the air between us, an invisible ledger where every wrinkle in my dress, every loose curl, was a mark against me. She moved through her world with the poise of a queen whose kingdom was the judgment of others, and I was her unruly subject, forever tugging at the hem of her carefully arranged life. Each word she spoke came tightly wrapped, suffocating in its restraint. It left me wanting to pull at the edges, to unspool the threads of her distance and find the woman underneath.

"Why can't we just be kind to them?" I asked once, too curious for my own good. I was thinking of Earline, her steady hands folding linens, or Miss Daisy from down the lane, whose laughter could fill the room even as her back bent under the weight of someone else's burdens. They worked with a grace that seemed unearned, given the hardness of their lives, and it baffled me how anyone could treat them as anything less than extraordinary.

"The Lord preaches not to get tangled in things that don't concern us, Shirley," she snapped, her voice like the crack of a whip on the air. The firmness in her tone was undeniable, but it was her eyes that betrayed her. In them, I saw silhouettes, deep and restless, speaking of grievances older than me, older than her. They weren't grievances with Earline or Miss Daisy, not directly, but with a life she must have once imagined for herself, one that had slipped through her fingers like water through a sieve. Her disapproval wasn't just about them; it was about her, about a world she had come to resent but couldn't leave.

In that moment, she wasn't just my mother. She was a woman ensnared by her own rules, trapped in a cage she had gilded herself. Her pride was both armor and prison, keeping her upright but forever bound. I wanted to hate her for it, for the coldness that had crept into her words and actions, but all I could feel was pity. For all her austerity, she was no freer than the women she watched over with such disdain, and in that recognition, I saw a sadness that neither of us could bear to confess out loud.

Daddy and I, on the other hand, shared a different rhythm. He was a riddle wrapped in contradictions and topped with a wide-brim hat, jauntily tilted just so. A hearty laugh came easily from him, filling the house like the smell of fresh-baked bread. And yet, beyond that laughter lay an air of harsh reality, one cloaked in the easy banter of a man cozy in his own world but grappling with something he hardly shared.

"Sometimes, Shirley, you just gotta' let life flow like the river," he'd say, tossing stones into the creek behind the house, each plunk echoing into the silence. "You fight the current, and it'll swallow your ass whole. Better to steer clear of the goddamned rocks." His voice held an inflection of wisdom, yet it seemed to shadow the weight of words left unspoken.

"Daddy," I replied, hesitant yet curious, "what if the current leads you somewhere you don't want to go?"

He would turn to me then, chewing on the words as though they were tough greens, revealing that fine line between care and ambiguity. "Life's got a way of throwing you in the deep end, whether you want it or not. Just learn to swim, gal. You'll be fine."

It was then I realized we lived not merely in the same house but within a theater of contradictions, each character trapped in their roles, performing for an audience of one. I felt like a puppet straining against my strings, caught between Mama's vigilant gaze and

Daddy's cheerful semblance of acceptance, perpetually wondering if I'd ever find a stage of my own.

Each evening brought its own peculiar ebb and flow as the sun slipped down, painting the sky with strokes of orange and violet, spilling over the edges of our routine.

I would hear them, with their overlapping conversations, sharp tones laced with unspoken truths as we sat around the kitchen table. "Did you see those colored women at the market today, Jim?" Mama would inquire, her eyes a mix of disdain and idle curiosity. "It's a shame they can't learn to keep their place."

Daddy would respond with his characteristic passive aggressive flair. "Well, but they sure do make good biscuits, don't they, dear?" His easy jest would draw a short laugh from me, but it never quite reached Mama, who merely tightened her grip on the linen napkin, folding it as if it were the fabric of her own frustrations.

Perhaps what haunted me most was the way their lives seemed to mirror and distort my own, familiar yet unknowable, like trying to trace the outline of your face in a darkened window. Each morning, I rose to the sound of Mother's sharp commands and the muffled clatter of Earline's steady work, tiptoeing through the tangled underbrush of their expectations, searching for some scrap of air I could call my own.

My spirit, untamed and restless, bristled against the orderliness of their world. I dreamed of being a wildflower, something unruly and unexpected, thriving in the careful confines of their manicured garden, but it was hard to bloom when the soil beneath you felt packed and dry. It was a silly dream, I knew—a young girl's rebellion against a world that had long since settled into its grooves—but the thought of it burned bright in me, a little light that refused to go out.

Still, the world doesn't care much for the dreams of a girl on the cusp of adulthood. Men like Father Lynch and others who set the rules and kept the order had no use for a woman interrupting the flow of a conversation, let alone an entire way of life. "The weaker sex," they'd say with a smirk, though the women I knew carried burdens that would leave most men on their knees. And yet, as much as my mind tried to make sense of things, the more the world pushed back, its weight pressing against my chest until breathing felt like a small act of defiance.

I thought of Earline then, her quiet dignity as she folded linens and polished silver, her hands moving with a grace that seemed to deny the injustices of her life. She walked through the world with a strength that didn't demand recognition but left an indelible mark all the same. How did she reckon with it all, I wondered? Keeping her head high in a town that barely acknowledged her humanity; and thinking me and Mother foolish for our tiresome complaints about being called the weaker sex.

As I stared out at the fading light, I wanted to believe I could be like Earline: strong, unyielding, finding meaning even in the confines of a small, divided place. But deep down, I wanted more. I wanted to be free of the fences altogether, to step beyond their lines and dance in the light of a world that didn't yet exist. It was a selfish thought, maybe even a dangerous one, but it was mine, and I held onto it as tightly as I could, even as the night settled over Springfield like a heavy quilt.

The truth that tugged at me, though, was that my freedom to dream, wild, boundless, selfish dreams, was a luxury not everyone shared. Earline didn't get to imagine a world beyond the fences, not in the way I did. For her and Mun, and their four children, the lines weren't just boundaries to push against; they were walls built high and hard, with sharp edges that cut deep if you dared lean too close. They didn't have the right to test the world's patience, to be ornery, to risk breaking the rules. The best hearts this county had to offer, steadfast and full of grace, and yet, they were denied the simple right to be restless, to wonder what might lie beyond the edges drawn for them.

Earline aroused a life of quiet dignity that I envied, though I didn't fully understand it. She bore the weight of things I'd never have to carry, things I couldn't even name. For every dream I conjured on a whim, Earline had a truth she couldn't escape. Her strength wasn't in defiance but in survival, in enduring a world that never let her forget her place. And as much as I admired her survival instincts, as much as I loved her, a part of me loathed her for accepting "her station" with a smile. I hated the world that asked so much of her while asking so little of me.

It struck me then, with a sharpness that left me breathless, that my freedom to dream came at a cost. It was paid for by the quiet sacrifices of people like Earline, who polished silver that wasn't hers and folded linens she'd never use. And yet, she never let bitterness settle in her like it did in Mother. Her strength came not from wanting something better for herself but from making something better for those she loved.

I turned away from the window, the dusk giving way to darkness. My dreams suddenly felt heavier, like they carried the weight of more than just my own desires. But even as the guilt settled in, a stubborn part of me held on to the hope that maybe, just maybe, there was a way to carry both, the wildness of my dreams and the quiet strength of hers.

I knew that I needed to stand up for myself, a flicker of resolve blooming like stubborn flowers pushing through cracked concrete. Earline had been my steadfast anchor, her loyalty unwavering even in the face of Mother's sharp tongue and cold shoulders, which could cut through gratitude like a hot knife through butter. Earline endured it all, an unappreciated testament to the depths of her quiet strength, but I could never allow myself to be swallowed by such a fate. I would carve out my own path, not marred by the specter of my mother's bitterness.

Tomorrow, I would find my voice. I would stand before Mother and speak the words that had burned in my throat for too long. Words about Bo, about the future I wanted, about the life I would claim whether she allowed it or not. I would no longer bend myself to fit the contours of her disappointment. I would no longer be a thing to be shaped by the weight of the past.

Tomorrow, I would step out from the fences that had been built around me. I would walk forward, not knowing where the road would lead, only that it would not end here. The past would always be waiting, coiled and patient, but I would not be one of those who stood still long enough to let it catch me.

THE WEIGHT OF BISCUIT AND BLOOD

Friday, First Week of August 1942

THE FOLLOWING MORNING unspooled itself slow and heavy, thick as molasses, the air damp with the dregs of August, pressing down like a lid over boiling water. Shirley stood in the kitchen, one hand braced against the counter, the other curled into a white-knuckled fist. The oven exhaled warm biscuit-scented breath, but the words her mother had flung at her minutes before still hung sharp in the air, barbed and biting, a thing that would not be swallowed.

Shirley had practiced the conversation a dozen times, standing in front of her vanity mirror, watching herself whisper defiance in the hush of night. The words had been strong then. They had stood tall inside her chest. Now, they wilted.

"Mother," she tried again, voice brittle as eggshells. "Bo's not what you think. He's—he's good to me. He makes me feel—" she hesitated, her breath shallow, a hot flush creeping up her throat, into her cheeks "—alive."

Her mother stood stiff-backed in her house dress, her silhouette a thing of sharp edges and rigid lines. A laugh rasped from her throat, humorous and clipped, like scissors snapping shut. "Good doesn't put food on the table, Shirley. And alive? What a foolish, flighty notion. Is that what you call sneakin' 'round with a boy who's spent more time on probation than in the classroom? Jesus watches you, young lady. Don't ever forget it."

Shirley flinched, her fingers curling at her sides. "He's not a criminal! He's on the baseball team and the football team. He might not be book smart, but at least he's tryin'. More than you ever give him credit for."

Her mother's gaze sharpened, cutting. Her voice dropped to a low, icy tone. "You're blinded by infatuation. A good man, a proper man, doesn't have to try. He's already there."

Something inside Shirley snapped. The weeks of stolen glances and breathless meetings at church, in town and at the creek, the way Bo made her feel like she was more than just the sum of her mother's expectations, it surged up, hot and fast, spilling over before she could stop it.

"Maybe if you weren't so damn busy trying' to control every inch of my life, you'd see that I'm happy for once! You don't know him. You don't even know me!"

The slap cracked through the small kitchen like a breaking branch. A jolt of white-hot shock spread across her cheek, her vision blurring for a half-second. She staggered, her hand flying to the place where her mother's palm had landed, her pulse a wild thing caged inside her ribs.

"You will not speak to me that way," her mother said, her voice trembling, though whether with anger or something else, Shirley couldn't tell. "You are my daughter, and you will behave like a proper lady in this house."

Shirley didn't answer. She turned on her heel and fled, her footsteps pounding down the hall, the slam of her bedroom door reverberating through the house.

The walls of her room pressed close, the ceiling too low, the air too thick. She slid to the floor, her knees drawn up to her chest, words bubbling to her lips in a whispered litany.

"I hate her," she whispered into the silence, tears spilling down her cheeks. "I hate her, I hate her, I hate her." The rhythm of those words echoed in her mind, mingling with the lingering stings of anger and hurt.

For a long while, Shirley sat there, the muffled sounds of her mother moving around the house the only indication that life continued outside her room. The afternoon passed in a haze of unspoken rage and muffled silence. Slowly, the tears subsided, replaced by a simmering resolve.

She read, or tried to, her fingers tracing over the pages of the dog-eared pages of *The Secret Garden*, her mind latching onto Mary Lennox and her wild, yearning heart. Freedom nestled in the spaces between the words. The thought of Bo stirred inside her, urgent, a current pulling her toward the edge of something vast and unknown. After a good long read, she fell asleep in her bed, only to have slept away the best part of the day.

Dusk draped itself over the town in long, languid strokes of blue and gold. Shirley pushed the book beneath her pillow, her pulse thrumming in her ears as she cracked open the door, stepping into the hush of the house. She slipped out of the back door, the air thick with the scent of damp grass and the faintest trace of honeysuckle, the streetlamps flickering to life like Morse code, casting spools of light that seemed fragile against the gathering gloom. She moved toward the shadowed tree line, glancing back only once to ensure her escape hadn't been noticed.

The creek curled through the wood like a dark vein, its waters slick and silvered in the failing light. And Bo was there, his back against the old oak, arms crossed, the easy slouch a stark contrast to the worry in his eyes.

"Hey," he greeted, his smile breaking past a façade of worry.

"Hi," she echoed, stepping into the quiet between them.

They sat on the moss-damp log, the night thick with the hum of cicadas, the creek babbling over stones like a secret passed hand to hand.

"Your mother?" Bo ventured cautiously, his voice low.

Shirley exhaled through her nose. "She doesn't understand. It's like trying to catch smoke with your bare hands."

Bo nodded, his fingers tracing idle patterns against the bark. "Sometimes I wonder if they even see us. Or just what they want us to be."

She turned toward him, searching his face, the sharp line of his jaw, the worry tucked into the corners of his mouth. "She says you're not good enough. That you never will be."

Bo let out a breath, slow and measured. "That so?"

"I don't care," she said quickly. "I don't care what she thinks."

He smiled then, small and crooked. "Yeah?"

"Yeah."

"Yeah, but sometimes it's hard to see past that," Shirley admitted, the weight of his words unraveling threads of concern she had tucked away.

And then his hand was on hers, calloused and warm, and the world shifted on its axis. His touch was careful, reverent, as if she were something fragile and holy. The night hummed around them, thick with the scents of earth and river, and for a moment, it felt like they were the only two people left in the world.

"For today," he said, squeezing her hand gently, "let's just figure out how to be us. We'll face everything else one step at a time. Together."

His words hung in the air, heavy with promise but accompanied by a shadow of doubt. The creek babbled nearby, oblivious to their silent pact, as they both sat in the gathering darkness, unaware of the tumult that awaited them down their winding path. Shirley gently tilted her head onto Bo's shoulder, her mind locked on the promise she'd made herself. Bo's demeanor changed suddenly, as if an ember from a campfire fell onto his lap.

"You afraid?" he asked, his voice quiet.

Shirley answered, her pulse hammering in her throat. "A little."

Bo leaned in, his breath a calculated whisper against her skin. "Me too."

And then his lips found hers, soft and insistent, the taste of summer and stolen time pressed between them. He mother's words rose up inside her like a warning, but she crushed them down, let herself be held in the moment, in the heat and the hush, in the trembling space between caution and want.

The creek murmured it approval. The trees stood witness. The night held its breath. And Shirley, for the first time in her life, felt unshackled.

*

I LIFTED MY HEAD, breath snagged in my throat as Bo slid his hand up inside of my thigh with the same unthinking ease he might rest a palm on the horn of a sun-warmed saddle. A hand that knew no hesitation, only the surety of a boy accustomed to taking what was offered, or, if need be, what could be coaxed.

"What do you think you're doing, Bo Harris?" My voice, meant to rebuke, betrayed itself as a grin flickered across my face, weak as morning light through a dirty pane. A warning without teeth. And he knew it.

"I came to rescue you, Miss Ragland," he murmured, fingers pressing just enough to remind me of their presence. "The danger of your mother is too great for a brave soul like yourself."

For a moment, the wreckage of the evening receded, the raised voices, the sharp-edged words that had rung through the walls of our house. And there was only Bo, the familiar heat of him, the steadiness, the promise of something reckless and free.

"You're a regular hero, aren't you?" I said, but my sarcasm carried no conviction, the excitement threading through my blood too urgent to suppress. He was a balm and a brand all at once, soothing the wounds and setting fresh ones alight.

"Just tryin' to keep you from losin' your mind." His voice dipped lower, teasing. "People say, behind every smart girl is a strong temptation to break plum free." He shifted closer, his breath against my cheek, and I tried to keep my composure, tried to pretend my pulse wasn't hammering against my ribs like a caged bird.

"Well," I said, straining for nonchalance, "I hear there are great adventures to be had out in the big world." But even I could hear the unsteadiness in my voice, the slight tremor betraying me.

"Adventures," he mused, his fingers advancing the smallest fraction, the act conspiratorial in its leisure. "I was thinkin' something a bit more… cloak and dagger."

The phrase danced through my mind, thick with intrigue, a whisper of mischief brushing up against my hesitation, tempting me to reach beyond the narrow walls of my life.

"What sort of adventure do you have in mind?" My own curiosity startled me. The part of me that should have been recoiling was instead leaning in, enticed by the unknown.

Bo flicked his wrist downstream, toward the murky blue hush of the creek where the trees bent low, their branches swaying like conspirators. "Why don't we wander a bit? Might find ourselves a place more private. No pryin' eyes, just open air and the sound of water. And who knows?" His voice lowered to something rough, something honey-slow. "Maybe we'll set the woods on fire."

His words sent a bolt through me, a reckless thrill, the kind that made your breath catch and your heart stammer.

"Wouldn't that be something?" I managed, though my mother's voice still curled through the back of my mind, an iron tether. *Shirley, dear, don't you step too far from the path.*

"Ah, who needs the path?" Bo laughed, as if he could read my mind, the sound rich and easy, like the hum of cicadas in the heat of summer. "Paths are for folks afraid of gettin' lost. We could make our own way. Make a little magic."

And there it was, the promise he always carried in his back pocket like a half-rolled cigarette, the suggestion that there was a world beyond the one carved out for me, a world not dictated by my mother's tight-lipped propriety or the careful whispers of church pews.

I hesitated, laughing a little too lightly, afraid to act too eager. But my body had already betrayed me, leaning closer, closing the space between us, my fingers catching against the rough callouses of his hand. His eyes held mine, and in that moment, the teasing fell away, replaced by something quieter, something deeper.

He kissed me, and my breath caught, the fight in me flaring bright and sharp before collapsing into something softer. His lips moved against mine with an insistent ease, and my tongue met his in a slow, languid war, the battle less about winning and more about surrender. His hand, unbidden, pressed higher, testing my resolve, testing the girl my mother had raised against the girl I might yet become.

"I—"

Bo broke the kiss, eyes gleaming with a knowing that sent heat racing through my skin. "Are you afraid, Shirley? Afraid of a little adventure? Or afraid of what's waitin' for you at home?"

A breath hitched in my throat. He was right. I was afraid. Afraid of both the consequences of getting caught and the consequences of letting fear keep me tethered to a life that no longer fit.

Bo knew. He knew as sure as he knew how to move through the world without apology. He guided me backward, the ground pressing cool and solid beneath my spine, his body settling against mine, his voice coaxing me further, fingers drawing slow, deliberate lines over my skin.

"You make it sound so easy," I whispered.

"It is easy," he murmured, his breath warm against my ear. "If you want to dance, you gotta' step away from the light."

His hands mapped me like an explorer learning new terrain, touching and retreating, a slow push and pull of temptation. The world tightened to the space between us, the quickened cadence of our breathing, the liquid pull of desire unfurling in the pit of my stomach.

But somewhere beneath the fevered heat, a voice still lived in me, stubborn, persistent, a tether I couldn't yet sever. I swallowed hard. "I... I have to go home."

Bo stilled. His expression flickered, disappointment curling the edges of his lips, but there was no anger, only resignation, as if he had always known this moment would come. "Shirley—"

"It's not just about us, Bo," I said, my voice quiet but firm, the finality settling between us like a stone dropped into still water.

He exhaled, a slow release, then brushed a piece of grass from my hair, his touch lighter than before. He sat back, rolling onto his elbows, watching me with that unreadable look, somewhere between amusement and something else, something I couldn't quite name.

"Well," he said at last, standing, dusting off his jeans, offering me a hand. "Guess I'll walk you home, then."

And so we walked, the summer night stretching around us, the cicadas droning their endless song, the air thick with the scent of honeysuckle and something else, something fleeting and half-formed, a moment that had nearly been and now never would be.

When we reached my house, I hesitated at the porch, the weight of the night pressing down on me. "Bo—"

But he only smiled, reaching out to tuck a loose strand of hair behind my ear, his fingers lingering just long enough to make me ache. "Goodnight, Miss Ragland."

And with that, he turned, disappearing into the dark, leaving me with nothing but the echo of his laughter and the slow, uncertain ache of something both lost and found.

SEVEN

THE HAMMER AND THE COLT

Summer 1899, Springfield, Tennessee

THE STORY OF Jim and Mun stretched back further than most folks in Springfield cared to remember. It began with a fight; the kind of bare-knuckled scuffle boys fell into when they had too much pride and not near enough sense. Mun had pilfered a shirt full of pears from young Jim's pull-cart and young Jim saw it.

Jim earned his dollars slow, selling fruit by the basket under the courthouse elm, each coin slipped into a rust-bit tobacco tin he kept buried beneath the hay in the back of the barn. He never said what it was for, not even to his mama, just shrugged and counted it again when no one was watchin'. But every nickel knew its purpose. It was for that buckskin colt out on Ollie Gentry's pasture, the one with the black mane like brushfire and eyes wild as creek water. Two years old and already thick through the chest, legs made for dust and thunder.

From the fenceline of his grandparents' farm in Franklin, Kentucky—just a stone's throw from Ollie's—Jim watches. Has been watchin', near every summer since the colt could stand. The bluegrass field, flecked with clover and the shade of hickory, turns holy ground when that horse runs. Not a gallop but a declaration. And Jim, barefoot and brown-armed, leans on that post rail with his soul turned inside out, praying quiet like, hard prayers that someday that horse will run for him.

Jim's father, a veteran of the great war and a man known in town to be a virulent racist, had insisted on the two boys settling the matter with fists. Mun's guilt had made him an easy target, and Jim had come out on top, though neither boy had much heart in the fight.

A week later, Jim spotted Mun working with a rank horse in the field behind his family's modest place, a plank shanty rented from old man Washington, the local trafficker of bootleg whiskey. There was a sober confidence in the way Mun moved with the horse without so much as crop nor strap, a natural rhythm and doughy baritone voice that Jim couldn't help but admire. He approached cautiously, half-expecting Mun to run or fight again, but instead, they talked. Slowly, the two boys found common ground in their shared love of horses, and a friendship began to take root.

Years later, that bond had only deepened. Jim had seen the scars Mun's father left on his back, had helped bandage him up more times than he cared to count. And Mun had listened to Jim's stories of his own father's cruelty, the man's many hatreds weeping like putrid wounds that would never heal.

They were two young men bound by pain and a quiet understanding that words could never quite capture. That is, until Mun's father fatefully crossed lines that couldn't be uncrossed and Jim showed up to find Mun in a shape unfit for any man.

Mun had watched his mother suffer at the hands of his troubled father for many years. Too young to do anything about it, he languished to help her, unable to summon the courage to lift a finger. Until the pain of inaction grew to be more horrid than the fear of trying. And in an instant, Mun became the object of his father's rage.

The barn was quiet but for the groaning timbers of the loft, a low chorus of creaks that reverberated the weight of its old timber and the confidences it had kept secret. The air inside was paunchy, sour with the musk of old straw dampened with pungent urea and sweat-stained saddle blankets. Mun had been here too many times to count, a boy growing under the shadow of a father who mistook cruelty for discipline. A rotten legacy taught to an innocent young boy by a merciless slave owner.

It was here that Jim found him, his back raw and streaked with welts, his face pressed into the rotten hay, drenched and bloated by a week's neglect, praying aloud for God to strike down the man who had put him there. Jim stood frozen that day, his fists clenched tight as though the force alone could make his own father better than what he was. But he knew better, even then.

It wasn't until a few weeks later, after one more drunken, frenzied thrashing, that Jim took the hammer in hand. It was heavy, ball-peen'd, and unbalanced, a thing meant for ten-penny nails, not the skulls of men. He waited, crouched by the stall door, watching through the slats as the drunken Mr. Johnson swung the leather crop in blind fury, drunk and red-faced.

The yearling colt inside the stall bucked and danced, wide-eyed with terror, but there was nowhere for the animal to go. When Mr. Johnson collapsed in a heap, snoring in the wet straw, Jim slipped inside. His hands shook as he hefted the hammer, the iron head catching the glint of the lantern light, and he brought it down with all the precision of a man twice his age—straight to the drunkard's temple. The sound it made was dull, wet, and final.

Jim didn't run. He walked home, the hammer hanging loose in his grip. He threw it into the creek behind his house, watching as it sank beneath the water, errant ripples erasing the violence of what he'd done. By morning, the thing that lived in his chest—the knotted ball of guilt and fear and rage—was gone, replaced by something colder, quieter.

The next day, he walked up on the porch of Mun's place, the board and batten façade, withered and rotten, barely a shelter at all. When he knocked on the door, he half-expected to see the man himself, looming in the doorway, belt in hand. Instead, Mrs. Johnson answered, her face calm, even serene, though her eyes seemed verbose—yet restrained.

"You here for Mun?" she asked, her voice soft but steady.

"Yes ma'am," Jim said. "Just wanted to check on him, see if he's alright."

She tilted her head, studying him as though she could see every thought in his young mind. "Well, you don't need to worry none 'bout Mr. Johnson no more," she said. "Drunk fool got himself kicked in the head by that colt last night. Dead as a stone."

Jim swallowed hard, the weight of her words, said without the trope of emotion, settling somewhere deep in his gut. "I'm real sorry to hear that, ma'am. If y'all need anything… I mean, if Mun needs help…"

Her lips curved in the faintest of smiles, a wry twist that said more than words ever could. "We'll be just fine, Mr. Jim. Thank you kindly, though."

Mun stepped into the doorway then, his face battered but his posture straight. "Mama, I'll talk to Jim outside," he said. She nodded and disappeared back into the house, leaving the two boys alone on the porch.

Mun didn't say anything at first. He just walked toward the barn, his steps slow but purposeful, and Jim followed. Inside, Mun stopped by the table where the sack of fence steeples still sat, though the hammer was gone. He stared at it for a long moment before turning to Jim, his face unreadable.

"I'm the man of the house now," he said finally. "And a man's gotta have a good hammer."

Jim opened his mouth to speak, but Mun cut him off, stepping closer and pulling him into a firm embrace. His arms were strong, his grip tight, and for the first time in years, Jim felt something like relief. Mun's voice was thick when he spoke. "Thank you," was all he said, the words heavy with meaning.

Jim nodded, his throat tight. "It's in the creek," he said. "I'll get it back for you."

And that was all they ever said about it.

BENEATH GILDED EYES

Saturday, First Week of August 1942

COMING INTO VIEW, the church steeple loomed over everything within sight, its tall slender shadow stretching long and sure, as if daring the sunlight to interrupt its dominion. The windows—those gilded, glowing panes—were more like eyes than glass, watching the town, watching me, with a scrutiny that seemed both gracious and accusatory.

They caught the sun rays just so, throwing colors onto the ground like breadcrumbs leading to an underwritten promise. But even a child could tell promises had layers, and the church's layers were thick as the incense that curled in the air escaping through its doors on Sunday mornings.

I had a lesson with Tom this morning, and I needed something, anything, to wrest my delicate thoughts away from Bo and the disquieting liberties I had allowed him last night.

Judgment settles on my shoulders like wet wool, dragging at the spine, shrinking me in a place meant to lift. The pews stretch long as shadows, worn smooth by knees and sorrow, but the holiness here feels almost borrowed, brittle. Still, I clutch belief like a shard of glass, bloodying no hands but my own—some stubborn glimmer of what the church might become if loosed from the merciless chokehold of Father Schadenfreude's sermons, sermons trimmed lean on truth and stripped of the messy grace that growing up demands. Just thinking of him curdles something low in my gut. His voice lingers even in absence, a brittle echo pretending to be song.

As I approached the heavy Romanesque steps—their shadows stretching obscured and somber in the morning light—I paused just before opening the door, drawn by the scent of the planters brimmed with Gerber daisies with a side of Caladium, a riot of color thriving defiantly in the large iron planters perched on either side. The flowers seemed to mock my troubles, vibrant and alive, a reminder that beauty could flourish even in the harshest conditions.

I stood there grappling with the weight of my own heart, caught between longing and regret. For a moment, the fragrance enveloped me, and I found myself wishing that the church would embrace the brilliance of life rather than wallow in its murky shallows; that it might discover a more honest way to grow. If only I could, too.

Inside, the air felt much heavier, like it was pressing me to the floor, making sure I knew my place. The statues stood frozen in their dramas, eyes cast upward in what I imagined was supposed to be rapture, but looked to me more like resignation. Gold glinted everywhere: on the candlesticks, on the trim of the priest's robes, even on the crucifix above the altar. It caught your eye and wouldn't let go, like a fishhook baited with something no longer resembling how it started off. It made you feel small, which I guessed was the whole point.

People spoke in veiled tones about the grandeur of it all as if it were a gift, but I couldn't help thinking it was more of a trick. There was something too precise about it, too practiced.

The way the sunlight splintered into arranged lines as it came through the windows, the way the hymns rose and fell just so, the way the priest's voice seemed to wrap itself around you like a snake; it all felt calculated, like someone had sat down and planned how best to make you believe the absurd.

I used to wonder if the church knew how fragile people are, how they cling to the symbols it dangles before them. Maybe that is the secret, the thing hidden under all that gold and stone, that it needs them just as much as they need it. For all its towering ceilings and ringing bells, the church is just another shop on the square, peddling security and comfort to those willing to pay the price.

Tom greeted me upstairs, our musical rituals by now becoming almost informal and routine. Tom left me alone in the loft, saying he'd be back soon after running errands for Father, leaving me to practice his daily lesson alone. The church was quiet except for the steady hum of the organ beneath my fingers, a slow hymn that hung heavy, almost formidable in the still air.

I liked it up there, away from everything, with just the light coming through the stained glass, soft and colored like something beatified. I played without thinking, my hands gliding over the keys, but my mind wandered.

Then I heard him. I knew him by the sound of his boots on the steps, careful and deliberate. I didn't have to look to know it was Bo Harris. My heart jumped, quick and wild, like it always did when he was near. I glanced up, and there he was, leaning in the doorway, his arms crossed like he owned the world. He looked at me like I was the only thing worth looking at, and I hated how much I loved it.

"Bo Harris," I said, standing up from the bench and smoothing my dress, my voice steady though my insides were anything but. "I wasn't expecting you."

"Wanted to see you," he said, stepping into the room, his eyes never leaving mine.

I walked toward him, feeling bold and nervous all at once. "I'm glad you came," I said, and I meant it, really meant it.

He took my hands in his, and I felt how warm they were, how strong. "You sure I'm not interrupting?" he asked, his voice low, like he was afraid to break the spell.

"You're never an interruption," I said softly, and it was true. If anything, he was the only thing I wanted to interrupt me.

He kissed me then, sudden and sure, and I let him. I melted into him, feeling his hands on my waist, his lips warm and insistent. It was like all the doubts and fears I'd had yesterday disappeared, leaving just this moment, just him. When he pulled back, I was breathless, my face hot, but I didn't care.

"Please meet me tonight," I said, surprising even myself with how steady my voice sounded. "At the creek, same as last night. I want to talk."

"Anything you want," he said, and then he kissed me again, softer this time, like a promise.

"Yes... there is something," I said, pulling back just enough to look at him. "I want to explain, and apologize. It's not right, Bo, for me to treat you so poorly. I mean—" I stopped, the words catching in my throat.

He tilted my chin up with his hand, making me look at him. "Shirley, I could never think less of you," he said, his voice so earnest it made my chest ache. "You're more than I deserve already."

I laughed softly, shaking my head. "You don't mean that."

"I do," he said, his voice firm. "But if you need to talk, I'll be there. No matter what."

His words settled over me like a blanket, warm and comfy. I reached out, my fingers brushing the collar of his shirt. "I really need to see you," I said, my voice dropping to a whisper. "And I want..." I couldn't finish, not like I wanted to.

But there was a shift then, a spark of something unspoken but understood. I smoothed a crease in his shirt, letting my hand linger just a little longer than I should have. "You'll be there, won't you?"

"Of course," he said, his voice rough, his eyes searching mine.

"Good," I said, letting my lips curve into a small smile. "Because I don't like waiting."

I surprised myself then, leaning in just enough so he could feel my breath against his cheek. "I thought about you all morning," I murmured, my excited voice barely more than a whisper.

The words had left me sharp and sudden, like a match flaring too close to the fingers, and for a breath or two I wasn't sure if I'd lit something or burned it down. But then there was that smile... slow, crooked, carved from memory. And without notice, the fear loosened its grip. Not all at once. Just enough to breathe again.

What passed between us wasn't language. It was consequence. Familiar and terrifying. Like standing barefoot on the tracks, hearing the hum long before the train rounds the bend.

He touched my face before leaving. Not a grand gesture, nothing to fill a frame or spin into a story. Just the barest sweep of skin on skin. But it landed brilliantly deep, rapt at the depth of bone. It hummed there waiting for a lyric yet unwritten.

When he turned away, I didn't call him back. I watched the space he left behind stretch wider than it should have, and I stood still inside it, hands at my side like I didn't know what to do with them anymore.

I stayed that way long after he was gone, held in the hush of it all, the world tilted slightly off its axis. I didn't know what tonight would be, whether he'd show or whether he wouldn't, whether I'd crumble or rise up in the dark, but I knew I'd meet it head on. With everything I was. And everything I wasn't yet.

MOONLIT RECKONINGS

Saturday, First Week of August 1942

THE WOODS HAVE a different weight to them, the air within, heavy with some unnameable tension, a noticeable hush lying thick as damp wool against the skin. The path winds ahead through the chestnut thicket, its edges furred with kudzu and the stammering remains of summer insects, their chirring now sporadic, uneasy. The moon sits swollen and pale above the black silhouette of trees, its light slanting through the underbrush in long, broken columns.

Shirley moves ahead, her grandmother's quilt draped and folded over one arm, the navy cloth of her dress catching briefly against low branches. She glances back at Bo with that small, knowing smile, the one that tugs at something loose in his chest. He follows, hands in his pockets, heart knocking a rhythm neither fast nor slow but something off-kilter, unsteady.

The clearing opens ahead like a wound in the woods, framed by the tangled fingers of kudzu and the gnarling, reaching limbs of an old magnolia, its leaves waxy and dark even under the moonlight. Shirley stops, shifting her weight, the toes of her shoes pressing into the dirt. She spread the quilt on the ground with careful, deliberate hands, smoothing it flat, then carefully straightens its geometry according to its exact orientation with the surroundings, brushing her palms together with a prideful finality. Her cheeks glowed faintly in the pale light, her hair coming loose from its pins.

"I brought us this quilt. It'll be a lot better than the grass," she says, voice quiet but holding.

Bo nods, the words drying up in his throat. His eyes fixed on the line of her shoulders, the way the dress dips there, fabric lying soft against skin pale as sun-dried river stone. She turns, hands at the hem, fingers kneading the fabric between them. A hesitation, then a breath.

"I hope you don't mind me doing this." A lilt of playfulness there, but something else too.

She turns from him and the zipper yields, slow and certain, each tooth unfastening with the hush of inevitability. The dress, blue as dusk, pools at her hips, then slips, serpentine, down the long pale incline of her back. Her spine reveals itself in small, clean notches, like a staircase no one dares ascend. She tilts her head, a motion both casual and absolute, and her eyes find his over her shoulder. The woods hold its breath. Even the light forgets to move.

"You better not laugh at me, Bo Harris," she says, and though her voice divulges a noticeable fragility, a warning glows bright beneath it.

Bo swallowed. "Laugh? Shirley, I'd have to be the biggest fool alive."

Her smile flickers before she steps free of the dress, folding it with careful hands, laying it over a low-hanging branch. Her beige slip shimmered in the light, the slippery fabric whispering against her skin as she pulls it over her head, its descent slow, deliberate. She stands there then, arms at her sides, the night wrapping around her nearly bare form, save a basic bra and scant panties. A breath, and then another.

"Well?" she asks, chin lifting, eyes dark and steady.

Bo exhales slow, shaking his head, words still nowhere.

"If I died right now, I'd die the happiest boy in Tennessee," he barely manages, voice rough.

A quiet laugh from her, breathy and uncertain. She steps forward, her feet light against the quilt, the air between them humming with something weighty and electric. Her hands find his chest, warm even through the fabric of his shirt.

"You're not saying much," she murmurs with a hint of insecurity.

Bo reaches for her, his hands skimming the bare curve of her back, fingers tracing the rise and fall of each slow breath. "I don't think I can," he admits. "You're knocking every damn word outta' my head."

She kisses him then, soft at first, tentative, then deeper, searching. He tastes her, the ghost of honeysuckle, something warm and sweet. His hands slide downward, finding the dip of her waist, the small of her back, the delectable place where satin and lace meet skin.

She presses into him, her body molding against his in a way that feels inevitable, like gravity pulling two objects into orbit.

The quilt cradles them like a hand worn by labor, frayed at the seams but sure in its grip. They fold inward, gravity. Not of the earth but of want, the world pressed small between breaths and bone. Her skin holds the moon still, its warmth sunk deep as seek in loam. He moves slow. No haste. No greed. Fingers drawn across her collarbone like a liturgy, trailing down the narrow cage of her ribs where breath stalls. She quivers—not from chill but from ignition, a live wire strung between impulse and awe. There is no name for it. Only the weight of it. The knowing before knowledge.

"Bo," she breathes, his name an anchor, a tether.

He stops, searching her face, waiting.

"I trust you," she whispers. The words land deep, striking something inside him that he hadn't known was there. He kisses her again, slower this time, tasting the promise in her voice. His hands skim lower, the silk of her undergarments cool and thin beneath his fingers.

She shivers, not from cold but from the collapse of waiting. His fingers work the silk away, fabric slipping like the end of a long-held lie, each intimate garment undone a yielding, a consent, a vow. The final layer of modesty falls. She does not. Instead, she reaches—need without language—and draws him into her, body answering what the mind has rehearsed in silence for months. They join without ceremony. Without pause. And the world, once stubborn in its shape, tilts. The night holds them like a witness. A magnolia exhales its heavy perfume into the damp air, thick enough to taste. Somewhere beyond, the creek gives its slow applause, water sliding across stone like time remembering itself.

She gasps, her spine arcs tight, a drawn bow. Fingers dig into his shoulders—no hesitation, no gentleness, only instinct and fire. He stills. Eyes fixed on hers. The world quiets. He waits—not out of fear, but reverence. Holding the moment like a lit fuse.

He freezes, hunting for the flicker, the recoil, the tell. Her gaze holds wide—startled, unblinking—caught somewhere between flight and fire. For a breathless beat, he braces for the break, the push, the undoing. But she exhales. Not a whisper, not a sob—something weightier, rounder. Her chest lifts against his, a slow tide rising. The sound she makes is low, nearly lost between them, not a sigh, not a quiet word. It carries heat. It carries ache. And in it, he hears the threshold— she has stepped across.

No fear, only something raw and unfamiliar. Another small sound, part sigh, and then she moves against him, welcoming.

Her body shifts to meet him, a slow undoing, each movement drawing him deeper into the storm of her. His head reels. Not from speed, but the enormity of it—the heat, the pull, the impossible tenderness laced with want. Her skin glistens, dewy slick beneath his palms, alive with sweat and smolder. He traces the ridge of her back, fingers moving like thought, feeling the tremble beneath—muscles clenching, loosening, her body recalibrating around him. He holds her. Not loosely. Not tight. With purpose. Hands wandering, not in search but in remembrance. Her pulse flutters beneath his lips.

She draws him in, legs circling tight, anchoring him to the heat of her, the want that no longer waits. She pulls without pleading. Her body speaks in pressure, in rhythm. The sounds she makes come soft at first, then rising, a note of wonder in them. He moves with her, slow, deliberate, every touch deliberate, every moment stretching wide, filling the spaces between words unspoken.

Her fingers, once clutching, now lace into his hair, pulling his face closer. Her lips part, and her head tilts back, her throat arches as she lets out a small, involuntary cry that sends a shiver down his spine. Her eyes find his again, but this time they are heavy-lidded, her pupils dark and full of something he's never seen before—pleasure, yes, but also trust.

Her mouth, slightly agape, seems to tremble with every measured motion he makes. She draws him closer, his body tighter against hers, her legs drape around him, hips locking in a hold that offers no distance, no exit. Only the quiet insistence of want made whole. A language without breath. The grip of her body speaks what her voice dare not: stay. Be held. Let this moment have you.

Bo marvels—not in thought, but in sensation, in the raw, unscripted poetry of how her body answers to his. Tremors chasing motion. The breathless staccato of her lungs. The scrape of her nails along his back, not pleading, not punishing, only reflex—an unthinking reply carved into skin. Her heart beating against this chest, untamed and erratic, matching beat for beat the riot inside him.

There's no speech between them. Only the sound of limbs entwining, the friction of skin, the hush of eyes held too long. Every motion braids them closer. Every breath taken in tandem tightens the seam. Until the notion of separation ceases to make sense. Until he no longer knows where her outline ends or where his begins.

And when the storm quiets, they fall into stillness. Bodies twined, quilt bunched beneath them, air weighted with sweat and magnolia and something else—something unnameable, but real enough to taste.

Shirley startles. Her voice small, sharp-edged. "What was that noise, Bo?"

She rolls to her stomach, fast, pulling the quilt up as if it could shield them from whatever comes next. He presses a finger to her lips, a hush without rebuke.

They listen.

Nothing.

But the silence feels loaded now, as if the world had paused to bear witness.

"It wasn't nothin', Shirley, just a rabbit or something."

Shirley calms herself, then rests her head against his chest, breath slow and even, fingers tracing small, idle circles on his skin. Bo stares at the sky, the stars burning cold and distant above them. "Sorry," she says, "I don't mean to spoil the moment." Bo smiles without saying anything.

After a long silence, she stirs.

"Bo?"

"Yeah?"

She lifts her head, resting her chin against the solid rise of his chest. Her eyes hold him steady—no flicker, no apology. Serious, yes, but gentled by something unguarded.

"I'll never regret this," she says. Voice low, certain. "Not with you. You know that, don't you?"

It isn't a question. It's a truth offered plainly, like water in an open palm.

Bo swallows hard, his hand cupping her face, thumb brushing along her cheekbone. "I do now."

She kisses him once more, lingering, before shifting away, reaching for her slip, the fabric catching moonlight as she pulls it over her head. Bo watches her dress, each motion slow and deliberate, the act itself carrying some quiet finality. She steps into her sandals, turns back to him, something unreadable in her expression.

"Come on," he says, voice low. "I'll walk you home."

The path curls back through the trees, narrow and root-bound, the night settling thick around them. No stars, only the hush of leaves overhead, the soft percussion of their steps in tandem. At her back door, she turns. Her fingers find his cheek, barely a touch, more memory than gesture. Her lips part as if to speak—one more word, one more truth—but nothing comes. She slips inside. The door shuts with a click.

Bo remains. Still as stone, breath held mid-chest. The porchlight glows for a beat, then dies. He doesn't move. Can't. The weight of the night has settled on him, not like a burden but like a mark—something carved and permanent, something that will follow.

Inside, Shirley folds beneath the covers. Sheets cool against her legs, the ceiling above vast and dim. Her heart still racing. Her thoughts spin like leaves in wind.

The night has altered its course. Not loudly. Not with fanfare. But surely.

Some unseen thread has been pulled, and now everything stretches forward—threadbare futures, imagined hands held across time, moments yet unlived laid out like constellations only she can see. And beneath it all, something ancient stirs. Not panic. Not fear. Something fixed and irrevocable.

She smiles into the dark. Closes her eyes. And lets the night take her whole.

EIGHT

PROMISE AND PERIL

Sunday, Second Week of August 1942

SUNDAY MORNING AND the sky above St. Cecilia's lay like a gauze of heat and pale light, the sun flat and pitiless against the white stone of the church. The congregants had spilled from the doors in their summer linens and polished shoes, the air thick with the scent of perfume and damp skin, the murmured pleasantries of another week survived; another Sunday endured. Shirley moved among them with the quiet urgency of a creature slipping unseen between the legs of giants, her heart a rabbit's gallop against the cage of her ribs.

Her mother had latched onto Mrs. Perkins, the two of them standing hip to hip, tongues clucking over some triviality: bad meat at the grocer, the heat in the sanctuary, who'd taken ill and who had failed to appear at all. Shirley cast one glance over her shoulder, her pulse a tight fist beneath her throat, then ducked through the side hall and past the door marked CHOIR ROBES.

The dim light of the room swallowed her whole. She pressed the door shut with careful fingers and turned. Bo Harris leaned against a stack of hymnals, the worn leather spines biting into the cotton of his Sunday shirt. He saw her and straightened, his mouth spreading into that slow, knowing grin, the one that curled at the edges like smoke from a burning field.

"Well," he drawled, his voice low and easy, the weight of his body shifting toward her in a way that made her insides twist, "ain't you a sight to make a man believe in miracles."

She was across the room before she could think, her hands sliding up the broad stretch of his shoulders, her mouth pressing into his, warm and urgent, the air between them thick with the hush of something reckless, something holy in its defiance. He pulled her in, his fingers spanning the small of her back, and for a moment they swayed there, pressed together in that stolen quiet, the world narrowed to the heat of breath and the press of fabric between them.

She broke first, dragging in air, her lips tingling. "Meet me," she whispered, her fingers still tangled in the rough curls at the nape of his neck, "at the thicket. Same place as before. I have to see you."

He hesitated, something passing behind those sharp blue eyes, the war of caution and want, the kind of hesitation that could unmake a moment. "You sure?" he murmured.

Her grip on him tightened. "I've never been more sure of anything in my life." And that was the truth, at least in that moment.

*

BO HARRIS WALKED THE gravel shoulder beside his mother, the sun mean and high and his collar damp with sweat that no church could wring clean. Blanche kept a steady pace, her bent parasol crooked against the sky, her silence louder than most women's scolding. She didn't ask what he was thinking—she already knew. That boy had the look of mischief stewing low and slow behind his eyes, and she'd birthed enough of his kind to recognize the boil before it bubbled over.

At the top of the hill, the Harris house waited like a judge behind a bench. George Harris stood in the doorway, sharpening his knife on an oil stone, slow and steady, the steel singing its warning in strokes. In his other hand, folded neat like Scripture, was a list that meant Bo's Sunday was already spoken for. No hello. No smile. Just the sound of that blade kissing stone, and the weight of a father's law fixing itself to Bo's shoulders before he ever crossed the threshold.

George worked him like a mule, set him to sweeping the porch, hauling water from the pump, scrubbing the kitchen floor where he swore he'd tracked in half the county. Even after all that, he wasn't done with him. Then Blanche chimed in with a chore of her own.

"Go on down to The Lady Bug," she said, dusting her hands on her apron. "Trixie's got my mending, said it'd be ready today."

A cold knot tightened in Bo's stomach. Trixie Simpson. That name, that woman, a wound he had tried not to pick at. But now he had no choice.

He imagined himself walking in there all upright and decent, his head high, his mouth set, asking for the package like a man with no history, no blood still drying in the cracks of his heart. A test of sorts, he figured. To see if he could look at her and not think of all the ways she had made him and unmade him in equal measure.

Little did he know, however, that Trixie was well aware of his impending arrival; she had learned about it from Blanche Harris herself, during her visit the day before. Trixie had completed the job, but with a sly wink of mischief, she'd told Blanche it would be finished the next day, asking her to send Bo after church, claiming she'd open the store just for a little while to make sure she handed over the mended things. Trixie had played her cards close to her chest, preparing for Bo's visit in a way that would turn his head.

And so, he set out, that single errand weighing heavier than all the chores before it.

*

SHIRLEY WALKED ALONE TO the grove, the quilt folded beneath her arm, the sound of cicadas buzzing thick as oil in the air. The path was familiar beneath her feet, the hush of trees arching overhead, the creek's slow churn a whisper in the distance. She spread the quilt with careful hands, smoothing its edges, and sat. The minutes stretched.

What she did not know, could not know, was that Benji Johnson had been watching.

Last night, he had seen her slip from her house and follow the path she followed now, had trailed her quiet as a ghost, his breath caught in the tight cage of his chest. He had seen what she had done with Bo Harris, had watched from the thick curtain of kudzu as she gave herself over to the boy he hated most in the world.

Benji stood now at the edge of the trees, his fists clenched, his stomach sick. Shirley, his Shirley, waiting for Bo. He could not unsee it, could not unmake it. A rage settled in his gut, old and gnawing, the kind that makes a man reckless, makes a man foolish.

*

BO WALKED INTO THE Lady Bug and was hit with the scent of pressed linen and perfume, the sharp bite of something that made his gut twist in recognition.

Trixie stood at the ironing board, a silk blouse draped over the frame, her own shirt abandoned somewhere, leaving only a skirt, crimson lace bra and bare skin. She turned, feigning surprise, one delicate hand slipping up to shield what it didn't intend to cover at all, artfully draped in alluring silk that shimmered under the light.

"Closed for Sunday, darling," she drawled, her voice was perfumed with an unexpected playfulness. "Well now," lips curved like a cat's. "Didn't expect to see you today."

Bo's jaw tightened. He knew this game.

"I just came for my mother's mending," he said, the words flat, firm. "Sorry, I didn't mean to surprise you like this."

Trixie tilted her head, eyes glinting with something unreadable. "And here I thought maybe you came for me." Trixie's laughter rang out, teasing and light, as though she was weaving a spell around him. "Oh, don't worry about that, Bo, It's fine. It ain't like you haven't seen it all before. Hard to impress a stud like Bo Harris."

Her words dripped in a honeyed indifference that simmered like the sultry warmth of the afternoon, setting the stage for a rendezvous that felt tantalizing and precarious; like the edge of a knife just before the plunge into the guts.

It should have been simple. Take the package, leave. But then she sighed, turning away, pressing a hand to her forehead like some tragic heroine in a play. Trixie let a single vulnerable tear fall. "I lost a dear friend this week," she murmured. "Been sittin' here thinkin' about all the things I lost." She let out a cry, then scurried back to the storeroom, pretending to be consumed by sorrow, or so she hoped Bo believed.

Bo swallowed hard, his hands twitching at his sides. The thing about Trixie was she always knew how to pull a man in.

Bo stood at the threshold of her familiar room, where the air was always thick with intoxicating scents that sparked memories deep within him. There she lay, sprawled and crying across the tiny bed, her skirt hiked precariously high above the tops of her stockings, garter straps clinging forbiddingly to her familiar milky thighs—and just enough of the crimson lingerie peeking into view that matched the lacy bra she was wearing.

And just like that, he was stepping toward her, caught in the gravity of her sadness, or the illusion of it.

*

IN THE GROVE, Shirley waits.

Footsteps behind her.

She turns, expecting Bo.

But it is Benji.

Her breath catches. "Benji? What are you doing here? You scared me half to death."

He steps forward, slow and deliberate, his face unreadable. His dark eyes lock onto hers, and for a moment, he says nothing. Then his gaze flicks to the quilt, to the space she had made, and something in him cracks.

"I might ask you the same damn thing, Shirley. You waitin' on him, ain't ya?" His voice is low, nearly tender, but coiled with something ready to strike. Not anger. Not yet. But the shadow of it. Something percolating and building steam.

She burns. The heat climbs up her neck and blossoms across her cheeks. She busies herself with brushing off her skirt, smoothing fabric that refuses to stay flat.

"That's none of your business," she says, lifting her chin like a dare. "You shouldn't be sneakin' 'round, spyin' on folks, Benji."

"I wasn't sneakin'," he bristles, voice rising. "I saw you," he says, and this time his voice comes rough. "I saw what you did with him last night."

Her heart kicks, and her voice hitches. "You don't know what you're talkin' about."

"I know enough."

He takes a step forward. She matches it backward.

"I saw it all! You think he loves you? You think he care 'bout you, like I do?"

"Benji, stop," she says, her voice cracking where it should rise. "You don't understand."

"I know more than you think. I've loved you—" his voice breaks against the edges of it, jagged and raw, "my whole damn life. And you… you threw it all away. For him."

The tears come fast now, hot and traitorous. She shakes her head like it might undo the world.

"Benji, it was never my choice. You know that. Your mother… she made sure of it. I never meant to hurt you. I never meant for any of this to happen."

"I don't care," The words spit from his mouth like sparks, his whole body shaking.

Silence swallows them. The creek behind them murmurs on, unbothered by heartbreak.

"I… I have to go," she whispers, already retreating in her mind.

"Don't go back to him," he pleads, his voice small now. "Please, Shirley. Don't let him ruin you." Benji reaches for her, hand trembling through the stillness, fingers fumbling until they find hers—grasping, clutching, not for comfort exactly, but for something rawer. A tether. A balm. A wordless plea for steadiness in the chaos of his mind.

Her lip trembles. She pulls her hand away from his. The tears come again, this time in earnest, tracking down her face unchecked.

She stays there for a moment longer, the space around her thick with what he's said, what he hasn't. Benji's words linger around her like fog—dense and impossible to shake. Her heart pounds against her ribs, like some wild animal desperate for sense. Guilt. Rage.

Ache. Love. All of it crowding inside her chest like too many people in one room.

She wipes her face with the back of her hand and turns her head. She doesn't want to let Benji see her cry any longer.

"You don't get to tell me what to do," she says, finally, her voice trembling but resolute. "You don't know what's in my heart."

Benji's jaw tightens. His broad shoulders stiffen.

"I know what's in his heart. And it ain't you, Shirley."

"You don't know anything about Bo." Her voice cuts through the space like a blade, sharpened by pain.

"I know he ain't here, don't I?" Benji throws out his arms like the empty woods are proof enough. "He don't care 'nough to show up, and you're just sittin' here waitin' like he hung the damn moon!"

She flinches. Her eyes flick to the path Bo should have taken.

"He'll come," she whispers, as if saying it out loud might summon him. "He will."

Benji laughs, bitter and cracked. "You keep on sayin' that. But I know boys like him. They take what they want. Sweet-talk gals 'til they've had their fill, and then they just split. And when they do, girls like you get left holdin' the bag, payin' the price for the games they play."

She doesn't answer. Her face goes hard, lips pressed together, arms crossed tight around herself like armor that won't hold.

Benji steps closer. His voice softens into something aching.

"You really think he's the only one who ever wanted you? Think I ain't been seein' you all these years? You think I don't see you now?"

She turns to him, eyes glassy, full of something distant and breaking.

"Benji, don't—"

But he's already moving, already closing the distance between them. His hands find her waist, his mouth on hers. It's a kiss that doesn't ask. It takes. Full of everything he's carried and couldn't say—his need, his hope, his desperation.

His mouth moves over hers, deep and searching, and for a flicker she lets him in, lets the past catch up to the present. His tongue brushes hers and for one dizzying second its five years ago, before Earline found them behind the bathroom door, before shame taught them to hide.

Then his hands begin to roam.

She jerks back, breathless, fingers flying to her lips.

"What are you doing?"

His eyes darken. "Tryin' to make you remember… I'm sorry," he says hoarsely. "I just—I just needed you to know. Needed you to remember."

She stares at him, her bones heavy with knowing. The trees blur at the edges of her vision. Everything tilts sideways. She feels exposed, vulnerable, as if the world has shifted beneath her feet.

Then, shaking his head, a wounded Benji turns. Just turns. And he disappears into the trees like he was never there at all.

She doesn't move. Not at first. The wind hums through the branches. The creek keeps on singing. The world forgets.

Eventually she picks up the quilt. Starts walking. The road home feels longer than it ever has.

*

WHAT HAPPENED NEXT AT The Lady Bug cracked open the old hinge of memory and let the heat spill in. Bo and Trixie—names once scrawled in the back of each other's skulls like matchstick graffiti—found the old fire not smoldering but raging, as if time had been holding its breath. And Trixie, hunger stitched into her spine, a hunger not for the boy but for the woman she used to be—beautiful, wanted, and dangerous—drifted toward the kid like a storm surge, slow and certain. Her touch was both a lesson and a confession. She spoke in glances, in half-laughed instructions, not of love but of power, of need shaped like lust. She walked him barefoot to the edge of innocence and dared him to jump, whispering all the while of deeper waters and darker thrills, spinning the moment into something dizzy and wicked and sweet. A dance of temptation promising a whirlpool of desire.

EPISTOLARY ECHOES

Monday, Second Week of August 1942

THE MORNING SETTLES like a spell, thick and unmoving, its silence not peace but a pause, an old house holding its breath. Light comes through the curtains in a weak spill, catching dust motes mid-air like the ghosts of things unsaid. I sit at the edge of the bed, heel to wood, skin to cold, listening—not for anything in particular, but for the world to begin again. A cart's wheel catches a stone in the road. A bird tries a note and then thinks better of it. Everything feels paused on the edge of something irreversible.

Benji.

His name alone is a splinter.

The way his face looked when I turned—God—it lives behind my eyes now, that expression. Not just surprise. Not just hurt. It was older than the moment, like he'd been carrying that wound a long time and I'd just ripped the tape off. There was a hollowness to it, a kind of silent accusation that didn't ask for explanation, didn't need one. The hurt was already shaped to fit him. I just confirmed its name.

No one should've seen.

That moment—that private undoing—wasn't meant for eyes. Not even mine, truth be told. It was something close to sacred, or maybe profane in its quiet intensity. Like catching a stranger whispering a secret into the black mouth of a confessional. It wasn't for him. But it was him, and that's what guts me. Because now the shame isn't just mine—its shared. Passed like a contagion from me to him, and I don't know what to call it. Not shame. Not really. Something far heavier. Something like grief wearing a mask of exposure.

I see him now—those hands of his, always sure, always ready, now curled into fists like he didn't trust what they'd do if left open. His face had gone blank, drained of its usual light, turned away not in anger but resignation, like he'd just been handed one more truth he never asked for. Did he mean to watch? Did he know what he was walking into? Or did the universe bend just wrong enough for both of us, and line up that single, brutal moment like a crosshair?

And now what? Now I'm left with the wreckage.

Do I write him? Do I go to him and pull the shame into the daylight like something that can be named and forgiven? Do I ask him to understand what I've barely begun to grasp? Or do I let it rot in silence between us, another thing we pretend we don't remember while it eats at us both, slow and low like a fever that never breaks?

That I love him in ways the language don't allow—yes. That we are something without a name, without a box to keep it in, a shape made of shadows and breath and the quiet space where two bodies once touched without touching. Not kin, not lovers, not what the world permits or even recognizes. Just us. Something older than permission. Wilder than rules.

I've never lied to myself about what lived between us. Of course I knew. You don't carry a wound that deep without knowing the shape of the blade. He loved me still—loved me the way children do before the world teaches them what love is supposed to look like, how to cut it into pieces and sort them by name: friend, sibling, sweetheart, sin. Back then, we didn't need words. We had a language of glances, of elbows brushing on porch steps, of laughter stolen at dusk. Now that language is gone, torn from us, syllable by syllable, until we are left with silence sharp as glass.

Five years. Five years of distance strung tight between us like a fenceline gone to rust and thorns. All we had were letters, trembling little bridges of ink and paper, where we spoke around the truth like dancers circling a fire they dared not touch. Until now. Until this—this break between us. Sudden as fever. Final as winter.

I press my fingers into my temples, the ache behind my eyes pulsing like something alive. I remember the way Earline used to cool my forehead with wet cloth, humming under her breath like she could *will* the sickness out of me with her voice alone. But that's another ache altogether—Earline. The way she stood between me and Benji that day, jaw tight, eyes glassy, her hand clenched on my arm like she was pulling me from a burning house. But who was she saving? Me? Him? Or something older and more broken than either of us?

The word comes, heavy and hard. *Bigotry.*

A stone in the throat. It doesn't explain. Doesn't excuse. Just sits there. A weight that changes nothing and explains everything. It wasn't ours, not at first. We didn't make it. But it was handed down to us just the same, sewn into family dinners and Sunday sermons, folded into the linen closets and buried with the dead.

It took Benji from me. Not his fault. Not mine. Just the old inheritance—the kind that slips in under your skin, passed like a disease from mother to son, from silence to silence. And Earline, God help her, she carries it too. Carries it in her bones, in her hands, in the way she won't speak of certain things and always knows *exactly* when to intervene. Maybe she thought she was protecting him. Or me. Or maybe she was just tired—tired of seeing the same pain circle back, again and again, dressed in new clothes but always the same wound.

Daddy never seemed to care what people said. He wore his friendship with Mun like a badge or a dare, grinning through it all. But he's a man. He can afford not to care. Men don't break the same way girls do. Their sins are swallowed, ours are *counted*.

And Benji—he's got the double curse. Being colored means the world looks past him until the second he steps out of line. Just like it does to me. We are ghosts until we aren't. And then we are punished for daring to exist—or, God forbid, have an idea.

I don't want to bring more hurt to him. God, I'd sooner set myself on fire. I just want to *see* him. To throw my arms around his neck and hold him like we did when we were small and the world hadn't touched us yet. To tell him none of it matters. That I love him. That I always have. That love don't shrink just because it gets crowded. That my heart has room for Bo, and still, always, for Benji.

But how do you *say* that? How do you explain a love that doesn't cancel out the others, that exists beside them like twin stars spinning around the same ache? How do you make someone understand you never learned how to love in pieces, only in wholes?

Maybe a letter isn't enough. Maybe words on a page can't hold this much sorrow, this much hope. Maybe I need to go. Find him. Sit across from him somewhere the world can't follow. Take his hands and speak without paper, without pretense. Just us. Just what we were before the world started carving us into roles.

I push to my feet. My palm finds the windowpane, the glass warm from morning sun. Somewhere out there, he's hurting. And I won't leave that pain unanswered. Not again.

Then a knock. Just one. And Earline steps in, slow and sure, holding an envelope like it weighs more than it should. Thick paper, the kind meant to impress or intimidate. My name written in careful, slanted ink— *Shirley Ragland*. Her hand trembles once before she lets it go.

I trace the letters with my fingertip, caught somewhere between dread and hunger. The seal breaks with a dry crack. The words inside are polished to a shine, precise and cold, like a knife behind a velvet curtain. Not an invitation. Not even a conversation. Just a gate, locked tight, dressed up in courtesy and cloaked in consequence.

William G. Crayton
1769 Germantown
Philadelphia, Pennsylvania

Dear Ms. Shirley Ragland,

I found myself somewhat taken aback upon receiving your letter last week, a missive that has prompted me to contemplate the motivations that underlie your inquiries. They strike me as rather personal, delicate in nature, and deserving of a measured response.

It is not my intention to appear discourteous, but I feel compelled to express that regardless of the nature of my relationship with Tom, I would no sooner divulge the intimacies of his private life to you, an unfamiliar correspondent, than pluck a delicate flower from the earth only to leave it withered in the dust. Indeed, to do so would betray not only Tom's dignity but also the sanctity of those complexities that bind us all.

As for Father Schadenfreude and his peculiar behavior toward Tom or others in your congregation, I find myself lacking in both breadth of acquaintance and the requisite depth of understanding to provide commentary on his character or his affairs. One cannot tread lightly in the realm of another's life without the firm foundation of genuine knowledge, an awareness that you appear to possess insufficiently in this case.

Thus, I would urge caution in your pursuit of answers concerning individuals with whom you have little familiarity, for the quest for truth can oftentimes spiral into the quagmire of conjecture and misunderstanding if not approached with the utmost care and humility.

With every good wish, I pray,

William G. Crayton, Esq.

I read the letter until the paper warmed beneath my touch, until the ink might as well have been blood. My fingers traced the loops and slants of his handwriting like they were scripture, or a cipher, or both. Breath caught in my chest, staggered and uneven. This was no casual refusal, no offhand dismissal wrapped in civility. There was *design* here. A restraint too elegant to be accidental. He knew more than he said. Perhaps more than he ever intended to say. And he would not be drawn.

A knot twisted tight in my belly, hard as wire. Could he not see it? Could he not fathom that a girl like me— barely grown, unknown to him, uninvited—does not reach across distance and reputation and the dignity of old paper unless the need is *real*? Urgent. Dangerous. That I would not put pen to page unless something terrible was pressing at the walls of our lives, threatening to bleed through?

The thing would not be silenced. It throbbed beneath the surface of every polite word, every calculated omission. I could *feel* it—like weather building behind a closed window. Something was coming. Something already here.

I folded the letter with the slow finality of ceremony. Slipped it back into the envelope like a priest tucking away a cursed relic. Crayton would not shake me off so easily. Not if Tom was tangled in it. Not if Bo, God help him, was drifting deeper into something vast and poisonous—a thing with many eyes and no face.

The letter was too precise. Too polished. This was no mere lawyer. This was a man who lived in language, who built walls with it, tall and bloodless and nearly seamless. But no wall is perfect. Every fortress has a flaw, a soft seam where the truth breathes. And if he had wrapped Tom in secrecy, drawn some clean perimeter around him for protection or pride or fear, I would find the frayed edge. I would worry it loose. I would press until the shape of the thing revealed itself.

Tonight, I would write again. Not with fury, but with force. Quiet force; the kind that comes not from screaming but from *knowing*. I would craft my words like a blade honed from silk, shaped to slip beneath his guard. I would not beg. I would persuade. And if Crayton suspected—if even the faintest shadow of Father Schadenfreude's name had passed through his thoughts like a storm cloud over a field—then he would *have* to choose: silence or salvation.

The letter lay heavy in my lap, a feather and a stone. I set it aside with care, like something sacred or poisonous or both. Already the reply began to take shape in my head—lines sharp enough to slice, questions coiled with just enough gentleness to make their sting undeniable.

This wasn't done.

Not yet.

Not even close.

NINE

SANCTITY AND SELF-DECEPTION

Sunday, Third Week of August 1942

TODAY IS SUNDAY, or as the congregation at St. Cecilia's might declare, the Lord's Day, though I suspect He rolls His eyes at the theatrics unfolding in His name. The pews will be filled with self-appointed saints, starched and pressed and reeking of cheap cologne and softer sins, their piety paraded like medals earned in battle, as though the Almighty has taken to distributing rewards for perfect attendance. They will murmur their hymns with the same conviction they whisper about one another's failings, their judgment as thick in the air as the scent of fading roses from the altar.

Mrs. Pickard, queen of all things sanctimonious, will tilt her chin just so, her gloved hands folded in devout repose as she drinks in Father Schadenfreude's sermon with the same relish she reserves for gossip. My mother, trailing in the pecking order just behind her, will play the role of dutiful acolyte, adjusting her position depending on whether Lucy Jo DuPree has deigned to grace us with her presence. If Lucy Jo is absent, Mother is a respectable fourth in rank. If she's here, then fifth. It matters little.

Presiding over this pageantry is Father Schadenfreude, his name an ill omen unrecognized by the flock. He has the air of a man who fancies himself divinely appointed, though his face, all angles and severity, reminds me of a butcher's knife held at an odd tilt. He speaks in measured tones, words rolling from his mouth like water from a cistern, too smooth, too controlled, the voice of a man who knows exactly when to lower it, when to pause, when to make you doubt whether you are hearing him correctly. He watches the congregation with an intensity that unsettles me, though the others seem blind to it, swallowing his words like bitter medicine they have been assured will heal them.

"Children of Springfield," he intones, "you must listen, for the truths of the Lord shall rain down like righteousness."

Righteousness might be nice, Father, but a little warmth wouldn't hurt either.

This morning's sermon is Jonah. Again. A prophet who thought he could outrun God and ended up in the belly of a fish for three days. One of those stories that makes you wonder if the Almighty isn't playing some long, elaborate joke. Schadenfreude leans into the lesson, his hands steepled as he speaks, his cadence slow and deliberate.

"Jonah struggled because he wanted justice, not mercy."

I stare at the stained glass above his head, at the swirling blues and crimsons, the faceless saints locked forever in acts of piety. Mercy and justice. Two sides of a coin that never lands the way you expect. Jonah, sulking beneath a shriveled plant, furious that God had the audacity to spare Nineveh. A man so wrapped in his own grievances that even salvation felt like a slight.

And yet. Isn't that all of us? Sitting here, judging who deserves what? Who gets grace, who gets cast out? I glance around the room and see them all—Mrs. Hargrove, her lips pursed in a way that suggests she finds herself on the better side of whatever dividing line she imagines. Mr. Connolly, dozing in his pew, his snores swallowed by the rising hymn. The girls who sit two rows ahead of me, heads bent together, whispering behind their hands about what, I can only guess, but their laughter is quick and sharp as a flint strike. The sinners in the back rows, their eyes downcast, their presence tolerated but never embraced.

And then Bo. Three pews back, right next to his mother Blanche, shoulders loose, one arm draped across the bench like he belongs nowhere and everywhere all at once. That easy grin, the one that can charm the scales off a snake. I watch him from the corner of my eye, wondering if he feels any remorse for standing me up last week, leaving me alone to be caught by the last person in my life that I'd ever wished it. If he notices what I'm noticing, the way Father Schadenfreude's gaze on him lingers a little too long, his expression inscrutable, as if measuring something only he can see.

The sermon rolls on. Jonah, swallowed whole. Jonah, crying out. Jonah, spat back onto the shore, reeking of fish guts and revelation. God doesn't let him go. That's the part that sticks.

God could have left him in the dark, in the stink, in the belly of something old and monstrous, but He didn't. He pulled him back out. Sent him on his way. And Jonah? Still bitter. Still angry that mercy was given to people he had already decided were beyond saving.

I think about that as the choir rises in song, their voices lifting toward the rafters, a harmony of devotion and obligation. Maybe that's the whole point. That we don't get to decide who gets saved. That the ledger we keep in our heads, tallying rights and wrongs, debts and dues, is nothing more than scribbles in the margins of a book too vast for us to read.

I sit there, the words of the hymn moving over me, and I feel something shift, some small crack in the carefully constructed wall of expectation and duty. Maybe mercy isn't about worthiness. Maybe it's about the fact that we are all, in some way, sitting in the dark, waiting to be pulled out.

When the final blessing is given and the congregation begins to stir, I linger, watching as Father Schadenfreude moves through the rows, offering nods, clasping hands. His gaze flickers to me, and for a moment, I think he might say something. He doesn't. Just a brief pause, then he is gone, lost in the swell of parishioners gathering their coats, smoothing their skirts, stepping back into the bright light of day.

Bo catches my eye as he stands, a half-smile tugging at the corner of his mouth. I don't smile back, not fully, but I hold his gaze a moment longer than I should. Long enough for something rank and unspoken to pass between us, something outside of mercy or justice, something he should know needs atonement.

I turn away before I can let myself think too hard.

Outside, the sun is blinding, the air thick with the heavy scent of pollen and summer grass and the distant tang of something rubber, like a tire burning off in the distance. The congregation spills into the street, voices rising, laughter mingling with the toll of the church bell.

And me? I walk home slow, the hem of my dress brushing against my calves, Jonah still turning over in my mind. How he ran. How he prayed. How he was swallowed whole. And how, despite everything, he was still given a second chance.

I could feel a smirk wrinkling my face, from the absurdity of Father Schadenfreude's sermon, Jonah and his whale and the Lord haggling over second chances, all that talk about sin and repentance, men tossed overboard and swallowed whole. I nearly laughed out loud. If the Lord had whales running errands, then maybe he had something worse waiting for me and poor Benji. Maybe Bo too, if he ever dared show his face.

He must have thought I'd come crawling to him, but he was wrong. I had no words for Bo Harris, not after he'd left me standing in the trees last week, clutching at my dress with shaking hands, measuring the smell of poor Benji's grief lingering on the damp earth.

Benji confronted me in the place where I'd stood waiting. *Foolish girl*, he'd imagined me—quiet and bare. He didn't say it out loud, but that's what he was thinking. Only it wasn't an insult, just something small and true and full of hurt, because he was right. I'd not been waiting for him, and he'd known it. But, if the world bent different—if it was made of kindness instead of sharp corners and bad timing—I would've been waiting for him. Not as an afterthought. Not as regret.

He should have known that. God, he should have.

He practically begged me not to ruin myself with Bo, had said my name out loud, only to look at me like I should have known all along. That his love was a child's love, something he'd held onto tightly, but something I had left behind when I'd been forced to leave Benji in the wake of our forbidden act; when I'd been peeled away from his body in the dim wash of the bathroom light five years ago and never returned. And it hit me. I was like Jonah.

Jonah had tried to run. That's what hit me, what I was thinking about. Not the whale, not the churning belly of the deep, but the moment just before. Jonah running, thinking he could outrun it. Thinking he could trick God, as if the sea did not stretch to the ends of the earth. As if God would not follow him there.

Jonah had been given a charge. He had been told, *Go*, and he had turned the other way, and still the thing had come for him, swallowed him down, kept him in the dark long enough for him to see himself for what he was.

In that same light, I could not run from Benji. I knew this now. I could not shake my thoughts of him, not the weight of him, the irrevocable shape of what we'd once been. And Bo—Bo had run. Maybe he knew before I did. Maybe he knew that I had things to make right before I could ever stand next to him, whispering vows to a priest. I couldn't move forward with Bo until I made things right with Benji, to smooth the jagged edges of what we were before I could step into what came next.

The dust curled up under my heels as I walked away from the church, my shoulders now squared up high and taut, and I unclipped the barrette from my hair, setting it free like Father Schadenfreude's ridiculous sermon set me free this morning.

I knew where to find him. I would not run, wouldn't write a coward's letter. The sea was coming, and I would not be caught unready.

ROOTS BOUND IN SILENT LONGING

Monday, Third Week of August 1942

THE MORNING HAD started like any other judgment-tinted Monday. Mother sat rigid in her oak rocker, a coffee cup cradled between two anxious hands, preaching about respect like it was something I could sew into my hem. "A girl who paints her nails like a Hollywood harlot invites nothing but rumor and regret," she'd said. "Respect is not earned by rouging up like some paramour." Her voice had that practiced disapproval in it, the kind that never quite cracked, but always cut.

I painted on anyway. Three nails done. Bette Davis red. A little rebellion in every brush stroke.

Then came the jeep.

Green like moss in the shade. Slow like something damned. It turned onto Willow Street, engine quiet, carrying two soldiers and what looked like a small trailer behind it. Government-issued. Precision in motion. The kind of slow that doesn't mean lost—it means looking.

Mother gripped my wrist mid-stroke, hard enough to jolt the bottle. The brush wobbled, a streak of red across my knuckle. Her fingers were cold, and she didn't let go. Her eyes locked on the jeep, and in that moment, she looked older than she ever had. Not aged—stripped.

The vehicle crawled closer. I half expected it to exhale.

"Jesus, Mary, and Joseph," she whispered, but her lips barely moved. Her whole body leaned forward, stone still, as if she could stop time by the force of her gaze alone.

They stopped directly in front of our house.

Two men. Crisp uniforms. Paperwork and precise movement. A slow ritual—hats straightened, buttons checked, papers shuffled like a gambler weighing odds he already knew were cursed.

Then a double take.

Then they crossed the street.

Mother didn't breathe until Mrs. Anderson screamed.

The kind of scream that doesn't rise—it spills.

We watched her crumple to the porch. Like a dropped quilt. Like a prayer that didn't work.

The soldiers helped her up, led her inside. Door closed behind them like a casket lid.

Mother's hand fell away from mine. I didn't realize until then how much it hurt. My wrist bore a faint red outline—another thing I wouldn't mention.

Twenty minutes passed like a whole childhood.

When the men came out, they didn't look back. They never do.

They drove away, hats in laps, slow as before, leaving behind a house forever changed and another still intact by the luck of a misread address.

Mother wiped her eyes. One slow gesture. Then straightened herself—chin up, grief tucked back into the creases behind her eyes.

But she didn't go inside.

She turned to me and said, "Come help me hang the wash."

No lecture. No sigh.

Just a request. Like a woman. Not a mother.

I set the polish down on the windowsill, two more left to paint, and followed her through the screen door. Cousin Ralph padded behind me, ears low like he knew sorrow when he smelled it.

We clipped shirts in silence, the clothesline swaying under the weight of damp cotton and unsaid things. She was folding a dish towel when her hands stopped moving. Her eyes fixed on the wind-blown hem of my dress.

"You know," she said, so quietly I barely caught it, "when I was your age, there was a boy named Ellis Beech who used to bring me blackberries in a paper sack. Wouldn't say a word. Just leave them at the well and walk away."

She smiled, but it was the kind that pulled inward, like she was apologizing to herself.

"My daddy caught him once. Said if Ellis ever stepped on our land again, he'd put buckshot in both knees. Next week, I found a sack of berries buried under a pile of straw. That's how boys loved girls back then. In secret. In fear."

She handed me a pillowcase. Her voice grew thinner.

"I never told anyone that. Not even your father."

I nodded. Not like a daughter. Like a witness.

She clipped the final clothespin and stood back. Wind snapped the sheets like flags.

"You looked so much like me just now, holding that polish. Same foolishness in my mouth. Same hope in the eyes."

She turned away. Not to hide. But because some memories are too sacred to be seen all the way through.

And I—I held my breath.

Because in that sliver of morning, I hadn't just seen my mother.

I'd met the girl she used to be.

I didn't know how long it would last, or when she would remember something to spoil the moment, but I stayed with her. I'd never craved anything like I'd craved a moment like this.

In those moments, it wasn't difficult to understand how she'd annealed her bulletproof exterior. How her own mother removed her from school and told her she'd learned enough. How her fertile mind had been forced to shrink inside the small clay pot of its making, the roots of it strangled into mediocrity in the quiet of what her daddy called *sufficient*.

She said it doesn't bother her, that she is grateful for her life, its simplicity, its order, but I see how her hands hover over magazine pages where proper ladies in silk dresses and pearls turn their faces to unseen cameras, their laughter frozen, weightless as cigarette smoke.

It was sufficient for her station. That phrase, polished like a silver relic, passed from mouth to mouth, an incantation muttered by men-in-charge with gold-tipped fountain pens, deciding the futures of others between the clink of whiskey glasses and the scratch of ink on paper. It is a phrase Mother repeats sometimes, though when she says it, it is quiet, like the low hum of a needle biting through fragile cloth.

She does, however, occupy important roles in the church—trusted with the budget by men who trust no one but themselves, handing the fate of its finances to the recognition of her well-known abilities without hesitation. And as Worthy Matron of the local Eastern Star chapter, she moves with a queen's authority, her every gesture a sermon in grace and control. Watching her glide through the church hall during a meeting or pause on the porch to adjust her hat before heading into town is like watching a play I've seen too many times—every line delivered perfectly, every cue hit with precision.

She hadn't, however, been formally trained. Not in finance or accounting or Latin or French or the sort of music that lifts the chin in mixed company. Her dresses were plain, her life plainer. As though a ribbon at the waist or a brooch at the collar might summon a terrible imbalance, might undo the careful geometry of a country girl's life.

Would she have been a sewing girl, a farmer's wife, a factory worker in the choking heat of the hosiery mill? The thought lingers, a bitter aftertaste on the tongue. Now, I wonder what she might have been good at, if all the doors hadn't been shut before she ever thought to knock. Not shut entirely, no, just off-limits to woman.

But the answer was given the moment Daddy entered her life, abrupt as a stone dropped into still water. Poof—housewife it was, and housewife she became. Her identity folding into itself like linens pressed smooth under the weight of her iron, edges sharp, pleats crisp, every trace of the woman she might have been hidden in the symmetry of domesticity.

Marrying Daddy was an escape, though not in the way stories tell it. There was no swoon, no breathless surrender to a love so vast it swallowed her whole. No, it was practical, swift as a trap snapping shut on the soft foot of a fat rabbit.

Her own father, fresh from prison, was a specter of bad debts and whiskey breath, a man with hands that knew only how to take. She saw the road ahead, its cobbles blood-warm beneath her feet, and she ran. Perhaps she believed marriage would be a kind of freedom. It's no wonder now why she resents Daddy's drinking so much.

A new cage is still a cage, but there are some you choose willingly, and she chose this one. She let it close around her, mistaking its walls for the shape of a home.

Somehow, we'd drifted from the backyard to the kitchen without my noticing, the screen door's creak and the shift of light swallowed by the sound of her voice. I was still riding the rhythm of her stories when

I found myself at the counter, apron tied, yolks already broken in the bowl, as if my hands had moved only to keep pace with her memory.

"I don't envy those ambitious men," she says, her voice even, untroubled, but her fingers tell a different story, tracing the edges of magazine pages, lingering on the pearls at the throat of a woman who looks out from a printed past she never lived. If life had bent another way, if the door had been left just slightly ajar, would she have stepped through it? Would she have turned her razor-sharp mind toward something greater than rationing flour, than stretching the wash water for one more round, than measuring the worth of a day by the weight of what has been mended and cleaned and put away?

She has the brains of two men and the grit of three, and yet here she stands, wrists dusted with flour, back turned as she kneads the dough into something pliable, something that can be shaped. "A housewife's work is never done," she tells me, and I almost believe she means it as a point of pride. I watch the way the flour lingers in the air, a fine white mist settling over the kitchen like snowfall, and I wonder at the things left unsaid, at the weight of things she chooses not to name.

"Where did you learn that?" I ask, after she has dismantled someone's argument with precision fit for a courtroom, the words sharp, unflinching. "The way you talk about those philosophers, Mother. You could have been a teacher. I'd sure love to see you up against Father Lynch—pick that man apart like a crow on a dead cat."

She throws back her head and laughs, a sound that seems to empty the room of its air for a moment. "Oh, but I am your teacher," she says, dusting her hands, her eyes flickering with something I cannot place. "This classroom just happens to have a skillet and a needle and thread."

She reads everything. Dog-eared books stacked in crooked towers, paperbacks that have begun to curl at the edges, hardbacks with their spines worn soft from handling. John Donne sits beside Twain, metaphysical ponderings tangled with the practical prayers of women who hold the world together in quiet, unseen ways.

"Each book is a doorway," she tells me, running a finger over the fragile pages, the words worn thin with rereading. "A world where I might have sipped tea in a parlor instead of dicing these onions."

And yet, for all her knowing, she wears the title housewife like a chain at her throat, an inheritance she never asked for but cannot remove. The word settles over her mouth like dust over an old photograph, dulling the sharpness, the clarity. "If only I were a woman of leisure," she says, later in the evening, her hands resting on the table, fingers curled inward. "Perhaps I would have written a novel. Or opened a school for girls."

"You could still write," I say, tentative, careful, because I know the way a thing can disappear the moment you give it a name. "Just a little every day."

She holds my gaze for a moment, something flickering behind her eyes, something half-buried, half-formed. "Oh, Shirley, that would mean writing before the dishes are washed and the floors are swept. And what would people think of a woman who puts words to paper before she's finished with her duties?"

She laughs then, a quick, sharp sound, but it does not touch her eyes.

I see it now, the tension once again tightening around her shoulders, the contradictions lining the walls like cracks in old plaster. I see the way she watches herself, a careful curator of her own performance. I wonder if she knows that I see it. That I have always seen it.

She changes the subject then, as she always does, washing away the moment like a stain on a dress, scrubbed until nothing remains but the memory of where it once was.

*

CHORES DONE, I SAT at the little desk by the window and tore a page from the back of my schoolbook, wrote his name neatly across the top. The words came slow, measured, the weight of them settling before I'd even finished the first line. 'Benji, meet me in the horse barn at nine. Let me explain.'

I folded the note, slid it into an envelope, pressed the seal closed with the flat of my palm. The house was quiet, the heat from the day still thick in the air, curling at the edges of my mother's drawn lace curtains. I stood, slipped out the door, let the screen door creak and settle behind me.

The walk to town was long enough to think twice, short enough to do nothing about it. The dirt road split the fields, the evening light turning the pasture grass dull gold. A dog barked somewhere down by the creek. The town rising slow before me, the scatter of lights, the shape of it familiar and indifferent.

Earline was where I knew she'd be, sorting through a bushel of peaches at the back of the farmer's market, her hands quick and knowing. She looked up, gave me the same measured glance she always did, neither welcoming nor wary, just steady. I held out the envelope.

"Earline, I need a favor. Can you give this to Benji when you get home? I think I hurt him, and I need to set things right. Mother can't know."

Earline took the letter but didn't look down at it. Her hands, dark and strong, folded it once, twice, pressed it into the top of her dress.

"Been wonderin' what had him all tied up in knots," she said, her voice low, even. "Figured it was something like this. I ain't one to pry, Miss Shirley, but that boy's my own. We both know what he wants. What he can't have. What ain't allowed. I hope you're fixin' to let him down soft."

I swallowed, shifted my weight.

"Benji was my best friend," I said, voice steady, quiet. "And I forgot that. I need him to know I'm sorry."

Earline's eyes sharpened, the softness gone.

"Then say you're sorry and be done with it."

I took a breath.

"I need to see him. I need to tell him face to face."

She stood silent a long moment, looking at me like she could see past my words to the shape of the thing underneath. Then, slow, deliberate, she nodded.

"You promise me this don't bring no trouble down on my boy. You swear it."

"I swear it."

A moment passed. Then Earline turned, went back to the peaches, sorting them one by one. The letter tucked safe, her mind made.

I left her there in the dimming light of the afternoon, the hush of a winds settling in, the weight of what this night will mean to me—us—and the metronome of time stretching long and uncertain before me.

WHAT THE WORLD REFUSES

THAT SAME AFTERNOON, Earline rounded the house one more time, looking to make sure every piece of furniture had been dusted and oiled. She went to the kitchen to grab her purse, sweater, and the bushel of peaches she bought to make Benji the peach cobbler he was asking for a few weeks back. She'd scrimped and saved, and was excited about going home to make her family something special.

As she walked home, a dread came over her about the contents of the letter she carried, saying a prayer to Jesus as her tender feet, sore from a sprained arch, carried her the mile from the Ragland house to her simple shack, that her son would be protected, no matter what.

She wasn't lying to Shirley when she said she trusted her—she did. She'd cared for that little white girl since she was barely an hour old, breast-fed her when Ora couldn't, and raised her like she was her own for all these years. She knew her, really knew her.

But trust was a different thing between colored folk and the white folk they worked for. She'd seen it time and time again.

How many sweet little white girls, good as gold when they were young, turn rotten when they grew up? At some point, these little girls become women who inherit and who marry and who end up owning things. And when a person owns things, they become protective of their property. Life and loss teaches people to become cruel protectors of things.

In Earline's troubled mind, she accepted that she possessed as close to a real love for Shirley as might be possible. But she knew it wasn't the same as the love she had for her own boys. Not when the bitterness of uncertainty gets factored in, like it always seems to do when it's between white folks and colored folks.

Earline walks in the door, feet tingling in pain like she's walked a mile on broken glass, and Benji comes running inside from the back yard to help his mother in the kitchen. He eyes the basket of peaches and a smile the size of the Mississippi River spreads across his face.

"Mama, you got us some peaches!"

"Now, Benji, don't you go and get all crazy for no cobbler—let Mama tend to that. I know you still got a few chores to do; I see them baskets of clean clothes over in there, need foldin' and puttin' away."

"Ok, Mama. Ok."

Benji got to work folding clothes and Mun came in to greet his wife. "Ya feets still feelin' bad, woman? Let me get some water boilin', I'll fetch some Epsom salts from the cupboard so you can soak 'em a while after dinner." Mun walked over and squeezed his strong arms around his wife, kissing her on the forehead.

Earline made a proper dinner for Mun and their two boys—salt-cured country ham, red-eye gravy, biscuits, turnip greens, and some peach cobbler for dessert. When the last dish had been scraped clean and the table wiped of crumbs, she turned to the boys with a quiet authority and asked them to help with the washing up. They didn't question it; Benji took the plates, Elijah the glasses, and together they moved like clockwork, dutiful sons trained by the rhythm of supper and silence. Elijah slipped out the screen door and made for the barn, a feed pail swinging at his side to feed the horse. Alone now, just her and Benji, the hush between them seemed to swell. Earline dried her hands on the hem of her apron, then reached beneath her blouse, fingers searching until they found the folded slip tucked warm against her chest. Without a word, she drew it out and placed it in her son's waiting hand.

"Shsssssh, don't tell nobody, this between you and me. I got this lil' note from Shirley, she wanna' talk to you. Say she got something important to say to you."

Benji didn't say a word, his face withdrawn but also alert and expectant. He opened the letter and read it, then folded it, only to unfold it and read it again. Afterwards, he folded the letter carefully, as if not to damage or bend it, then put it in his pocket for safe keeping.

"Mama, did you read it… the letter?"

"No, child, I didn't. Ain't my troubles, baby, these belong to you and that white child. But I trust you both, whatever it say, I think you can deal with it. You strong, Benji. Strong like your daddy. I trust you."

"Thank you, Mama. Thank you."

The two of them put their thoughts elsewhere and cleaned up the mess made from cooking dinner.

*

IT WAS THE KIND of heat that made the air thick, viscous, like moving through some slow-dying dream. The cicadas had wound themselves into a frenzy, high in the hickories and sweetgums, their bodies thrumming against the night like the world was ending and they were the first to know. Benji had spent the evening pacing the width of the small bedroom he shared with Elijah, who was busy with Mun at the barn. Four steps across, four back, then sitting on the edge of the bed, head in hands—then standing again, restless, waiting for nine o'clock, when he would slip from the house and find Shirley waiting where she said she'd be. He told himself he wasn't afraid. He told himself a lie.

The back door groaned against its hinges, a whisper of protest. He stepped onto the packed dirt, the scent of hay and manure thick in his nose, the distant creak of the windmill turning slow. The barn sat low against the dark, the wood worn silver by sun and time, a place older than both of them, standing before either had drawn breath, before either had learned what it meant to love something the world forbade. He kept to the far side, away from the chicken coop, where the birds, stirred from their roosts, would raise a racket that could wake the dead.

Inside, the smell of earth and old grain, the dust suspended in the moonlight that slanted through the rafters. Shirley sat atop the feed bin, her back to him, wearing a white nightgown with a pink sweater over it, one hand resting on the worn edge as if considering whether to take something or leave it behind.

"Shirley."

She turned, her face breaking into something neither smile nor frown, something in between, some fragile place that lived between joy and sorrow. "Benji." She dropped down from the bin, light-footed, the hem of her gauzy nightgown brushing against the straw-littered floor. "I wasn't sure you'd come."

He shifted, feeling the weight of his own uncertainty. "I wanted to. Needed to. And I needed to tell you, I'm sorry for spying, for sneaking around. I saw you and him, I did. And I ain't proud of it. I just—" He paused, shaking his head, the words knotted inside him. "I shoulda walked away. I shoulda—"

"It's all right, Benji." She stepped closer, her hands empty, but still he felt as though she carried something heavy. "You don't have to say nothing else."

"But I do." He lifted his chin, met her eyes head-on. "I have to know. If you love me. If you ever did."

Shirley exhaled, slow, controlled, her fingers tracing the fabric of her gown where it lay tight against her stomach. "I did. I do." She swallowed. "I always have. But I lost you, Benji. I lost you when your mama sent you away from me. Five years is a long time to forget how to hold onto something that was never yours to begin with."

"If you love me," he said, "why Bo?"

Her gaze flickered to the darkness beyond the barn door. "Because the world ain't built for us. Because people with power made it so." Her voice was quiet, but full. "Because they've passed laws that say what me and you feel is a sin, that our love is a crime because you're black and I'm white. And because if they caught us, you'd be swinging from the big oak on Carter's land before the sun rose."

Benji felt it then, the tight, trembling heat in his chest. The fire and the fury of it, and the helplessness, too. "So, what does that mean—for us?"

Shirley stepped close enough that he could feel the warmth of her. "It means, Benji, darling, you and I have to be c-a-r-e-ful." Shirley finished the sentence slow and sugar-smooth, a half-smile playing at the corners of her mouth, her brow arched just enough to suggest she knew more than she was saying.

"It means, if we're to be happy on this earth, we have to live two lives." Her voice was unsteady. "It means you find a black wife, hopefully ugly, and I marry Bo, and in the spaces between, we find each other and make our moments in secret places. Or, we decide to sacrifice our happiness, and just try to be friends, careful not to hurt the other's feelings."

He reached for her with the kind of slowness that made time feel deliberate, his hands finding the hollow where her back met the swell of her hips. His thumb wandered upward, a lazy pilgrimage along the ridge of her spine, the fabric slick and whisper-thin against his skin. He kissed her then, and she kissed him back, and the heat that lived in the walls of that old barn grew hotter still. Her hands found their way to his neck, to his shoulders, to the sharp angle of his jaw, to the ridges of thick muscle that ran the length of his spine.

When he lifted her, she wrapped her legs around him, her arms clinging, her breath shallow and quick. He moved toward the feed bin, setting her down, her legs still curled around him. He pressed his lips against hers, felt the shape of her mouth beneath his, the press of her fingers at the nape of his neck. The lost years unraveled between them, unwinding with the slow, breathless force of a coiled spring long held in check—releasing not in violence, but in aching waves, each movement a surrender to all they had buried in silence. They don't speak; words are flimsy things—too small—no match for the heat thrumming between them, for the ache that could never fit inside a sentence.

His hand slipped beneath the hem of her gown, fingers ghosting over the thin silk between them, the only thing protecting her from the inevitable. He didn't ask, he just did.

Her breath hitched, her grip tightening, her body yielding. Her hand, uncertain but deliberate, found the buckle of his belt, then lower, the fabric shifting, parting, and then she was holding him, her fingers tracing what had once been imagined but was now real.

She looked down, her lips parted, her gaze fixed. And then she lifted her eyes back to his, searching, asking. And he answered, not with words but with movement, his body meeting hers, their limbs tangled, their breath mingling, the night pressing close around them. And in that moment, they were neither black nor white, neither sinner nor saint, neither right nor wrong. They were only Benji and Shirley, only flesh and heat and a love that the world refused to make room for.

And when it was over, they lay still, the weight of what had passed settling between them. He traced the curve of her cheek, watched the way her lashes fluttered, the way her lips parted as if to speak but held no words. He wanted to tell her that he would stay, that he would fight, that the world be damned if it tried to keep them apart. And this time, he did.

"No," he said, voice low but firm. "I won't play at pretending, Shirley. I won't watch you put on a white dress for some boy just because the world's too narrow to hold what we are. I won't smile and tip my hat while you lay beside someone else, and I, wide awake, knowing you're not mine—not really. That ain't living. That's survival with a noose tied 'round it."

She blinked, caught in the sudden gravity of him, but he didn't stop.

"I know what's out there. I know the law don't protect me, and it sure as hell don't love me. But that don't mean I bow to it. I won't give them the right to tell me who I can love. I'll be careful, yes—I'm not stupid. I won't put your life or my mama's in the crosshairs of fools who carry badges and hate in the same pocket. But don't ask me to pretend this ain't real."

He brought her hand to his chest, held it there like he was making a pledge.

"I will not let you go. Not in truth. Not in soul. They can write their rules and burn their crosses, but they don't own me, and they sure as hell don't own what we have."

She spread open her balled hand, clutched his clenched fist, lacing her fingers with his, then pulled his hand over to her, pressing his palm to her chest. And he felt it, the steady drumbeat of her heart, the proof of her, the proof of them. And for that moment, for that breath of time, it was enough.

Outside, the cicadas had gone quiet, as if even they understood that something had changed. That nothing, after this, would ever be the same.

TEN

A CONFIDANT'S PLEA

Tuesday, Third Week of August 1942

THE NEXT LETTER from William Crayton arrived in a stiff envelope, the seal unbroken, the weight of it carrying more than paper and ink. It sat on the table for a time before I dared touch it, as though my hand upon it would bring forth an inevitable reckoning, some hidden mechanism springing into place, setting events beyond my control into motion. But the truth was already in motion. I had only to lift the waxed flap and let it spill into my lap.

I unfolded the letter. The penmanship was meticulous, slanted slightly leftward with purpose, a calculated distance. The words leapt from the page in a voice I could almost hear, steady and deliberate, a voice that had measured its syllables before pressing them into permanence. He was careful. The nature of his relationship with Tom lay coiled between the lines, not named but not hidden, an intimacy wrapped in the austerity of his prose, a thing that would only be misunderstood if exposed to the wrong set of eyes.

Tom had sent letters. Letters burdened with the weight of something unspeakable. I imagined the ink, hurried and smudged, the pressure of the pen breaking through the paper in places, evidence of a hand that trembled as it wrote. The shape of the words mattered, the lean of them, the choice of phrase betraying the desperation he had tried to suppress. A debt. A confession. A fear thick enough to smother him. Father Schadenfreude's name surfaced again and again, suspicions running through each paragraph, clenching tight around the elements of Tom's disappearance.

The money was missing. Vanished. The church's coffers emptied, the accusations lingering in the rafters, waiting to settle on a scapegoat. Tom's sudden departure had been no coincidence, and now I saw what William saw, what Tom had feared. A trap laid beneath the guise of providence. A hand extended, not to save, but to claim. I saw the priest in my mind's eye, the gleam of his eyeglasses, the careful arrangement of his features, every word he spoke designed to turn the cogs and gadgetry of fate to his favor. He had been uncharacteristically patient. Had watched. Had waited for the right moment to tighten his grip.

Tom had been taken.

Not in the manner of the law, no chains around his wrists, no sentence read from a judge's bench. Taken in a way more insidious. Persuaded. Worn down like a stone beneath the slow trickle of a stream until he no longer recognized the shape he had been before. I could see it now, the slow and steady gnawing away of his will, the priest's words dripping into his ear, filling the empty spaces inside his head until he believed they had always been there. Until he believed they were his own.

Had he gone willingly?

That was the wrong question.

The letter trembled in my grip. I set it aside and leaned back, pressing my palms flat against the table, grounding myself against the burden of what I now knew. I had been too late to stop it. But not too late to pull him back.

The priest had underestimated the strength of what tethered Tom to this world. He had miscalculated. He had taken something that did not belong to him, and I intended to take it back.

I would go to Philadelphia if I had to. I would find the man who had orchestrated this and lay bare every hidden thing. The priest had built his house upon stolen gold and borrowed time. He had spun his web and sat fat in the center, waiting for his prey to tire, to stop struggling.

He had not accounted for me.

I rose, the chair scraping against the floor, the sound sharp in the silence of the room. The letter remained on the table, ink drying, words waiting. William Crayton had given me what I needed. Now it was my turn to act.

OBSERVING THE WOVEN FAÇADE

Wednesday, Third Week of August 1942

I WATCH PEOPLE. I don't know why. Perhaps if Mother permitted visitors, my mind wouldn't be such a captive audience to itself. But she does not, and I am. And so, I observe.

I am afflicted with a peculiar talent, an accursed knack for dissecting movements, parsing the subtleties of limbs and fingers and fleeting expressions that, when coupled with words, spin a dialect of their own. A secondary language if you will, oblique and double-edged, as though meaning itself conspires against the speaker, saying one thing aloud and another in silence.

With each Mass, the parish practically hums with the uneasy shuffle of patent-leathered feet and silk skirts flouncing like banners, signaling misgivings beneath the thick varnish of righteousness. One needs only to know where and how to look.

The air is close with the scent of wax and incense, ancient things meant to smother doubt, but doubt clings all the same. I sit, fourth row, dead center, stiff-backed in my starched dress, legs crossed at the ankle, and I watch them shift and twitch, adjusting collars and cuffs with nervous fingers.

Their eyes dart, erratic, pupils contracting in the dim candlelight, restless birds flitting before the storm breaks. I see them evade each other's glances, shifting up to the rafters as though waiting for some divine intervention, or down to their laps, picking at invisible specks of dust on their skirts. If the body betrays, the eyes convict. They know this. And so, they look everywhere but where they ought to.

One woman chews her lower lip raw, her hands folded too tightly in her lap, like she's strangling some hidden truth between her palms. A man two pews up crosses himself twice instead of once, fingers shaking at the temple. They all carry it—the twitch, the tremble, the small rehearsed devotions that almost mask the rot beneath. But I see it. I see how shame leaks into movement, how sin clings to the skin like smoke. And just like that, my mind slips—slides somewhere low and warm and wrong.

Bo's breath in the dark, the cut of his jaw when he looks at me like I'm a thing to be ruined. Benji's hands, steadier than any prayer, and the way they trembled once, just once, when they touched my wrist. The pew creaks beneath me as I shift, trying to shake them loose, but it's no use. The thought is already there—ripe, wet, obscene. And I know better than to pretend it came from anywhere but me.

Father Schadenfreude gives me one of those looks, as if to say, "Shirley, my child, are you listening?" Despite his composure, I know he's not happy with me.

And just like that, I'm wandering off again. Just as I meander back into consciousness, the priest catches me adrift once more, eyes forward but soul elsewhere, wandering the worn paths of memory where no scripture could ever compete. His imagined voice slips through the gates of my indelicate distractions, soft but edged, like warm water poured over a blade. I blink, torn from the muddled thicket of Bo's mouth on mine, Benji's eyes—hurt, damaged—and all the things I've done or might still do if left unchecked by grace.

Father Schadenfreude's voice has a way of cleaving through the murmuring quiet, thick as the incense that wavers in ghostly tendrils high above the altar. His accent, a heavy thing of Polish origin, lends gravity to his words, turns the simplest phrase into something profound, something unavoidable. His pale hands are pressed together in that peculiar way of his, fingers interlocked so tightly the knuckles blanch.

"You must learn to distinguish the true from the false. This is paramount, is it not?"

His eyes do not blink. The parishioners nod and chant an affirmation in practiced unison—"Amen!" I think perhaps, he knows. That he senses this conflict within me, the yearning for truth amid the murk of deceit. But perhaps I give him too much credit. The righteous have their own blindness.

He nods, satisfied with the effectiveness of his message. Turns back to his sermon, to his flock, and as he continues to deliver his Mass, they bow their heads in meek agreement, supplicant to his will. A chorus of murmured *Amens*, and a rustle of fabric as they settle back into place, as though they believe sitting still might still their own treacherous hearts.

Bo Harris slips into the pew at the back. His mother offers a disapproving glare. He is late, as usual, but he wears his tardiness like a laurel wreath, unbothered by the priest's glare. He sinks into the seat, runs a hand through his already messy hair, and catches my eye as he does. A flicker, no more, but it sends the breath tight in my chest.

He hasn't spoken to me in a week from Sunday. Not since that night by the creek when he stood me up. Or, rather, not since the silence that followed. But I do intend to break it, to speak. I just don't know exactly when. I have a plan I need to follow. One that gets me a dumb hunky husband, and a prize to boot, a secret friend that loves me and knows exactly how to make me happy. And just as Bo gets settled into the pew, Mass is over.

Mother's voice, brittle as cracked glass, had followed me through the house that morning: "Confess. You must confess, Shirley. I asked Father Schadenfreude; he said it's been three months." But I lean against the idea. Not because I am afraid, but because I do not regret. And that is, perhaps, the greatest sin of all. Besides, all I'd intended to confess was the kiss, and the feelings that went with it. Since I first considered my next confession, I've done way worse. Uhm, way, way worse.

Once Mass is over, I see Father Schadenfreude make his way to the confession booth. I decide that it's best not to avoid, but to just lie. The confessional is a spooky thing: narrow, wooden, as though carved from the ribs of some great ancient beast that intends to eat you if the sin is too big to easily reconcile. I look over at Bo as I approach the booth. The expression on his face is priceless, which makes me grin. The door creaks on its hinge as I push it open, and inside, the dark is almost complete, save for the thin lattice of carved wood that separates me from the priest.

"Bless me, Father, for I have sinned." The words taste foreign on my tongue, touched with trepidation as if they might unravel something I barely understand myself.

"O my God, I am heartily sorry for having offended Thee, and I detest all my sins, because I dread the loss of Heaven and the pains of Hell; but most of all because I have offended Thee, my God, who art all-good and deserving of all my love. I firmly resolve, with the help of Thy grace, to confess my sins, to do penance, and to amend my life. Amen." The Father's authoritative voice flowing like a river wrought from ages past.

The ritual words spill from my lips, but they do not fit right. They are borrowed clothes; too stiff, too formal. I wring my hands in my lap. The bench is hard beneath me, pressing straight lines into my oh so sinful skin.

The priest exhales, a slow and measured thing, a sound that makes the small space feel smaller. "Go on."

I wet my lips. Hesitate. Then—

"I kissed him."

The words hang, suspended in the hush. I do not know what I expected—sharp censure, perhaps, a gasp of disappointment. But Father Schadenfreude only inclines his head, an invisible motion beyond the screen, a movement I feel more than see. I didn't say to whom it was I kissed. I dare say, he wouldn't have suspected not one, but two boys, one... untouchable.

"And?"

"And... uh, nothing," I whisper. "That's all."

A pause. A long one. Then—

"My child," he says, and his voice is softer now, an edge smoothed away. "These matters of the heart are perilous. Temptation, when indulged, grows roots."

"I know. That's exactly why I came to you, Father." Spoken like Hedy Lamarr, if I say so myself.

"And yet."

"Yes," I say. "And yet." Does he know I'm being furtive? I strike back a grin as I think about what happened two nights ago. If the Father knew that, would I be burned at the stake? Is that what they do in Poland?

Father Schadenfreude gruffs his way through the rite, his voice thick with impatience, as though mercy were a tax he paid begrudgingly. He offers no warmth, no gentle encouragement, only the dry decree of 'two good deeds' and a prayer scraped clean of compassion. "God frees you from your sins," he says, clipped and final. "Go in peace."

My lips move on instinct—"Thanks be to God"—the words falling out like coins dropped in a collection plate, more habit than conviction. I slip from the kneeler like a soul escaping a coffin, breath held, body stiff, eager to be free of the stale breath of judgment.

When I step out, the air is cool against my flushed skin. Outside, the sky is vast and unbothered, a deep blue untouched by my confession. I am lighter, but not absolved.

Bo is waiting. Leaning against the church wall, hands in his pockets, the slant of his shoulders careless, but his eyes, they are watching me.

"Shirley," he says. "You alright?"

I consider lying. But the truth is an unshakable thing between us. It lingers. A third presence in this space.

"I don't know," I say.

He nods, slow, as though he understands something I do not. And maybe he does.

The silence stretches, thickens. Then—

"I'm sorry," he says. "For before."

I want to ask—for what? For pulling away? For looking at me like I was something special, then vanishing into silence like it never happened? I want to demand the truth, strip it bare, hold it to the light until it flinches.

But I don't.

Because maybe there is no truth to hold. Maybe the moment never meant what I thought it did. Maybe this is what it is to be young—raw and reaching, aching without knowing why. To be caught in that strange corridor between girl and woman, where every glance is a question and every silence feels like a door closing.

Maybe he didn't stay because there was nothing to stay for.

Instead, I say, "It doesn't matter. I'm becoming accustomed to your meanness, or is it just you being inconsiderate? Maybe I need a new boyfriend anyway. I gotta be thinkin' about marriage pretty soon. Bridgette and Phylis already have dates set after graduation."

"Shirley, I said I'm sorry, somethin' came up. My parents. You know."

"What do I know, Bo? Look, I don't have time to waste on a boy who doesn't know if I'm worth his time or not. I've given you everything, Bo, everything that's precious to give, and you stood me up; you didn't even try to talk to me. I'm going home, Bo. If you take me, us, serious, let me know when you're ready to talk."

Bo watches me for a moment longer. Then he nods.

And just like that, he is gone.

ELEVEN

WHAT GROWS IN THE DARK

Wednesday, Third Week of August 1942

TRIXIE HAD KNOWN long before the visit, before the bathroom light flickered against the water damaged pine floor, before her best friend spat out her verdict in stark, unmerciful dialogue. She had known in the way her body spoke its old, quiet realization, in the way her belly held a curious weight, not yet visible but there, pressing against her restless bones, against the architecture of her ribs.

The nausea came first—not sudden, not violent, but insistent and stealthy, the way a tide rises so slowly you don't notice until the sands are gone. Poof. And the dreams. Lord, the crazy dreams.

Strange, spectral things—dust-thick houses with doors that led to nowhere, roads that split in directions that could not be followed. And the hunger, not for food necessarily, but for something she couldn't describe, not in words, more like something that had lain dormant in her chest for years, waiting for just the right moment to claw its way back into the light.

She sat in Dr. Herbert's office, spine straight as a fence post, hands folded so tightly in her lap she could feel the blood struggling beneath her arthritic knuckles. He spoke in the careful, measured rhythm of a man who had seen it all before, who had delivered news both blessed and damning in nearly equal measure, who had learned long ago to keep his voice smooth, his expression unreadable.

Eight weeks along, healthy, progressing as expected. He handed her a pamphlet, thin and pink, the paper slick between her fingers, its edges curling where the air was damp. As if she were some girl just out of high school, some bright-eyed thing who needed diagrams and reassurances, who did not already understand the weight of what she was feeding and toting around.

By the time she locked up her shop that afternoon, she had made her decision. Bo had to hear it from her first. Not from the town, not from some old man at the gas station, not from whispered rumors that she knew would grow like kudzu around every porch and telegraph wire in this place. And certainly not from his mother. He had to hear it from her, for better or worse, because no matter what came next, it was his to know.

Bo came by after sundown, smelling of sweat and cheap beer, of leather and the musk of whatever unholy thing had dragged him through the day. He stood in the doorway, a dark silhouette against the last bruised remnants of dusk, his skewed image, a shadow on the floor, stretched long across the wooden floorboards.

When she told him, he didn't go quiet.

"The hell you mean you're pregnant?" he snapped, voice louder than the room could hold. He paced, kicked at nothing, ran both hands through his hair until it stuck out like straw. "You're sure it's mine?" he added, then regretted it before the words had even cooled on his tongue.

Trixie flinched, just slightly, her eyes hardening. She didn't answer. She didn't need to. Bo turned his back, fists pressed into his hips, the beer still doing its talking. But then something shifted, something in the silence between her breath and his guilt, in the way she looked at him like he was both storm and shelter. That old, stupid ache he had for her stirred, pulled him back down from the place his anger had taken him.

He sighed, shook his head. "Well, I'll be damned. You're gonna be the sexiest mother in Robertson County," he muttered, forcing a crooked grin as he turned back to her. "You'll have that baby strapped to your hip and every man in town wishing he was me."

Trixie exhaled, the tension leaving her shoulders in a slow, reluctant wave. The fight drained from the air. She smirked despite herself, rolled her eyes, and before she could talk herself out of it, she reached for him.

Bo took that for permission.

There was a rhythm to it, to the way his hands found her waist, to the way his body pressed against hers, a silent request, a grasping for something neither of them could deny. And she let him take her there, on that narrow cot in the back of the shop, let his weight press her into the mattress, let him take what he needed, because maybe, just maybe, it was what she needed too.

Afterward, she lay beside him, tracing the ridges of his scarred knuckles, the boyish strength still in them, though his hands had known too much work for too many years. She let the silence stretch between them, waiting, letting the news sink in, to let him feel it. Then, softly, she said, "We need to talk about what comes next."

Bo exhaled, long and slow, like a man who already knew he was cornered. "What's there to talk about? You're pregnant and I'm seventeen."

"You know exactly what I mean, Bo."

A sharp tension rippled through him, a shudder that ran from his shoulders down to the coiled muscle in his thighs. He sat up, raking a hand through his hair, eyes dark and unreadable. "Jesus, Trixie," he said, voice rough. "You should've been more careful."

Her stomach twisted, but she refused to show it. "I'm forty-two, Bo. I've buried a husband. I never had kids. This might be my only chance, and I'm not throwing it away because you're too young and stupid to handle your own responsibilities. It takes two, Bo; surely this isn't news to you."

His head snapped toward her, anger flashing behind his eyes. "You think this is my fault? You think I wanted this?"

"What I think is that it happened," she said, voice steady, "and now you and I have to deal with it."

Bo stood, yanking his shirt over his head, muscles rigid beneath his skin. "Then get rid of it."

The words landed like a slap, sharp and final.

Trixie sat up, the sheet pooling around her waist, her heart a stone in her chest. "No," she said simply.

Bo clenched his fists, the tendons in his forearms straining like cables about to snap. "You're out of your damned mind if you think I'm ready for this."

"Then don't be," she said, watching him dress, her voice cold now. "But I am."

For a moment, he stood there, fists flexing at his sides, something unreadable in his face. Then, without another word, he turned and stormed out, the door slamming behind him with a force that rattled the walls.

Trixie lay back against the pillow, listening to the echo of his footsteps fading into the night. She pressed a hand to her stomach, felt the faintest rise, a promise of something new, something real, something undeniable.

Bo Harris be damned. This baby was hers. And no matter what the town said, no matter what her daddy thought, she was going to have this child, with or without its father.

GROUNDED BY MIDDLE C

Thursday, Third Week of August 1942

YESTERDAY, I STOOD before the gathered faithful in the church hall, nerves bristling under the weight of a hundred expectant stares. The smell of mildew, wax and polished wood thickened in the air, and beyond the tall, arched windows, the dusk settled in violet bruises over the town. The moment had come, the long-awaited recital where I was to prove myself worthy of the lessons, the discipline, the hours spent chained to ivory and mahogany while the world outside wheeled forward without me.

Mother, dressed in her Sunday silk with her hair pinned high and merciless, had fussed over my collar until the starch felt fused to my skin. "Shirley, you'll shine like the full moon tonight," she declared, voice buoyant with a certainty I could not share. Her hands flitted, tugged, smoothed, her eyes scanning for imperfections and lint she would not abide. "They'll see. They'll all see. Some Yankee man from New York will hear you, and before you know it, you'll be playing to crystal chandeliers and velvet seats."

Daddy—looking all spiffy in his black suit, pressed waistcoat, polished wingtips, and a solemn air he dusted off for special occasions—sat planted in his rocking chair like he was fixin' to narrate the whole spectacle for the neighbors. He didn't say much, just watched us with that same half-smirk he wore when the hens got loose in the yard. Mother and I were flurrying about the house in a whirlwind of curlers, face powder, and perfume so thick it near 'bout peeled the wallpaper. Between the two of us, we'd tried on every dress from here to Memphis and still weren't one hundred percent sure we'd picked right.

Daddy pretended to be interested, lifting his chin every now and then like he was weighin' in, but truth be told, his face looked downright bewildered—like a coon dog at a tea party—just sittin' there trying to make sense of all the fussing and fluttering. I paused at the hall mirror, halfway pinned into a dress that may or may not have been mine, and turned to him.

"Daddy," I asked, "you learnin' anything over there?"

He glanced up, his spectacles drooping low on the bridge of his nose, and with the kind of slow drawl that carried both wisdom and the refusal to use it, said, "Well, they say a man's education is a path from cocky ignorance to miserable uncertainty. I reckon I prefer to be ignorant and cocky."

Mother swatted at him with her lint brush on her way past, muttering something about how men wouldn't last five minutes in a woman's world. Daddy just rocked, peaceful as an opossum in a patch of sun, and we went right back to flappin' like hens before the preacher comes to dinner.

The pressure coiled 'round my ribs like piano wire. I wanted to tell her that I had no interest in chandeliers or velvet seats, no desire for limelight or rapturous applause. I wanted to tell her that music lived in the quiet places, in the long hush after a storm, in the spaces where words failed. But she was already gone, whisked away to claim her seat among the town's grand dames, *her* pride balanced precariously on the edge of my performance, or, I fear, the lack thereof.

The grand piano stood like an altar at the front of the hall. I took my place upon the bench, spine straight, hands poised. The keys gleamed, each a small door to some other world. My fingers hovered over middle C, the anchor, the eye of the storm, the note upon which all others hinged. I closed my eyes. Breathed. Let the first sound ripple through the hush, a single, crystalline tone blooming in the silence.

Chopin first. Prelude No. 4 in E minor. A piece so deceptively simple it felt like a trick, like a hush that held more power than a shout. My fingers pressed and lifted, the melody curling through the air, sorrow layered beneath restraint. Each note fell like rain upon parched earth, sinking into something deep and dry, something aching for it. I played as if my life depended on it, as if by giving them this music I might be offering some piece of myself that could not be ignored.

And then, Beethoven. *The Moonlight Sonata*, the first movement. The notes wove together like thread, long and aching, a lament stretched across time. My mother's face hovered in my mind's eye, her proud tilt of chin, her belief that this moment would set me on some grand and shining path. But what if I did not want to be set? What if I wanted only to stay, to play not for adoring crowds but for myself, for the sake of the sound alone?

The audience was still, rapt, their faces touched by the music's ghostly fingers. But somewhere in the back, I felt Bo watching. He was always watching. Silent and steady, a presence weighted with judgment or expectation or something else, an expected failure and his rescue; asshole! And though my hands did not falter, though I played on, the knowing of him there unsettled the melody.

So I broke it.

Joplin next. *The Entertainer*. A wink, a joke, a bit of rebellion. My fingers skipped, trilled, leapt across the keys, the melody bounding forth like Benji's laughter on a summer evening. I could almost hear him, could almost feel the sun-warmed grass beneath my bare feet, holding his hand. I could almost forget for a moment that I was on display, a performer in my mother's grand design.

But Bo. Bo, who sat still and unamused, the corners of his mouth drawn tight, the weight of him pressing against my joy like a hand against my throat. I changed course again, let the bright notes fade into the slow unraveling of Grieg's *Åse's Death*. A sorrowful descent, a piece that spoke of things lost before they could be grasped. I thought of Bo. Thought of the tangled thing between us, the questions I did not dare to ask. Could we, one day, marry? Could I keep Benji a secret? Could I ever become what was expected of me?

The fugue came last. Bach. A grand and shining thing, a piece of jubilance, of triumph, of order brought to chaos. It built and climbed and stretched toward heaven, the notes folding over one another in exquisite logic—the place I lived. I let myself disappear into it. For seven perfect minutes, I was nothing but the music.

And then silence.

The last notes hung, fading. I lifted my hands, let them rest in my lap. The hall itself exhaled, and then the applause broke forth, a torrent of sound that rattled the tin chandeliers. I stood, bowed, felt my mother's eyes upon me, shining with something fierce and desperate.

Daddy had tucked three pink roses into the inside pocket of his waistcoat, the petals still cool from the air, delicate things against the worn lining. He said nothing when I stepped off the stage, just stood there at the foot of the steps like a man trying not to look too proud of himself for planning ahead. The flowers crinkled slightly as he handed them over, his calloused fingers brushing mine, rough from the years of work that didn't ask for applause. He didn't speak—not really his way—but his face held a light I hadn't often seen in him, something quiet and wide and almost boyish, as if pride had caught him off guard and decided to stick around.

The walk home was slow, the moon riding high above the oaks like a silent chaperone, casting silver across the pavement. My shoes pinched at the heels and the satin of my recital dress itched at the seams, but I said nothing. Mother's stride had turned airy, her heels tapping like applause still echoing in her head, her voice full of praise that landed oddly in the space between us—not on me, but floating somewhere above, addressed more to the air, to the idea of me, the version she'd spent years sculpting.

"You played beautifully," she said, her voice bright with a strange triumph. "I was so proud. Everyone was watching. They'll remember this night."

The words felt practiced, polished, set out like crystal on a table no one had asked to sit at. Daddy walked beside us without comment, his hands in his coat pockets, the faint scuff of his steps keeping time on the sidewalk like a metronome.

"Yes, Mother," I said, measuring each word. "Thank you for preparing me for this night. Thank you for the lessons and your steadfast efforts that made me what people got to see tonight. You're due all the credit, Mother."

The silence that followed was not the peaceful kind. It was the sort that pressed down on your shoulders, as if the words had turned into weights the moment they left your mouth. Her steps slowed. I heard the flutter of fabric as she stopped, the rhythm of her walk broken by the gears turning behind her eyes.

She said nothing for a few paces more, then caught up, her breath a little tighter now.

"Oh, Shirley," she said at last, her voice softer, bending at the edges, "You can lead a horse to water, but you can't make 'em drink. The praise and the glory are all yours, gal. You were amazing tonight. No one can take that from you."

She reached for my hand then, not like a mother claiming a child, but like someone suddenly aware of distance. "You showed me tonight that everything your father and I put into you—every lesson, every practice, every penny and prayer—it wasn't wasted. You honored us tonight. Not just with the music, but by proving you understood what it meant."

Her fingers were warm. A little trembling. And for the first time that evening, her voice sounded less like a performance and more like a woman unsure if she'd done right by the daughter walking beside her.

I nodded. Said nothing. Because already I felt it coming. The shift, the crack that would widen until all of this, the music, the moment, the fragile closeness—it could easily collapse beneath the weight of the world she had built around us. The world I'd become more and more reluctant to abide.

I wondered how long it would be before we fought again. How long before this night, this fragile peace, was nothing but another note swallowed by silence.

LUMPS IN THE GRAVY

ENTERING THE HOUSE, dampened notes played incorrectly and a few dragged-out key changes rummaged through my memory, creating mental fix-it remedies for my next practice. I hated making mistakes, even the one's no one notices. Particulars about the recital performance would be pestering my practices for weeks, maybe months.

Daddy was crouched next to the radio, its weak signal echoing through the house like a staticky ghost muttering the news of the war, the voices drowned beneath the crackle of signal interference, no more discernible than chickens clucking. The thing's half-swallowed words were dissolving into the kitchen's dim hum. Daddy sat back in his chair, plopped down in frustration over the signal, now unmoving but for the steady rhythm of his hand over his jaw, listening the way a man listens who has heard more than he will ever speak.

Mother had left dinner in the oven, its warmth and the odor of pork fat dulling into the evening air, and now she moved through the kitchen with the purpose of a woman who understood the importance of hot biscuits even in the midst of a tired meal. God bless her loyalty; please excuse the hubris.

I watched her—the way her hands worked the dough, knuckles pressing deep into the soft mound before gathering it again, folding, pressing. She was talking, though the words drifted over me, breaking apart and reassembling in phrases that meant little beyond the cadence of her voice. Her favorite subject was herself and the particular shape of her own martyrdom. Her second favorite subject—the righteousness of her judgments.

There was something in her tone that made my stomach tighten, a slow wringing of patience, and I turned my thoughts elsewhere, away from her sermonizing, away from the lilt of her certainty, and toward the tangled mess of my own unrest.

Bo and Benji. What to do? The sheer weight of it settled sharp and mean at the base of my ribs, the way hunger settles when you've missed too many meals. I had grown weary in the past month, and it was not the kind of weariness that sleep could mend. It was the push and pull, the dance of the affections from a pair of beaus.

It was the way one moment Bo was all sunlit laughter, and the next, he was cold-boned silence. The absence of his apology burned in me like sweat on a raw wound, the kind that festers, turns ugly with time. He had left me waiting, the place where he should have stood gone hollow.

And wasn't that the way of things? Leaving me alone and subject to the shame of being watched by a boy I've loved and respected since I was old enough to form sentences. That a girl is made to feel like something misplaced, an afterthought, the shape of longing mistaken for love. Did Bo use me? The question curled against my ribs, sharp-toothed and restless. Would Benji use me up too? Had I gone too far, too deep to fail?

And as if my own heartache weren't enough, Mother's voice cut through my thoughts with the dull edge of a sermon practiced too long, the words thick with condescension, sweetened with false kindness, musing on her usual diatribe about the ignorance of the colored person.

"They'd be better off, Shirley, if they stuck to the simple scriptures. Not all things are meant to be understood by simple minds. It's just their nature, and we must be patient, give them grace."

Grace? The bile rose hot in my throat. As if she were some great dispenser of charity, doling out wisdom from the high seat of her conviction. As if patience were the same as understanding. As if grace were a thing to be measured and portioned out like flour.

Her words settled over the dinner table, heavy as the lumped-up gravy she spooned onto our plates, thick and bitter; unpalatable.

I felt the burn in my chest, the deep throb of anger, the old knowing that some words are too wrong to let pass unchallenged. My hands curled into my lap. My mother, who had taught me prayers but never how to wield them. My mother, who would rather see the world made small enough to fit inside her own understanding than stretch herself to see beyond it.

I tried with every ounce of my being to drown out her bigotry with thoughts of cicadas buzzing about in the humid air, the sounds of the occasional car rumbling in the distance, children playing, trains streaking by in the night. Nothing would quiet my offended mind.

And so, I spoke.

"I wonder, Mother, how it is that you, with all your so-called grace, have never considered the ignorance of so many educated people, yourself included, and how their certainty does far more harm than the innocence you so easily condemn."

The words dropped between us, the weight of them undeniable. I saw the way her fork froze midair, the way her lips parted just slightly, the sharp intake of breath.

"And what of your Father Schadenfreude?" I continued, the words burning as they left me. "That man and his so-called sermon on 'The Spirituality of Negroes', the audacity of him to claim *insight*, as if his judgment were anything but a veil over his own arrogance. If anything, he sins against himself, against any half-decent hope of humanity, against the very people he claims to uplift. The word *'insight'* does not belong in his mouth. It is a thing too delicate for hands as brutal as his."

The silence stretched long. And then the door opened, the creak of the swinging door spilled across the kitchen like something living. Daddy's footsteps, slow and measured, the pause before he entered the room. He was a man of few words, but his presence carried more weight than any sermon. He stood just at the threshold, watching. And though he said nothing, I felt the moment shift, the air in the room becoming something tight and brittle.

And I wasn't finished.

"It is people like him, like you, Mother, who patronize both the coloreds and God himself. Who twist words into tools of judgment, who mistake condescension for kindness. And tell me, how can you honor what you patronize? If you truly believe in the righteousness of your heart, then tell me this, Mother: who stands before God with cleaner hands? The man who sees his neighbor as an equal, or the man who cloaks himself in the arrogance of pity?"

My mother's face burned with something too fierce for words, and I saw in her eyes the fire of a woman who had lost the argument before she had spoken a single word. She stood abruptly, the chair legs scraping against the floor, her departure a retreat, a battle unfinished. She left without so much as a bite of biscuit, and I was never forced to resort to pious Latin phrases, not once.

Daddy watched me over the wire rims of his spectacles, then smiled faintly, shaking his head as he tore into a piece of chicken from the bone. He chewed, swallowed, wiped his hands against his knees before speaking.

"Patience, sweetheart," he said at last. "Patience is a hymn best sung slow."

"But Daddy—"

"Did you hear me, gal? Must I educate you on your place?"

"Daddy, I know the word. I just don't know how it applies to a wrong that demands to be made right."

He sighed, leaned forward, set his plate aside. "Made right, or made right by you? You are your mother's child. A parent, even when they deserve it, even when they can learn from it, will find it hard to take the wisdom of a child.

"And the way you delivered yours, well, you took a stick to a hornet's nest, didn't you? Patience, girl, is the slow work of change. It's a thing that hums under the skin, that waits in the quiet spaces, that shapes the world not with fire but with time. My mother always told me the peach ripens sweetest on the branch left unshaken, and a life lived well is the same. Time is the hand that smooths the edges, polishes the heart, makes it shine. Some folks need more time, sweetheart. And nothing wrong with having an opinion, but being mean about it, rushing the truth when your anger is still hot, well, that's just another kind of ignorance."

I stared at him, my chest tight, my hands—fists in my lap.

"You finish your supper, gal," he said, easing back into his chair. "And when you're done, you go find your mother. Show her what grace really looks like, since you seem to be the expert on it in this house."

"But Daddy—"

"You heard me, Shirley."

WHAT LIES BETWEEN MELODIES

Friday, Third Week of August 1942

MORNING WAS A slow and sullen thing, curling in thick ribbons through the kitchen where the light cut pale angles on the floor. Mother moved with a kind of practiced economy, setting the table with the same precise hands that folded vestments at the church, ironed sheets to a crisp perfection, wiped at stray specks of dust as though their presence was an offense to God Himself. She had not yet spoken more than a word or two, nodding to the open chair across from her as if I needed an invitation.

I had apologized, but only after a night spent twisting between sleep and something that gnawed at the edges of it, regret calcifying into something honest, something inescapable. She had received my words with a quiet that did not quite signal forgiveness, but neither did it cast me wholly beyond redemption. She had looked at me once, the morning light catching the sharp ridge of her cheekbone, and said simply, "Eat."

My organ lessons with Tom had been progressing well enough, measured in the slow, deliberate inches that marked all manner of mastery. He had a way of shaping my hands on the keys, adjusting the stops with the softest touch, his fingers feather-light but certain. There was a method to it, a language that existed beyond words, the press and pull of sound forming something close to understanding between us.

He would watch as I struggled, the tension in my fingers betraying the effort it took to make the thing look effortless, and he would offer a quiet correction, a suggestion rather than a command. "S-Slower," he would say, or, "Let the note sit j-just a second l-l-longer," and I would obey, because to do otherwise would feel like an insult to the music itself.

He had come to supper once, maybe twice, and Mother had received him with the kind of polite interest reserved for visiting clergy, offering up her stories of the parish in neat, measured portions. He listened well, nodding at all the right places, answering questions in that soft, deliberate way of his, as though he were tuning his words to the same careful pitch he used on the organ.

Tonight, Tom would be over for supper with us. On his last visit, he spoke of Notre Dame, of how his time spent in the cathedrals had shaped his hands into something useful, of Pennsylvania and the paths that had led him here, to Springfield, to this quiet parish where the Father had given him safe harbor. No family named. Nothing beyond the breadcrumbs one might leave if they meant never to be followed.

The man had the stillness of a person trained in restraint, his words weighted, held in suspension before release, as though they belonged first to God, and only second to himself. Tonight would mark his third appearance at our table, and with it, the quiet hope I harbored—that Mother, for once, might allow space for him to speak freely, to hear his opinion of my performance at the recital. I wanted to know his thoughts on my fingers' reach, the tone I drew from Bach's sorrow and Chopin's longing.

There were things he could tell me, if she'd only let the room breathe long enough for him to tell them. But Mother has never understood the silence necessary for revelation; she fills it instead, seizes the air with her own voice, her own view, and leaves the rest of us nodding like parishioners to a sermon that cannot be questioned.

Still, I watch him carefully. Not for politeness, not for duty, but with a sharpened interest. Because I know there is more to him than he allows. I've seen it in the way he carries himself in the doorway, not with the awkwardness of the shy, but the calculation of the once-wounded. There is a history behind his wire-framed glasses.

I believe myself a fair judge of character. And Tom is, by all appearances, kind. But I am certain he has come here not just for ministry or calling. He has arrived from elsewhere, carrying a past whose doors he's quietly closed. Not a killer, no, but a man who has stood close enough to ruin that it left a heat on his skin. And whatever it is he's run from, he has not come to confess it. Only to rest.

Father Schadenfreude had found him in Philadelphia, pulled him from some darkness Tom has not yet named, and set him here with the church's blessing. That was the story, or at least the version of it that was safe to share. There were surely debts somewhere in the telling, unpaid or unpayable, but Tom spoke only of the light that had found him, never the darkness that had preceded it. I had watched Mother nod along, her expression placid, her hands stilling on the table's edge when Tom mentioned the Father's name, her mouth pressing into a thin line that might have been disapproval, or understanding, or something in between.

At the recital, Tom had lingered at the back of the hall where the light was softest, where the sound of my playing could reach him without the weight of my gaze pinning him to the moment. He had clapped when it was done, that same slow, measured applause that made it seem as if he were listening not to the music itself, but to the silence that followed it, the space between notes where meaning was made.

"You p-played b-b-beautifully, Shirley," he'd said afterward, his voice low and warm, and Mother beamed as though she had played each note herself. I nodded, accepting the praise, because to deny it would be dishonest, because in that moment, I had felt something close to pride. I desperately wanted to know more. I wanted the good, the bad, the indifferent—whatever I needed to improve.

Tom has spoken of the Father often, his words always lined with a reverence that felt out of place on his tongue, as though he had borrowed someone else's faith and had yet to wear it in. He said the Father had come from Poland—that much was known—had suffered beneath the weight of war, had escaped with his life but not his family, had arrived here with nothing but his faith and the wounds that carved their stories across his skin. He had lived through fire and come out the other side, and Tom, in his quiet devotion, has fashioned him into something close to holy; yet still this unspoken fear. Mother eats it up. I, on the other hand, can't help but feel things just doesn't add up.

The morning stretched, time moving in slow ripples around us. The weight of what tonight's conversation might be is settling heavy in the air. With Earline off work today, Mother cleaned and organized the house with the same careful precision as she did all things, her silence measured and absolute. I could hear the clock in the hallway, its steady ticking marking the space between breaths, between thoughts.

It would be some time before I would understand the fullness of what had been set into motion, before I would come to see the fractures in the stories I had been told, the places where truth had been bent to fit into the shape of something more palatable.

And beneath it all, the quiet knowledge that between melody and silence, between faith and doubt, between truth and the fictions we tell ourselves to survive, there was a space where something else lived, something vast and unnameable, waiting to be heard.

TWELVE

WHAT A MAN OWES

Saturday, Third Week of August 1942

CALVIN JOHNSON HAD always carried himself with the quiet assurance of a man who understood the weight of his own hands, the worth of his labor. For twenty-five years, he had been the steady hand behind Dr. Herbert's prized Tennessee Walkers, those high-stepping, coal-black marvels that floated through the county fairs as if they had been spun from silk and sinew, God's own showpieces. He knew the temper of each, the mood and the mettle, how to read a horse by the set of its ears or the ripple along its flank, the way a man who's lived long enough learns to read the sky before a storm.

He was trusted, well paid, and loyal past what some folks might have considered wise. People talked. They always did. Springfield was a town where rumor curled through the streets like fog, slipping into parlors and barbershops, settling in the rafters of old men's recollections. They said Calvin's duties stretched beyond the stable, that he had a particular fondness for young Mrs. Herbert, and she for him, and that when Dr. Herbert traveled, as he often did, Calvin spent his nights in finer company than he ought to. But talk was talk, and Calvin had never been a man to waste breath setting folks straight.

Earline had muttered something once to Mun about his little brother Calvin loving that job like pear preserves on a hot buttered biscuit, and Mun had told her to hush before she said something she couldn't take back. It didn't matter what Calvin was up to at the Herbert house. What mattered was that a man in his position picked up things, things that could cut when turned the right way, things best left buried until the hour required them to surface.

When he came up the steps of Mun's porch that Wednesday, the air was thick with the smell of the stables, of sweat and saddle leather, horse dung and the damp rot of old hay. His boots scuffed the boards as he leaned against the railing, hat tipped low, the line of his mouth set firm.

"Evenin', Mun," Calvin said, voice slow as a creek running low in the heat of summer.

Mun looked up from where he sat, a rusty pocketknife turning over in his hands. "Evenin'. You got the look of a man with bad news and nowhere to put it."

Calvin let out a short breath, something close to a laugh but lacking any real humor. "Ain't much for sugarcoatin'. Got somethin' you need to hear."

Mun set the knife aside and leaned forward, elbows on his knees, his face unreadable. "Well, go on then. I got a long night ahead of me already."

Calvin glanced toward the road, making sure no ears were turned their way. He lowered his voice. "It's about Miss Trixie Simpson. Ora's cousin. Seems she's in a way. Got herself knocked up by Bo Harris."

Mun's expression didn't change, but something in his posture went tight, a man bracing against a blow. "You sure?"

Calvin nodded once, deliberate. "Ain't no mistake. Herbert's wife told it to me straight. And you know that woman don't open her mouth less she's got a reason."

Mun let out a slow breath through his nose, jaw tight. "Damn fool boy," he muttered. "Ain't that Harris boy runnin' around with Miss Shirley? You know, my boy Benji is sweet on that lil' white girl too. That'll tear him up. Gonna' make a mess of things."

"Well," Calvin said, shifting his weight, "ain't the first time somebody's got caught up where they ought not to be. Benji can figure it out. But this? This thing with the Harris boy is different. Ain't no way it stays quiet."

Silence stretched between them, the cicadas screaming from the trees, the boards beneath Mun's feet creaking as he shifted. He stared out at the yard, the light slanting low, the grass burning gold in the last of the sun. The weight of it settled in his chest, heavy as a storm about to break.

"You know what this means," he said finally. "Jim's gotta' hear about it. Ain't no way 'round it. A man gotta' figure that boy sniffin' up one skirt, he likely sniffin' up two."

Calvin's eyes met his, steady as river stone. "Figure you're the one to tell him. He'll take it better from you."

Mun nodded, rubbing a hand over his jaw, feeling the rough scrape of stubble, the bone-deep weariness of a man who knew trouble when it came knocking.

"Well," he said. "Best get it done, then."

Calvin straightened, pushing off the railing, his gaze still fixed on his brother. He had said what needed saying. The rest wasn't his to carry.

He tipped his hat, turned, and walked back down the steps, boots kicking up dust as he made his way down the road, the sun sinking behind him, the weight of it all left in Mun's hands.

TEMPTATION AND THE TRUTH

Sunday, Fourth Week of August 1942

THE PRIEST STOOD before us, hands folded over the lectern like a man gripping the rail of a ship listing in a slow, inevitable wreck. The congregation sat in neat, pious rows, backs straight against the wooden pews, the air thick with incense and the slow-baked reek of sweat. Not fresh from honest exertion, but sour, like old unwashed bedsheets sealed in a trunk—earthy, intimate, unclean—a damp, rank sweetness of flesh pushed beyond decency and hoping the Father hadn't noticed. Father Schadenfreude cleared his throat, the sound rasping through the quiet like a blade across a whetstone. His eyes swept the crowd, deep and dark, as though he were searching for something hidden, something lurking just beneath the flesh of the faithful.

"And how strange it is," he intoned, voice rolling over the pews, "that when faced with the divine, it is the dumb beast who understands, while the wise man falters."

He let the words settle like dust in an abandoned house.

Bo sat three rows back, his attention pulled between the gilded altar and the resonance of the priest's voice. His fingers twitched against the hem of his shirt, a nervous habit he never quite outgrew, and though his face was carved in the casual indifference he had mastered, I could see the storm in him. The struggle. A boy on the precipice of becoming something, though what, neither of us knew yet.

The story the priest told was a well-worn fable, the kind that held just enough absurdity to make you wonder if it was meant to be taken literally at all. Balaam and his mule, a beast that saw the angel before the man did, that opened its mouth and spoke wisdom where the wise man saw only empty road.

And yet, the man argued. The miracle was not enough to stop him. A creature of service rose up and named the truth, and still, he refused to see.

A lesson in humility, the priest said. A warning, a parable, a divine irony, a hand pressed firm against the shoulders of the arrogant, forcing them to bow. But my mind snagged on another thought, another lesson lingering at the edges of the story: the burden of seeing, the curse of knowledge, the way truth does not make the path easier but heavier, more treacherous.

I could feel my brow furrow at priest's theatrics as I stole a glance at Bo, whose presence sent my stomach into a flutter of nausea, of a particularly erratic and recurrent nature. He looked gruesomely handsome, God save me, but beneath his typical casual demeanor, I was over-the-moon happy to notice what looked a lot like turmoil, like a cow caught in the invisible vortex of a tornado.

The priest delivered this offensive bit as though it were the centerpiece of a Shakespearean drama, pausing for effect, his voice trembling with the effect of awe. Meanwhile, I was sitting there wondering why no one else seemed to be asking the obvious question: Why is Balaam arguing back? A donkey talks to you, and your first reaction isn't to faint or run or, I don't know, check what's in your canteen? It's to have a full-blown argument?

And here's Father Schadenfreude's grand takeaway: God uses the most unexpected voices to reach us. Sure. Fine. But if God has to resort to donkeys to deliver His message, doesn't that say something about the state of His audience? And honestly, why stop there? Why not pigeons or raccoons? Imagine a gospel according to houseplants: And lo, the ficus did say, "Stop overwatering me, thou fool." Bo exhaled slow but raucously through his nose. I could feel the weight of it from where I sat, and so could his mother who seemed to recognize the disrespectful tone of her son's exhalation from six pews away.

Father Schadenfreude turned his gaze to him then, sharp as the edge of a broken bottle, voice shifting from reverence to something closer to a threat. "Beware that which leads you astray. A man's choices follow him, even into the house of God."

A slow, creeping thing unfurled in my gut. The words were not meant for the whole of us, though they reached every ear. They were a knife honed for a single target.

The priest's voice took on the cadence of the old prophets, of the fire-and-brimstone preachers who carved fear into the marrow of the faithful, who wove shame like a tapestry and draped it across the shoulders of boys who had dared to look at the world and find it wanting.

I could see it working. Bo's jaw tightened, his hand clenched in his lap. I wanted to stand, to call the priest a liar, to tell the whole congregation that they were letting a wolf live among them. But my tongue was a stone in my mouth, and I was afraid.

This week has unraveled in strange, looping threads—a slow tumble into a kind of quiet chaos that hums beneath every breath. The joy of having Benji again, of his hands, his voice, and the familiar burn of wanting something forbidden and real. It all clashes with the dull throb of Bo, who lingers like a promise I never meant to make. My piano recital still lingers too, a high note struck days ago that hasn't quite faded, its echo trailing me like perfume: sharp and sweet and vaguely unreal.

Each of these things—Benji, Bo, the music—pulls at me for first dibs to my waking thoughts, jostling for shape and attention, as though I am more stage than self.

The fight with Mother left us both mutes. We pass each other like ghosts now, barely speaking, each convinced the other should be the first to fold. And threading through all of it are the quiet weights of the men who are gone. James, off in basic training, his letters fewer and thinner now, his name still warm in my mind but fading around the edges. And then the older boys—Raymond and Thomas—cast out into whatever corner of the world this war has flung them, their voices still hanging in these walls like old wallpaper. Both were married before I was born, so are more like cousins than brothers. I care, of course—just not as deeply as my feelings for James. He still lived at home when I was born and spoiled me like a proper big brother.

Mother flinches at every radio broadcast, jumps at the mail slot, spills flour on the counter when their names are spoken. She tries to fold their absence into the rhythm of her days, but she's always offbeat, always catching breath like grief is a thing that might knock on our screen door at any second.

Nothing feels settled. Not the house, not the town, not the sky. The trees seem to lean a little heavier and the moss a little lower, as if they too are waiting for news. Even the wind feels nervous, like it doesn't know which way to turn.

I thought I might cry when James' pitiful wife Sally and their adorable daughter Suzanne drove away yesterday, headed to her parents' place in Shelbyville. But I didn't. I just stood there like a fence post, the hem of my dress snapping in the dust her truck kicked up. She hadn't said it plain, but we all understood— this wasn't a visit. This was her saying goodbye until the war gave her back a husband. If it gave her one at all. None of us knew when we'd see each other next. Maybe it would be when James came home in a box.

What does it say about me, I wonder, that I couldn't cry, even then? Does it make me heartless, or just hollowed out from trying too long to feel the proper thing at the proper time? It seems the whole world has misplaced its compass, and we're all just standing around pretending we know where we're going.

And then there's Bo—with his stupid smile and all his devilish charm—who hasn't spoken more than ten words to me in almost two weeks, not since I told him off. He just stares at me like I'm some kinda' dingbat that did him wrong. I told myself I'd never speak to him again, not because I hate him but because I hate the way he makes me feel: small, unsure, like a child playing dress-up in a grown woman's life.

A girl needs someone she can trust, doesn't she? Someone like Benji who stands beside her when the days are heavy, when the world's a mess of war and whispered prayers. Benji's there for me with the risk of a rope around his neck. That's Benji's kinda' loyalty. Bo proved he isn't that same kinda' someone. Not for me.

And yet, if he were to show up right now, or even tomorrow, some part of me—some soft, stupid part— might still let him in. Isn't that the trouble with boys like Bo? They leave you feeling bruised but hopeful, as though next time will be different, even when you know it won't.

While the world requires me to hide Benji, and Benji to hide me, Bo could really be my beau. Or maybe beaux, yes, *Les beaux que tu connais* ... The handsome one that you know about; a much better description.

I broke away from my drifting reverie just as the Father's voice stumbled to a halt, the tale of Balaam and his talking mule delivered with such sweat-slick conviction you'd have thought that the lathered-up donkey was seated among us. The congregation coughed itself awake in that curious hush that follows holy absurdity, hymnals fluttering closed like startled birds. Sunlight had shifted down the aisle, dust rising like incense in its path, and the day, despite the sermon's strangest intentions, moved forward all the same.

Afterward, Bo disappeared into the depths of the church, moving like a man led to the gallows, and I followed. Not closely. Not enough to be seen. But I needed to know where he was going, what was being said in those darkened corridors beyond the altar where the priest whispered his true sermons.

I caught pieces of it, enough to feel the wrongness, the sickness at the core of it. The priest's voice, smooth, coaxing, full of a certainty that smelled of rot. "She is a distraction. A temptation that will drag you down from the light to the bed of a whore. You are meant for something greater than a girl who will never understand the burden you carry. You do not need her. You do not want her."

Then Bo, his voice cracked open with rage. "You don't want what's best for me, Father. You just want me. You're sick! Don't you ever say that about Shirley, never again, you hear me?"

The silence that followed was thick and waiting. A blade held just above the skin, trembling, ready to fall.

Then footsteps. The heavy tread of Bo, his breath ragged, his body carrying the storm he had held back for too long. He came out of the room like a shot fired from a rifle, and I pressed myself against the cool stone wall, heart hammering. He did not see me. He did not see anything but the path ahead, and whatever lay at the end of it.

The priest followed slower, composed, his hands still folded, but something in his eyes told me the battle had been lost. The war, perhaps, was still to be decided.

I did not know then what I knew now—what I should have known the moment I read the sermon notes, saw the heavy hand that had pressed ink into the page with more force than necessary, the tension behind every word that spoke of control not freely given but wrestled from the bones of the unwilling. I did not know what made my stomach churn as I watched him smooth his robes and place a hand on the shoulder of Tom Walker, who had lingered too long in the wrong places, had heard too much without knowing how to carry it.

I only knew that Bo had spoken the truth in a room where truth was not welcome, and he had come out of it shaken but whole, while the priest remained inside, still smiling, still preaching, still waiting for the next boy, weakened by a world of contradictory rules, to walk through his godless door.

I stood in the hallway a long time, listening to the echoes of voices beyond the sanctuary, to the murmur of prayers and the shuffle of feet. The congregation moved like sleepwalkers, unaware, untouched.

And I thought of Balaam. I thought of the mule, the burden of sight, the weight of knowledge.

The punishment for seeing was always the same.

The world would call you a beast.

The world would silence you.

The only question was whether you would let them.

THE CHAPEL AT DUSK

Sunday Evening, Fourth Week of August 1942

THE AIR INSIDE St. Cecilia's bore the weight of old hymns and unspoken confessions, thick as incense, stale as regret. The walls, the vaulted ceiling, the quiet presence of all things holy—none of it moved, none of it breathed. Not anymore. The hush had settled too deep, as if even the stones knew to listen.

It was late. Hours past the sermon, past the murmured *Amens* and the scraping shuffle of departing parishioners. Mother had pulled me along under the guise of work, but work was a flimsy excuse. We both knew what we sought. Something more than duty, something neither of us would name.

I had snuck off to spend some time with Benji after the morning service, still in my uniform skirt. Mother doesn't allow me to wear pants, says pants are for white trash girls. Oh, how I want to be a white trash girl—maybe now I am.

After getting my emotional batteries charged, my equilibrium balanced by Benji's unbridled and uncensored affection, I returned to my home and helped Mother can a bushel of green beans. Afterwards she asked if I would walk with her to the parish. She had work to do and it was getting dark, so I agreed.

We walked the path from home to chapel as the sun folded itself into the hills, the last gold light pouring through the stained glass, igniting the saints in fire and blood.

Inside, Mother disappeared into her office, ledger-bound, her fingers quick, precise. I left her to it and let my feet guide me elsewhere, past the pews, past the heavy scent of wax and dust. Something old called to me, something buried in forgotten corners. I found it in the apocryphal Acts of Peter, bound in cracked leather, its Latin curling up like chimney smoke across the brittle pages. A relic of a lesson from school, a language I had once struggled with, but one that now spoke to me in whispers only I could hear.

Yet my eyes did not stay on the text. They drifted. They caught movement at the altar.

Father Schadenfreude. A name that clung to the tongue like damp cloth dipped in vinegar. He stood before the chalice, the paten, the plate of the holy host. But something in his movements betrayed him. The meticulous care, the trembling fingers, the weight in his hands—each piece of silver might as well have been lead. His lips moved, but not in prayer.

A noise. Small, but sharp.

The priest stiffened. The host slipped from his grasp and scattered in a dry hush against the stone floor. He turned, quick as a startled beast, his gaze locked on the confessional booth. The curtain stirred—not a gust, not a draft. Someone had passed through.

He swallowed hard, the column of his throat shifting, his Adam's apple bobbing like a buoy in stormy waters, his very own Judas, informing a vulnerability never revealed to the congregation.

I saw it then, the truth of him. Not the towering figure of righteous sermon, but something else. Something frayed. The man beneath the robes. I, ever the observant one, rose to my feet, my school uniform skirt rustling softly as I moved toward him, fueled by a mix of mischief and intrigue. Enjoying the way the silence stretched tight between us.

"*Quo vadis*, Father?" (Cool, amused). The words fell easy from my lips—crisp Latin, deliberate. A knife slid between ribs. My voice flowed calm and measured, though underpinned with just enough sharpness to indicate that I was playing a game of my own design, one whose rules only I seemed to comprehend. With that, the dance between us began, two souls locked in a brief, delicate tension, under the watchful gaze of the sacred and the profane. He had insulted me in his sermon; now it was my turn.

Father Schadenfreude blinked, his face went pale.

"I—excuse me?"

I let my head tilt, let my lips curl just enough to unsettle. "*Quo vadis?* Where are you going?"

The grip on the chalice tightened. A beat of silence. A frayed breath. He forced a chuckle, but it landed wrong, thin and reedy in the cavern of the church. It was my turn to put him in his place, a female, just fifteen. The trapped priest forces another strained snicker, attempting to gather himself, but his fingers tighten more zealously around the chalice, too hard, his knuckles whitening.

"Or should I say—" I leaned in, voice dipping to a whisper, soft as a prayer, cruel as revelation. "Exit stage left?"

Something broke in his gaze.

My work was done. I let the moment hold, then turned, my footsteps echoing as I left him there, clutching the altar as if it alone could keep him upright. But I did not leave. Not entirely. I lingered at the edges, waiting. Watching. There was something here, something deliciously wrong. And I meant to find it.

Father Schadenfreude's breath hitched. He clutched the edge of the altar, his gaze darting once more toward the confessional, then to the heavy oak doors at the back of the chapel.

I caught it; that look of confusion on his face. I no longer need a confession to know. Something, or someone, is hiding in that booth. And whatever it is, it has Father Schadenfreude scared senseless.

I decided to let the moment hang, then I gave him a knowing wink before turning on my heels and strolling toward the door, leaving the priest rooted in place, still clutching the altar as if it was the only thing keeping him upright.

But behind me, the silence of the chapel felt heavier than it should.

Something was terribly, deliciously wrong. And I was going to find out exactly what it was.

The chapel was too quiet, the kind of hush that carries weight, like a held breath before a confession that might damn the penitent.

I took my time. I felt no rush, only excitement.

Father Schadenfreude, however, looked like a man who very much wishes time would speed up and carry him far, far away.

I allowed the tension to sit, marinate like a Sunday roast, before strolling toward the confessional with the ease of someone inspecting the frescoes.

Allowing my fingers to trail along the edge of the curtain, pausing just slightly before I gave it a gentle, almost lazy tug.

Tom Walker was not what I expected.

I pulled the confessional curtain back, slow as peeling skin, and there he sat. The esteemed organist of St. Cecilia's. Not in his vestments, not in the pressed solemnity of his Sunday best. No. Boxers, cherub-patterned. An undershirt clinging damp to his overstuffed chest. Black socks stretched to his knees. And beside him, a half-emptied bottle of altar wine.

The silence ripened between us. Then, his mouth opened, worked, failed to find footing.

"S-S-Shirley?"

His voice wavered.

I smiled.

"Oh, Tom," I sighed, like we were old friends catching up over coffee, like I hadn't just caught him drunk and bare-legged in the house of God. My gaze flicked to the discarded choir robe, to the bottle, then back to him.

He stammered something useless. "I—This is n-n-not—I wasn't—" A hoarse, panicked whisper fumbled from his lips. I let him drown in it. I gave him a nod, then looked over to the priest, as if he had just confirmed something very important.

"Oh, of course, Tom. I mean, it would be silly to think that the esteemed organist of St. Cecilia's, a man of great musical discipline, whose posture at the keys is always so precise, would simply abandon the dress code entirely when it came to private practice."

"The w-w-wine…, f-for c-circulation?"

I mused, when he finally cobbled together an excuse. "How reassuring. Shall I let Mother know? Perhaps the congregation would benefit."

His skin burned red.

"And the undress? Is this an advanced technique? A method you forgot to include in my lessons?"

Tom closed his eyes, briefly contemplating whether or not he was already in purgatory.

I turned toward the Father, slow and deliberate, taking in his ashen complexion.

"Oh—Father," gesturing vaguely at Tom, as if only now remembering that this might be worth comment. "Shouldn't you… say something?"

Father Schadenfreude had not moved. He watched from the altar, the chalice still clutched in his hands. But something in his face had changed. Not the weight of scandal, not the simmer of suppressed rage. No.

Relief.

A different fear had been gripping him. And this, this sorry display, was not it.

The priest met my gaze, and I knew. Whatever haunted him, whatever had drawn his hand to tremble over the sacraments, had nothing to do with Tom Walker.

And I had missed it.

I knew that look. It was not the *Oh dear, my organist is a scandalous fool* look.

It was the *This isn't what I was afraid of* look.

Which means—

I allow the moment to settle between them before offering him a smile, gentle and curious.

"Father, are you familiar with *Mundus vult decipi*?" I say softly, as if I've just remembered something.

Father Schadenfreude's breathing stutters.

I wait, giving him every opportunity to pretend he doesn't recognize the phrase, to lie to me in his own house of worship.

He doesn't take it.

His throat works painfully, but his voice, when it finally forces itself free, is hollow.

"The world... wants to be deceived," Father Schadenfreude mutters, barely above a whisper.

I offer an approving nod. "Exactly. And I suppose that's true."

My gaze flickers, just for a second, back toward the confessional booth.

"But every now and then," I gently add in higher octaves, "someone decides to open the curtain."

I let the moment linger. I let it stretch long and thin, until Tom's breath turns shallow, until Father Schadenfreude's fingers loosen around the cup. Then I leave them to their separate shames, slipping back into the dark belly of the church, where answers wait in silence.

I do not go far. The stairwell is cold beneath my fingers as I climb, pressing myself into the narrow alcove above the nave, where the pipes of the organ loom like ribs. I crouch low, unseen, watching.

Tom leaves, shooting some sort of curious look toward the Father. His shoes clap against the stone floor, his shoulders hunched in shame. The priest barely spares him a glance. He waits. He paces. And then he moves.

He slips behind the altar, to the vestment storage. A place rarely used.

A clink of glass.

Then he emerges, his collar unbuttoned, a crystal tumbler in hand. Amber liquid swirls in the dim light.

I exhale slowly, the weight of the question coiling behind my teeth, never spoken but sharp all the same. *Drinking on church property, Father? How very Protestant of you.*

He throws back the whiskey in one swallow. A bitter laugh. Then, to no one in particular, "You watch everything, don't you? Every miserable second of it!"

He lets out a breath. Stares up at the ceiling, the great stretch of stone and silence.

"I wonder if you enjoy this—watching me clean up messes that aren't mine, pretending that I believe in redemption."

I almost pity him.

Almost.

Then the chapel doors creak open, and the pity vanishes.

Mrs. Dolores Hardwick. Widow. Catholic to her bones. A woman who sharpens her faith like a blade. She moves without hesitation, straight to the altar, and Father Schadenfreude pours her a drink without a word.

Not scandal. Not crime. Just hypocrisy, plain and stinking.

I am ready to leave. Until I see it.

That look. The one Tom had given him.

I haven't placed it before—had chalked it up to curiosity, maybe even respect. But it comes back to me now, clear as candlelight on polished brass. The way his eyes linger too long. The way his mouth stays parted just enough, like he is weighing something unholy in his cheek. Not reverence. Not admiration. Not guilt. Something else.

Something hungry. Something depraved.

And in that moment, I know.

Father Schadenfreude is not my biggest concern.

Tom Walker is.

And there are bigger mysteries waiting, houses that need burning down.

THIRTEEN

UNDER THE WEIGHT OF UNSPOKEN RULES

Monday, Fourth Week of August 1942

THE WEEK THAT followed, I held the knowledge of Bo's severed tether to the priest like a hand cupped over a candle, sheltering its flickering light from errant winds. Relief, muted and cautious, settled into the corners of my mind. He was safe. And yet safety was a mercurial thing, a phantom that vanished at the moment of pursuit. I had no certainty of what remained between him and me, of what terrain we might still share. That was a question I had yet to ask, and an answer I dreaded to receive.

The days stretched on in their predictable rhythms, the mechanical churn of small-town life: school, organ and piano lessons, Latin Club, the endless cycle of routine that only later, with time's cruel hindsight, reveals itself as the architecture of memory. I did not speak of the priest's proclivities, not to Bo, not to anyone, but in my quiet moments I imagined him still, imagined his reach even now extending beyond what had been severed.

That Bo had been securely placed in his hands, his parents fastening their trust to a man who cloaked his appetites in reverence, remained an unbearable thought. Had Bo been different, had he not been the boy he was, the boy who could not be bent or broken, I had no doubt that he would have been lost to unspeakable sins. The calculation of that horror stayed with me like a slow poison in the blood.

And then there was reliably perfect Benji Johnson, his presence slipping back into my life like a song half-remembered, a thing that had always belonged but had been absent long enough to feel brand new and excitingly unfamiliar. With him came a peace that I had not known I was missing, the quiet assurance of someone who had nothing to take from me, nothing to gain. And with that peace, I found myself softening toward Bo once more, though whether out of habit or desire, I could not yet say. He had begun walking me home again, the return of an old ritual, one that carried the ghosts of other walks, of other times, of secrets and betrayals, of a past I was loath to put much thought into.

I had not expected to want him back, not in the way I had before, but rather in the way one tolerates a thing that has been part of them for too long to cast aside, a dog that barks too loud but nestles warm at the foot of the bed, a broken chair that still holds its shape when sat upon. And there he was, waiting beneath the oak at the edge of the schoolhouse, as he always had, as if nothing had changed at all.

Bo doesn't go to Our Lady. Never did. He belongs to the public school—the one with rust on the lockers and gum under every desk. The one where kids eat lunch out of paper sacks and nobody prays before arithmetic. His parents couldn't afford parochial, not even close. The divide's not written down, but *tuition* is a word of French origin we all know.

Still, he waits for me outside the limestone steps, hangs back like he's got business nearby, though he doesn't. Sometimes Lynch walks past on his way to the rectory, eyes cutting sideways, like Bo's presence is a stain on the brick.

There are questions. I carry them like coins in my purse, worn smooth from turning. Things I've seen. Glances that lasted too long. Words spoken in tones that didn't match their shape. The way Father Schadenfreude watches Bo at Mass, like a man weighing a threat. The way Bo watches back, unblinking. But I don't ask. I never do.

We took the long route home. Bo's idea, though he let me pretend it was mine. The sun stretched low, the kind of gold that makes even the gravel look forgiving. I hoped to get him to open up, to let me in on the thing that makes him mute.

He walked beside me, close but not touching, satchel slung like he was in a picture of someone who's sure of where he is going.

"Father Lynch is the worst," he said, right as we passed the general store, not looking at me. "If he pulls my ear one more time, I swear I'll—"

I squinted at him. "What?" I teased. "Tell him to stop? Oh Lord, I'd pay good money to see that."

He let out a sharp, barking laugh. "I was gonna' say I'll run off and join the circus. But yeah, maybe I'll just tell him to stop. Might hurt less."

His fingers found his ear without him knowing it. There was no bruise, but that didn't mean it isn't tender.

At St. Cecilia's they all share one pew and one priest. Springfield's too small for a second opinion. It's at Sunday school where Lynch gets hold of him. Not often. Just enough to make a boy flinch when someone lifts a hand too quick.

Father Lynch, assistant priest to Father Schadenfreude, is the one we kids fear the most. All collar and quiet rage, the sort of man who sees a crooked nail and doesn't hesitate to hammer it straight, even if it ain't his fence. A sledgehammer in vestments. A *Sargent-at-Arms* with a rosary. Which makes him perfect for headmaster at a school built on guilt and discipline.

Bo grinned, rubbing his ear like a habit.

"He likes you, you know," I said, half-smirking.

"Yeah, well," Bo muttered, "he's got a real funny way of showin' it."

I laughed—it was real, but it came from somewhere a little off-center. My ponytail brushed against my back as I walked, and for a moment the rhythm felt easy. Familiar. Bo's always had that way—pulling the laughter from me when everything else felt too quiet.

And still, I don't ask.

At Our Lady, Ruthie Mae could make anyone laugh, but not when she tried. Just that morning, she had raised her hand during arithmetic and asked, "If two trains leave the station at the same time, how does anyone know which one's happier?" The class had erupted while Lynch turned the color of a boiled beet.

Then there was Bessie Jane, who had a face so serious it could sour milk, who claimed she had a pet raccoon named Whiskers that could play the harmonica, though no one had ever seen it. Ruthie Mae swore it was a lie, that raccoons didn't have lips, and the resulting argument had nearly landed them both in the corner.

I told Bo everything—every lopsided tale, every word Ruthie Mae ever twisted into a sermon, every look she'd given that could slice the knees off a grown man. The stories tumbled out fast, reckless, like I had to empty them before the spell broke. Bo had seen her at church, of course, but he didn't really know her. As I repeated her absurdities with all the animation of an automaton, he watched and listened close, head tilted like he was memorizing the shape and timbre of my voice.

And when he finally tried his hand at her—chin tucked, lips pursed, brows knitted in righteous indignation—Lord help me, it was her. Or close enough to drop me where I stood. I doubled over, wheezing, holding my sides like something might split. It wasn't Ruthie Mae he'd drawn from, not really. It was me—my retellings, my rhythm, my tilted lens.

For that breathless moment, it was enough. The shadows stayed quiet. The past and all its dark corridors held its tongue.

We reached the corner of Elm and Third, the place where he always stopped, where I always continued. A quiet understanding. But I had led him here with purpose, and now I wanted the thing I had baited.

"Bo," I said, careful, slow. "I hate to speak ill of anyone, but that Tom Walker, my organ teacher, there's something about him. I don't know what it is, but it sets my nerves wrong."

Bo's expression flickered, a thing unspoken shifting behind his eyes. "I hear you, Shirley," he said, voice measured. "It's just... he has a way of getting into your head, doesn't he? I can't quite put my finger on it either. But let's not dwell on it too much."

"Bo." I stopped walking, forcing him to turn back to me. "I saw him yesterday. In the church. He was watching you. Watching you and Father Schadenfreude. He was angry. He looked like he was going to come in."

Bo stilled. A moment stretched between us, taut as a wire. Then, his voice, low and edged. "You shouldn't eavesdrop on things that don't concern you."

Anger flashed through me, hot and sudden. "You don't get to say that. Not to me. Not after—" I wanted to govern my contempt, but I couldn't. "If the Father tells you that *'nothing but a distraction. A temptation that will drag you down from the light to the bed of a whore,'* then I would think it does concern me.

He exhaled sharply, rubbing the back of his neck. "It's nothing, Shirley."

"It's not nothing. You don't even know what I had to suffer. You don't know because you weren't there. My best friend in the world saw us, saw the whole thing. And he confronted me about it while you were doing whatever it was you wanted to do besides being with me."

He looked at me then, really looked at me, and for a moment, I thought he might show me something besides indifference, or tell me the truth about something. But then the walls went up again, the practiced mask of nonchalance sliding into place. "I'm late for home," he said. "We'll talk later."

"Bo—"

He hesitated, his weight shifting from foot to foot, an unspoken thought balanced between action and retreat. And then, as if making some final, silent decision, he turned.

I watched him go, the last light of the afternoon catching in his hair. I stood there long after he had disappeared from view, the unanswered questions pressing against me like a thing alive.

When I turned for home, I did so with the knowledge that something had shifted between us. And in the days to come, that knowledge would press closer, closer still, until at last, I could no longer turn away.

*

SHIRLEY PEELED THE LAST potato, her fingers slick with starch, the peels curling in damp ribbons at the edge of the sink. Her mother had left strict instructions: dinner at six sharp, the clothes on the line before dusk, the floors swept before she returned.

The window above the sink was open, and she could hear the cicadas droning for mates in the trees, the rise and fall of their song like something ancient and eternal. A breeze moved through the kitchen, stirring the lace curtains, lifting the hair at the nape of her neck. She let her eyes close for a moment, just a moment, before she straightened and reached for the colander, letting the water run cold over the peeled potatoes, the smell of earth and root filling the small space.

Outside, the sun was engulfed by thick clouds, dropping lower to the horizon. The clothesline strained tight between two trees, the damp linens shuddering in the sporadic winds, snapping like the sails of a boat. Shirley moved with the rhythm of policy, the wooden clothespins smooth in her hands, the laundry basket pressing against her hip. Her mother would inspect her work later, pursing her lips in that way she did, never outright scolding, just letting the silence stretch longer than necessary.

She was reaching for the last sheet when she felt him before she saw him. A presence at the edge of her vision, something pulling her attention like a magnet grasping at iron.

Behind the garage apartment, where the afternoon light could not quite reach, Benji waited. His form half-obscured by the angle of the building, but unmistakable. She didn't turn immediately. Didn't want to seem too eager, too obvious. Instead, she pinned the last sheet, smoothed the fabric between her fingers, felt the heat of her pulse in her wrists.

And then she went to him.

He pulled her close the moment she was within reach, arms wrapping around her like he could somehow press the two whole days spent apart into nonexistence. His mouth found hers, insistent, desperate, the kind of kiss that stole both breath and reason, that made the world narrow to just this: his body against hers, his hands mapping familiar territory.

She knew the risk. Knew that at any moment, someone could pass by, that a neighbor could glance out a window, that his own mother Earline could step onto the porch, broom in hand. But none of that stopped her from melting into him, from clutching the back of his shirt to anchor herself.

He pulled away first, just enough to look at her, his eyes dark, intensely brown, his voice low. "I couldn't wait. Not another day."

She swallowed, still breathless.

"Benji, we can't—"

"I don't care. I haven't seen you in two days. You know how long that is? It's too long."

"You're being reckless. My mother—"

"Isn't here."

She exhaled sharply, glancing toward the house, then back to him. "You need to be gone before she gets back."

He grinned, the mischief in it something that both thrilled and unsettled her. "Then let's go inside. Where no one can see."

She hesitated only a second before taking his hand, fingers tightening in that way that meant her resolve had already collapsed. They slipped through the side door of the garage, past the old tool bench and the shelves still cluttered with her father's jars of rusted bolts and paint can lids. The stairs creaked beneath their feet, wood swollen with summer damp.

Above the garage sat the apartment her parents had built when the house was too full of children and not enough walls. It had been meant for Thomas, the eldest, who'd grown too large and too proud for bunk beds and brotherly squabbles. Later, once he'd married and moved to Nashville, it had become a rental—extra money for the Raglands, a tidy little place for transients and temporary folk.

The last tenant, Mr. Lancashire, an insurance adjuster from Life & Casualty, had stayed for two months while he catalogued storm damage from the early June squalls. Three weeks ago, he packed up, left behind only a mug in the sink and a calendar turned to July. A place that had been empty for weeks, yet now felt charged, humming with something alive.

The air was thick with heat, the stale kind that settles when doors stay shut too long. Dust curled in the corners, sun pressing through the gauzy curtains like breath held too long. The bed was there, the small table, the counter with its single cooking eye, the tiny bathroom tucked into the corner.

She sat on the bed, and he sat beside her, and then there was no space between them, no hesitation. Hands finding skin, lips parting with words half-formed, swallowed by urgency. The clamor of clothes and shoes hitting the floor. In those hallowed moments, however impulsive and reckless, the world outside ceased to exist. Time unraveled, minutes stretching, folding in on themselves until nothing mattered except this. The shape of him beneath her fingertips, the taste of him on her tongue, the way his breath hitched when she whispered his name.

Later, when the air cooled and their bodies were tangled, limbs heavy, breaths slowing, she turned to him, pressing her forehead against his shoulder. "Benji, I..."

He ran a hand down her bare back, slow, lazy. "What is it?"

She hesitated. The words sat heavy on her tongue, thick with something she couldn't coax out of her mouth. "I haven't been feeling quite right."

He stilled. "What do you mean?"

"I've been sick. In the mornings."

The silence stretched, too taut, too loud. His fingers tightened against her skin. "Shirley… my oh my."

"I think, I think I might be—" She couldn't say the word. Wouldn't let herself.

He sat up, dragging a hand through his hair. "Are you sure? And you still—today—even though…"

"No, I don't know. I didn't say before because you were so excited. I didn't want to ruin our time. I just— I keep thinking about it. I can't stop thinking about it. What if I have your baby?"

His jaw clenched. He looked away, out the window where the last light of the day bled into the horizon. "It could be Bo's."

The words hung between them, heavy and undeniable. She knew that was what he wanted to believe. What he needed to believe. But the doubt was there, in the space between his words, in the way his hands had curled into fists.

She reached for him, pressing her palm against his cheek, forcing him to look at her. "No matter what happens, I won't lose you again. Even if we have to move away."

He exhaled, long and slow, then covered her hand with his own. "I don't want to lose you either."

She closed her eyes, allowing herself to sink into the warmth of him, the steady rise and fall of his breath. But beneath it all, beneath the quiet comfort of his touch, the fear remained. A thing uncertain, waiting. An inevitability that neither of them could yet see, but that loomed just beyond the edge of this moment, coiled and patient, biding its time.

WHAT THE RIVER CARRIES

Monday, Fourth Week of August 1942

EARLINE'S SUSPICIONS BEGAN weeks ago, as these things often do, with small signs. A shift in the weight of fabric as she lifted Shirley's dress from the washbin, damp cotton heavier than it should be, like it held more than water. A grass stain along the hem, deep and stubborn. Red dirt smudged into the weave, not the kind that comes from an accidental brushing against a porch step, but the kind that speaks of time spent low to the ground, of knees pressed into earth, of hands bracing against soil as the body above them moves.

Earline turned the dress in her hands. She was not a woman given to illusions. A child who lays in the grass daydreaming does not wear the kind of stains that refuse the washboard, that seep into the seams. The knowing was a slow thing, creeping up on her like a sickness, revealing itself in pieces: the way Shirley's eyes lingered out the window toward the forest, the hurried smoothing of her skirts when she thought no one was watching, the slight bloom in her cheeks that hadn't been there before.

She did not speak of it. Not yet. She held it inside her like a stone in the belly. But then came the final proof, irrefutable, laid bare in a soiled wisp of silken cloth, Shirley's undergarment; she had no wish to examine but could not ignore. The ruin of innocence, proof of the threshold Shirley had crossed, and the only name that could be spoken in its wake: Bo Harris.

Earline sat with the knowledge a long time before she spoke it aloud, because once it left her lips it would be real in a way that could not be undone. After supper, when the dishes were dried and stacked, she turned to Mun, who had settled into his chair with the weight of a man who had done an honest day's work and was looking for nothing more than a quiet end to it.

"Mun," she said, her voice not the voice of a woman settling into the night. "I'm worried about Miss Shirley."

Mun shifted, looking at her over his glasses. "What about?"

"Bo Harris been sniffin' round her. And I don't think it stopped at sniffin'."

His mouth set in a line, the way it always did when trouble came knocking. "What you talkin' bout, Earline?"

She told him. The laundry, the stains, the look in Shirley's eyes. The small things, the big things, the things she had not wanted to know but knew all the same. He listened in silence, jaw tight, hands clasped over his belly. When she was done, he sighed, long and slow.

"You reckon Jim oughta know?"

"He need to know," she said with a raised voice. "But it ain't gonna be me tellin' him. That's yo job, Mun Johnson. He yo best friend."

Mun nodded, pressing his palms against his knees. "I'll talk to him tomorrow."

But tomorrow came and went, and so did another. And then, without fanfare, without any great revelation beyond the steady ticking of days, Shirley missed her monthlies.

Earline knew before Shirley did. She kept track the way she kept track of everything, in the quiet accounting of a woman who measures the world by its patterns. One week passed. Now two. No sign. No sign at all.

She waited until the house was still that night, until Mun had set his pipe down and the clock had struck past a decent hour. Then she turned to him, voice low. "Mun, she's with child. I'm sure of it."

Mun rubbed his hands over his face, slow, as if he could wipe away what she'd just said. "Lord help us," he muttered. "Jim's gonna lose his goddamn mind."

"He need to know," she said again, and this time her voice left no room for argument. "Better he hear it from you than find out some other way."

Mun nodded, but there was no ease in his agreement. Jim Ragland was a hard man. He had been shaped by the land he worked and the weight of expectations pressed into his bones from the day he was born. And Shirley, Shirley had always been wild. Wild in a way that didn't know fences, that didn't understand lines, that didn't see laws, or race, or consequences. It had been bound to happen.

Earline sighed, and there was something in the sound that was more than exhaustion, more than frustration. "I always knew she was too wild for this little town," she said, more to herself than to Mun. "That child been interested in boys since she was five years old. You know what I had to do with Benji. You remember what I caught that child doin' to him, don't you?"

Mun's face darkened. "Now, Earline, don't go bringin' that up again. That was the two of them, not just Miss Shirley. That boy of yours, he ain't no saint. He's a boy, same as any other, with urges same as any other. And Shirley, she do got the devil in her, just a little, but it's there. Like her daddy. She don't see the walls 'round her. She don't see nothin' that tells her no." He paused. "But Benji. He like his daddy, too. He sniff of something that smell good, that boy gonna take a bite if he get a chance."

Mun laughed, shook his head like a man remembering the heat of his own youth. But Earline was not laughing. Her face was set in something close to anger, but deeper. Closer to sorrow.

"Maybe you right about that," she said. "But I'll tell you one thing, I'm just glad it's that white boy sniffin' 'round her and not our boy. 'Cause you know exactly what would happen if it was. That reckless, lawless little girl be on Benji like a hair stuck in a biscuit, and then what? Then what happens?"

But it wasn't about Benji. It was about Shirley, and what had already happened. It was about the road she had stepped onto without knowing where it led, and the weight of it, the way it would follow her for the rest of her life, whether she understood that yet or not.

Earline stood, hands gripping the edges of the washbasin, and looked out the window. The dark stretched out beyond the glass, silent and endless. She thought of Shirley, of the child she had watched grow, the girl she had scolded and protected in equal measure. She thought of the world and the way it closed its teeth around a girl like that, a girl who did not see fences. A girl who ran too fast and laughed too loud and never thought the things she wanted could be denied her.

She had wanted to protect her. She had wanted to shield her from the weight of knowing. But knowing had come, all the same. It always did.

She was not Shirley's mother. But she had raised her, in all the ways that counted. And she would not let her stand alone now.

The road ahead was steep. Earline did not know if Shirley would find footing or if she would tumble, arms flailing, into something she could not escape. But there was one thing she did know.

She would be there. Same as she had always been. Same as she always would be.

FOURTEEN

THE RECKONING

Tuesday, Fourth Week of August 1942

THE WOODEN CRUCIFIX above the chalkboard hung crooked, skewed to the right as though burdened beyond its design, as though Christ himself had leaned just so, whispering some terrible secret into the ear of the world. The thing had been that way for weeks. Maybe months. No one had fixed it. Shirley sat beneath its gaze, her fingers curled loose around a pencil, the edges of her notebook smudged from the oil in her skin. The heat pressed heavy through the schoolhouse windows, syrup-thick, the scent of sun-warmed dust and scorched ink curling through the air like some silent, creeping thing.

Sister Lytle's chalk scratched sharp against the board, a sound like bones crushing under a cart's wheel.

Mens sana in corpore sano.

Shirley's lips moved in silent translation. "A sound mind in a sound body." A fine thing to aspire to, if a person had been built for it. But she had never been built for symmetry. She was loose at the seams, a thing cobbled together out of borrowed cloth, pressed at the corners where she did not quite fit.

She snickered at her thoughts. The irony of this particular Latin maxim was not lost on the precocious student, nor, she imagined, on the rest of her classmates, though none dared laugh outright. Not while Sister Lytle stood guard at the head of the class, her knuckles tight against the edge of the podium, her sharp eyes slicing through their uniforms, their polished Mary Janes, their hastily scribbled notes.

The bell rang, a shrill, iron-throated wail that split the air like an old wound reopened; chairs scraped the floor, a sea of adolescence in a flurry of plaid skirts murmured their goodbyes. Shirley rose slow from her desk, bag slung over her shoulder, head bent in the quiet pretense of study. But Bridgette was already there, sidling up beside her, close enough that their skirts brushed in passing.

"You hear what that little weasel Prentice Bunson's been sayin'?" Bridgette's voice was low, sly. Her mouth curled like she already knew the answer. "Says you been spreadin' your legs for Bo Harris behind the shed like some barn cat in heat."

Shirley did not flinch. Did not betray the heat rising slow beneath her collar. "Bunson oughta worry less about me and more about that pimple farm on his forehead and his mama's lazy eye."

Bridgette grinned. "Ain't stopped him from runnin' his mouth, though. Said Bo told the boys he's got you right where he wants you. That you're sweet on him. That you don't make him work too hard for it."

Shirley's stomach turned. Not sudden. Not sharp. Just a slow, sick roil, a thing buried deep that had been waiting for an excuse to rise. "Bo said that?"

Bridgette shrugged, adjusting her sweater. "I ain't one to tell tales. Just sayin' what's been said."

They stepped out into the afternoon, the heat settling thick against their skin. Shirley did not see him at first, but she felt him, leaning against his daddy's old Ford, one boot braced against the bumper, hands in his pockets, a grin cut sharp and sure across his face. There had been a time when that grin had made her stomach dip low, made her heart stammer like a bird against glass. That time had passed. Shirley had other things on her mind.

But there was something else. Something worse.

The other truck. Rolling up beside them, slow and heavy, the door creaking as it swung open. And her father, Jim Ragland, tipping a brown bottle against his knee, the sweet smell of sour mash and sweat lifting off him in waves.

Jim Ragland never picked her up from school.

Her blood ran cold before she even saw the bottle. She didn't even say goodbye to Bridgette.

Bo straightened, tipped his chin, gave her that look. That *Come over here, sweetheart, let's talk about this* look.

Shirley's feet moved before she had decided to move them. She turned, climbed into the truck without a word. Her hand closed around the handle, pulled the door shut behind her with a finality she felt in her bones.

The truck groaned forward, the road kicking up dust behind them. Shirley stared ahead, her hands clenched tight in her lap. On the seat, the brown glass catching the light, half-drained but full enough to make a man loose-tongued and reckless. The cab reeked of whiskey and sweat, of cheap tobacco and something sour, something like a half-eaten bologna sandwich on the floor, left too long in the heat. Jim rolled the bottle between his fingers.

"Trixie Simpson's got herself in a fix, gal."

Shirley's stomach went still. A dead kind of still. A pond when the wind has stopped.

"What—" The word caught, too raw. She swallowed. "What kinda fix?"

Jim exhaled slow through his nose. "A damn fine fix, that's what kind, gal. She's knocked up, Shirley. Bo's the father. Her daddy's raisin' hell. Says Bo's gonna marry her or else he'll kill the lil' son of a bitch."

It did not land like a blow. Blows come sudden, sharp, and expected. This was worse. This was a bomb, detonating deep in her chest. This was a slow collapse, a gutting from the inside out. A dead branch finally giving under the slow crush of rot.

Her breath came in shallow gasps. She turned to the window, pressed her forehead against the glass. The truck rocked beneath her, a shuddering, rattling thing, old bolts straining, wooden slats shaking loose in their nails.

Her body convulsed, a sudden lurch, and she barely had time to shove her head through the open vent before she was heaving, her stomach emptying itself in a thin, sour stream that caught the wind and splattered back against the rusted door, dripping off the door handle onto her uniform skirt. The truck skidded to a stop. Jim's arm shot out, a clumsy attempt at steadiness.

"Jesus, Shirley—"

Jim's voice cracked. He reached across her, fumbled for the door handle, for anything. She shoved him off. Sucked in a ragged breath, wiped her mouth with the back of her sleeve. She turned to him, face blotchy, eyes raw, breath still coming in uneven gasps, and something in his face broke.

She did not sob. Did not wail. The sound that came from her was low, guttural, some deep primitive agony that resembled nothing her father had ever witnessed. And she knew, with the plainness of a switchblade pressed to skin, that it was not only Bo Harris she mourned.

Jim sat still. Hands curled loose around the wheel, the tendons in his wrists drawn taut. He was not a man built for softness, but his fingers twitched, hesitant, before reaching for the nape of her neck. A gesture so small, so lost in the vastness of her grief, but it steadied her. His hand, calloused and rough, just resting there.

For a moment, she tensed. He felt it, the instinct to pull away, to shove him off, to prove she was still strong. But she didn't.

She let him stay.

He had never seen his daughter like this, never seen his girl, his Shirley, bright and sharp as cut glass, come undone. Not like this. Not sobbing, not breaking, not spilling over like a dam finally cracked.

And when she finally sat back, sucked in a breath, wiped the wet from her face, he did not move away first. He let her be the one to go.

Jim exhaled, rough, tired. "You know what's funny?" she said, her voice hoarse, her hands slack in her lap. "I spent half my life thinkin' men like Bo Harris could love a girl like me. Turns out, men like Bo Harris only love what girls like me can give 'em."

She exhaled through her nose, turned to the window.

Jim did not answer. Did not move. Did not look at her. Just put the truck in gear, turned onto the square, and stopped in the dust-choked light of evening.

"Go on and walk home from here," he said, voice low, steady. "Ain't no sense in stirrin' your mama up with this."

Shirley nodded. Reached for the door. And then—

"But listen to me, gal." His hand, catching her wrist, firm but not rough. She turned. Met his eyes. "If anything else happens, if you hear anything else, you come to me first. You don't go handling it alone. You understand me?"

A long silence. Then, a nod.

Jim squeezed her hand. "I love you, gal."

She stepped out. Latched the door behind her. Did not look back.

She walked toward home, through the slow-falling dusk, and the air smelled different. The town looked different. She felt different, in more ways than one.

And it was time she started acting like it.

ECHOES OF JEALOUSY

Wednesday, Fourth Week of August 1942

THE ORGAN GROANED beneath Tom Walker's hands, a chaotic discordance shivering up the nave, rattling in the beams, pouring like an oil spill over the empty pews. His fingers struck keys without thought, the sound a fevered prayer with no object, only need. Then silence. Sudden and absolute. He turned.

Father Schadenfreude stood in the doorway of the organ loft, his face lit only in slants of waning light that slithered through the high stained glass.

Tom swallowed the acid in his throat. "He's yur-yur-your favorite," he said, the words brittle, trembling at the edges. "Don't d-d-deny it."

The priest's expression did not change. He stepped forward, measured, composed, like a man moving through water. "You're being absurd, Tom."

"Am I?" Tom laughed, short, sharp, a thing with teeth. "Y-You've barely looked at m-me s-since he s-showed up. Y-You think I d-don't see it? The wu-wu-way you d-dote on him, the wu-way you—" He stopped, voice breaking against something jagged, dire, mortal.

The priest folded his arms. "You're jealous."

Tom's breath came fast. "Of course I'm j-jealous! You p-p-pulled me out of h-h-hell, and now you t-throw me over-b-b-board, for s-some ignorant f-farm boy who doesn't even know wu-wu-why he's here!"

Something in the priest's face shifted, a quiet, cold thing settling in the corners of his mouth, in the narrowing of his gaze. "Watch your tone." The words were even, but the space between them carried the authority of a judge's gavel. "You forget the risks I took. The strings I pulled. The debts I incurred. You think Philadelphia simply let go of you? You think I didn't fight for you?"

The air in the loft was suddenly small, thick. Tom's body stiffened, his mind playing at something he did not want to see, but saw anyway.

The priest exhaled, slow, as though tempering himself. "And then there was your little display last Sunday." He did not blink. "That was a mistake."

Tom's mouth went dry.

"In front of Shirley, no less." Father Schadenfreude's voice was smooth, clipped, efficient. "I won't imagine she won't tell her mother. And anyone else who will listen."

Tom's spine curled in on itself. The girl. The gossip. The stories spreading like rot in the church's foundation. His own undoing, the slow unravel of the careful, fragile web that had held him above ruin.

"That's right," the priest continued, his voice low, calculated, a blade turned precisely at the seam between ribs. "I saved you from ruin, and yet you insist on making yourself a liability. Do you have any idea what they would have done to you if I hadn't intervened? And this—" He gestured, a hand flicking in the dim light. "This little tantrum. Your drunken spying. You will not make a fool of me, Tom."

Tom pressed his back against the organ, his hands gripping at nothing. "I..." The words were gone before he could find them.

Father Schadenfreude stepped closer, tenderly placing a hand on Tom's back, and his expression was unreadable. "You are special to me, Tom," he said, soft now, softer than Tom could bear. "But you must understand. Bo is lost. He needs me. What I do for him, I do for his soul."

Tom nodded, barely seeing, barely breathing. "Yes, Father."

The priest watched him a moment longer, then turned, his robes whispering as he disappeared down the stairwell, leaving Tom alone in the hollow loft, the organ silent, his pulse loud in his ears.

Somewhere below, the last light of the afternoon bled through the nave's great window, throwing long streaks of gold across the stone floor. Tom's fingers hovered over the keys again, but the music did not return.

GAMES BENEATH THE OAK CANOPY

Thursday, Fourth Week of August 1942

BO STOOD WAITING as the last bell rang, a fixture against the schoolhouse wall, arms crossed, face turned slightly away as if he had tired of the waiting. I knew better. He wanted to be seen, to be admired, to be whispered about. And he was. The girls behind me murmured in jealous awe, their words rising like dust behind me, but my mind was elsewhere. I saw him and felt the dull, feverish hum beneath my skin, the war drum of want and knowing. I thought of his body, the way it moved, the way it had felt under my hands. I thought of how I had let him take me, how I had wanted him to. I thought of Trixie Simpson, the woman he had been with when I had been waiting for him, a woman I had once thought of as family.

He did not know that I knew.

He caught my arm and led me away, and I let him, let him believe for this moment that I was his to guide. The streets were quiet, the heat of late August pressing against us, heavy and thick, but there were secrets, plenty of them.

I'd teetered on the precipice of modern womanhood, had tasted the sweet air of burgeoning sexual freedom, but I felt a stirring within that suggested our journey was far from over. Bo and I were at war, his vanity against my aspirations to be a modern, adventurous woman without boundaries. He just didn't know it yet.

When we reached the intersection of Oak and 7th, I tugged him toward the grove, toward the place that had, for a short time, belonged to only us.

The trees curled above, their limbs tangled, their bark scarred by carvings of names long forgotten. The air smelled of wildflowers, thick earth, damp roots. I had hidden something here earlier, a small mason jar of my father's dandelion wine, its golden liquid burning in the light that filtered through the canopy. I picked it up, turning to face Bo, my fingers curling tight around the glass.

"Thought we might try this," I said, my voice light, almost playful. "Daddy won't miss it."

Bo smirked, that lazy, knowing tilt of his lips, an understanding passing between us that neither of us spoke aloud. He took the jar from me, unscrewed the lid, and took a long, careless gulp. When he handed it back, I only pretended to drink. I had no love for the taste, but the act was something else entirely.

"Hold your horses, playboy," I said, reining him in as I slipped my heels off with a determined twist. "I'll need to shed these shoes. I can walk down to the part where it gets rocky, then you can carry me the rest of the way."

Bo held on to my shoes for me then we resumed our scandalous traipse. The tug of his arm around my waist and his misbehaving hand stretching downward to cup the cheek of my bottom set a tone of glamorous disobedience, grounding us in a moment that felt electric, daring, and delightfully wicked. I'm pregnant anyway. May as well have some fun without consequences. Maybe scare him just a little.

We walked deeper into the grove, past the edge where the trees gave way to a clearing. An old stone wall stood there, crumbling at its edges, half-lost to moss and creeping vines. Beyond it, the cemetery sloped into view, crooked markers jutting from the ground like broken teeth. Shadows danced under the sprawling canopy of chestnuts, the dappled sunlight spilling like coins onto the soft, grassy meadow, a place I'd not yet explored. I paused at the edge of the clearing, my breath catching at the sight before me.

"I told you it was somethin'," Bo said, his voice low, almost reverent.

I nodded, running my fingers over the white petals of a daisy. "You come here often?"

He shrugged. "Used to. When I was a kid. When I needed to be alone." A pause. Then, quieter, "Figured you might like it."

I did. More than I wanted to admit.

Bo reached for me then, fingers brushing my wrist before sliding down to lace through my own. A touch meant to reassure. A touch meant to claim. I let him hold my hand as we walked to the center of the clearing, his grip firm, his palm warm and rough. I let him believe I was his.

We sat together in the grass, and I watched him take another long drink, his Adam's apple shifting as he swallowed. I thought of Trixie, of the way he must have touched her, the words he must have whispered against her skin. The sickness of it curled inside me, cold and sharp, but I did not let it show.

Instead, I smiled. Reached out. Let my fingers drift over his sleeve, tracing the curve of his arm. He turned toward me, his expression shifting, something soft in his eyes. Something tender.

And I kissed him.

It was slow at first. Measured. His lips warm, his breath carrying the faint burn of the wine. Then he was pulling me closer, fingers at my waist, at the small of my back, his touch insistent. My dress rustled against my skin, the fabric shifting as his hands moved, and I let him. I let him believe this was for him. That this was love. That this was something more than the war I had already won.

He pulled me down into the grass, and I let him do that too. The earth was warm beneath me, solid, unyielding. My fingers found the buttons of his shirt, slipping them free one by one. He shivered under my touch, and I smiled against his mouth. I let my hands wander, let them linger. I let him believe I was his.

His gaze lingered, tracing my profile, the delicate angle of my jaw, the slight upturn of my nose, the shape of my mouth, cataloging me as something to be kept. "You look happy, Shirley. I like seein' you like this."

I might've told him it was the glow of pregnancy, the one he'd seen fit to burden me with, but I did not. I smiled instead, let the lie breathe between us like something living, something waiting to be given a surname.

I turned toward him, the curve of my lips softening, and felt the weight of weeks uncoil inside me, the sharp edge of my mother's voice, the stifling silence of home, the ache of loneliness that had settled in my bones. Trixie's betrayal. His. The knowing that he had lain with her while I sat waiting for him in the woods, scolded by a broken Benji. Her pregnancy. My own. And still, the damn fool wanting of him.

"You make me happy, Bo," I said, and the words felt brittle, not quite whole, but he did not seem to notice.

He swallowed, throat working, his gaze falling to the ground between us. "You don't know what that means to me."

I reached out, brushed my fingers against the edge of his sleeve, felt the warmth of him through the thin cotton, something raw unspooling in my chest. I did not think. I leaned in, let my lips touch his cheek, a whisper of a thing, fleeting, barely there before I pulled away.

His breath hitched. "Shirley—"

But whatever he meant to say was lost as I kissed him again, and this time, he did not hesitate. His hands found my waist, unsure at first, then firm. The world quieted. The grove wrapped itself around us, leaves whispering, the distant hum of cicadas thick in the air. The sun cut through the canopy in pale gold slants, and the scent of warm earth and wildflowers filled my lungs.

I leaned back, pulling him with me, the grass cool against my skin. His buttons came undone beneath my fingers, his breath quickening as I traced the solid plane of his chest. He trembled beneath my touch, and a part of me, the part still raw from knowing, from Trixie, recoiled at the idea of him pretending, of him playing at inexperience. And yet, in that moment, I did not stop him.

I sat there in the dappled light of the forest, allowing my dress to fall to the forest floor like the last vestiges of the innocence Bo took from me. The undergarments followed, pooling at my feet like relics of something already lost. The wind stirred, lifting the hem of his shirt, and he watched me, unmoving, a soldier at the gates.

There I stood before him, bared and unadorned, a wild enchantress embodying the vibrant allure of starlets I'd seen flickering across the screen at the picture show.

With a boldness I scarcely recognized in myself, I sauntered over to Bo, my heart pounding with a playful urgency, unfastening his suspenders and trousers with a practiced ease. I pushed him down to the earth, which seemed to tremble beneath the weight of our reckless abandon, and there I straddled him, reveling in the sheer majesty of his form, the embodiment of a gladiator in the midst of a battle that was all our own.

As I lowered myself down, my gaze locked into his deep-set blue eyes, their depths steadying my descent while I gripped his broad, muscular shoulders as if they were my lifeline. Channeling the bold spirit of his own secret lover, Trixie Simpson, I found my voice, bold and unyielding, proclaiming the woman I had long envisioned myself becoming, today fully realized.

I felt the muscle tense beneath my fingers, positioned my body strategically, and met his gaze. "Bo Harris," I said, and my voice was steady, unyielding. "This ain't about you. I don't love you. I'm not a child. I'm doing this for myself one last time, so don't you dare treat me like you love me or like I'm a girl who don't know better. I want you to treat me just like you did Trixie Simpson."

Mouthing the words "Trixie Simpson," I slid my body downward simultaneously, planting myself firmly, gluing my body to his, leaving his escape utterly impossible.

And then at once, he understood what I was doing, what this was. And there was something close to admiration in the way he looked at me, something almost reverent. "Don't you fret none about that, Shirley Ragland. The good Lord knows you ain't no damn child."

His voice settled over me like an oath, a promise, an undoing. And then there was only the two of us, tangled in the grass, the sunlight pressing hot against our skin, the slow and deliberate breaking of something sacred, something that had already been broken long before this moment.

And when it was his time to finish the job, when he desperately tried to buck me from his body, I feigned a plea of passion too far gone to come back from, then begged him to give me an exact dose of what he'd given Trixie.

And he did.

When it was over, when the breath had left us both and the grove had returned to its quiet, I turned to him, voice lilting with something sharp, something knowing. "Maybe you got me pregnant too, Bo. Wouldn't that be somethin'?"

A smirk played at my lips, the taste of dandelion wine still lingering there. "Two babies, same age, different mothers. That's really a thing to be proud of, Bo."

He did not answer. Could not. And as I lay back against the earth, my pulse steady, my breath even, I knew the war was already won. The weight of him, the weight of this, all of it had settled into something different. Something inevitable.

And Bo? Bo would never see it coming.

A TANGLE OF LONGING AND FATE

Saturday, Fourth Week of August 1942

THE HEAT LINGERED, dense and breathless, until the wind tore it apart. The air shifted, sudden and bracing, carving hollows through the silence, threading itself between the warped slats of the porch, through the narrow gaps of window shutters, through the brittle reeds bending at the creek's edge. The pines beyond the grove swayed in the dying light, their dark limbs shuddering as if they too felt what was coming. The horizon burned gold, then fell away into an iron dusk, the glow of the setting sun swallowed whole by the slow-closing mouth of night.

I stood at the threshold of the woods where Bo and I had left something undone the day before, something raw and knotted that now pulsed at the edges of my mind. The clearing beyond the trees felt ancient, the kind of old that held its breath when you entered, watching, waiting. Wildflowers curled in the dim, their petals heavy as though bowed by some unseen burden. The earth beneath me hummed low, a pulse beneath the dirt, the weight of all that had come before pressing up through the roots, into my bones. I wanted to turn back. I wanted to press my forehead against the cool glass of my bedroom window and let the hours slip past in silence. But the woods called me forward, and I followed.

Mama had tried to keep me inside that morning, fussing over my hemline, sighing into the thick air as she scolded. Said I was overtaken by airs, thinking myself better than the rest, since I had been slipping from church, slipping from her reach. But there had been something in her voice this time, something just shy of fear. I met her gaze without flinching, felt something rise in me, hot and unrelenting.

"You think you're so holy, Mama," I said, voice quiet but certain, "but holiness ain't supposed to look like meanness. And it sure don't look like how you've treated Earline all these years. She's loved this family. She's loved me more than you ever have."

Her hand stopped mid-air, the dish towel twisting in her grip. The room went still, everything hovering in the wake of my words. She did not strike me, nor did she speak. And I did not wait for permission to leave.

I knew where I would find him. Bo never went to the store or the pool hall on days like this. Days when the air grew restless and the crows lined the fences, their black eyes knowing. He would be in the grove, rifle slung across his shoulder, the scent of spent gunpowder clinging to his shirt. My steps carried me forward, through the meadow where bramble caught at my skirts, the sharp kiss of thorns against my ankles. The sun was nothing more than a suggestion, its light weak and weary, spilling long and broken through the trees.

Then the clearing opened up before me, and the world buckled inward. A stillness, profound and unnatural, pressed in against my ribs. The air thickened, the sound of my breath loud in my own ears. The chestnut grove stood dark and quiet, the branches heavy with a silence that did not belong. High above, crows sat in twisted lines, perched like omens. Their wings slack, their throats closed, too sick, too knowing to utter a sound, as if they had seen something and did not care to speak of it.

The feeling of it felt wrong, jarring, even against the stillness that settled in my chest when I saw the rifle. Bo's father's .22 rifle lying half-hidden in the grass, the barrel slick with the breath of evening. Then the figure slumped against the base of the old oak, limbs folded inward, his face turned toward the sky but his eyes unseeing. And the note, pinned above him.

My knees buckled before I even reached it, then my hands shivered wildly as I pulled it free, the paper worn soft at the edges. Drops of rain began to drip and patter on the page as I read, the ink bleeding at the creases.

I read it once. Then again. The words crawling up my throat like bile.

Dear Mama, Daddy… and Shirley,

I don't reckon there's a right way to say what I got to say, so I'll just get to it.

I'm sorry. I'm sorry for all of it.

It feels like my heart's done turned to rock, sittin' heavy in my chest day and night. I can't seem to shake it no more. Feels like I'm stuck down in a deep hole and the sky's just gone from it. I tried to climb out, I did, but it keeps pullin' me under like mud after a big rain.

I been doin' wrong. I told lies. Big ones. And I let things into me that shouldn't never've got in. Dark things. Mean things. And they ain't leavin'. They sit with me now like old kin, whisperin' awful things in my ear, makin' me remember all I've done and what I can't never fix. Y'all should know it all by now, the whole thing gnaws at my insides, my darkest secrets now laid bare to the whole town, but to you mostly.

I used to laugh. Used to feel light. Used to think of Shirley and smile like it was springtime in my chest. But even that's gone now. Even thinkin' of Trixie don't help none. I see her eyes in my mind and it just hurts worse, 'cause I know I let her down too. I broke stuff there ain't no way I can mend.

Shirley… sweet Shirley. I never wanted you to know what kind of mess I made. But I reckon everybody knows now. And what eats at me most is knowin' you see me different. I was tryin' to be somebody you could be proud of, but I reckon I went and became the opposite. I'm so sorry, darlin'. I'm so sorry.

I don't hardly know who I am anymore. This mornin' I looked in the mirror and saw a stranger starin' back. He looked tired and low, like a dumbass boy who dug his own grave and just sat down in it.

It don't feel real no more. None of it. It's like I'm walkin' in a bad dream and can't wake up.

I don't want y'all to think I done this 'cause I don't love you. I do. Lord, I do. That's why it hurts so much. I can't carry this weight no more. It's tied 'round my neck like a rope, and I can't breathe.

Please remember me from before, all those good days, the ones where the sun was shinin' and I still laughed. Not this shell I turned into.

Tell Shirley I loved her best. Tell her not to cry too long.

Goodbye,

Bo

The note slipped from my fingers. The air held no scent of gunpowder, no echo of the moment he had torn himself from this world. He had done it hours ago, perhaps when the sun still sat high, when the wind still carried the last of summer's warmth. I had been too late.

I sank to my knees beside him. His lips parted as if caught mid-sentence, his hands limp against his lap, the rain cruelly obscuring the last of his face I would ever see. My hands hovered above him, unsure where to land, and I whispered his name as if it might still hold power.

I did not run at first. I sat. I listened to the stillness, to the quiet hymn of the wind in the leaves.

The rain came sudden and hard, a blind and feral thing loosed from the heavens, its descent not in drops but in sheets, a vast and unbroken curtain of water that swallowed the chestnut grove whole, the wind tearing through its blanketed canopy with a howl that sent limbs groaning and snapping, leaves ripping free and flung into the torrent like birds caught mid-flight and dashed against the unseen; the undergrowth shuddered, the ground churned to a cold black soup.

Then, finally, I rose and I ran, through the meadow and wood, as fast as I could, hoping not to be swallowed whole by the storm. Large pondings and puddles formed in my path, forcing shifts and straying along the path that left me exposed to the storm for a longer duration than expected, my new route obstructed by limbs and briars and rock outcrops.

Rivulets were forming in the ruts of old deer trails, spilling over banks, twisting into gullies that frothed and swelled as thunder detonated overhead, rolling through the treetops in great, slow percussions that rattled my eardrums and the windows of houses crouched at the edge of the woods, porches and their swings shuddering beneath the battering gale. Still the rain did not relent, only deepened, only gathered, turning the neighborhood roads into churning arteries of mud and floodwater.

My dress, tattered and frayed by the briars and the velocity to which I negotiated them, legs no less ruined, the air thick with the acrid scent of ozone and wet earth, the storm thrumming against rooftops, pressing its fury into the world until all that remained was the sound of it, the endless hammering of sky upon earth, until I finally made it through the open door of my house, into my father's arms, the words tumbling from my mouth before I could stop them.

*

THEY FOUND HIM WHERE I left him. The sheriff came, his voice low and gruff, his boots heavy against the earth. The neighbors whispered. The women in their summer dresses folded their arms across their stomachs, speaking in hushed tones about the way boys get lost in their own foolishness, about the way some hearts are born too tender for this world.

The days that followed were thick with quiet. Benji came to see me, Mun too, and Earline, who held me tight and told me that grief has its own language, one the heart speaks long before the mouth finds the words. Tom Walker came to the house uninvited, his smile thin, his words slick as oil.

"You must've known he was troubled," he said. "Father Schadenfreude always said Bo needed guidance. Some boys just can't be saved."

I met his gaze, felt the fury rise in me. "At what point does a person know another is so troubled they would do something like that?"

He did not answer.

It wasn't until later, when I found Bo's old journal hidden under the seat of his truck, that I began to understand. The pages were chocked full with sketches of the grove, of wildflowers and gravestones, and of figures that seemed to shift between menacing and mournful. A few entries stopped me cold:

"Father says I can be whole again, but I don't know which part of me he wants to keep and which to kill?"

"Shirley makes me feel alive, but what if she is the sin he means to burn out of me?"

"Trixie is indescribable. Intoxicating. Manipulative."

There were other notes about him and Trixie too, notes I didn't want to read, but... I just wanted to throw it away, but I was afraid someone would find it and tell all about me and all of the things Bo and I had done together. I ripped out the pages with private things about us on them, then burned them in the barrel out back.

I couldn't bring myself to show the journal to anyone, not even Mother, who had taken to hovering outside my bedroom door as if waiting for me to crumble. Instead, I sat alone in the grove each evening, piecing together the fragments of Bo's life and the shadow Father Schadenfreude had cast over it. Even though I know that Bo escaped the Father's wrath, whatever it would have been, I still hated him for who and what he is.

And then there's me. I put pressure on him. Pressure that he might not have handled. The idea of having two girls pregnant at the same time would be a daunting thing to contemplate. If I had not done that, had I just left well enough alone and sent him on his merry cheating way, he might be alive today.

The next week, at the funeral, Father Schadenfreude spoke of sin, of redemption, of a soul lost to darkness. I watched him as he spoke, saw the calculation behind his words, the careful arrangement of his sorrow.

Afterward, there was a hush, a kind of reverent rustling, as the crowd began to break apart like dry leaves scattered on the wind. Mother and I drifted toward George and Blanche Harris—not because it was expected, but because it was owed. George stood stiff as a fence post, his face carved from something much harder than grief. He nodded when we approached, knife-sharp eyes giving nothing, not even to Mother, whom he'd known since childhood. Blanche, though— her glance sliced clean through me. I offered her my hand and a soft, small "I'm so sorry." She took it as if it offended her, held it just long enough to show me she could, then dropped it like something rotten.

"I reckon sorrow wears different faces," she said. "Some of 'em prettier than others."

I blinked, caught between shame and fury. Before I could speak, Mother stepped in—not warm, not angry, just steel covered in silk. "We all carry what we must, Blanche. And we carry it how we can. Let's not mistake grief for license."

Blanche pursed her lips but said no more. George gave the smallest nod again, maybe to me, maybe to the ground. Then they turned.

When the service ended, I caught Father Schadenfreude's sleeve before he could slip away.

"You knew," I said, my voice low, steady. "You let it happen."

He looked at me with the practiced sorrow of a man accustomed to wearing grief like a well-fitted suit. "My child, we can't always save those who are lost."

"No," I said, my hand tightening around his sleeve, "you're the one who lost him."

I let go of him. Walked past the enfeebled Besse Kimbro, past the rows of mourners, down the church steps worn smooth by the weight of the faithful. I stepped into the sun, and I did not look back. Mother was waiting by the car, her face drawn and weary. She opened her mouth to speak, but I held up a hand.

"Not today, Mother," I said, stepping past her. "Not today."

FIFTEEN

THE BOY IN THE WOODS

Saturday, Fourth Week of August 1942

RUMORS OF BO Harris' macabre discovery began to wind their way through the streets of Springfield before the sheriff had even made it back from the woods. Folks in town talked in suppressive, not necessarily respectful, tones—behind curtains, in their beds, and on porches—like the summer heat had wrung them dry of anything but speculation. Why would Bo Harris, a boy with good looks and better prospects, snuff himself out in such a way? It didn't sit right with anyone, least of all Sheriff Emory Cobb, whose sense of order didn't allow for loose ends, let alone a tragedy that seemed stitched together with innuendo and speculation.

Sheriff Cobb had seen more grief than most men ought to, had stood at the edges of too many lives unraveled, had watched the weight of calamity settle onto shoulders already bent with the burdens of the South, its heat, its poverty, its unspoken rules that bound men just as surely as they broke them. There was not a house in the county, not a dim-lit church parking lot or an abandoned stretch of blacktop, not a fishing hole sunk deep in the tangle of cypress and water oak, that had not borne witness to some kind of ruin.

A body found gutted and left for the sun and the buzzards. A car curled around a tree, its driver still clutching the wheel like it might save him. A woman whose last breath had been stolen in the hands of the man who once swore to love her. These places, these lawman landmarks of violence and misfortune, had become part of the landscape in Cobb's mind, fixed in his memory the way an old surveyor marks the lines between one man's land and another's.

Yet for all the ways a man could die, for all the ways he had seen life torn from bone, it was the parents that unsettled him the most.

That wretched and raw thing, the way a father will stand with fists clenched high in the air, lips moving but making no sound, a prayer or a curse or both, while a mother keens like some ancient ritual, something feral, undiscovered and untouched by the veneer of civility.

Cobb had seen many a man dead before his time, but there was a peculiar cruelty in seeing a boy, almost grown but not quite, still at the threshold of what he might have been, laid out cold while his parents, their faces carved by years of toil, looked on and understood, maybe for the first time, that the world would keep turning, and their grief would not stop it.

Cobb carried himself with the slow, calculated gait of a man who had long since given up any pretense of hurry. His khaki uniform, once stiff and ironed with fresh starch, had long since surrendered to time and lackadaisical habit, its creases now a distant memory, its fabric faded to the color of old parchment. The patches on his sleeves, once bold in embroidery, had bled into the weave like the ink of a wet newspaper, and the five-pointed star upon his chest sat at a slight angle, pinned without care, as if the law itself had grown tired and leaned a little under the pressure of its responsibilities.

His belly, a grand thing, announced itself before the man did, rounding out just beneath the crease where his shirt met his waistband, the fabric stained dark with errant drops of spittled snuff that had settled there like punctuation marks in the slow-told story of his day. That belly had been earned, not gifted, fifteen years walking the beat in Franklin, Kentucky, where the sidewalks cracked under the summer sun, before moving his wife and young'uns down to Springfield to chase the sharper angles of detective work.

That was sixteen years ago, before the silver crept into his hair, before his patience wore thin, before he had took the bold notion to run for sheriff.

Two years past, he had beat the incumbent, a firebug if there ever was one, a man with the peculiar habit of setting houses alight just to watch the flames dance, then arriving in a flourish to help douse them. Cobb had taken the office by a trifling sixty-three votes, a margin just wide enough to keep the man from contesting but slim enough to remind him he hadn't won by much more than the width of the incumbent's matchstick.

Now, Cobb sat with the casualness of a man who had made peace with his own gravity. His stained tie, a relic of a time when he still pretended to care, hung short by a good eight inches from reaching the top of his belt, suspended mid-air like an unfinished thought. The odorous cab of his patrol car smelled of gun leather and stale tobacco, combined with the sweat of him and the three feral lawmen before him, baked into its cloth seats. The rubber back seat, another story altogether, a superfecta of vomit, beer, sweat, and blood. Cobb's age and occupation told a story, while the graveness of his eyes and the slow measured drawl of his voice carried the weight of a hundred stories told too many times. Pulling up on the scene, he rubbed at his chin, let the silence linger.

He wasn't a fast man, nor an uncommonly sharp one, but he was steady, and in a county where steadiness counted for more than brilliance, that was enough.

By the time he stepped from his patrol car, the crickets and earthworms had begun their evening dirge, the rasp and clatter of them swelling into the air like the sound of something unkillable. August's post-rain humidity clung to the earth and curled up in wavering apparitions from the blacktop road, and the wet woods beyond the road stood solemn and unmoving, the trees like watchers, their branches heavy with damp and the knowledge of something that could not be spoken aloud.

The scene in the woods offered little clarity. There were no footprints; if there had been any, the deluge of rain would have made them a jumble too tangled to read. Shirley had been the one to find him, she'd told her daddy. Said she'd smelled the odor of gunpowder upon her arrival. The spot, a clearing where Bo lay, still as death, because death had claimed him proper.

The boy had been found before midday, body slackened in the dirt, eyes open to the indifferent morning sky. Bo Harris, seventeen, with a future clean as a starched collar, now slumped against the bole of a chestnut tree with his father's Winchester levered across his lap. The rifle's blueing had long since rubbed thin from years of oiling and handling, the stock stained dark where a man's calloused grip had worn it down, and somewhere near the barrel, a fleck of blood had dried or been baked by the heat of the barrel into a tiny rust-colored crescent. A neat, small hole at the temple. One shot, dead clean.

The scene was otherwise untouched, pristine as if the woods themselves had turned solemn, a strange, perfect stillness of it, except for the presence of a half-empty can of snuff discarded near the boy's body. Cobb turned it over in his palm, rolling the truth of it around in his mind, the metal cool and slick with dew. Bo wasn't known to dip snuff. The sheriff noted that detail in his steno pad, then stuffed it in his back pocket, just in case.

The Winchester rifle was another thing entirely. Bo's daddy kept it in the floorboard of his old truck, primed for rabbits and squirrels. Sheriff Cobb knew the gun well. Even though the gun smelled of being freshly fired and one lone spent cartridge case of .22 long ammunition was found near the body, the gun didn't speak to motive, and neither did the note Shirley had found pinned against the tree near Bo's remains. The note lying next to Bo's cold remains, dropped by the terrified girl, now waterlogged with its ink forever maligned by the unmerciful storm.

Written in Bo's hand, everyone said, though Shirley had mentioned the script, when it was still dry and legible, looked hurried, panicked even.

"People 'bout to kill themselves, their hands ain't exactly steady," he'd muttered to no one in particular. Still, it didn't explain much.

Cobb had seen death in many permutations. The slow ruin of a man who drank himself empty. The sudden, senseless violence of a pistol fired in anger. A woman with hands still curled as if to claw her way back from the abyss. But this—this carried a different weight. A boy barely unlatched from childhood, his life clipped short with all the care of a man trimming the wick of a candle. And that note, ragged and rain-blurred, tacked into the tree like an afterthought. The words scrawled in an uneven hand. The kind of writing that spoke of something desperate and hurried.

And then there was the snuff can. Half-full, cast aside. Bo didn't dip snuff.

The Ragland girl had been the one to find him. Shirley. Fifteen, slender, raven-haired, the kind of young girl men watched longer than they should. She'd come racing back to the house white as a sheet, legs and arms engraved by briar patches and broken limps, her voice a tangle of sobs and syllables that her father had barely unraveled before grabbing his shotgun and calling for the sheriff.

Cobb turned the cylindrical snuff can over in his hand, rubbing a thick thumb across the ridged metal lid. The whole thing felt off-kilter, a story told wrong, its seams showing but not enough. A boy like Bo, good grades, decent hand at baseball, set to work his uncle's farm till he found something better. The kind that married young and died old, worn out by the sun and a lifetime of cutting the same fields his father had cut before him.

And yet here he was. And here was Cobb, looking for a truth that felt as slippery as oil poured over water.

Springfield was a town that collected secrets like dust in the rafters, and by sundown, the terrifying news had woven itself through every porch and parlor, every back pew and bait shop, the details shifting with each retelling, like river stones rubbed smooth by the current. Cobb had long since learned that the truth was a thing that moved, like a hog snake in high grass, and if a man wanted to catch it, he had to move slow, deliberate, let it come to him.

It was the rumors about Trixie Simpson that sent the sheriff down a different path. Ms. Trixie Simpson, a wealthy handsome widow with a reputation for keeping to herself, had found her name dragged into the murky waters of juicy town gossip. It had been said she was carrying Bo's child. Sheriff Cobb didn't like to chase bawdy rumors, but this one wouldn't go away, so he dusted off his hat and paid Ms. Trixie a surprise visit.

The knock at her door was slow, booming, and deliberate; the sound of inevitability. When Trixie opened the door, her face was pale and drawn, her hands clasped tightly in front of her as if she were attempting to hold herself together, piece by piece. She gestured for the sheriff to come in, and they sat in her dimly lit parlor, the afternoon light slicing through the curtains in thin, accusing lines.

The air in the parlor was thick, scented with lilac powder and the ghosts of old tobacco money. The disoriented widow sat rigid in her chair, fingers clasped, the white creases at her knuckles betraying the stillness of her face.

"You know why I'm here," Cobb said, his voice as steady as a man setting a nail with a hammer.

Trixie hesitated, her lips trembling. "It got out of hand," she said finally, her voice barely above a whisper. "I take full responsibility, Sheriff. I... I'm so sorry, I thought he was eighteen," she said nervously. "He told me he was," she said at last. "I didn't mean for it to happen."

Cobb watched her, his eyes the color of river silt, unreadable. "You take responsibility for what, exactly?"

The silence stretched.

Cobb leaned back in his chair, his gaze fixed on her like a hawk sizing up prey. Cobb scratched down a few notes in his stained and abused spiral-bound steno pad. "And you believed him?"

She nodded quickly, too quickly.

"He said he'd failed a grade. I didn't question it. I should have, but..." Her voice broke, and she pressed a hand to her mouth, a gesture of apology or regret or both. "What now, what can I do? I'm pregnant!" Trixie's voice cracked.

The words hung there, thick in the still air.

The old floorboards beneath Cobb's chair creaked as he shifted his weight.

"I didn't question it," Trixie added.

Cobb let the words settle like dust in a still room. He had seen women lie, and he had seen women tell the truth, and more often than not, the difference was in the way they held their hands. Trixie's hands were rigid, fingers interlocked, arms folded over her chest, but her thumb twitched at the nail of her index finger, a nervous tic, the tell of a woman who wanted to say more but feared what the saying might bring.

Cobb sat there, unmoved, eyes fixed on Trixie, as if to say, *I need more*. "And you told him," Cobb said, not a question.

Trixie nodded, a slow, reluctant thing. "Last week, Wednesday, I think. He wasn't happy."

Cobb watched her, measuring the small details. The way she licked her lips before speaking. The way her gaze flicked, just for a second, toward the window.

"What do you mean, wasn't happy?"

Her jaw tightened, eyes fixed somewhere just past him. "He told me to get rid of it. I told him no. Said this was my last chance to be a mother."

Cobb rubbed his thumb over the calloused ridge of his palm. The widow had a reputation. That was a word polite people used, a word that covered more ground than it had any right to. Reputation. Like a sickness passed from mouth to ear, whispered in church pews and back rooms where men leaned too close over half-empty glasses.

"You tell anyone else?" Cobb asked.

Trixie shook her head. "Only Dr. Herbert."

"And Dr. Herbert didn't think to advise you better?" Cobb's voice carried an edge, sharp as the glint of his badge in the sunlight.

"He's my doctor, Sheriff Cobb, not my keeper," she shot back, then softened, voice dropping, shoulders sagging. "I didn't want this. None of it. Bo... he was young, yes, but he came to me. I... I didn't seek him out."

Cobb grunted. "That man's got a mouth looser than a rusted hinge."

She didn't answer. Just sat there, hands clenched, waiting for something that might save her.

Cobb studied her face, weighing the space between her words. "That the truth?"

"Yes."

Cobb's expression didn't change. He'd heard plenty of lies in his time, but the truth was rarely far off, even when it was buried under a trash-heap of excuses.

Cobb stood, the chair scraping against the worn wood. Tipped his hat to her, the small courtesy of a man who knew there was no need for cruelty where truth was enough.

"Now, Ms. Trixie, you got yourself a situation. And situations like this got a way of making people act foolish. So, I'd advise you to sit tight, keep to yourself, and let me do my work."

She nodded, but he could see the fear in the way she held herself, in the tight press of her lips.

Cobb stepped onto the porch, the air thick with the scent of honeysuckle and something else turned sour in the heat. The sun was sinking, dragging the sky down in streaks of blood and fire, and in the distance, the woods stood silent, waiting.

Truth was a thing that moved, but Cobb had spent his life tracking it, and tonight, he had the scent.

*

COBB STEERED HIS CRUISER down Willow Street, the tires humming low against the pavement, the old car groaning with the heat that had settled heavy on the town since morning. He eased it beneath the tangled limbs of a maple and an oak locked in some silent, patient duel, the wiry fingers of Spanish moss grazing the windshield like something blind feeling its way through the dark. He shut the engine off, sat a moment in the oppressive hush of early evening, the cicadas wound tight in their endless thrum, their bodies hidden among the branches, their voices pulsing through the air like a thing alive.

He climbed out slowly, his boots crunching on the gravel as he adjusted the wearing weight of his gun belt, then his hat. The Ragland house stood before him, the white paint on its ornate fenestrations peeling in long curls like a dead man's fingernails.

Jim Ragland met him on the porch, his face set with the grim determination of a man about to do something he'd rather not. His stance was stiff as a fence post, the set of his jaw betraying a weariness that had settled deep in the bone; thumbs hooked in his suspenders. Cobb took his time, his movements deliberate, letting the moment stretch between them.

"Sheriff," Jim said, his voice low, weighted. "I'll let you talk to Shirley, but I'll be there too. She's been through enough."

Cobb studied him a moment, then nodded. "Fair enough, Jim. But let's keep it honest. My patience in this case is holding tight like a hair in a biscuit, and Shirley might be the only witness I got with no reason to lie."

A scene inside the parlor initially perplexed the good Sheriff: a black family, Mun and Earline Johnson, with one of their four sons, Benji, all sat nervously, Mun taking a dip of snuff and Benji soothing a callus on his hand with his pocketknife. The Sheriff knew of the tight knit friendship between Mun and Jim, so the scene went unquestioned. He tipped his hat to the Johnsons.

Inside, Shirley's room was small, thick with the scent of lavender and linens dried in the sun. Cobb took in the floral wallpaper, the trinkets lining the shelves—small things, delicate things, things that had been touched and arranged with care—and, most impressively, books.. The bookshelf looked as if it'd been first commenced as a child's modest built-in, but enlarged and expanded, the joints and seams showing signs of two, distinct but not altogether contrasting, enlargements. As if the child's interests had grown beyond all expectation, the shelves now full, with neatly stacked sets of books scattered about the room, a copy of *Hagar's Daughter* and *Kneel to the Rising Sun* bedside. Cobb wrote the titles down in his steno pad.

She sat on the bed, hands clutched, twisting a handkerchief over and over like a thing wound too tight and needing someplace to spill. Jim hovered by the door, arms folded, his presence a thing both protective and uncertain, as though torn between guarding his daughter and letting her speak her own piece.

Cobb settled into the chair beside her, his voice quiet, steady. "Shirley, I need to ask you about Bo. I know this is hard, but I need to understand what happened."

She swallowed, nodded. "Alright."

"Was he acting different lately? Anything unusual in his mood?"

A flick of her gaze toward her father, a breath drawn thin and shaky. "He was upset. The priest,

Father Schadenfreude. His parents made him spend the summer with him, and… I don't know. They argued a lot. I saw them talking, but it was always heated. I could feel it even when I couldn't hear it. It all seemed so strange for a priest."

Cobb's brow creased. "What kind of arguments?"

She shook her head. "I don't know. But I saw Tom Walker once, up in the organ loft. He was crying, reading a letter the priest had written him. He had his diary out too, writing something, but he wouldn't tell me what it was."

"Did you trust the priest?"

Her head snapped up, something hard in her eyes. "No. Never. He made Bo think things. Like he might be something he wasn't. I think that's why Bo…" She stopped short, pressing the handkerchief to her lips.

"What things, Shirley? Be straight with me."

Another glance at her father, her grip tightening on the cloth. "I… uh, I was thinking maybe Father fancies boys, boys like Bo. Maybe he wanted Bo to fancy him too. In ways he shouldn't. But I don't know, not really. Maybe Bo was confused; I tried to ask, he wouldn't talk. Maybe he wasn't. But I know that priest… I seen things; I know he ain't no saint."

Cobb leaned back, let the silence stretch. "Alright. I needed you to be straight with me, and you were. Now I need to be straight with you too." He shifted, adjusting his hat, his tone changing, softer, but firm. "Shirley, were you and Bo… together?"

Shirley froze, her breath catching in her throat. She darted a look at her father, pleading. Jim stepped forward, but Cobb raised a hand, holding him still.

"Ain't looking to shame you. Just trying to understand where his mind was. It matters."

She closed her eyes, the tears welling and falling before she could stop them. "Yes. We were. The day before he…" Her voice broke. "Same place he was found. That's why I went back. I thought he'd be there." Shirley's face leapt back at her father again. "I… yesterday, I told him I was pregnant too, but I… I don't really know for sure. I been sick some."

Jim exhaled slow, his jaw tight. Cobb nodded, rubbing a thumb over the crease in his pants. "Did he seem happy? Sad? What was he thinking?"

"He told me he loved me," she whispered, her voice barely more than air. "And I believed him. But… I told him I didn't love him."

Cobb's voice was gentle, but unyielding. "Shirley, I need to tell you something, and it ain't easy. Bo was involved with Ms. Trixie Simpson. She's carrying his child."

Shirley flinched, the color draining from her face. "That's… that's why he was acting strange. Makes sense now. Him being hot and cold." Shirley couldn't betray the confidence of her daddy's warning; she performed an ostensible act of surprise and anger.

Jim moved closer, put a hand on her shoulder. Cobb sat back, letting the room settle around them. "I'm sorry," he said. "But you deserved to know."

Jim's voice came low, steady. "Appreciate you telling us, Sheriff. But I think Shirley's had enough for today."

Cobb nodded, standing. "One last thing, Jim. Shirley. You ever see him with a can of snuff? Found one near him."

Shirley shook her head, firm. "Bo didn't dip. Never. I'd swear on it."

Jim scratched his chin, thoughtful. "Now, I don't know. A boy his age, they all dip and smoke. Maybe not around certain folks, but that don't mean he didn't. He knew Shirley thought it was a disgusting habit. No secret 'bout that."

Cobb studied them both, then tipped his hat. "I'll be heading to the parish. Got a few more questions for the good Father. Appreciate the hospitality."

Outside, the heat pressed close, thick and unmoving. Cobb walked slow to his cruiser, his mind sifting through the pieces. A boy dead. A widow and a girlfriend, both pregnant. A note that answered nothing. A can of snuff that didn't belong. And the priest, his name surfacing again and again, like something bloated rising to the top of dark water.

Cobb settled into the driver's seat, the cloth beneath him creaking, the engine grumbling as it turned over. He stared out at the horizon, the sinking sun casting the sky in hues of copper and blood.

The priest would answer. One way or another.

QUIET SINS

THE CRUISER'S TIRES whispered calmly across the gravel, a hush of stone against rubber, as Sheriff Cobb pulled into the lot of St. Cecilia's.

The rain had passed but left its breath on the air, the damp earth mingling with the scent of magnolia. He cut the engine and stepped out slow, the heat of the day now dissipated, but the humidity thick with the promise of more rain or worse.

The impressive church stood ahead, its steeple pricking the overcast sky, pale stone darkened in patches by the passing storm. A holy thing but no refuge. Cobb had long learned that men could pray with their mouths and lie with their hands, and nothing about a house of God changed the nature of what people were capable of, always willing to do if circumstances demanded it.

Near the rectory, Tom Walker paced, his movements sharp, restless, erratic, like a beast that had been cornered and knew it but hadn't yet decided whether to fight or run. Cobb watched him a moment, adjusting his hat. A man on edge often stumbled over the truth before he had the chance to steady himself.

"Afternoon, Tom," the sheriff called, his voice even, unhurried. "Mind if I have a word?"

Tom froze, mid-step, as though the words had reached inside him and locked his limbs. His face was pale, drawn tight. "Sheriff," he said, barely above a whisper. "Of course. W-Whatever you need."

Cobb nodded toward a bench, the wood warped from years of sun and storm, the edges splintered where the varnish had long given up its purpose. "Let's sit," he said. "I've got a few questions, and I'd appreciate your honesty."

Tom hesitated, then sat, his fingers curling over the seat like a man gripping the edge of something unsteady. Cobb leaned back, studying him, letting the quiet settle over them like the thickening humidity before a downpour.

"You been here long enough to see things," Cobb said, his tone almost conversational. "And I've already talked to a few folks. Heard some things about the Father. About his relationship with Bo Harris." He let the words sit, the weight of them pressing into the air between them. "Conversations. Arguments. Maybe more."

Tom swallowed hard. His throat bobbed with it. "The Father," he said, his voice tight, "he c-c-cared for Bo. J-Just w-wanted to help him, w-w-with his troubles. That's all." His fingers worked at the hem of his sleeve, rolling the fabric between them. "Bo... he wouldn't open up. T-That frustrated h-h-him, s-sure. But it w-w-wasn't... it wasn't anything improper."

Cobb narrowed his eyes. He knew the shape of a lie even when it wasn't fully formed. The edges soft. The middle full of nothing.

"You seem nervous, Tom," he said, voice low, steady. "I'm just asking about the priest. You covering for something?"

"No, Sheriff, I'm n-not hiding anything." The words rushed out too fast, too eager. Tom's hands twisted in his lap, knotted up like rope. "The Father, he's a g-g-good man. H-H-He only ever tried to help Bo. I s-s-swear to God, that's the truth."

Cobb leaned forward, elbows on his knees, eyes locked on the younger man. Cobb, like any seasoned lawman, knew a man needn't swear on something believable. If a man's words were true, he expects them to be believed. No need to embellish or ask the Lord to back him up.

"What about you, Tom? Anything you've done that might complicate this investigation?"

"No!" Tom's voice cracked, sharp as snapped wood. "Absolutely not. l-l-loved Bo. H-He was a good kid. Troubled, y-y-yeah, but he deserved better than… than this."

The silence stretched between them, thick as the coming rain. Cobb let it. He knew the power of quiet. How a man would fill it if he was desperate enough.

Then, softer, almost gentle, "Tell me about yourself, Tom. Where'd you come from before this parish? What brought you here?"

The tension in Tom's hands went still, but his shoulders tensed, his body locking up tight. "The Father… he b-b-brought me here from Philadelphia." The words came slow, reluctant. "I w-w-was an organist. Small parish outside the city." His voice thinned, barely more than breath. "I fell in l-love with someone."

Cobb didn't speak. Just let the silence keep working.

"A p-parishoner," Tom added, voice rough. "They w-w-were married."

A flicker of something crossed his face—regret, shame, something else—but he pressed on, as if speaking fast enough would outrun it. "We never—" His lips parted, shut again. Then, quieter, "It was just a kiss." His hands flattened against his thighs. "They confessed it t-t-the next week. The priest there l-l-let me go. Said it wasn't appropriate. And m-m-maybe it wasn't. But I loved them. And I—" He shook his head. "The Father found me. G-Gave me a chance to start over. I owe him everything."

Cobb watched him. The way his eyes flickered, the tremor in his fingers, the shift of his breath when he spoke. The things a man couldn't fake. The things he didn't even know were betraying him. He wrote something in his steno pad.

"That kind of loyalty," Cobb said after a moment, voice measured, "it ever make you lie for him? Even now?"

Tom's eyes widened, his breath hitching. "If you had p-p-proof, real proof—" His voice caught, "I'd stop defending him." A pause, thick with something close to grief. "But I'd still s-s-see the good in him. P-People are complicated, S-Sheriff. We're all capable of both."

Cobb let the words sit between them, let them breathe. Then he pushed himself up from the bench, dusted his hands off on his thighs. "Fair enough," he said. "Now, take me to the Father's office."

Tom stood, his movements jerky, stiff, like something pulling him in two different directions. As they walked toward the rectory, Cobb's mind turned over everything the boy had said. Truth and lies lived close together, held hands in the dark. And guilt, he knew, wasn't always loud. Sometimes it was quiet, trembling just beneath the surface, waiting for someone to press hard enough to let it spill.

THE WEIGHT OF HOLLOW MEN

THE SHERIFF'S BOOTS struck against the flagstone, slow and deliberate, each step hammering down the silence that thickened in the corridor like tar cooling in the seams of the world. The air held the acrid tinge of sweat rising from the back of Tom Walker's neck. The stones beneath them had been walked upon for nearly a century, pressed smooth beneath the weight of the town's men and women burdened by confession and the men who demanded it of them.

Tom hesitated at the threshold of the priest's private office, his hand floating over the brass handle like a thing untethered, some small part of him unwilling to close the distance, to seal himself inside that room where he would sit, bookended by the weight of judgment—one who meant to control him, the other meaning to ruin him. He knew already how the priest would be sitting, how the thin skin at his temples would tighten when the sheriff spoke, how the light behind him would frame him in something akin to holiness, though holiness had long since abandoned that body.

Tom pushed the door open, stepped back, voice tight and small in his throat. Father Schadenfreude was seated behind a broad wooden desk, his hands folded neatly atop a stack of correspondence.

"Father, this is Sheriff Cobb. He's got s-s-some questions for you."

The priest lifted his head, slow as if unburying himself from thought, then rose slowly to his feet, careful not to shatter his thin veneer of calm. The sheriff studied him in that brief quiet: a man of paper-thin skin stretched over a body disciplined into restraint. Standing, he carefully extended a hand. "Sheriff."

Cobb did not take it.

Tom stepped back to the doorway, the priest's gaze cutting into him as he did, but he did not leave the building. He moved down the darkened alcove at the end of the hall and slid into the small closet there, pressing himself into the cold, stale space, ear close to the wood, breath shallow. He had done this before, this listening, but never had his hands shaken this way, never had his own pulse beat so heavy against his skull, knocking like a hammer at his temples.

Inside, Cobb surveyed the room, then eyed a tall wooden chair in the back corner pushed under a small writing desk. The chair was a good three inches taller than the two leather club chairs across from the priest's desk. Cobb walked over, grabbed hold of the wooden chair, and dragged the thing over to the side of the desk, its legs screeching across the stone floor like fingernails across a blackboard.

When he dropped into the chair beside the priest's desk, hat resting against his knee, he was a good three or four inches taller than the priest, and up close and personal, just like the sly old Sheriff liked it. "I'll cut to it, Father. I've had witnesses say Bo Harris was troubled by some… actions of yours. They say he was confused. Some think it went so far as inappropriate. And maybe that's why he's dead."

The priest's face did not flicker. He sat, spine straight, fingers still pressed together in that practiced fold. But his knuckles went pale, the smallest gesture of tension breaking through the surface. "Sheriff," he said, voice soft, precise, "I assure you, I have done nothing but counsel Bo. He carried burdens he refused to speak aloud. I was his confessor, nothing more, my goal to help him. If he misunderstood my intentions, I cannot answer for that, only tell you that my conscience is clean."

Cobb's eyes narrowed, mouth curled at the corner. "That so?"

"I would not lie to you, Sheriff."

Cobb leaned forward, his eyes darker than before. "You ever argue with Bo?"

The priest's breath pressed against the silence. "We had disagreements."

"Disagreements?"

"Bo was private to the point of stubbornness. He rejected authority when it did not serve him. I admit, I lost my patience at times. But only out of desperation to help him."

Cobb nodded, let that settle, his gaze fixed on the priest like a predator studying its prey. "You ever see him and Tom argue?"

The priest sighed, gaze shifting toward the narrow window, the light there dying against the pane, dim and sickly, as if something had been set between it and the sun. "Yes," he said, after a long moment. "The day before Bo was found. They were in the lot outside. Tom was angry. Bo was shouting. I did not intervene."

The sheriff watched him. "Why not?"

"I did not think it odd. Bo... he was often at odds with the world around him."

Cobb let the silence stretch, let the weight of it settle between them like the slow creep of rot beneath floorboards. Then he stood, hat back in his hands. "Father," he said, voice low, "inside this church, you might be the closest thing to God. But out there, I am. And I mean to find out why Bo Harris is dead. Doesn't matter to me who gets caught up in it, even you."

The priest's expression did not change. He sat still, measured. "Sheriff, Bo took his own life. I do not see what else there is to determine."

Cobb stepped toward the door. "Why, Father—that's what's left," he said. "Why would a boy with everything ahead of him end it all? Everything was conveniently in place, except a reason. Don't you want to know?"

The priest exhaled, the smallest thread of impatience winding through it. "Of course I do," the priest replied, his voice quieter. "My priority has always been his soul. Have you spoken to the Ragland girl? Shirley?"

"I have," Cobb said. "Why do you ask?"

"The two of them were close," the priest offered. "Perhaps... intimate. If things ended badly between them, that could be the cause."

Cobb shook his head slowly. "I know all about Shirley. What you might not know is that Bo had another relationship before her, one that persisted after he started seeing Shirley. With Trixie Simpson. The two were intimately involved for months before Bo's parents noticed the change in his behavior that caused them to bring him here to you. Maybe that's what he didn't want to share with you, not something sinister, just... human."

Father Schadenfreude's eyes widened slightly, but he said nothing. Cobb pressed on. "When Trixie learned about Shirley, she pulled Bo back in. And that... that led to her getting with child. But Bo didn't want it, he wanted her to end it; she wouldn't. He'd already chosen Shirley. So why does a boy who's made his choice, who has everything lined up, suddenly take his own life? That's what I'm here to figure out. And if you were jealous, of Shirley... if you wanted an indecent thing from that child, then perhaps you had a motive. Does that sound like you, Father?"

In the closet, Tom's breathing quickened. He clenched his fists, his heart pounding in his chest.

And then, the door burst open.

Tom Walker fell forward, knees striking the stone, the sound of it breaking something in the air between them. His voice was ragged, broken at the edges. "It was m-m-me, Father. Please forgive me!" He gasped, hands shaking, eyes wild with it now. "I t-t-told him to do it."

Tom was sobbing convincingly, his voice cracking. "I thought h-he was c-c-corrupting you, Father, that h-h-he loved you in a w-w-wicked way. I didn't think he'd actually do it. I s-s-swear, I didn't know."

Cobb turned, slow, the look on his face shifting from something hard to something colder. "What," he said, not a question but an order, "did you just say?"

Tom's chest heaved, each breath thick in his throat. "I t-t-told him he was going to r-r-ruin everything," he whispered. "I t-t-told him it'd be better if h-he were gone."

The room froze, the air heavy with the weight of Tom's confession.

Cobb crouched down beside him, voice calm now, a sharp contrast to the storm unraveling in the man before him. "And now he is."

Tom shut his eyes, his body folding further in on itself. "I didn't m-m-mean it," he choked. "I swear, I didn't m-m-mean it."

Cobb stepped forward, his shadow falling over the crumpled figure on the floor. His voice was cold, sharp as winter frost. "You just confessed to pushing a boy toward his death, Tom Walker. Now you're gonna tell me everything. And you're gonna do it right here, right now, or at the jailhouse."

Cobb reached into his coat and pulled out a pair of hand irons, the metal catching the dim light, glinting like something final.

"Now listen here, you two. Either y'all gonna tell me the whole truth, or I'm gonna rip a hole in y'all's asses that a three-bedroom, two-bath house won't fit through. Ya hear me?"

The sheriff bent down to Tom and forcefully gathered his hands together, then locked the irons on each wrist to the front of his chest. Tom started crying immediately.

The priest sat, hands still folded, eyes fixed on some distant point beyond them both. He did not move as Cobb took Tom by the arms, lifted him to his feet, and started pulling him toward the door. The priest watched, seemingly unaffected.

The room fell into a tense silence; the priest stood, still as a statue, his face unreadable. Outside, the sun had disappeared, the wind picked up, rattling the windows like a ghost demanding to be let in. Then, it started to rain.

The air in the office had become so thick it'd become hard to breathe. Cobb stood next to Tom, his massive hands gripping Tom's bicep, sensing the broken man surrender what little vanity to which he still clung, his shoulders curved inward like he'd been gut-punched by Joe Louis.

Cobb exhaled, slow. He slowly dragged his chair back across the floor, the scrape of it loud, unsettling, then he looked at Tom again, pressing his heavy foot on Tom's in-step, applying pressure. Tom winced in pain. The sheriff ordered, "Start talkin' or your coming with me!" his voice flat.

Tom swallowed hard, nodded, but still didn't look up. "I was afraid," he whispered. "Of Bo. Of w-w-what he felt. What h-he might do."

Father Schadenfreude shifted uncomfortably, his cassock rustling as he moved, but he said nothing. His face unreadable, carved from something patient and eternal.

Tom let out a shuddering breath. "I think B-B-Bo was in love with h-him," he said, glancing at the priest, then back down, shame crawling up his throat like bile. "I saw t-t-the way he looked at h-him. Like h-h-he was struggling with something d-d-dark inside. I'd s-s-see them talk, sometimes arguing, low v-v-voices in the church when they thought n-no one else was listening. And it… it d-d-didn't sit right. Not with me."

Cobb narrowed his eyes. "You telling me you thought the boy was…" He stopped, disgust curling the edges of his mouth. "Christ, Walker!"

Tom flinched like he'd been struck. "Y-Y-You don't understand. I've s-s-seen what happens to men like that. To b-b-boys like that."

The priest's voice came quiet but firm. "Tom."

Cobb gave a stern look to the priest. "Are you tryin' to interfere with my investigation, preacher man?"

But Tom shook his head. "No, Father. Let m-m-me say it. Let m-me finish." He turned back to Cobb, eyes red-rimmed, desperate. "I knew. I knew because I r-r-recognized it. Because I l-l-lived it."

The room stilled.

Tom's breath grew heavy. "I had a man, b-back in Philadelphia. A l-l-lawyer. William G. Crayton. He was g-g-good to me. K-Kind. Made m-m-me feel like I was worth something. And then—then Buck W-Wallden caught me. He found out. C-Caught me in something that wasn't meant to be s-s-seen."

His hands were wringing with distress.

"Buck s-stole from the parish office. Twelve hundred dollars, right out of Father O'Connor's d-d-desk. I caught him in the act. But before I could s-s-say a word, he smiled at me. Said if I t-t-told a soul, he'd tell O'Connor what I w-w-was. What I am. Said he'd r-r-ruin me."

Tom let out a bitter laugh.

"And I knew he c-c-could. Knew he would. Knew it w-w-would work. I had no choice b-b-but to leave. To run."

Tom looked at the priest now, something like apology in his expression.

"Father Schadenfreude s-s-saved me. Brought me here. Gave me a p-p-place to start over. And I—I thought m-m-maybe he was like me. That m-m-maybe he saw something in Bo. And I was afraid."

The priest's face did not change, announcing, "I am not a homosexual, Tom."

Tom's throat bobbed. "I thought, I thought you might be."

Cobb scoffed, shaking his head. "Christ Almighty." He turned back to the priest. "And what do you got to say about all this, Father? About Bo?"

Schadenfreude exhaled through his nose, slow, measured.

"I did not encourage anything improper, Sheriff. Bo was—troubled. He came to me for guidance, for counsel. I tried to help him, to steer him toward righteousness."

Cobb stopped at the threshold, turned once more. "You never wanted him?"

The priest blinked, slow, measured. "I have sworn an oath, Sheriff. Just like you. Mine was to God Almighty."

Cobb let out something like a laugh, bitter, hollow. "Yeah," he said. "So had this idiot."

Tom wiped at his face, sniffling. "I told Bo h-h-he was going to r-r-ruin everything," he said, wiping his shoulder against his snotty nose. "I told h-him if he kept on this path, h-he'd destroy himself. I said, I said maybe it'd be b-b-better if he were gone." He let out a sharp, shaking breath. "And n-n-now he is."

The room held its silence.

The priest closed his eyes. "May I pray?"

Cobb hesitated. "Suit yourself."

Schadenfreude bowed his head, his hands clasped before him, his voice steady as he began:

"Pater noster, qui es in caelis, sanctificetur nomen tuum. Adveniat regnum tuum, fiat voluntas tua, sicut in caelo et in terra..."

The Latin rolled off his tongue smooth and practiced, the ancient rhythm of it like a drumbeat through the heavy air. He prayed for wisdom. For clarity. For mercy.

And Cobb listened, indifferent.

Cobb scratched at his scalp like something foul had taken root beneath the skin. The two men stood before him, sweat-thick and silent, and the sight of them turned his stomach in ways he couldn't rightly say. Between them, the truth flickered—a slick thing, eel-like, just out of reach. But Cobb knew. Knew in the way a man knows when a storm's coming, deep in the joints.

He gave his hat a hard slap against his thigh, knocking loose the dust and the moment with it. Then, slow as if testing the weight of his own conscience, he reached forward and undid the irons from Tom's wrists. Steel clinked. Skin rubbed raw. No charge held weight without proof, and suggestion, no matter how foul, weren't proof enough. The law had its codes. And the sheriff—damned as he was by pride and weariness—still clung to those codes like scripture.

He'd let them both walk. For now.

But the air felt wrong. Like something unfinished had been set loose in the room.

"That'll be all for now," he said.

And they both stood there, as if they were schoolchildren waiting to be dismissed.

Cobb set his hat low on his brow, palm firm against the crown like a man sealing in more than hair, then gave a short nod or parting, no more than breath and motion. Father Schadenfreude said nothing, only watched as the sheriff disappeared in the dim warren of inner rooms, boots echoing faintly through plaster and stone, each step dragging silence in its wake. Somewhere deep in the building, a door slammed—sharp, final— like a verdict laid bare.

His gut twisted.

He had heard plenty of liars before.

And maybe, just maybe, he had heard two more.

A HAND EXTENDED, A HAMMER RAISED

Tuesday, Fourth Week of August 1942

LAST MONDAY NIGHT, Earline spoke cautiously to her husband about a most sensitive subject. She explained how for weeks, Shirley had been slipping garments into the wash, garments marked with stains that spoke plainly of knees pressed into earth, grass, and gravel. But there was more. She'd found other things too, delicate fabrics stained in ways that carried no mystery, only the blunt, undeniable truth of what Shirley had become.

Earline's words came slow, each one measured, as she confessed she'd tracked Shirley's monthly cycles from the day the girl got her first period a week after she turned thirteen. And now, on this particular Monday, Shirley was precisely two weeks overdue. Earline met Mun's gaze directly then, her expression unwavering, her voice bearing the certainty of storms looming over fields of wheat. It was time Mun knew. Time Jim knew. Shirley was with child.

The next morning, Mun found Jim in the barn, saddling up his horse. Jim's movements were deliberate, his hands steady as he tightened the cinch. He looked up when Mun entered, his face breaking into a faint smile.

"Morning, Mun," Jim said. "You here to tell me I'm overdue for my sins again?"

Mun let out a dry chuckle. "Ain't that your preacher's job?" Mun joked. "Nah, I need to talk to you. Thought we might ride a ways."

Jim glanced at him, his pale blue eyes narrowing slightly. He nodded and swung up into the saddle. "Alright then. Let's ride."

The two men rode in silence for a while, the rhythm of the horses' hooves settling into a steady cadence. Mun's hands rested loosely on the reins, but his thoughts were tangled up like a bad piece of fishing line. Finally, he cleared his throat.

"Jim," he said slowly, "there's something you ought to know about that boy Bo Harris—one datin' Miss Shirley."

Jim turned his head slightly, his jaw tightening. "Goddamn Mun, what about him?"

Mun shifted in the saddle. "Seems he's got Miss Ora's cousin Trixie Simpson in trouble… with child, Jim. Brother Calvin told me so last weekend. Said it was straight from the doc's wife."

Jim pulled his horse up short, the animal snorting and pawing at the ground. He turned to Mun, his face hard as granite. "You're telling me Bo's fooling around with Shirley *and* Trixie, and Trixie is with child?"

Mun nodded, his expression grave. "That's what I'm saying. And if Shirley's acting off lately, well, I reckon you can guess why." Mun paused, studying his next words carefully. "And Jim, Earline believes Shirley might be with child too. She told me 'bout some signs, and…" Mun didn't finish—no need.

Jim sat silent for a moment, his gaze fixed on the horizon. When he spoke, his voice was low and even. "What do you think I ought to do about it?"

Mun shook his head. "Ain't my place to say. But you've got to think about what's best for Shirley. That girl don't deserve to get caught up in something like this, Jim."

Jim nodded slowly, his face unreadable. "You're right," he said finally. "She don't."

Mun stood still, the weight of years resting in the lines of his face, in the way his hands curled and uncurled at his sides, steady as the tides. He looked at Jim, his voice low, firm, carrying the kind of finality that left no room for argument. "You been like my big brother near my whole life. Stood for me when nobody else would. Saved me, Jim. Likely saved Mama too. Ain't no telling where we'd be if not for you. But I need you to listen now. Ain't nothing you gotta say. Just nod. That's all. Just nod."

Jim didn't move, not yet. His breath came slow, measured, his eyes fixed on Mun, reading the spaces between the words, the years behind them, the thing that had been growing long before this moment.

Mun's hands settled at his sides. He exhaled once, slow, like he was making peace with what was to come.

"This time, brother," he said, quiet, sure, "I got the Goddamn hammer."

Mun extended his hand, the movement slow, deliberate, a gesture weighted with things long unspoken, things understood. A quiet truce, a reckoning. Jim hesitated, eyes dark with something Mun had only seen once before—the day his daddy died, the day the world had shifted beneath his feet and left him standing in its aftermath.

Jim's gaze dropped to Mun's outstretched palm, fingers rough, calloused, a man's hand but somehow still, the hand of the boy he once knew.

And then, an exhaled breath, a decision made final.

Jim extended his own, clasped Mun's hand in the way only men of their kind did, the grip firm, precise, the ancient sign of the Freemasons, the quiet confirmation of brotherhood, of loyalty sealed in silence.

The moment held.

Then Jim let go.

And the world, unchanged, kept turning.

THE SILENCE THE TREES KEPT

Thursday, Fourth Week of August 1942

SISSY JACKSON LIVED in the breath between memory and myth, a body grown small from the years, her name spoken only when necessity demanded it. Wessyngton Knob knew her not as woman but as relic, a whisper of history still moving through the world, her years counted in stories that were older than most of the town's dead.

The knob itself rose like a blister from the edge of the Cumberland Valley, rocky and unwilling, a patch of land no white man every broke properly. After the war, when the Jeffersons of Wessyngton Plantation— lords of thirteen thousand acres and three generations of human bondage—found themselves land-rich and labor-poor, they offered it up like a prize. Not out of mercy, but calculation. A craggy hill of poor soil and bent pines, the Knob wasn't worth the iron on a plowshare, but it was land, nonetheless. In exchange for a promise—a kind of quiet indenture dressed up in contract and coin—the freedmen were granted parcels, a corner of the plantation's ruin, just enough to tether them back to the place they thought they'd left behind.

So, they built. With scrap wood and clay and breath held between generations, they made homes where the wind cut cruelly, and the ground refused seed. They stayed because they had to, and over time, the Knob took on a life of its own—unclaimed by the county, uncharted by maps, known by name but not invitation. Wessyngton Knob was a world apart, a place where white folks did not venture unless invited or bleeding. Not out of law, but out of wisdom. And Sissy, older than the place itself in spirit if not in fact, lived at its heart, where memory never let the ground forget what it had once refused to hold.

She had drawn her first breath on land and law that did not belong to her, her body counted among the holdings of the Jefferson family, a girl born in chains and shaped by the slow, grinding cruelty of the years that followed. A healer, a midwife, a root doctor, a woman whose hands knew how to bring forth life and, when the hour called for it, how to silence it.

The knowledge Sissy carried came from her mother, a Caribbean midwife, passed down the secrets of roots, berries, and seed, the power of which Sissy turned into teas and salves for all manner of ailments. In a world where white doctors turned their noses up at treating colored folk, root doctors like Sissy were the only hope for healing, their purpose clear: get the sick slaves back to the fields.

Sissy's remedies were well known. Her skills respected, though whispered about. Even in her frail old age, there was an unmistakable strength about her, a fire in her hollowed frame that hinted at the iron resolve it took to survive, let alone thrive, in a world designed to crush her.

She sat before Mun, a frail frame wrapped in muslin, the small room smelling of dried herbs and old sweat, air thick with desperation. Mun needed something special, something dark and final, that he'd promised Jim he'd deliver.

The years carved deep into Sissy's skin like the rings of an ancient tree. Her fingers worked steadily at the mortar, crushing jimson seeds into a fine powder, her lips moving in a soundless rhythm, a hymn to the old gods who had long since ceased answering.

Poke berries crushed and left to thicken in the sun for three days, then mixed with jimson powder and cloves to make the tea.

Sissy's hair, streaked silver, curled free beneath the knot of her headwrap, her dark eyes sharp and knowing as she measured out the poison.

She poured the dark brew into a small mason jar containing another goldish-colored powder—the final concoction, a viscous thing meant to be mixed with hot tea or coffee to thin it out.

"A teaspoon," she said, handing him the jar. "No more." Sissy's toothless mouth worked words in a voice stripped of its sharpness by time and loss.

Mun took it without a word, slid her the money, and touched the brim of his hat in deference. When he left, she did not watch him go. Just turned back to the work, grinding life into dust.

A TOAST BEFORE DEATH

Friday, Fourth Week of August 1942

EVENING HUNG HEAVY over the dirt road, the sun's last breath turning the earth to gold beneath the tired Ford as it rattled toward the chestnut thicket. The mason jar sat warm against Mun's leg, the poison long since dissolved into the dandelion wine he had spent the morning stirring, watching the liquid darken, waiting for it to swallow the bitter concoction whole. Beside him, Benji sat quiet, fingers curled against his knee, his eyes ahead, unblinking.

Bo Harris waited where he said he would, his truck idling just off the road. He'd skipped school that morning to kill a mess of squirrels, parking his truck out of sight from the truancy cop's prying eyes. The air was thick with the scent of wet leaves and engine heat. Mun killed his own engine, soon as he pulled up alongside Bo's pickup, turning to face Benji. "Lead with a smile, boy. Folks trust a smile."

Benji nodded, though his throat felt tight. He climbed out, forced his face into something close to a grin, then lifted a hand in greeting. "Hey, Bo. Got any squirrel to sell? Daddy's got a mind for dumplin's."

Bo grinned, easy, unworried. "Ain't got none yet, but I'm workin' on it. Y'all wanna' come along, you're welcome."

Mun stepped out, the jars in his grip. Held one up like a peace offering. "Figured I'd bring somethin' for the hunt. Dandelion wine. My own brew."

Bo's grin widened, and he took it with a laugh. "Strong as the last? I done had a lil' bit, earlier today, matter of fact. Damn good stuff."

Mun nodded. "Strong's what makes it good."

Bo tilted back the jar, took a swig. Caught his breath, coughed, then grinned wide. "Hell yeah. I'll drink to that."

*

THE FOREST SWALLOWED THEM whole. They moved beneath the canopy, the crows silent now, watching, the low, lumpy clouds creeping into the corners of the sky. Bo leaned against a tree, limbs heavy with drink, the rifle loose in his grip, his breath slowing. His mouth shaped words that didn't quite make it past his lips.

"My head," Bo murmured, words slurring. "Feels like I'm floatin'."

Mun nodded, crouched beside him, voice low. "Just rest a spell," he said. "Ain't no rush."

Bo nodded, his head falling back, his eyes slipping shut. "You good folk, Mun."

Mun exhaled. "Close your eyes, Bo."

Bo did as he was told.

The rifle cracked.

Crows shrieked from the trees, flying off in every direction. A black cloud rising. Bo's body jerked once, then stilled, folding inward like a discarded coat. The earth, indifferent as always, accepting him without question.

Mun wiped his hands on his shirt, turned to Benji. "Gimme the note."

Benji pulled it from his pocket, his hands trembling. Mun took his knife, drove it into the tree trunk, pinning the paper there like an epitaph. Then he turned Bo's corpse, set the rifle against him, positioned his hand just so. The silence settled again. The cadaver loose as sleep.

Father and son walked back slow, the chestnut branches bowing under their own weight, the path behind them already erasing itself in the falling dusk. The sky drained of color, bruised and waiting. Mun twisted the lid on the mason jar until it held firm. One less thing to carry.

A can of snuff slipped from his pocket, landed soft in the pine needles. Rolled once, twice. Settled. Neither man noticed.

Benji's voice came quiet. "It don't feel right, Daddy."

Mun didn't look at him. "Right don't always matter, boy. Now maybe things be different, him out of the way."

Benji let the words from his father sink deep, wondering should he share the secrets between him and Shirley.

No, Benji kept it.

They climbed into the truck, the road stretching ahead, the trees behind them keeping their silence. As they always had. As they always would.

SIXTEEN

THE WEIGHT OF WHAT REMAINS

THE STORY OF Bo's death settled into the town like the dust on the road, fine and inevitable, and no more to be disturbed than the church bells on Sunday. They called it what they needed to, whispered what made the most sense. That he'd done it himself. That there were things a man could not bear. That he had slipped loose from the world as quietly as a fish sliding under the current.

His family carried it with the tired shame of a coat worn too long in the heat. But Sheriff Cobb wasn't the type to let go, not even when the town turned its head and let the silence do its work. That snuff can sat on his desk, a tin circle of quiet accusation, and he pressed his thumb over its lid so many times it shone in the lamplight, as if his persistence alone might call up a ghost to tell him what was true.

Years passed by, and the world moved on, as the world is prone to do. Rhys Pritchard, sharp-eyed and even sharper-tongued, unhorsed Cobb in the next sheriff's race—a younger man with paper-thin patience for old ghosts.

He laughed about that can of snuff in the back room of the jailhouse, leaned his chair back against the wall and told the other deputies that Cobb had been a good man but a damn fool, and that it was time to let cadavers grow daisies. A majority of the town agreed. Cobb packed up his office, shaking hands and swallowing pride, the little can tucked into his pocket, evidence he could never leave behind.

Meanwhile, Jim and Ora saw their opening, grief turning to calculation as fast as breath turns to fog in the cold. Shirley was heavy with child, and shame curled in Ora's stomach like a slow-burning coal.

Ora went to Bo's family with a plan that landed heavy, threats dressed up as wherefores, reminders of what a scandal could do to a name already moth-eaten. Money changed hands, silent and loathe, a transaction made in the feeble light of a back room, and the town turned its face the other way, preferring to forget.

Shirley was sent to Nashville, where unwed pregnant women disappeared behind lace curtains and strict rules, where the walls were thick enough to swallow all regrets. The lie Ora spun was practiced and perfect. An ailing grandmother in Tupelo. A good deed, a necessary kindness.

The town nodded along, accepting it as they accepted all the other small fictions that made life easier. Shirley sat alone in that room, hand over the swell of her belly, the future unfolding before her like a long, dark road with no turnoffs. It was a heavy thing, knowing you're carrying a life whose story is already being written by hands not your own, and still not knowing the race of your own baby.

But Shirley had never been one to surrender easy. Her aunt and uncle came to visit, their presence a brief warmth against the cold. She planted seeds in their minds, careful and deliberate, the same way Bo had once taught her to plant tomatoes in the hard-packed earth behind the barn. Uncle Rhea was soft, eager to be swayed. But Aunt Lois, Ora's sister, was made of sterner stuff.

"You don't know what you're asking," Lois told her, hands folded tight in her lap. "Your mama, she'd never forgive us."

Shirley didn't flinch. "She don't have to know."

Each visit, she worked them like a gambler playing a long hand. Love. Trust. The promise that it was the right thing. That if they raised the child, she could still be near, still be part of her child's life. It wasn't easy. Lois held out, fingers tapping the side of her teacup, the weight of her conscience something she wasn't quick to ignore. But Uncle Rhea leaned forward, the longing in his face laid bare like a wound.

"We could move," Lois said finally, voice slow, like the words had to be measured before being spoken. "Somewhere far enough. Start fresh."

So they did. Sold their store in Springfield, packed their belongings in the back of a truck, and left before the baby could be born. Moved to Adairsville, Kentucky, thirty miles north, where the past wouldn't follow so easy. Shirley's daughter was born on a gray morning, rain streaking the hospital window, and when Lois carried her away, Shirley let them, her arms aching with the loss even as she told herself it was the right thing. The only thing.

Back home, the years turned like pages in a book left open to the wind. The Raglands carried their own burdens, silent and unspoken. Mun and Earline worked for them near half a century, till the weight of age pressed too heavy on their bones. Their oldest boys never made it back from the war. But Benji and his older brother Elijah both graduated high school, Benji goin' on to trade school to be a mechanic.

When they left, Ora barely spared them a glance. But Jim—Jim lingered. Took Mun's hand in his own, gripped it like something solid in a world that wouldn't stay still. It wasn't just parting. It was an ending. The kind of thing that sits heavy in a man's chest and never quite leaves.

Trixie Simpson lost her baby.

The life of her young child disappeared to a thief she couldn't quite see, small breaths stolen in the dark, a quiet unknotting of a life that had barely started.

The town called it crib death. A sigh of serendipity, no one to blame. But Trixie moved through her days like something missing, stitched her sorrow into dresses she sewed for other people's daughters, never speaking of the little girl she had once held close. Grief settled into her like a stone dropped in deep water, never making a sound, only sinking, sinking, sinking.

And Shirley, she built a life out of what was left. Moved to Nashville, took a job at Sears counting numbers into order, the rhythm of it a comfort she hadn't expected.

She met Louis there, a man who knew how to smile in a way that made the world seem lighter. He loved her in a way that made the past feel distant, made it easier to pretend she had never stood in a hospital room watching another woman carry her child away. But mostly, he was a path to instant parenthood.

They married. Had children. Cindy, Bo's daughter, was brought into the fold, wrapped in a lie that was almost tender in its necessity.

But secrets are patient deeds. They wait. And when the truth finally found its way, it didn't come with anger, but with understanding. Cindy saw her mother for what she really was, a woman who had done what she thought was right in a world that had given her no choices. And Shirley, for the first time, felt something close to release.

Mun passed in the fall of 1975, and Jim Ragland stood at the grave, hat in his hands, looking down at the earth like it held every word he'd never said. The town whispered his name, wondered what it was that sat so heavy on his shoulders. But Jim, he just stood there, the past pressing close—the only time Shirley saw her father crying.

After the service, Benji found Shirley, placed an envelope in her palm, his voice low. "Daddy wanted you to have this."

Benji said he'd call her sometime to check on her. But the tone was off, staged. Louis never caught on. It'd been thirty years. Benji had gone through three wives and still no children.

Benji's face had been a war of memory and restraint, the flicker of old possession in his gaze veiled by the decorum required. Her husband, Louis, had stood steady beside her, but it was Benji's eyes that had burned. And Chris, her youngest, had seen it, understood in some nameless way that the man looking at his mother carried the same quiet knowing that curled like smoke in his own bones.

The letter had trembled in her hands as Benji passed it to her, fingers brushing in a ghost of what had been. And when he said, in that low, honeyed drawl, that he might call in a few weeks just to check on her, the air between them had thickened like July heat, like the old unspoken things that neither time nor vows could ever put to rest.

She read the letter that night, the house quiet, the paper trembling in her hands. Mun's words were careful, deliberate, weighed with years of silence. He spoke of debts that couldn't be repaid, of bonds formed in blood and shadow. Of the things a man does in loyalty and love, even when they sit uneasy in the soul.

Shirley finally understood. And she was fine.

She folded the letter, pressed it against her chest. The room felt small around her, the past too large to escape. And yet, the world turned. The children laughed in the next room. The telephone sat within reach. She picked it up, dialed the number she had known since before she was a mother, before she was a wife. Before she had learned what it meant to carry a secret and bear its weight.

Her delicate fingers, like the petals of a rose unfurling, carefully spun the dial of the old rotary phone, each click echoing the rhythm of her heart, counting down the precious seconds until she could hear his voice again. She held the receiver to her ear, waiting, breath caught in the space between one life and another.

Now, in the hush of her house, she heard the intake of her own breath on the line, felt it answer something restless inside her. The decades secretly shared between them fell away, and she knew, as she always had, that this, this was forever.

Benji answered on the second ring.

ACKNOWLEDGMENTS

You know this story already. A friend writes a book. You want to support him, buy the book, you open it and turn to the back—the acknowledgments section—with high hopes. Just maybe, your name is there—etched in the deckled edged paper, between the sacred and the absurd—but it never is. Not this time, Bruh. Because this one is for you. Whether we passed each other once at a Buc-ee's gas station in Georgia or held each other's awkward gaze over top of a bloodstained ticket book, as you decided whether my fate would be a warning citation or a trip to court. Whether you've forgotten me entirely or held a small corner of your heart open, and a plate of cold biscuits, just in case I came back. Whether you're flesh and blood or long buried beneath it. I am writing to you, and for you. With all that's left in me. You'll know what that means when you read this. You probably already do.

There are people who helped me write this book, and I owe them more than language can carry. And there are others—ghosts from my past—who left fingerprints on my stories without ever knowing they were helping to shape them. Like the man in the Giant Foods aisle, bent over the frozen food section, who shouted hellfire at a child who didn't yet know what those words meant. You should know, sir, I never forgot you. I was six. My brother was a prisoner of circumstance and trapped in a runaway cart. You shouted like I had broken something sacred, and maybe I had. You taught me, however unwillingly, that words are weapons and shame can pass down like a kind of inheritance. So no, I won't thank you. But I'll remember you. That's worse.

Now to those I *can* thank:

To Nina Bryce Cobb—thank you for your stories, your strength, your unflinching honesty. Your fingerprints are on more pages than you know.

To my mother and father—you gave me the tools: common sense, quiet courage, the ability to think for myself. You also gave me a voice I've been trying to write in for decades. Thank you for letting me go and not changing your mind when you realized I might be a danger to myself or others. And mostly to my mother for giving me the story, royalty free.

To my wife, Emily. You never asked for this. But you bore it just the same. Every late night, every tantrum, every empty look across the dinner table. You told me once, in a moment of beautiful fury, "When are you gonna' finish that fucking book?" And that was the moment I knew I had to. For you. Because you believe in me with a fierceness that frightens and saves me all at once.

To Elizabeth Davis—fellow traveler, co-conspirator, book buddy—thank you for the long road to Savannah and the better plot and sentences it led me to.

To Walter White, my dog. My shadow. My sounding board. Thank you for listening without judgment and for sticking closer than any friend I've ever had.

To Curt Cobb—if you think a certain character feels familiar, he probably is. That's on you. Thank you for the quirks.

To Josh Carney—*see* Dedication.

To Christian Hidalgo—your genius bailed me out more than once. Thank you for your patience, for elevating my story even when my sentences deserved detention.

To Olivia Eisinger—thank you for making me face the mess I'd made, for closing the loops and stitching up the wounds in the prose and plot. And to Zara Thatcher—thank you for sweeping up the debris, tightening the bolts, and handing me back something that felt not just readable, but whole.

To my sisters, Lisa and Cindy—thank you for your steadfast loyalty and sharp wit, for never once flinching when I told you I'd taken our mother's secret story and dressed it in scandal—and for saying what I already knew—that Mama was a born provocateur, and would've relished the chance to be the whore of the tale, so long as her name was spelled right and the dialogue was clever.

And finally, to Tennessee. You strange, lovely, wounded place. You made me. You filled my lungs with honeysuckle and my gut with grits, raised me on hymns and in hollers, and taught me what it meant to belong to something larger than my own pitiful ego. If this book falters—if it doesn't live up to the place it came from—then let's pretend it never happened. But if there is truth here, if there is southern gothic beauty in these pages, you'll find it came straight from Tennessee's red clay, tangled kudzu, and long, humid memory.

To everyone who made me the writer I am—thank you. And to those who didn't—I still owe you something, and here it is.